Nora Roberts is the number one *New York Times* bestselling author of more than one hundred novels. She is also the author of the bestselling futuristic suspense series written under the pen name J.D. Robb. With over 150 million copies of her books in print, and more than seventy *New York Times* bestsellers to date, Nora Roberts is indisputably the most celebrated and beloved women's fiction writer today.

Visit her website at www.noraroberts.com

D0774312

*Also by Nora Roberts writing as J.D. Robb:*

Glory in Death
Immortal in Death

*Also by Nora Roberts*

Homeport
The Reef
River's End
Carolina Moon
The Villa
Midnight Bayou
Three Fates
Birthright

*Three Sisters Island Trilogy:*

Dance Upon the Air
Heaven and Earth
Face the Fire

*Chesapeake Bay Quartet:*

Sea Swept
Rising Tides
Inner Harbour
Chesapeake Blue

# Naked in Death

*Nora Roberts*

writing as

*J.D. Robb*

PIATKUS

## ♋ Visit the Piatkus website!

Piatkus publishes a wide range of bestselling fiction and
non-fiction, including books on health, mind, body & spirit,
sex, self-help, cookery, biography and the paranormal.

*If you want to:*
- read descriptions of our popular titles
- buy our books over the internet
- take advantage of our special offers
- enter our monthly competition
- learn more about your favourite Piatkus authors

VISIT OUR WEBSITE AT: www.piatkus.co.uk

All the characters in this book are fictitious and any resemblance to real persons,
living or dead, is entirely coincidental.

Copyright © 1995 by Nora Roberts
Material excerpted from *Glory in Death* by Nora Roberts writing as J.D. Robb
copyright © 1995 by Nora Roberts

This edition published in Great Britain in 2003 by
Piatkus Books Ltd of
5 Windmill Street, London W1T 2JA
email: info@piatkus.co.uk

Reprinted 2004 (twice), 2005

First published in the United States in 1995 by Berkley Publishing Group,
a division of Penguin Putnam Inc., New York

**The moral right of the author has been asserted**

*A catalogue record for this book is available from the British Library*

ISBN 0 7499 3406 9

Typeset by Palimpsest Book Production Limited,
Polmont, Stirlingshire
Printed and bound in Great Britain by
Mackays of Chatham Ltd, Chatham Kent

What's past is prologue.

WILLIAM SHAKESPEARE

Violence is as American as cherry pie.

RAP (HUBERT GEROLD) BROWN

# Chapter One

She woke in the dark. Through the slats on the window shades, the first murky hint of dawn slipped, slanting shadowy bars over the bed. It was like waking in a cell.

For a moment she simply lay there, shuddering, imprisoned, while the dream faded. After ten years on the force, Eve still had dreams.

Six hours before, she'd killed a man, had watched death creep into his eyes. It wasn't the first time she'd exercised maximum force, or dreamed. She'd learned to accept the action and the consequences.

But it was the child that haunted her. The child she hadn't been in time to save. The child whose screams had echoed in the dreams with her own.

All the blood, Eve thought, scrubbing sweat from her face with her hands. Such a small little girl to have had so much blood in her. And she knew it was vital that she push it aside.

Standard departmental procedure meant that she would spend the morning in Testing. Any officer whose discharge of weapon resulted in termination of life was required to undergo emotional and psychiatric clearance before resuming duty. Eve considered the tests a mild pain in the ass.

She would beat them, as she'd beaten them before.

When she rose, the overheads went automatically to low

setting, lighting her way into the bath. She winced once at her reflection. Her eyes were swollen from lack of sleep, her skin nearly as pale as the corpses she'd delegated to the ME.

Rather than dwell on it, she stepped into the shower, yawning.

'Give me one oh one degrees, full force,' she said and shifted so that the shower spray hit her straight in the face.

She let it steam, lathered listlessly while she played through the events of the night before. She wasn't due in Testing until nine, and would use the next three hours to settle and let the dream fade away completely.

Small doubts and little regrets were often detected and could mean a second and more intense round with the machines and the owl-eyed technicians who ran them.

Eve didn't intend to be off the streets longer than twenty-four hours.

After pulling on a robe, she walked into the kitchen and programmed her AutoChef for coffee, black; toast, light. Through her window she could hear the heavy hum of air traffic carrying early commuters to offices, late ones home. She'd chosen the apartment years before because it was in a heavy ground and air pattern, and she liked the noise and crowds. On another yawn, she glanced out the window, followed the rattling journey of an aging airbus, hauling laborers not fortunate enough to work in the city or by home-links.

She brought the *New York Times* up on her monitor and scanned the headlines while the faux caffeine bolstered her system. The AutoChef had burned her toast again, but she ate it anyway, with a vague thought of springing for a replacement unit.

She was frowning over an article on a mass recall of droid cocker spaniels when her tele-link blipped. Eve shifted to communications and watched her commanding officer flash onto the screen.

'Commander.'

'Lieutenant.' He gave her a brisk nod, noted the still wet hair and sleepy eyes. 'Incident at Twenty-seven West Broadway, eighteenth floor. You're primary.'

Eve lifted a brow. 'I'm on Testing. Subject terminated at twenty-two thirty-five.'

'We have override,' he said, without inflection. 'Pick up your shield and weapon on the way to the incident. Code Five, lieutenant.'

'Yes, sir.' His face flashed off even as she pushed back from the screen. Code Five meant she would report directly to her commander, and there would be no unsealed interdepartmental reports and no cooperation with the press.

In essence, it meant she was on her own.

Broadway was noisy and crowded, a party where rowdy guests never left. Street, pedestrian, and sky traffic were miserable, choking the air with bodies and vehicles. In her old days in uniform she remembered it as a hot spot for wrecks and crushed tourists who were too busy gaping at the show to get out of the way.

Even at this hour there was steam rising from the stationary and portable food stands that offered everything from rice noodles to soydogs for the teeming crowds. She had to swerve to avoid an eager merchant on his smoking Glida-Grill, and took his flipped middle finger as a matter of course.

Eve double-parked and, skirting a man who smelled worse than his bottle of brew, stepped onto the sidewalk. She scanned the building first, fifty floors of gleaming metal that knifed into the sky from a hilt of concrete. She was propositioned twice before she reached the door.

Since this five-block area of Broadway was affectionately termed Prostitute's Walk, she wasn't surprised. She flashed her badge for the uniform guarding the entrance.

3

'Lieutenant Dallas.'

'Yes, sir.' He skimmed his official compu-seal over the door to keep out the curious, then led the way to the bank of elevators. 'Eighteenth floor,' he said when the doors swished shut behind them.

'Fill me in, officer.' Eve switched on her recorder and waited.

'I wasn't first on the scene, lieutenant. Whatever happened upstairs is being kept upstairs. There's a badge inside waiting for you. We have a Homicide, and a Code Five in number Eighteen-oh-three.'

'Who called it in?'

'I don't have that information.'

He stayed where he was when the elevator opened. Eve stepped out and was alone in a narrow hallway. Security cameras tilted down at her and her feet were almost soundless on the worn nap of the carpet as she approached 1803. Ignoring the handplate, she announced herself, holding her badge up to eye level for the peep cam until the door opened.

'Dallas.'

'Feeney.' She smiled, pleased to see a familiar face. Ryan Feeney was an old friend and former partner who'd traded the street for a desk and a top level position in the Electronics Detection Division. 'So, they're sending computer pluckers these days.'

'They wanted brass, and the best.' His lips curved in his wide, rumpled face, but his eyes remained sober. He was a small, stubby man with small, stubby hands and rust colored hair. 'You look beat.'

'Rough night.'

'So I heard.' He offered her one of the sugared nuts from the bag he habitually carried, studying her, and measuring if she was up to what was waiting in the bedroom beyond.

She was young for her rank, barely thirty, with wide brown

4

eyes that had never had a chance to be naive. Her doe-brown hair was cropped short, for convenience rather than style, but suited her triangular face with its razor-edge cheekbones and slight dent in the chin.

She was tall, rangy, with a tendency to look thin, but Feeney knew there were solid muscles beneath the leather jacket. More, there was a brain, and a heart.

'This one's going to be touchy, Dallas.'

'I picked that up already. Who's the victim?'

'Sharon DeBlass, granddaughter of Senator DeBlass.'

Neither meant anything to her. 'Politics isn't my forte, Feeney.'

'The gentleman from Virginia, extreme right, old money. The granddaughter took a sharp left a few years back, moved to New York, and became a licensed companion.'

'She was a hooker.' Dallas glanced around the apartment. It was furnished in obsessive modern – glass and thin chrome, signed holograms on the walls, recessed bar in bold red. The wide mood screen behind the bar bled with mixing and merging shapes and colors in cool pastels.

Neat as a virgin, Eve mused, and cold as a whore. 'No surprise, given her choice of real estate.'

'Politics makes it delicate. Victim was twenty-four, Caucasian female. She bought it in bed.'

Eve only lifted a brow. 'Seems poetic, since she'd been bought there. How'd she die?'

'That's the next problem. I want you to see for yourself.'

As they crossed the room, each took out a slim container, sprayed their hands front and back to seal in oils and finger-prints. At the doorway, Eve sprayed the bottom of her boots to slicken them so that she would pick up no fibers, stray hairs, or skin.

Eve was already wary. Under normal circumstances there would have been two other investigators on a homicide scene,

5

with recorders for sound and pictures. Forensics would have been waiting with their usual snarly impatience to sweep the scene.

The fact that only Feeney had been assigned with her meant that there were a lot of eggshells to be walked over.

'Security cameras in the lobby, elevator, and hallways,' Eve commented.

'I've already tagged the discs.' Feeney opened the bedroom door and let her enter first.

It wasn't pretty. Death rarely was a peaceful, religious experience to Eve's mind. It was the nasty end, indifferent to saint and sinner. But this was shocking, like a stage deliberately set to offend.

The bed was huge, slicked with what appeared to be genuine satin sheets the color of ripe peaches. Small, soft focused spotlights were trained on its center where the naked woman was cupped in the gentle dip of the floating mattress.

The mattress moved with obscenely graceful undulations to the rhythm of programmed music slipping through the headboard.

She was beautiful still, a cameo face with a tumbling waterfall of flaming red hair, emerald eyes that stared glassily at the mirrored ceiling, long, milk white limbs that called to mind visions of *Swan Lake* as the motion of the bed gently rocked them.

They weren't artistically arranged now, but spread lewdly so that the dead woman formed a final X dead center of the bed.

There was a hole in her forehead, one in her chest, another horribly gaping between the open thighs. Blood had splattered on the glossy sheets, pooled, dripped, and stained.

There were splashes of it on the lacquered walls, like lethal paintings scrawled by an evil child.

So much blood was a rare thing, and she had seen much too

much of it the night before to take the scene as calmly as she would have preferred.

She had to swallow once, hard, and force herself to block out the image of a small child.

'You got the scene on record?'

'Yep.'

'Then turn that damn thing off.' She let out a breath after Feeney located the controls that silenced the music. The bed flowed to stillness. 'The wounds,' Eve murmured, stepping closer to examine them. 'Too neat for a knife. Too messy for a laser.' A flash came to her – old training films, old videos, old viciousness.

'Christ, Feeney, these look like bullet wounds.'

Feeney reached into his pocket and drew out a sealed bag. 'Whoever did it left a souvenir.' He passed the bag to Eve. 'An antique like this has to go for eight, ten thousand for a legal collection, twice that on the black market.'

Fascinated, Eve turned the sealed revolver over in her hand. 'It's heavy,' she said half to herself. 'Bulky.'

'Thirty-eight caliber,' he told her. 'First one I've seen outside of a museum. This one's a Smith & Wesson, Model Ten, blue steel.' He looked at it with some affection. 'Real classic piece, used to be standard police issue up until the latter part of the twentieth. They stopped making them in about twenty-two, twenty-three, when the gun ban was passed.'

'You're the history buff.' Which explained why he was with her. 'Looks new.' She sniffed through the bag, caught the scent of oil and burning. 'Somebody took good care of this. Steel fired into flesh,' she mused as she passed the bag back to Feeney. 'Ugly way to die, and the first I've seen it in my ten years with the department.'

'Second for me. About fifteen years ago, Lower East Side, party got out of hand. Guy shot five people with a twenty-two before he realized it wasn't a toy. Hell of a mess.'

'Fun and games,' Eve murmured. 'We'll scan the collectors, see how many we can locate who own one like this. Somebody might have reported a robbery.'

'Might have.'

'It's more likely it came through the black market.' Eve glanced back at the body. 'If she's been in the business for a few years, she'd have discs, records of her clients, her trick books.' She frowned. 'With Code Five, I'll have to do the door-to-door myself. Not a simple sex crime,' she said with a sigh. 'Whoever did it set it up. The antique weapon, the wounds themselves, almost ruler straight down the body, the lights, the pose. Who called it in, Feeney?'

'The killer.' He waited until her eyes came back to him. 'From right here. Called the station. See how the bedside unit's aimed at her face? That's what came in. Video, no audio.'

'He's into showmanship.' Eve let out a breath. 'Clever bastard, arrogant, cocky. He had sex with her first. I'd bet my badge on it. Then he gets up and does it.' She lifted her arm, aiming, lowering it as she counted off, 'One, two, three.'

'That's cold,' murmured Feeney.

'He's cold. He smooths down the sheets after. See how neat they are? He arranges her, spreads her open so nobody can have any doubts as to how she made her living. He does it carefully, practically measuring, so that she's perfectly aligned. Center of the bed, arms and legs equally apart. Doesn't turn off the bed 'cause it's part of the show. He leaves the gun because he wants us to know right away he's no ordinary man. He's got an ego. He doesn't want to waste time letting the body be discovered eventually. He wants it now. That instant gratification.'

'She was licensed for men and women,' Feeney pointed out, but Eve shook her head.

'It's not a woman. A woman wouldn't have left her looking both beautiful and obscene. No, I don't think it's a woman.

Let's see what we can find. Have you gone into her computer yet?'

'No. It's your case, Dallas. I'm only authorized to assist.'

'See if you can access her client files.' Eve went to the dresser and began to carefully search drawers.

Expensive taste, Eve reflected. There were several items of real silk, the kind no simulation could match. The bottle of scent on the dresser was exclusive, and smelled, after a quick sniff, like expensive sex.

The contents of the drawers were meticulously ordered, lingerie folded precisely, sweaters arranged according to color and material. The closet was the same.

Obviously the victim had a love affair with clothes and a taste for the best and took scrupulous care of what she owned.

And she'd died naked.

'Kept good records,' Feeney called out. 'It's all here. Her client list, appointments – including her required monthly health exam and her weekly trip to the beauty salon. She used the Trident Clinic for the first and Paradise for the second.'

'Both top of the line. I've got a friend who saved for a year so she could have one day for the works at Paradise. Takes all kinds.'

'My wife's sister went for it for her twenty-fifth anniversary. Cost damn near as much as my kid's wedding. Hello, we've got her personal address book.'

'Good. Copy all of it, will you, Feeney?' At his low whistle, she looked over her shoulder, glimpsed the small gold-edged palm computer in his hand. 'What?'

'We've got a lot of high-powered names in here. Politics, entertainment, money, money, money. Interesting, our girl has Roarke's private number.'

'Roarke who?'

'Just Roarke, as far as I know. Big money there. Kind of

9

guy that touches shit and turns it into gold bricks. You've got to start reading more than the sports page, Dallas.'

'Hey, I read the headlines. Did you hear about the cocker spaniel recall?'

'Roarke's always big news,' Feeney said patiently. 'He's got one of the finest art collections in the world. Arts and antiques,' he continued, noting when Eve clicked in and turned to him. 'He's a licensed gun collector. Rumor is he knows how to use them.'

'I'll pay him a visit.'

'You'll be lucky to get within a mile of him.'

'I'm feeling lucky.' Eve crossed over to the body to slip her hands under the sheets.

'The man's got powerful friends, Dallas. You can't afford to so much as whisper he's linked to this until you've got something solid.'

'Feeney, you know it's a mistake to tell me that.' But even as she started to smile, her fingers brushed something between cold flesh and bloody sheets. 'There's something under her.' Carefully, Eve lifted the shoulder, eased her fingers over.

'Paper,' she murmured. 'Sealed.' With her protected thumb, she wiped at a smear of blood until she could read the protected sheet.

### ONE OF SIX

'It looks hand printed,' she said to Feeney and held it out. 'Our boy's more than clever, more than arrogant. And he isn't finished.'

Eve spent the rest of the day doing what would normally have been assigned to drones. She interviewed the victim's neighbors personally, recording statements, impressions.

She managed to grab a quick sandwich from the same

Glida-Grill she'd nearly smashed before, driving across town. After the night and the morning she'd put in, she could hardly blame the receptionist at Paradise for looking at her as though she'd recently scraped herself off the sidewalk.

Waterfalls played musically among the flora in the reception area of the city's most exclusive salon. Tiny cups of real coffee and slim glasses of fizzling water or champagne were served to those lounging on the cushy chairs and settees. Headphones and discs of fashion magazines were complementary.

The receptionist was magnificently breasted, a testament to the salon's figure sculpting techniques. She wore a snug, short outfit in the salon's trademark red, and an incredible coif of ebony hair coiled like snakes.

Eve couldn't have been more delighted.

'I'm sorry,' the woman said in a carefully modulated voice as empty of expression as a computer. 'We serve by appointment only.'

'That's okay.' Eve smiled and was almost sorry to puncture the disdain. Almost. 'This ought to get me one.' She offered her badge. 'Who works on Sharon DeBlass?'

The receptionist's horrified eyes darted toward the waiting area. 'Our clients' needs are strictly confidential.'

'I bet.' Enjoying herself, Eve leaned companionably on the U-shaped counter. 'I can talk nice and quiet, like this, so we understand each other – Denise?' She flicked her gaze down to the discreet studded badge on the woman's breast. 'Or I can talk louder, so everyone understands. If you like the first idea better, you can take me to a nice quiet room where we won't disturb any of your clients, and you can send in Sharon DeBlass's operator. Or whatever term you use.'

'Consultant,' Denise said faintly. 'If you'll follow me.'

'My pleasure.'

And it was.

Outside of movies or videos, Eve had never seen anything

so lush. The carpet was a red cushion your feet could sink blissfully into. Crystal drops hung from the ceiling and spun light. The air smelled of flowers and pampered flesh.

She might not have been able to imagine herself there, spending hours having herself creamed, oiled, pummeled, and sculpted, but if she were going to waste such time on vanity, it would certainly have been interesting to do so under such civilized conditions.

The receptionist showed her into a small room with a hologram of a summer meadow dominating one wall. The quiet sound of birdsong and breezes sweetened the air.

'If you'd just wait here.'

'No problem.' Eve waited for the door to close then, with an indulgent sigh, she lowered herself into a deeply cushioned chair. The moment she was seated, the monitor beside her blipped on, and a friendly, indulgent face that could only be a droid's beamed smiles.

'Good afternoon. Welcome to Paradise. Your beauty needs and your comfort are our only priorities. Would you like some refreshment while you wait for your personal consultant?'

'Sure. Coffee, black, coffee.'

'Of course. What sort would you prefer? Press *C* on your keyboard for the list of choices.'

Smothering a chuckle, Eve followed instructions. She spent the next two minutes pondering over her options, then narrowed it down to French Riviera or Caribbean Cream.

The door opened again before she could decide. Resigned, she rose and faced an elaborately dressed scarecrow.

Over his fuchsia shirt and plum colored slacks, he wore an open, trailing smock of Paradise red. His hair, flowing back from a painfully thin face echoed the hue of his slacks. He offered Eve a hand, squeezed gently, and stared at her out of soft doe eyes.

'I'm terribly sorry, officer. I'm baffled.'

'I want information on Sharon DeBlass.' Again, Eve took out her badge and offered it for inspection.

'Yes, ah, Lieutenant Dallas. That was my understanding. You must know, of course, our client data is strictly confidential. Paradise has a reputation for discretion as well as excellence.'

'And you must know, of course, that I can get a warrant, Mr—?'

'Oh, Sebastian. Simply Sebastian.' He waved a thin hand, sparkling with rings. 'I'm not questioning your authority, lieutenant. But if you could assist me, your motives for the inquiry?'

'I'm inquiring into the motives for the murder of DeBlass.' She waited a beat, judged the shock that shot into his eyes and drained his face of color. 'Other than that, my data is strictly confidential.'

'Murder. My dear God, our lovely Sharon is dead? There must be a mistake.' He all but slid into a chair, letting his head fall back and his eyes close. When the monitor offered him refreshment, he waved a hand again. Light shot from his jeweled fingers. 'God, yes. I need a brandy, darling. A snifter of Trevalli.'

Eve sat beside him, took out her recorder. 'Tell me about Sharon.'

'A marvelous creature. Physically stunning, of course, but it went deeper.' His brandy came into the room on a silent automated cart. Sebastian plucked the snifter and took one deep swallow. 'She had flawless taste, a generous heart, rapier wit.'

He turned the doe eyes on Eve again. 'I saw her only two days ago.'

'Professionally?'

'She had a standing weekly appointment, half day. Every other week was a full day.' He whipped out a butter yellow

13

scarf and dabbed at his eyes. 'Sharon took care of herself, believed strongly in the presentation of self.'

'It would be an asset in her line of work.'

'Naturally. She only worked to amuse herself. Money wasn't a particular need, with her family background. She enjoyed sex.'

'With you?'

His artistic face winced, the rosy lips pursing in what could have been a pout or pain. 'I was her consultant, her confidant, and her friend,' Sebastian said stiffly and draped the scarf with casual flare over his left shoulder. 'It would have been indiscreet and unprofessional for us to become sexual partners.'

'So you weren't attracted to her, sexually?'

'It was impossible for anyone not to be attracted to her sexually. She . . .' He gestured grandly. 'Exuded sex as others might exude an expensive perfume. My God.' He took another shaky sip of brandy. 'It's all past tense. I can't believe it. Dead. Murdered.' His gaze shot back to Eve. 'You said murdered.'

'That's right.'

'That neighborhood she lived in,' he said grimly. 'No one could talk to her about moving to a more acceptable location. She enjoyed living on the edge and flaunting it all under her family's aristocratic noses.'

'She and her family were at odds?'

'Oh definitely. She enjoyed shocking them. She was such a free spirit, and they so . . . ordinary.' He said it in a tone that indicated ordinary was more mortal a sin than murder itself. 'Her grandfather continues to introduce bills that would make prostitution illegal. As if the past century hasn't proven that such matters need to be regulated for health and crime security. He also stands against procreation regulation, gender adjustment, chemical balancing, and the gun ban.'

14

Eve's ears pricked. 'The senator opposes the gun ban?'

'It's one of his pets. Sharon told me he owns a number of nasty antiques and spouts off regularly about that outdated right to bear arms business. If he had his way, we'd all be back in the twentieth century, murdering each other right and left.'

'Murder still happens,' Eve murmured. 'Did she ever mention friends or clients who might have been dissatisfied or overly aggressive?'

'Sharon had dozens of friends. She drew people to her, like . . .' He searched for a suitable metaphor, used the corner of the scarf again. 'Like an exotic and fragrant flower. And her clients, as far as I know, were all delighted with her. She screened them carefully. All of her sexual partners had to meet certain standards. Appearance, intellect, breeding, and proficiency. As I said, she enjoyed sex, in all of its many forms. She was . . . adventurous.'

That fit with the toys Eve had unearthed in the apartment. The velvet handcuffs and whips, the scented oils and hallucinogens. The offerings on the two sets of colinked virtual reality headphones had been a shock even to Eve's jaded system.

'Was she involved with anyone on a personal level?'

'There were men occasionally, but she lost interest quickly. Recently she'd spoken about Roarke. She'd met him at a party and was attracted. In fact, she was seeing him for dinner the very night she came in for her consulation. She'd wanted something exotic because they were dining in Mexico.'

'In Mexico. That would have been the night before last.'

'Yes. She was just bubbling over about him. We did her hair in a gypsy look, gave her a bit more gold to the skin – full body work. Rascal Red on the nails, and a charming little temp tattoo of a red-winged butterfly on the left buttock. Twenty-four-hour facial cosmetics so that she wouldn't smudge. She looked spectacular,' he said, tearing up. 'And she kissed me and told me she just might be in love this time. "Wish me luck, Sebastian." She said that as she left. It was the last thing she ever said to me.'

# Chapter Two

No sperm. Eve swore over the autopsy report. If she'd had sex with her killer, the victim's choice of birth control had killed the little soldiers on contact, eliminating all trace of them within thirty minutes after ejaculation.

The extent of her injuries made the tests for sexual activity inconclusive. He'd blown her apart either for symbolism or for his own protection.

No sperm, no blood but for the victim's. No DNA.

The forensic sweep of the murder site turned up no fingerprints – none: not the victim's, not her weekly cleaning specialist, certainly not the murderer's.

Every surface had been meticulously wiped, including the murder weapon.

Most telling of all, in Eve's judgment, were the security discs. Once again, she slipped the elevator surveillance into her desk monitor.

The discs were initialed.

Gorham Complex. Elevator A. 2–12–2058. 06:00.

Eve zipped through, watching the hours fly by. The elevator doors opened for the first time at noon. She slowed the speed, giving her unit a quick smack with the heel of her hand when the image bobbled, then studied the nervous little man who entered and asked for the fifth floor.

A jumpy john, she decided, amused when he tugged at his

collar and slipped a breath mint between his lips. Probably had a wife and two kids and a steady white-collar job that allowed him to slip away for an hour once a week for his nooner.

He got off the elevator at five.

Activity was light for several hours, the occasional prostitute riding down to the lobby, some returning with shopping bags and bored expressions. A few clients came and went. The action picked up about eight. Some residents went out, snazzily dressed for dinner, others came in to keep their appointments.

At ten, an elegant-looking couple entered the car together. The woman allowed the man to open her fur coat, under which she wore nothing but stiletto heels and a tattoo of a rosebud with the stem starting at the crotch and the flower artistically teasing the left nipple. He fondled her, a technically illegal act in a secured area. When the elevator stopped on eighteen, the woman drew her coat together, and they exited, chatting about the play they'd just seen.

Eve made a note to interview the man the following day. It was he who was the victim's neighbor and associate.

The glitch happened at precisely 12:05. The image shifted almost seamlessly, with only the faintest blip, and returned to surveillance at 02:46.

Two hours and forty-one minutes lost.

The hallway disc of the eighteenth floor was the same. Nearly three hours wiped. Eve picked up her cooling coffee as she thought it through. The man understood security, she mused, was familiar enough with the building to know where and how to doctor the discs. And he'd taken his time, she thought. The autopsy put the victim's death at two A.M.

He'd spent nearly two hours with her before he'd killed her, and nearly an hour more after she'd been dead. Yet he hadn't left a trace.

18

Clever boy.

If Sharon DeBlass had recorded an appointment, personal or professional, for midnight, that, too, had been wiped.

So he'd known her intimately enough to be sure where she kept her files and how to access them.

On a hunch, Eve leaned forward again. 'Gorham Complex, Broadway, New York. Owner.'

Her eyes narrowed as the date flashed onto her screen.

Gorham Complex, owned by Roarke Industries, head-quarters 500 Fifth Avenue. Roarke, president and CEO. New York residence, 222 Central Park West.

'Roarke,' Eve murmured. 'You just keep turning up, don't you. Roarke?' she repeated. 'All data, view and print.'

Ignoring the incoming call on the 'link beside her, Eve sipped her coffee and read.

Roarke – no known given name – born 10-06-2023, Dublin, Ireland. ID number 33492-ABR-50. Parents unknown. Marital status, single. President and CEO of Roarke Industries, established 2042. Main branches New York, Chicago, New Los Angeles, Dublin, London, Bonn, Paris, Frankfurt, Tokyo, Milan, Sydney. Off-planet branches, Station 45, Bridgestone Colony, Vegas II, Free-Star One. Interests in real estate, import-export, shipping, entertainment, manufacturing, pharmaceuticals, transportation. Estimated gross worth, three billion, eight hundred million.

Busy boy, Eve thought, lifting a brow as a list of his companies clicked on-screen.

'Education,' she demanded.

Unknown.

'Criminal record?'

No data.

'Access Roarke, Dublin.'

No additional data.

19

'Well, shit, Mr Mystery. Description and visual.' *Roarke. Black hair, blue eyes, 6 feet, 2 inches, 173 pounds.*

Eve grunted as the computer listed the description. She had to agree that in Roarke's case, a picture was worth a couple hundred words.

His image stared back at her from the screen. He was almost ridiculously handsome: the narrow, aesthetic face; the slash of cheekbones; and sculpted mouth. Yes, his hair was black, but the computer didn't say it was thick and full and swept back from a strong forehead to fall inches above broad shoulders. His eyes were blue, but the word was much too simple for the intensity of color or the power in them.

Even on an image, Eve could see this was a man who hunted down what or who he wanted, bagged it, used it, and didn't bother with frivolities such as trophies.

And yes, she thought, this was a man who could kill if and when it suited him. He would do so coolly, methodically, and without breaking a sweat.

Gathering up the hard data, she decided she'd have a talk with Roarke. Very soon.


By the time Eve left the station to head home, the sky was miserably spitting snow. She checked her pockets without hope and found she had indeed left her gloves in her apartment. Hatless, gloveless, with only her leather jacket as protection against the biting wind, she drove across town.

She'd meant to get her vehicle into repair. There just hadn't been time. But there was plenty of time to regret it now as she fought traffic and shivered, thanks to a faulty heating system.

She swore if she got home without turning into a block of ice, she'd make the appointment with the mechanic.

But when she did arrive home, her primary thought was food. Even as she unlocked her door, she was dreaming about a hot bowl of soup, maybe a mound of chips, if she had any left, and coffee that didn't taste like someone had spilled sewage into the water system.

She saw the package immediately, the slim square just inside the door. Her weapon was out and in her hand before she drew the next breath. Sweeping with weapon and eyes, she kicked the door shut behind her. She left the package where it was and moved from room to room until she was satisfied she was alone.

After holstering her weapon, she peeled out of her jacket and tossed it aside. Bending, she picked up the sealed disc by the edges. There was no label, no message.

Eve took it into the kitchen, tapping it carefully out of its seal, and slipped it into her computer.

And forgot all about food.

The video was top quality, as was the sound. She sat down slowly as the scene played on her monitor.

Naked, Sharon DeBlass lounged on the lake-size bed, rustling satin sheets. She lifted a hand, skimming it through that glorious tumbled mane of russet hair as the bed's floating motion rocked her.

'Want me to do anything special, darling?' She chuckled, rose up on her knees, cupped her own breasts. 'Why don't you come back over here . . .' Her tongue flicked out to wet her lips. 'We'll do it all again.' Her gaze lowered, and a little cat smile curved her lips. 'Looks like you're more than ready.' She laughed again, shook back her hair. 'Oh, we want to play a game.' Still smiling, Sharon put her hands up. 'Don't hurt me.' She whimpered, shivering even as her eyes glinted with excitement. 'I'll do anything you want. Anything. Come on over here and force me. I want you to.' Lowering her hands, she began to stroke herself. 'Hold that big bad gun on me while you rape me. I want you to. I want you to—'

The explosion had Eve jolting. Her stomach twisted as she

21

saw the woman fly backward like a broken doll, the blood spurting out of her forehead. The second shot wasn't such a shock, but Eve had to force herself to keep her eyes on the screen. After the final report there was silence, but for the quiet music, the fractured breathing. The killer's breathing.

The camera moved in, panned the body in grisly detail. Then, through the magic of video, DeBlass was as Eve had first seen her, spread-eagled in a perfect x over bloody sheets. The image ended with a graphic overlay.

## ONE OF SIX

It was easier to watch it through the second time. Or so Eve told herself. This time she noticed a slight bobble of the camera after the first shot, a quick, quiet gasp. She ran it back again, listening to each word, studying each movement, hoping for some clue. But he was too clever for that. And they both knew it.

He'd wanted her to see just how good he was. Just how cold.

And he wanted her to know that he knew just where to find her. Whenever he chose.

Furious that her hands weren't quite steady, she rose. Rather than the coffee she'd intended, Eve took out a bottle of wine from the small cold cell, poured half a glass.

She drank it down quickly, promised herself the other half shortly, then punched in the code for her commander.

It was the commander's wife who answered, and from the glittering drops at her ears and the perfect coiffure, Eve calculated that she'd interrupted one of the woman's famous dinner parties.

'Lieutenant Dallas, Mrs Whitney. I'm sorry to interrupt your evening, but I need to speak to the commander.'

'We're entertaining, lieutenant.'

'Yes, ma'am. I apologize.' Fucking politics, Eve thought as she forced a smile. 'It's urgent.'

'Isn't it always?'

The machine hummed on hold, mercifully without hideous background music or updated news reports, for a full three minutes before the commander came on.

'Dallas.'

'Commander, I need to send you something over a coded line.'

'It better be urgent, Dallas. My wife's going to make me pay for this.'

'Yes, sir.' Cops, she thought as she prepared to send the image to his monitor, should stay single.

She waited, folding her restless hands on the table. As the images played again, she watched again, ignoring the clenching in her gut. When it was over, Whitney came back on-screen. His eyes were grim.

'Where did you get this?'

'He sent it to me. A disc was here, in my apartment, when I got back from the station.' Her voice was flat and careful. 'He knows who I am, where I am, and what I'm doing.'

Whitney was silent for a moment. 'My office, oh seven hundred. Bring the disc, lieutenant.'

'Yes, sir.'

When the transmission ended, she did the two things her instincts dictated. She made herself a copy of the disc, and she poured another glass of wine.

She woke at three, shuddering, clammy, fighting for the breath to scream. Whimpers sounded in her throat as she croaked out an order for lights. Dreams were always more frightening in the dark.

Trembling, she lay back. This one had been worse, much worse, than any she'd experienced before.

She'd killed the man. What choice had she had? He'd been too buzzed on chemicals to be stunned. Christ, she'd tried, but he'd just keep coming, and coming, and coming, with that wild look in his eyes and the already bloodied knife in his hand.

The little girl had already been dead. There was nothing Eve could have done to stop it. Please God, don't let there have been anything that could have been done.

The little body hacked to pieces, the frenzied man with the dripping knife. Then the look in his eyes when she'd fired on full, and the life had slipped out of them.

But that hadn't been all. Not this time. This time he'd kept coming. And she'd been naked, kneeling in a pool of satin. The knife had become a gun, held by the man whose face she'd studied hours before. The man called Roarke.

He'd smiled, and she'd wanted him. Her body had tingled with terror and sexual desperation even as he'd shot her. Head, heart, and loins.

And somewhere through it all, the little girl, the poor little girl, had been screaming for help.

Too tired to fight it, Eve simply rolled over, pressed her face into her pillow and wept.

'Lieutenant.' At precisely seven A.M., Commander Whitney gestured Eve toward a chair in his office. Despite the fact, or perhaps due to the fact that he'd been riding a desk for twelve years, he had sharp eyes.

He could see that she'd slept badly and had worked to disguise the signs of disturbed night. In silence, he held out a hand.

She'd put the disc and its cover into an evidence bag. Whitney glanced at it, then laid it in the center of his desk.

'According to protocol, I'm obliged to ask you if you want to be relieved from this case.' He waited a beat. 'We'll pretend I did.'

'Yes, sir.'

'Is your residence secure, Dallas?'

'I thought so.' She took hard copy out of her briefcase. 'I reviewed the security discs after I contacted you. There's a ten minute time lapse. As you'll see in my report, he has the capability of undermining security, a knowledge of videos, editing, and, of course, antique weapons.'

Whitney took her report, set it aside. 'That doesn't narrow the field overmuch.'

'No, sir. I have several more people I need to interview. With this perpetrator, electronic investigation isn't primary, though Captain Feeney's help is invaluable. This guy covers his tracks. We have no physical evidence other than the weapon he chose to leave at the scene. Feeney hadn't been able to trace it through normal channels. We have to assume it was black market. I've started on her trick books and her personal appointments, but she wasn't the retiring kind. It's going to take time.'

'Time's part of the problem. One of six, lieutenant. What does that say to you?'

'That he has five more in mind, and wants us to know it. He enjoys his work and wants to be the focus of our attention.' She took a careful breath. 'There's not enough for a full psychiatric profile. We can't say how long he'll be satisfied by the thrill of this murder, when he'll need his next fix. It could be today. It could be a year from now. We can't bank on him being careless.'

Whitney merely nodded. 'Are you having problems with the rightful termination?'

The knife slicked with blood. The small ruined body at her feet. 'Nothing I can't handle.'

'Be sure of it, Dallas. I don't need an officer on a sensitive case like this who's worried whether she should or shouldn't use her weapon.'

'I'm sure of it.'

25

She was the best he had, and he couldn't afford to doubt her. 'Are you up to playing politics?' His lips curved thinly. 'Senator DeBlass is on his way over. He flew into New York last night.'

'Diplomacy isn't my strong suit.'

'I'm aware of that. But you're going to work on it. He wants to talk to the investigating officer, and he went over my head to arrange it. Orders came down from the chief. You're to give the senator your full cooperation.'

'This is a Code Five investigation,' Eve said stiffly. 'I don't care if orders came down from God Almighty, I'm not giving confidential data to a civilian.'

Whitney's smile widened. He had a good, ordinary face, probably the one he was born with. But when he smiled and meant it, the flash of white teeth against the cocoa colored skin turned the plain features into the special.

'I didn't hear that. And you didn't hear me tell you to give him no more than the obvious facts. What you do hear me tell you, Lieutenant Dallas, is that the gentleman from Virginia is a pompous, arrogant asshole. Unfortunately, the asshole has power. So watch your step.'

'Yes, sir.'

He glanced at his watch, then slipped the file and disc into his safe drawer. 'You've got time for a cup of coffee . . . and, lieutenant,' he added as she rose. 'If you're having trouble sleeping, take your authorized sedative. I want my officers sharp.'

'I'm sharp enough.'

Senator Gerald DeBlass was undoubtedly pompous. He was unquestionably arrogant. After one full minute in his company, Eve agreed that he was undeniably an asshole.

He was a compact, bull of a man, perhaps six feet, two hundred and twenty. His crop of white hair was cut sharp and thin as a razor so that his head seemed huge and bullet sleek. His eyes were nearly black, as were the heavy brows over them. They were large, like his nose, his mouth.

His hands were enormous, and when he clasped Eve's briefly on introduction, she noted they were smooth and soft as a baby's.

He brought his adjutant with him. Derrick Rockman was a whiplike man in his early forties. Though he was nearly six-five, Eve gave DeBlass twenty pounds on him. Neat, tidy, his pin-striped suit and slate blue tie showed not a crease. His face was solemn, attractively even featured, his movements restrained and controlled as he assisted the more flamboyant senator out of his cashmere overcoat.

'What the hell have you done to find the monster who killed my granddaughter?' DeBlass demanded.

'Everything possible, senator.' Commander Whitney remained standing. Though he offered DeBlass a seat, the man prowled the room, as he was given to prowl the New Senate Gallery in East Washington.

'You've had twenty-four hours and more,' DeBlass shot back, his voice deep and booming. 'It's my understanding you've assigned only two officers to the investigation.'

'For security purposes, yes. Two of my best officers,' the commander added. 'Lieutenant Dallas heads the investigation and reports solely to me.'

DeBlass turned those hard black eyes on Eve. 'What progress have you made?'

'We identified the weapon, ascertained the time of death. We're gathering evidence and interviewing residents of Ms DeBlass's building, and tracking the names in her personal and business logs. I'm working to reconstruct the last twenty-four hours of her life.'

'It should be obvious, even to the slowest mind, that she was murdered by one of her clients.' He said the word in a hiss.

'There was no appointment listed for several hours prior to her death. Her last client has an alibi for the critical hour.'

'Break it,' DeBlass demanded. 'A man who would pay for sexual favors would have no compunction about murder.'

Though Eve failed to see the correlation, she remembered her job and nodded. 'I'm working on it, senator.'

'I want copies of her appointment books.'

'That's not possible, senator,' Whitney said mildly. 'All evidence of a capital crime is confidential.'

DeBlass merely snorted and gestured toward Rockman.

'Commander.' Rockman reached in his left breast pocket and drew out a sheet of paper affixed with a holographic seal. 'This document from your chief of police authorizes the senator access to any and all evidence and investigative data on Ms DeBlass's murder.'

Whitney barely glanced at the document before setting it aside. He'd always considered politics a coward's game, and hated that he was forced to play it. 'I'll speak to the chief personally. If the authorization holds, we'll have copies to you by this afternoon.' Dismissing Rockman, he looked back at DeBlass. 'The confidentiality of evidence is a major tool in the investigative process. If you insist on this, you risk undermining the case.'

'The case, as you put it, commander, was my flesh and blood.'

'And as such, I'd hope your first priority would be assisting us to bring her killer to justice.'

'I've served justice for more than fifty years. I want that information by noon.' He picked up his coat, tossed it over one beefy arm. 'If I'm not satisfied that you're doing everything in your power to find this maniac, I'll see that you're removed from this office.' He turned toward Eve. 'And that the next thing you investigate, lieutenant, will be sticky fingered teen-agers at a shop-com.'

After he stormed out, Rockman used his quiet, solemn eyes to apologize. 'You must forgive the senator. He's overwrought. However much strain there was between him and his grand-daughter, she was family. Nothing is more vital to the senator than his family. Her death, this kind of violent, senseless death, is devastating to him.'

'Right,' Eve muttered. 'He looked all choked up.'

Rockman smiled; he managed to look amused and sorrowful at once. 'Proud men often disguise their grief behind aggression. We have every confidence in your abilities and your tenacity, lieutenant. Commander,' he nodded. 'We'll expect the data this afternoon. Thank you for your time.'

'He's a smooth one,' Eve muttered when Rockman shut the door quietly behind him. 'You're not going to cave, commander.'

'I'll give them what I have to.' His voice was sharp and edged with suppressed fury. 'Now, go get me more.'


Police work was too often drudgery. After five hours of staring at her monitor as she ran makes on the names in DeBlass's books, Eve was more exhausted than she would have been after a marathon race.

Even with Feeney taking a portion of the names with his skill and superior equipment, there were too many for such a small investigative unit to handle quickly.

Sharon had been a very popular girl.

Feeling discretion would gain her more than aggression, Eve contacted the clients by 'link and explained herself. Those who balked at the idea of an interview were cheerfully invited to come into Cop Central, charged with obstruction of justice.

By midafternoon she had spoken personally with the first dozen on the client list, and took a detour back to the Gorham.

DeBlass's neighbor, the elegant man from the elevator,

was Charles Monroe. Eve found him in, and entertaining a client.

Slickly handsome in a black silk robe, and smelling seductively of sex, Charles smiled engagingly.

'I'm terribly sorry, lieutenant. My three o'clock appointment has another fifteen minutes.'

'I'll wait.' Without invitation, Eve stepped inside. Unlike DeBlass's apartment, this one ran to deep, cushy chairs in leather and thick carpets.

'Ah . . .' Obviously amused, Charles glanced behind him, where a door was discreetly closed at the end of a short hallway. 'Privacy and confidentiality are, you understand, vital to my profession. My client is apt to be disconcerted if she discovers the police on my doorstep.'

'No problem. Got a kitchen?'

He let out a weighty sigh. 'Sure. Right through that doorway. Make yourself at home. I won't be long.'

'Take your time.' Eve strolled off to the kitchen. In contrast to the elaborate living area, this was spartan. It seemed Charles spent little time eating in. Still, he had a full-size friggie unit rather than a cold cell, and she found the treasure of a Pepsi chilling. Satisfied for the moment, she sat down to enjoy it while Charles finished off his three o'clock.

Soon enough, she heard the murmur of voices, a man's, a woman's, a light laugh. Moments later, he came in, the same easy smile on his face.

'Sorry to keep you waiting.'

'No problem. Are you expecting anyone else?'

'Not until later this evening.' He took out a Pepsi for himself, broke the freshness seal from the tube, and poured it into a tall glass. He rolled the tube into a ball and popped it into the recycler. 'Dinner, the opera, and a romantic rendezvous.'

'You like that stuff? Opera?' she asked when he flashed a grin.

'Hate it. Can you think of anything more tedious than some big-chested woman screaming in German half the night?'

Eve thought it over. 'Nope.'

'But there you are. Tastes vary.' His smile faded as he joined her at the little nook under the kitchen window. 'I heard about Sharon on the news this morning. I've been expecting someone to come by. It's horrible. I can't believe she's dead.'

'You knew her well?'

'We've been neighbors more than three years – and occasionally we worked together. Now and again, one of our clients would request a trio, and we'd share the business.'

'And when it wasn't business, did you still share?'

'She was a beautiful woman, and she found me attractive.' He moved his silk-clad shoulders, his eyes shifting to the tinted glass of the window as a tourist tram streamed by. 'If one of us was in the mood for a busman's holiday, the other usually obliged.' He smiled again. 'That was rare. Like working in a candy store, after a while you lose your taste for chocolate. She was a friend, lieutenant. And I was very fond of her.'

'Can you tell me where you were the night of her death between midnight and three A.M.?'

His brows shot up. If it hadn't just occurred to him that he could be considered a suspect, he was an excellent actor. Then again, Eve thought, people in his line of work had to be.

'I was with a client, here. She stayed overnight.'

'Is that usual?'

'This client prefers that arrangement. Lieutenant, I'll give you her name if absolutely necessary, but I'd prefer not to. At least until I've explained the circumstances to her.'

'It's murder, Mr Monroe, so it's necessary. What time did you bring your client here?'

'About ten. We had dinner at Miranda's, the sky café above Sixth.'

'Ten.' Eve nodded, and saw the moment he remembered.

'The security camera in the elevator.' His smile was all charm again. 'It's an antiquated law. I suppose you could bust me, but it's hardly worth your time.'

'Any sexual act in a secured area is a misdemeanor, Mr Monroe.'

'Charles, please.'

'It's a nitpick, Charles, but they could suspend your license for six months. Give me her name, and we'll clear it up as quietly as possible.'

'You're going to lose me one of my best clients,' he muttered. 'Darleen Howe. I'll get you the address.' He rose to get his electronic datebook, then read off the information.

'Thanks. Did Sharon talk about her clients with you?'

'We were friends,' he said wearily. 'Yeah, we talked shop, though it's not strictly ethical. She had some funny stories. I'm more conventional in style. Sharon was . . . open to the unusual. Sometimes we'd get together for a drink, and she'd talk. No names. She had her own little terms for them. The emperor, the weasel, the milkmaid, that kind of thing.'

'Was there anyone she mentioned who worried her, made her uneasy? Someone who might have been violent?'

'She didn't mind violence, and no, nobody worried her. One thing about Sharon, she always felt in control. That's the way she wanted it because she said she'd been under someone else's control most of her life. She had a lot of bitterness toward her family. She told me once she'd never planned on making a career out of professional sex. She'd only gotten into it to make her family crazy. But then, after she got into it, she decided she liked it.'

He moved his shoulders again, sipped from his glass. 'So she stayed in the life, and killed two birds with one fuck. Her phrase.'

He lifted his eyes again. 'Looks like one of the fucks killed her.'

'Yeah.' Eve rose, tucked her recorder away. 'Don't take any out-of-town trips, Charles. I'll be in touch.'

'That's it?'

'For the moment.'

He stood as well, smiled again. 'You're easy to talk to for a cop . . . Eve.' Experimentally, he skimmed a fingertip down her arm. When her brows lifted, he took the fingertip over her jawline. 'In a hurry?'

'Why?'

'Well, I've got a couple of hours, and you're very attractive. Big golden eyes,' he murmured. 'This little dip right in your chin. Why don't we both go off the clock for awhile?'

She waited while he lowered his head, while his lips hovered just above hers. 'Is this a bribe, Charles? Because if it is, and you're half as good as I think you are . . .'

'I'm better.' He nibbled at her bottom lip, let his hand slide down to toy with her breast. 'I'm much better.'

'In that case . . . I'd have to charge you with a felony.' She smiled as he jerked back. 'And that would make both of us really sad.' Amused, she patted his cheek. 'But, thanks for the thought.'

He scratched his chin as he followed her to the door. 'Eve?'

She paused, hand on the knob, and glanced back at him. 'Yes?'

'Bribes aside, if you change your mind, I'd be interested in seeing more of you.'

'I'll let you know.' She closed the door and headed for the elevator.

It wouldn't have been difficult, she mused, for Charles Monroe to slip out of his apartment, leaving his client sleeping, and slip into Sharon's. A little sex, a little murder . . .

Thoughtful, she stepped into the elevator.

Doctor the discs. As a resident of the building, it would

have been simple for him to gain access to security. Then he could have popped back into bed with his client.

It was too bad that the scenario was plausible, Eve thought as she reached the lobby. She liked him. But until she checked his alibi thoroughly, Charles Monroe was now at the top of her short list.

# Chapter Three

Eve hated funerals. She detested the rite human beings insisted on giving death. The flowers, the music, the endless words and weeping.

There might be a God. She hadn't completely ruled such things out. And if there were, she thought, It must have enjoyed a good laugh over Its creations' useless rituals and passages.

Still, she had made the trip to Virginia to attend Sharon DeBlass's funeral. She wanted to see the dead's family and friends gathered together, to observe, and analyze, and judge.

The senator stood grim-faced and dry-eyed, with Rockman, his shadow, one pew behind. Beside DeBlass was his son and daughter-in-law.

Sharon's parents were young, attractive, successful attorneys who headed their own law firm.

Richard DeBlass stood with his head bowed and his eyes hooded, a trimmer and somehow less dynamic version of his father. Was it coincidence, Eve wondered, or design that he stood at equal distance between his father and wife?

Elizabeth Barrister was sleek and chic in her dark suit, her waving mahogany hair glossy, her posture rigid. And, Eve, noted, her eyes red-rimmed and swimming with constant tears.

What did a mother feel, Eve wondered, as she had wondered all of her life, when she lost a child?

Senator DeBlass had a daughter as well, and she flanked his right side. Congresswoman Catherine DeBlass had followed in her father's political footsteps. Painfully thin, she stood militarily straight, her arms looking like brittle twigs in her black dress. Beside her, her husband Justin Summit stared at the glossy coffin draped with roses at the front of the church. At his side, their son Franklin, still trapped in the gangly stage of adolescence, shifted restlessly.

At the end of the pew, somehow separate from the rest of the family, was DeBlass's wife, Anna.

She neither shifted nor wept. Not once did Eve see her so much as glance at the flower-strewn box that held what was left of her only granddaughter.

There were others, of course. Elizabeth's parents stood together, hands linked, and cried openly. Cousins, acquaint-ances, and friends dabbed at their eyes or simply looked around in fascination or horror. The President had sent an envoy, and the church was packed with more politicians than the Senate lunchroom.

Though there were more than a hundred faces, Eve had no trouble picking Roarke out of the crowd. He was alone. There were others lined in the pew with him, but Eve recognized the solitary quality that surrounded him. There could have been ten thousand in the building, and he would have remained aloof from them.

His striking face gave away nothing: no guilt, no grief, no interest. He might have been watching a mildly inferior play. Eve could think of no better description for a funeral.

More than one head turned in his direction for a quick study or, in the case of a shapely brunette, a not so subtle flirtation. Roarke responded to both the same way: he ignored them.

At first study, she would have judged him as cold, an icy fortress of a man who guarded himself against any and all. But there must have been heat. It took more than discipline and intelligence to rise so high so young. It took ambition, and to Eve's mind, ambition was a flammable fuel.

He looked straight ahead as the dirge swelled, then without warning, he turned his head, looked five pews back across the aisle and directly into Eve's eyes.

It was surprise that had her fighting not to jolt at that sudden and unexpected punch of power. It was will that kept her from blinking or shifting her gaze. For one humming minute they stared at each other. Then there was movement, and mourners came between them as they left the church.

When Eve stepped into the aisle to search him out again, he was gone.

She joined the long line of cars and limos on the journey to the cemetery. Above, the hearse and the family vehicles flew solemnly. Only the very rich could afford body internment. Only the obsessively traditional still put their dead into the ground.

Frowning, her fingers tapping the wheel, she relayed her observations into her recorder. When she got to Roarke, she hesitated and her frown deepened.

'Why would he trouble himself to attend the funeral of such a casual acquaintance?' She murmured into the recorder in her pocket. 'According to data, they had met only recently and had a single date. Behavior seems inconsistent and questionable.'

She shivered once, glad she was alone as she drove through the arching gates of the cemetery. As far as Eve was concerned, there should be a law against putting someone in a hole.

More words and weeping, more flowers. The sun was bright as a sword but the air had the snapping bite of a petulant child. Near the gravesite, she slipped her hands into her pockets. She'd forgotten her gloves again. The long, dark coat she wore was borrowed. Beneath it, the single gray suit she owned had a loose button that seemed to beg her to tug at it. Inside her thin leather boots, her toes were tiny blocks of ice.

The discomfort helped distract her from the misery of headstones and the smell of cold, fresh earth. She bided her time, waiting until the last mournful word about everlasting life echoed away, then approached the senator.

'My sympathies, Senator DeBlass, to you and your family.'

His eyes were hard; sharp and black, like the hewed edge of a stone. 'Save your sympathies, lieutenant. I want justice.'

'So do I. Mrs DeBlass.' Eve held out a hand to the senator's wife and found her fingers clutching a bundle of brittle twigs.

'Thank you for coming.'

Eve nodded. One close look had shown her Anna DeBlass was skimming under the edge of emotion on a buffering layer of chemicals. Her eyes passed over Eve's face and settled just above her shoulder as she withdrew her hand.

'Thank you for coming,' she said in exactly the same flat tone to the next offer of condolence.

Before Eve could speak again, her arm was taken in a firm grip. Rockman smiled solemnly down at her. 'Lieutenant Dallas, the Senator and his family appreciate the compassion and interest you've shown in attending the service.' In his quiet manner, he edged her away. 'I'm sure you'll understand that, under the circumstances, it would be difficult for Sharon's parents to meet the officer in charge of their daughter's investigation over her grave.'

Eve allowed him to lead her five feet away before she jerked her arm free. 'You're in the right business, Rockman. That's a very delicate and diplomatic way of telling me to get my ass out.'

'Not at all.' He continued to smile, smoothly polite. 'There's simply a time and place. You have our complete cooperation, lieutenant. If you wish to interview the senator's family, I'd be more than happy to arrange it.'

'I'll arrange my own interviews, at my own time and place.' Because his placid smile irked her, she decided to see if she could wipe it off his face. 'What about you, Rockman? Got an alibi for the night in question?'

The smile did falter – that was some satisfaction. He recovered quickly, however. 'I dislike the word alibi.'

'Me, too,' she returned with a smile of her own. 'That's why I like nothing better than to break them. You didn't answer the question, Rockman.'

'I was in East Washington on the night Sharon was murdered. The senator and I worked quite late refining a bill he intends to present next month.'

'It's a quick trip from EW to New York,' she commented.

'It is. However, I didn't make it on that particular night. We worked until nearly midnight, then I retired to the senator's guest room. We had breakfast together at seven the next morning. As Sharon, according to your own reports, was killed at two, it gives me a very narrow window of opportunity.'

'Narrow windows still provide access.' But she said it only to irritate him as she turned away. She'd held back the information on the doctored security discs from the file she'd given DeBlass. The murderer had been in the Gorham by midnight. Rockman would hardly use the victim's grandfather for an alibi unless it was solid. Rockman's working in East Washington at midnight slammed even that narrow window closed.

She saw Roarke again, and watched with interest as Elizabeth Barrister clung to him, as he bent his head and murmured to her. Not the usual offer and acceptance of sympathy from strangers, Eve mused.

Her brow lifted as Roarke laid a hand on Elizabeth's right cheek, kissed her left before stepping back to speak quietly to Richard DeBlass.

He crossed to the senator, but there was no contact between them, and the conversation was brief. Alone, as Eve had suspected, Roarke began to walk across the winter grass, between the cold monuments the living raised for the dead.

'Roarke.'

He stopped, and as he had at the service, turned and met her eyes. She thought she caught a flash of something in them: anger, sorrow, impatience. Then it was gone and they were simply cool, blue, and unfathomable.

She didn't hurry as she walked to him. Something told her he was a man too used to people – women certainly – rushing toward him. So she took her time, her long, slow strides flapping her borrowed coat around her chilly legs.

'I'd like to speak with you,' she said when she faced him. She took out her badge, watched him give it a brief glance before lifting his eyes back to hers. 'I'm investigating Sharon DeBlass's murder.'

'Do you make a habit of attending the funerals of murder victims, Lieutenant Dallas?'

His voice was smooth, with a whisper of the charm of Ireland over it, like rich cream over warmed whiskey. 'Do you make a habit of attending the funerals of women you barely know, Roarke?'

'I'm a friend of the family,' he said simply. 'You're freezing, lieutenant.'

She plunged her icy fingers into the pockets of the coat. 'How well do you know the victim's family?'

'Well enough.' He tilted his head. In a minute, he thought, her teeth would chatter. The nasty little wind was blowing her poorly cut hair around a very interesting face. Intelligent, stubborn, sexy. Three very good reasons in his mind to take a second look at a woman. 'Wouldn't it be more convenient to talk someplace warmer?'

'I've been unable to reach you,' she began.

40

'I've been traveling. You've reached me now. I assume you're returning to New York. Today?'

'Yes. I have a few minutes before I have to leave for the shuttle. So . . .'

'So we'll go back together. That should give you time enough to grill me.'

'Question you,' she said between her teeth, annoyed that he turned and walked away from her. She lengthened her stride to catch up. 'A few simple answers now, Roarke, and we can arrange a more formal interview in New York.'

'I hate to waste time,' he said easily. 'You strike me as someone who feels the same. Did you rent a car?'

'Yes.'

'I'll arrange to have it returned.' He held out a hand, waiting for the key card.

'That isn't necessary.'

'It's simpler. I appreciate complications, lieutenant, and I appreciate simplicity. You and I are going to the same destination at the same approximate time. You want to talk to me, and I'm willing to oblige.' He stopped by a black limo where a uniformed driver waited, holding the rear door open. 'My transport's routed for New York. You can, of course, follow me to the airport, take public transportation, then call my office for an appointment. Or you can drive with me, enjoy the privacy of my jet, and have my full attention during the trip.'

She hesitated only a moment, then took the key card for the rental from her pocket and dropped it into his hand. Smiling, he gestured her into the limo where she settled as he instructed his driver to deal with the rental car.

'Now then.' Roarke slid in beside her, reached for a decanter. 'Would you like a brandy to fight off the chill?'

'No.' She felt the warmth of the car sweep up from her feet and was afraid she'd begin to shiver in reaction.

41

'Ah. On duty. Coffee perhaps.'

'Great.'

Gold winked at his wrist as he pressed his choice for two coffees on the AutoChef built into the side panel. 'Cream?'

'Black.'

'A woman after my own heart.' Moments later, he opened the protective door and offered her a china cup in a delicate saucer. 'We have more of a selection on the plane,' he said, then settled back with his coffee.

'I bet.' The steam rising from her cup smelled like heaven. Eve took a tentative sip – and nearly moaned.

It was real. No simulation made from vegetable concentrate so usual since the depletion of the rain forests in the late twentieth. This was the real thing, ground from rich Columbian beans, singing with caffeine.

She sipped again, and could have wept.

'Problem?' He enjoyed her reaction immensely, the flutter of the lashes, the faint flush, the darkening of the eyes – a similar response, he noted, to a woman purring under a man's hands.

'Do you know how long it's been since I had real coffee?'

He smiled. 'No.'

'Neither do I.' Unashamed, she closed her eyes as she lifted the cup again. 'You'll have to excuse me, this is a private moment. We'll talk on the plane.'

'As you like.'

He gave himself the pleasure of watching her as the car traveled smoothly over the road.

Odd, he thought, he hadn't pegged her for a cop. His instincts were usually keen about such matters. At the funeral, he'd been thinking only what a terrible waste it was for someone as young, foolish, and full of life as Sharon to be dead.

Then he'd sensed something, something that had coiled his

muscles, tightened his gut. He'd felt her gaze, as physical as a blow. When he'd turned, when he'd seen her, another blow. A slow motion one-two punch he hadn't been able to evade.

It was fascinating.

But the warning blip hadn't gone off. Not the warning blip that should have relayed *cop*. He'd seen a tall, willowy brunette with short, tumbled hair, eyes the color of honeycombs and a mouth made for sex.

If she hadn't sought him out, he'd intended to seek her.

Too damn bad she was a cop.

She didn't speak again until they were at the airport, stepping into the cabin of his JetStar 6000.

She hated being impressed, again. Coffee was one thing, and a small weakness was permitted, but she didn't care for her goggle-eyed reaction to the lush cabin with its deep chairs, sofas, the antique carpet, and crystal vases filled with flowers.

There was a viewing screen recessed in the forward wall and a uniformed flight attendant who showed no surprise at seeing Roarke board with a strange woman.

'Brandy, sir?'

'My companion prefers coffee, Diana, black.' He lifted a brow until Eve nodded. 'I'll have brandy.'

'I've heard about the JetStar.' Eve shrugged out of her coat, and it was whisked away along with Roarke's by the attendant. 'It's a nice form of transportation.'

'Thanks. We spent two years designing it.'

'Roarke Industries?' she said as she took a chair.

'That's right. I prefer using my own whenever possible. You'll need to strap in for takeoff,' he told her, then leaned forward to flip on an intercom. 'Ready.'

'We've been cleared,' they were told. 'Thirty seconds.'

Almost before Eve could blink, they were airborne, in so smooth a transition she barely felt the g's. It beat the hell, she thought, out of the commercial flights that slapped you back in your seat for the first five minutes of air time.

They were served drinks and a little plate of fruit and cheese that had Eve's mouth watering. It was time, she decided, to get to work.

'How long did you know Sharon DeBlass?'

'I met her recently, at the home of a mutual acquaintance.'

'You said you were a friend of the family.'

'Of her parents,' Roarke said easily. 'I've known Beth and Richard for several years. First on a business level, then on a personal one. Sharon was in school, then in Europe, and our paths didn't cross. I met her for the first time a few days ago, took her to dinner. Then she was dead.'

He took a flat gold case from his inside pocket. Eve's eyes narrowed as she watched him light a cigarette. 'Tobacco's illegal, Roarke.'

'Not in free air space, international waters, or on private property.' He smiled at her through a haze of smoke. 'Don't you think, lieutenant, that the police have enough to do without trying to legislate our morality and personal lifestyles?'

She hated to admit even to herself that the tobacco smelled enticing. 'Is that why you collect guns? As part of your personal lifestyle?'

'I find them fascinating. Your grandfather and mine considered owning one a constitutional right. We've toyed quite a bit with constitutional rights as we've civilized ourselves.'

'And murder and injury by that particular type of weapon is now an aberration rather than the norm.'

'You like rules, lieutenant?'

The question was mild, as was the insult under it. Her shoulders stiffened. 'Without rules, chaos.'

'With chaos, life.'

Screw philosophy, she thought, annoyed. 'Do you own a thirty-eight caliber Smith & Wesson, Model Ten, circa 1990?'

He took another slow, considering drag. The tobacco burned expensively between his long, elegant fingers. 'I believe I own one of that model. Is that what killed her?'

'Would you be willing to show it to me?'

'Of course, at your convenience.'

Too easy, she thought. She suspected anything that came easily. 'You had dinner with the deceased the night before her death. In Mexico.'

'That's right.' Roarke crushed out his cigarette and settled back with his brandy. 'I have a small villa on the west coast. I thought she'd enjoy it. She did.'

'Did you have a physical relationship with Sharon DeBlass?'

His eyes glittered for a moment, but whether with amusement or with anger, she couldn't be sure. 'By that, I take you to mean did I have sex with her. No, lieutenant, though it hardly seems relevant. We had dinner.'

'You took a beautiful woman, a professional companion, to your villa in Mexico, and all you shared with her was dinner.'

He took his time choosing a glossy green grape. 'I appreciate beautiful women for a variety of reasons, and enjoy spending time with them. I don't employ professionals for two reasons. First, I don't find it necessary to pay for sex.' He sipped his brandy, watching her over the rim. 'And second, I don't choose to share.' He paused, very briefly. 'Do you?'

Her stomach fluttered, was ignored. 'We're not talking about me.'

'I was. You're a beautiful woman, and we're quite alone, at least for the next fifteen minutes. Yet all we've shared has been coffee and brandy.' He smiled at the temper smoldering in her eyes. 'Heroic, isn't it, what restraint I have?'

'I'd say your relationship with Sharon DeBlass had a different flavor.'

'Oh, I certainly agree.' He chose another grape, offered it.

45

Appetite was a weakness, Eve reminded herself even as she accepted the grape and bit through its thin, tart skin. 'Did you see her after your dinner in Mexico?'

'No, I dropped her off about three A.M. and went home. Alone.'

'Can you tell me your whereabouts for the forty-eight hours after you went home – alone?'

'I was in bed for the first five of them. I took a conference call over breakfast. About eight-fifteen. You can check the records.'

'I will.'

This time he grinned, a quick flash of undiluted charm that had her pulse skipping. 'I have no doubt of it. You fascinate me, Lieutenant Dallas.'

'After the conference call?'

'It ended about nine. I worked out until ten, spent the next several hours in my midtown office with various appointments.' He took out a small, slim card that she recognized as a daybook. 'Shall I list them for you?'

'I'd prefer you to arrange to have a hard copy sent to my office.'

'I'll see to it. I was back home by seven. I had a dinner meeting with several members of my Japanese manufacturing firm – in my home. We dined at eight. Shall I send you the menu?'

'Don't be snide, Roarke.'

'Merely thorough, lieutenant. It was an early evening. By eleven I was alone, with a book and a brandy, until about seven A.M., when I had my first cup of coffee. Would you like another?'

She'd have killed for another cup of coffee, but she shook her head. 'Alone for eight hours, Roarke. Did you speak with anyone, see anyone during that time?'

'No. No one. I had to be in Paris the next day and wanted

a quiet evening. Poor timing on my part. Then again, if I were going to murder someone, it would have been ill advised not to protect myself with an alibi.'

'Or arrogant not to bother,' she returned. 'Do you just collect antique weapons, Roarke, or do you use them?'

'I'm an excellent shot.' He set his empty snifter aside. 'I'll be happy to demonstrate for you when you come to see my collection. Does tomorrow suit you?'

'Fine.'

'Seven o'clock? I assume you have the address.' When he leaned over, she stiffened and nearly hissed as his hand brushed her arm. He only smiled, his face close, his eyes level. 'You need to strap in,' he said quietly. 'We'll be landing in a moment.'

He fastened her harness himself, wondering if he made her nervous as a man, or a murder suspect, or a combination of both. Just then, any choice had its own interest – and its own possibilities.

'Eve,' he murmured. 'Such a simple and feminine name. I wonder if it suits you.'

She said nothing while the flight attendant came in to remove the dishes. 'Have you ever been in Sharon DeBlass's apartment?'

A tough shell, he mused, but he was certain there would be something soft and hot beneath. He wondered if – no, when – he'd have the opportunity to uncover it.

'Not while she was a tenant,' Roarke said as he sat back again. 'And not at all that I recall, though it's certainly possible.' He smiled again and fastened his own harness. 'I own the Gorham Complex, as I'm sure you already know.'

Idly, he glanced out the window as earth hurtled toward them. 'Do you have transportation at the airport, lieutenant, or can I give you a lift?'

# Chapter Four

Eve was more than tired by the time she filed her report for Whitney and returned home. She was pissed. She'd wanted, badly, to zing Roarke with the fact that she knew he owned the Gorham. His telling her in the same carelessly polite tone he used to offer her coffee had ended their first interview with him one point up.

She didn't like the score.

It was time to even things up. Alone in her living room, and technically off the clock, she sat down in front of her computer.

'Engage, Dallas, Code Five access. ID 53478Q. Open file DeBlass.

*Voice print and ID recognized, Dallas. Proceed.*

'Open subfile Roarke. Suspect Roarke – known to victim. According to Source C, Sebastian, victim desired suspect. Suspect met her requirements for sexual partner. Possibility of emotional involvement high.

'Opportunity to commit crime. Suspect owns victim's apartment building, equaling easy access and probably knowledge of security of murder scene. Suspect has no alibi for eight-hour period on the night of the murder, which includes the time span erased from security discs. Suspect owns large collection of antique weapons, including the type used on victim. Suspect admits to being expert marksman.

'Factor in personality of suspect. Aloof, confident, self-indulgent, highly intelligent. Interesting balance between aggressive and charming.

'Motive.'

And there, she ran into trouble. Calculating, she rose, did a pass through the room while the computer waited for more data. Why would a man like Roarke kill? For gain, in passion? She didn't think so. Wealth and status he would, and could gain by other means. Women – for sex and otherwise – certainly he could win without breaking a sweat. She suspected he was capable of violence, and that he would execute it coldly.

Sharon DeBlass's murder had been charged with sex. There had been a crudeness overlaying it. Eve couldn't quite reconcile that with the elegant man she'd shared coffee with.

Perhaps that was the point.

'Suspect considers morality a personal rather than legislative area,' she continued, pacing still. 'Sex, weapon restriction, drug, tobacco, and alcohol restrictions, and murder deal with morality that has been outlawed or regulated. The murder of a licensed companion, the only daughter of friends, the only granddaughter of one of the country's most outspoken and conservative legislators, by a banned weapon. Was this an illustration of the flaws the suspect considers are inherent in the legal system?

'Motive,' she concluded, settling again. 'Self-indulgence.' She took a deep, satisfied breath. 'Compute probability.'

Her system whined, reminded her it was one more piece of hardware that needed replacement, then settled into a jerky rum.

*Probability Roarke perpetrator given current data and supposition, eighty-two point six per cent.*

Oh, it was possible, Eve thought, leaning back in her chair. There was a time, in the not so distant past, when a child could be gunned down by another child for the shoes on his feet.

What was that if not obscene self-indulgence?

He had the opportunity. He had the means. And if his own arrogance could be taken into account, he had the motive.

So why, Eve thought as she watched her own words blink on the monitor, as she studied her computer's impersonal analysis, couldn't she make it play in her own head?

She just couldn't see it, she admitted. She just couldn't visualize Roarke standing behind the camera, aiming the gun at the defenseless, naked, smiling woman, and pumping steel into her perhaps only moments after he'd pumped his seed into her.

Still, certain facts couldn't be overlooked. If she could rather enough of them, she could issue a warrant for a psychiatric evaluation.

Wouldn't that be interesting? she thought with a half smile. Traveling into Roarke's head would be a fascinating journey.

She'd take the next step at seven the following evening.

The buzz at her door brought a frown of annoyance to her eyes. 'Save and lock on voice print, Dallas. Code Five. Disengage.'

The monitor blipped off as she rose to see who was interrupting her. A glance at her security screen wiped the down away.

'Hey, Mavis.'

'You forgot, didn't you?' Mavis Freestone whirled in, a jangle of bracelets, a puff of scent. Her hair was a glittery silver tonight, a shade that would change with her next mood. She flipped it back where it sparkled like stars down to her impossibly tiny waist.

'No, I didn't.' Eve shut the door, reengaged the locks. 'Forgot what?'

'Dinner, dancing, debauchery.' With a heavy sigh, Mavis dropped her slinkily attired nighty-eight pounds onto the sofa where she could eye Eve's simple gray suit with disdain. 'You can't be going out in that.'

Feeling drab, as she often did within twenty feet of Mavis's outrageous color, Eve looked down at her suit. 'No, I guess not.'

'So.' Mavis gestured with one emerald-tipped finger. 'You forgot.'

She had, but she was remembering now. They had made plans to check out the new club Mavis had discovered at the space docks in Jersey. According to Mavis, the space jocks were perennially horny. Something to do with extended weightlessness.

'Sorry. You look great.'

It was true, inevitably. Eight years before, when Eve had busted Mavis for petty theft, she'd looked great. A silk swirling street urchin with quick fingers and a brilliant smile.

In the intervening years, they'd somehow become friends. For Eve, who could count on one hand the number of friends she had who weren't cops, the relationship was precious.

'You look tired,' Mavis said, more in accusation than sympathy. 'And you're missing a button.'

Eve's fingers went automatically to her jacket, felt the loose threads. 'Shit. I knew it.' In disgust she shrugged out of the jacket, tossed it aside. 'Look, I'm sorry. I did forget. I had a lot on my mind today.'

'Including the reason you needed my black coat?'

'Yeah, thanks. It came in handy.'

Mavis sat a minute, tapping those emerald-tipped nails on the arm of the couch. 'Police business. Here I was hoping you had a date. You really need to start seeing men who aren't criminals, Dallas.'

'I saw that image consultant you fixed me up with. He wasn't a criminal. He was just an idiot.'

'You're too picky – and that was six months ago.'

Since he'd tried to get her in the sack by offering a free lip tattoo, Eve thought it was not nearly long enough, but kept the opinion to herself. 'I'll go change.'

'You don't want to go out and bump butts with the space boys.' Mavis sprang up again, the shoulder-length crystals at her ears sparkling. 'But go ahead and get out of that ugly skirt. I'll order Chinese.'

Relief had Eve's shoulders sagging. For Mavis, she would have tolerated an evening at a loud, crowded, obnoxious club, peeling randy pilots and sex-starved sky station techs off her chest. The idea of eating Chinese with her feet up was like heaven.

'You don't mind?'

Mavis waved the words away as she tapped in the restaurant she wanted on the computer. 'I spend every night in a club.'

'That's work,' Eve called out as she went into the bed-room.

'You're telling me.' Tongue between her teeth, Mavis perused the menu on-screen. 'A few years ago I'd have said singing for my supper was the world's biggest scam, the best grift I could run. Turns out I'm working harder than I ever did bilking tourists. You want egg rolls?'

'Sure. You're not thinking of quitting, are you?'

Mavis was silent a moment as she made her choices. 'No. I'm hooked on applause.' Feeling generous, she charged dinner to her World Card. 'And since we renegotiated my contract so I get ten percent of the gate, I'm a regular businesswoman.'

'There's nothing regular about you,' Eve disagreed. She came back in, comfortable in jeans and a NYPSD sweatshirt.

'True. Got any of that wine I brought over last time?'

'Most of the second bottle.' Because it sounded like the best idea she'd had all day, Eve detoured into the kitchen to pour it. 'So, are you still seeing the dentist?'

'Nope.' Idly, Mavis wandered to the entertainment unit and

programmed in music. 'It was getting too intense. I didn't mind him falling in love with my teeth, but he decided to go for the whole package. He wanted to get married.'

'The bastard.'

'You can't trust anybody,' Mavis agreed. 'How's the law and order business?'

'It's a little intense right now.' She glanced up from the wine she was pouring when the buzzer sounded. 'That can't be dinner already.' Even as she said it, she heard Mavis clipping cheerfully toward the door in her five-inch spikes. 'Check the security screen,' she said quickly and was halfway to the door herself when Mavis pulled it open.

She had one moment to curse, another to reach for the weapon she wasn't wearing. Then Mavis's quick, flirtatious laugh had her adrenaline draining again.

Eve recognized the uniform of the delivery company, saw nothing but embarrassed pleasure in the young, fresh face of the boy who handed the package to Mavis.

'I just love presents,' Mavis said with a flutter of her silver-tipped lashes as the boy backed away, blushing. 'Don't you come with it?'

'Leave the kid alone.' With a shake of her head, Eve took the package from Mavis and closed the door again.

'They're so cute at that age.' She blew a kiss at the security screen before turning to Eve. 'What are you so nervous about, Dallas?'

'The case I'm working on has me jumpy, I guess.' She eyed the gold foil and elaborate bow on the package she held with more suspicion than pleasure. 'I don't know who'd be sending me anything.'

'There's a card,' Mavis pointed out dryly. 'You could always read it. There might be a clue.'

'Now look who's cute.' Eve tugged the card out of its gold envelope.

As she read over Eve's shoulder, Mavis let out a low whistle. 'Not *the* Roarke! The incredibly wealthy, fabulous to look at, sexily mysterious Roarke who owns approximately twenty-eight percent of the world, and its satellites?'

All Eve felt was irritation. 'He's the only one I know.'

'You know him.' Mavis rolled her green shadowed eyes. 'Dallas, I've underestimated you unforgivably. Tell me everything. How, when, why? Did you sleep with him? Tell me you slept with him, then give me every tiny detail.'

'We've had a secret, passionate affair for the last three years, during which time I bore him a son who's being raised on the far side of the moon by Buddhist monks.' Brows knit, Eve shook the box. 'Get a grip, Mavis. It has to do with a case, and,' she added before Mavis could open her mouth, 'it's confidential.'

Mavis didn't bother to roll her eyes again. When Eve said *confidential*, no amount of cajoling, pleading or whining could budge her an inch. 'Okay, but you can tell me if he looks as good in person as he does in pictures.'

'Better,' Eve muttered.

'Jesus, really?' Mavis moaned and let herself fall onto the sofa. 'I think I just had an orgasm.'

'You ought to know.' Eve set the package down, scowled at it. 'And how did he know where I live? You can't pluck a cop's address out of the directory file. How did he know?' she repeated quietly. 'And what's he up to?'

'For God's sake, Dallas, open it. He probably took a shine to you. Some men find the cool, disinterested, and understated attractive. Makes them think you're deep. I bet it's diamonds,' Mavis said, pouncing on the box as her patience snapped. 'A necklace. A diamond necklace. Maybe rubies. You'd look sensational in rubies.'

She ripped ruthlessly through the pricey paper, tossed aside the lid of the box, and plunged her hand through the gold-edged tissue. 'What the hell is this?'

But Eve had already scented it, already – despite herself – begun to smile. 'It's coffee,' she murmured, unaware of the way her voice softened as she reached for the simple brown bag Mavis held.

'Coffee.' Illusions shattered, Mavis stared. 'The man's got more money than God, and he sends you a bag of coffee?'

'Real coffee.'

'Oh, well then.' In disgust, Mavis waved a hand. 'I don't care what the damn stuff costs a pound, Dallas. A woman wants glitter.'

Eve brought the bag to her face and sniffed deep. 'Not this woman. The son of a bitch knew just how to get to me.' She sighed. 'In more ways than one.'

Eve treated herself to one precious cup the next morning. Even her temperamental AutoChef hadn't been able to spoil the dark, rich flavor. She drove to the station, with her faulty heater, under sleeting skies, in a wild chill that came in just under five degrees, with a smile on her face.

It was still there when she walked into her office and found Feeney waiting for her.

'Well, well.' He studied her. 'What'd you have for breakfast, ace?'

'Nothing but coffee. Just coffee. Got anything for me?'

'Ran a full check on Richard DeBlass, Elizabeth Barrister, and the rest of the clan.' He handed her a disc marked Code Five in bold red. 'No real surprises. Nothing much out of the ordinary on Rockman, either. In his twenties, he belonged to a paramilitary group known as SafeNet.'

'SafeNet,' Eve repeated, brow wrinkling.

'You'd have been about eight when it was disbanded, kid,'

Feeney told her with a smirk. 'Should have heard of it in your history lessons.'

'Rings a distant bell. Was that one of the groups that got worked up when we had that skirmish with China?'

'It was, and if they'd had their way, it would have been a lot more than a skirmish. A disagreement over international space could have gotten ugly. But the diplomats managed to fight that war before they could. Few years later, they were disbanded, though there are rumors on and off about a faction of SafeNet going underground.'

'I've heard of them. Still hear about them. You think Rockman's involved with a fanatic splinter group like that?'

It only took Feeney a moment to shake his head. 'I think he watches his step. Power reflects power, and DeBlass has plenty. If he ever gets into the White House, Rockman would be right beside him.'

'Please.' Eve pressed a hand to her stomach. 'You'll give me nightmares.'

'It's a long shot, but he's got some backing for the next election.' Feeney moved his shoulders.

'Rockman's alibied, anyway. By DeBlass. They were in East Washington.' She sat. 'Anything else?'

'Charles Monroe. He's had an interesting life, nothing shady that shows. I'm working on the victim's logs. You know, sometimes if you're careless in altering files, you leave shadows floating. Seems to me somebody just kills a woman could get careless.'

'You find a shadow, Feeney, clear away the gray, and I'll buy you a case of that lousy whiskey you like.'

'Deal. I'm still working on Roarke,' he added. 'There's a guy who isn't careless. Every time I think I've gotten over one wall of security, I hit another. Whatever data there is on him is well guarded.'

'Keep scaling those walls. I'll try digging under them.'

When Feeney left, Eve shifted to her terminal. She hadn't wanted to check in front of Mavis, and preferred, in this case, using her office unit. The question was simple.

Eve entered the name and address of her apartment complex. Asked: Owner?

And so the answer was simple: Roarke.

Lola Starr's license for sex was only three months old. She'd applied for it on her eighteenth birthday, the earliest possible date. She liked to tell her friends she'd been an amateur until then.

It was the same day she'd left her home in Toledo, the same day she'd changed her name from Alice Williams. Both home and name had been far too boring for Lola.

She had a cute, pixie face. She'd nagged and begged and wept until her parents had agreed to buy her a more pointed chin and a tip-tilted nose for her sixteenth birthday.

Lola had wanted to look like a sexy elf and thought she'd succeeded. Her hair was coal black, cut in short, sassy spikes. Her skin was milk white and firm. She was saving for enough money to have her eyes changed from brown to emerald green, which she thought would suit her image better. But she'd been lucky enough to have been born with a lush little body that needed no more than basic maintenance.

She'd wanted to be a licensed companion all of her life. Other girls might have dreamed of careers in law or finance, studied their way into medicine or industry. But Lola had always known she was born for sex.

And why not make a living from what you did best?

She wanted to be rich and desired and pampered. The desire part she found easy. Men, particularly older men, were willing to pay well for someone with Lola's attributes. But the expenses of her profession were more stringent than she'd anticipated when she'd dreamed away in her pretty room in Toledo.

The licensing fees, the mandatory health exams, the rent, and sin tax all ate into profits. Once she'd finished paying for her training, she'd only had enough left to afford a small, one-room apartment at the ragged edges of Prostitute Walk.

Still, it was better than working the streets as many still did. And Lola had plans for bigger and better things.

One day she'd live in a penthouse and take only the cream of clients. She'd be wined and dined in the best restaurants, jetted to exotic places to entertain royalty and wealth.

She was good enough, and she didn't intend to stay at the bottom of the ladder for long.

The tips helped. A professional wasn't supposed to accept cash or credit bonuses. Not technically. But everyone did. She was still girl enough to prefer the pretty little gifts some of her clients offered. But she banked the money religiously and dreamed of her penthouse.

Tonight, she was going to entertain a new client, one who had requested she call him Daddy. She'd agreed, and had waited until the arrangements were made before she allowed herself a smirk. The guy probably thought he was the first one to want her to be his little girl. The fact was, after only a few short months on the job, pedophilia was rapidly becoming her specialty.

So, she'd sit on his lap, let him spank her, while telling her solemnly that she needed to be punished. Really, it was like playing a game, and most of the men were kind of sweet.

With that in mind, she chose a flirty skirted dress with a scalloped white collar. Beneath she wore nothing but white stockings. She'd removed her pubic hair, and was as bare and smooth as a ten year old.

After studying the reflection, she added a bit more color to her cheeks and clear gloss on her pouty lips.

At the knock on the door she grinned, and her young and still guileless face grinned back in the mirror.

She couldn't yet afford video security, and used the Judas hole to check her visitor.

He was handsome, which pleased her. And, she assumed, old enough to be her father, which would please him.

She opened the door, aimed a shy, coy smile. 'Hi, Daddy.'

He didn't want to waste time. It was the one asset he had little of at the moment. He smiled at her. For a whore, she was a pretty little thing. When the door was shut at his back, he reached under her skirt and was pleased to find her naked. It would speed matters along if he could become aroused quickly.

'Daddy!' Playing her part, Lola let out a shrieking giggle. 'That's naughty.'

'I've heard you've been naughty.' He removed his coat and set it neatly aside while she pouted at him. Though he'd taken the precaution of clear sealing his hands, he would touch nothing in the room but her.

'I've been good, Daddy. Very good.'

'You've been naughty, little girl.' From his pocket he took a small video camera, which he set up, aimed toward the narrow bed she'd piled with pillows and stuffed animals.

'Are you going to take pictures?'

'That's right.'

She'd have to tell him that would cost him extra, but decided to wait until the deed was done. Clients didn't care to have their fantasies broken with reality. She'd learned that in training.

'Go lie down on the bed.'

'Yes, Daddy.' She lay among the pillows and grinning animals.

'I've heard you've been touching yourself.'

'No, Daddy.'

'It isn't good to tell lies to your Daddy. I have to punish

you, but then I'll kiss it and make it better.' When she smiled, he walked to the bed. 'Lift your skirt, little girl, and show me how you touched yourself.'

Lola didn't care for this part. She liked being touched, but the feel of her own hands brought her little excitement. Still, she lifted her skirt, stroked herself, keeping her movements shy and hesitant as she expected he wanted.

It excited him, the glide of her small fingers. After all, that was what a woman was made for. To use herself, to use the men who wanted her.

'How does it feel?'

'Soft,' she murmured. 'You touch, Daddy. Feel how soft.'

He laid a hand over hers, felt himself harden satisfactorily as he slipped a finger inside her. It would be quick, for both of them.

'Unbutton your dress,' he ordered, and continued to manipulate her as she opened it from its prim collar down. 'Turn over.'

When she did, he brought his hand down on her pert bottom in smart slaps that reddened the creamy flesh while she whimpered in programmed response.

It didn't matter if he hurt her or not. She'd sold herself to him.

'That's a good girl.' He was fully erect now, beginning to throb. Still, his movements were careful and precise as he undressed. Naked, he straddled her, slipped his hands beneath her so that he could squeeze her breasts. So young, he thought, and let himself shudder from the pleasure of flesh that had yet to need refining.

'Daddy's going to show you how he rewards good girls.'

He wanted her to take him into her mouth, but couldn't risk it. The birth control her file listed she used would eradicate his sperm vaginally, but not orally.

Instead, he vaulted up her hips, taking the time to stroke

his hands over that firm, young flesh as he drove himself into her.

He was rougher than either of them expected. After that first violent thrust, he held himself back. He had no wish to hurt her to the point where she would cry out. Though in a place such as this, he doubted anyone would notice or care.

Still, she was rather charmingly unskilled and naive. He settled on a slower, more gentle rhythm, which he discovered drew out his own pleasure.

She moved well, meeting him, matching him. Unless he was very mistaken, not all her groans and cries were simulated. He felt her tense, shudder, and he smiled, pleased that he'd been able to bring a whore to a genuine climax.

He closed his eyes and let himself come.

She sighed and cuddled into one of the pillows. It had been good, much, much better than she'd expected. And she hoped she'd found another regular.

'Was I a good girl, Daddy?'

'A very, very good girl. But we're not done. Roll over.'

As she shifted, he rose and moved out of camera range. 'Are we going to watch the video, Daddy?'

He only shook his head.

Remembering her role, she pouted. 'I like videos. We can watch, and then you can show me how to be a good girl again.' She smiled at him, hoping for a bonus. 'I could touch you this time. I'd like to touch you.'

He smiled and took the SIG 210 with silencer out of his coat pocket. He watched her blink in curiosity as he aimed the gun.

'What's that? Is it a toy for me to play with?'

He shot her in the head first, the weapon barely making more than a pop as she jerked back. Coolly, he shot again, between those young, firm breasts, and last, as the silencer eroded, into her smooth, bare pubis.

Switching the camera off, he arranged her carefully among blood-soaked pillows and soiled, smiling animals while she stared up at him in wide-eyed surprise.

'It was no life for a young girl,' he told her gently, then went back to the camera to record the last scene.

# Chapter Five

All Eve wanted was a candy bar. She'd spent most of the day testifying in court, and her lunch break had been eaten up by a call from a snitch that had cost her fifty dollars and gained her a slim lead on a smuggling case that had resulted in two homicides, which she'd been beating her head against for two months.

All she wanted was a quick hit of sugar substitute before she headed home to prep for her seven o'clock meeting with Roarke.

She could have zipped through any number of drive-through InstaStores, but she preferred the little deli on the corner of West Seventy-eighth – despite, or perhaps because of the fact that it was owned and run by François, a rude, snake-eyed refugee who'd fled to America after the Social Reform Army had overthrown the French government some forty years before.

He hated America and Americans, and the SRA had been dispatched within six months of the coup, but Francois remained, bitching and complaining behind the counter of the Seventy-eighth Street deli where he enjoyed dispensing insults and political absurdities.

Eve called him Frank to annoy him, and dropped in at least once a week to see what scheme he'd devised to try to short credit her.

Her mind on the candy bar, she stepped through the automatic door. It had no more than begun to whisper shut behind her when instinct kicked in.

The man standing at the counter had his back to her, his heavy, hooded jacket masking all but his size, and that was impressive.

Six-five, she estimated, easily two-fifty. She didn't need to see Francois's thin, terrified face to know there was trouble. She could smell it, as ripe and sour as the vegetable hash that was today's special.

In the seconds it took the door to clink shut, she'd considered and rejected the idea of drawing her weapon.

'Over here, bitch. Now.'

The man turned. Eve saw he had the pale gold complexion of a multiracial heritage and the eyes of a very desperate man. Even as she filed the description, she looked at the small round object he held in his hand.

The homemade explosive device was worry enough. The fact that it shook as the hand that held it trembled with nerves was a great deal worse.

Homemade boomers were notoriously unstable. The idiot was likely to kill all of them by sweating too freely.

She shot Francois a quick, warning look. If he called her lieutenant, they were all going to be meat very quickly. Keeping her hands in plain sight, she crossed to the counter.

'I don't want any trouble,' she said, letting her voice tremble as nervously as the thief's hand. 'Please, I got kids at home.'

'Shut up. Just shut up. Down on the floor. Down on the fucking floor.'

Eve knelt, slipping a hand under her jacket where the weapon waited.

'All of it,' the man ordered, gesturing with the deadly

little ball. 'I want all of it. Cash, credit tokens. Make it fast.'

'It's been a slow day,' Francois whined. 'You must understand business is not what it was. You Americans—'

'You want to eat this?' the man invited, shoving the explosive in Francois's face.

'No, no.' Panicked, Francois punched in the security code with his shaking fingers. As the till opened, Eve saw the thief glance at the money inside, then up at the camera that was busily recording the entire transaction.

She saw it in his face. He knew his image was locked there, and that all the money in New York wouldn't erase it. The explosive would, tossed carelessly over his shoulder as he raced out to the street to be swallowed in traffic.

She sucked in a breath, like a diver going under. She came up hard, under his arm. The solid jolt had the device flying free. Screams, curses, prayers. She caught it in her fingertips, a high fly, shagged with two men out and the bases loaded. Even as she closed her hand around it, the thief swung out.

It was the back of his hand rather than a fist, and Eve considered herself lucky. She saw stars as she hit a stand of soy chips, but she held on to the homemade boomer.

Wrong hand, goddamn it, wrong hand, she had time to think as the stand collapsed under her. She tried to use her left to free her weapon, but the two hundred and fifty pounds of fury and desperation fell on her.

'Hit the alarm, you asshole,' she shouted as Francois stood like a statue with his mouth opening and closing. 'Hit the fucking alarm.' Then she grunted as the blow to her ribs stole her breath. This time he'd used his fist.

He was weeping now, scratching and clawing up her arm in an attempt to reach the explosive. 'I need the money. I got to have it. I'll kill you. I'll kill you all.'

She managed to bring her knee up. The age old defense bought her a few seconds, but lacked the power to debilitate.

She saw stars again as her head smacked sharply into the side of a counter. Dozens of the candy bars she'd craved rained down on her.

'You son of a bitch. You son of a bitch.' She heard herself saying it, over and over as she landed three hard short arm blows to his face. Blood spurting from his nose, he grabbed her arm.

And she knew it was going to break. Knew she would feel that sharp, sweet pain, hear the thin crack as bone fractured.

But just as she drew in breath to scream, as her vision began to gray with agony, his weight was off her.

The ball still cupped in her hand, she rolled over onto her haunches, struggling to breathe and fighting the need to retch. From that position she saw the shiny black shoes that always said beat cop.

'Book him.' She coughed once, painfully. 'Attempted robbery, armed, carrying an explosive, assault.' She'd have liked to have added assaulting an officer and resisting arrest, but as she hadn't identified herself, she'd be skirting the line.

'You all right, ma'am? Want the MTs?'

She didn't want the medi-techs. She wanted a fucking candy bar. 'Lieutenant,' she corrected, pushing herself up and reaching for her ID. She noted that the perp was in restraints and that one of the two cops had been wise enough to use his stunner to take the fight out of him.

'We need a safe box – quick.' She watched both cops pale as they saw what she held in her hand. 'This little boomer's had quite a ride. Let's get it neutralized.'

'Sir.' The first cop was out of the store in a flash. In the ninety seconds it took him to return with the black

66

box used for transporting and deactivating explosives, no one spoke.

They hardly breathed.

'Book him,' Eve repeated. The moment the explosive was contained, her stomach muscles began to tremble. 'I'll transmit my report. You guys with the Hundred and twenty-third?'

'You bet, lieutenant.'

'Good job.' She reached down, favoring her injured arm and chose a Galaxy bar that hadn't been flattered by the wrestling match. 'I'm going home.'

'You didn't pay for that,' Francois shouted after her.

'Fuck you, Frank,' she shouted back and kept going.

The incident put her behind schedule. By the time she reached Roarke's mansion, it was 7:10. She'd used over the counter medication to ease the pain in her arm and shoulder. If it wasn't better in a couple of days, she knew she'd have to go in for an exam. She hated doctors.

She parked the car and spent a moment studying Roarke's house. Fortress, more like, she thought. Its four stories towered over the frosted trees of Central Park. It was one of the old buildings, close to two hundred years old, built of actual stone, if her eyes didn't deceive her.

There was lots of glass, and lights burning gold behind the windows. There was also a security gate, behind which evergreen shrubs and elegant trees were artistically arranged.

Even more impressive than the magnificence of architecture and landscaping was the quiet. She heard no city noises here. No traffic snarls, no pedestrian chaos. Even the sky overhead was subtly different than the one she was accustomed to farther downtown. Here, you could actually see stars rather than the glint and gleam of transports.

Nice life if you can get it, she mused, and started her car again. She approached the gate, prepared to identify herself.

She saw the tiny red eye of a scanner blink, then hold steady. The gates opened soundlessly.

So, he'd programmed her in, she thought, unsure if she was amused or uneasy. She went through the gate, up the short drive, and left her car at the base of granite steps.

A butler opened the door for her. She'd never actually seen a butler outside of old videos, but this one didn't disappoint the fantasy. He was silver haired, implacably eyed and dressed in a dark suit and ruthlessly knotted old-fashioned tie.

'Lieutenant Dallas.'

There was an accent, a faint one that sounded British and Slavic at once. 'I have an appointment with Roarke.'

'He's expecting you.' He ushered her into a wide, towering hallway that looked more like the entrance to a museum than a home.

There was a chandelier of star-shaped glass dripping light onto a glossy wood floor that was graced by a boldly patterned rug in shades of red and teal. A stairway curved away to the left with a carved griffin for its newel post.

There were paintings on the walls – the kind she had once seen on a school field trip to the Met. French Impressionists from what century she couldn't quite recall. The Revisited Period that had come into being in the early twenty-first century complimented them with their pastoral scenes and gloriously muted colors.

No holograms or living sculpture. Just paint and canvas.

'May I take your coat?'

She brought herself back and thought she caught a flicker of smug condescension in those inscrutable eyes. Eve shrugged out of her jacket, watched him take the leather somewhat gingerly between his manicured fingers.

Hell, she'd gotten most of the blood off it.

'This way, Lieutenant Dallas. If you wouldn't mind waiting in the parlor, Roarke is detained on a transpacific call.'

'No problem.'

The museum quality continued there. A fire was burning sedately. A fire out of genuine logs in a hearth carved from lapis and malachite. Two lamps burned with light like colored gems. The twin sofas had curved backs and lush upholstery that echoed the jewel tones of the room in sapphire. The furniture was wood, polished to an almost painful gloss. Here and there objets d'art were arranged. Sculptures, bowls, faceted glass.

Her boots clicked over wood, then muffled over carpet.

'Would you like a refreshment, lieutenant?'

She glanced back, saw with amusement that he continued to hold her jacket between his fingers like a soiled rag. 'Sure. What have you got, Mr—?'

'Summerset, lieutenant. Simply Summerset, and I'm sure we can provide you with whatever suits your taste.'

'She's fond of coffee,' Roarke said from the doorway, 'but I think she'd like to try the Montcart forty-nine.'

Summerset's eyes flickered again, with horror, Eve thought. 'The forty-nine, sir?'

'That's right. Thank you, Summerset.'

'Yes, sir.' Dangling the jacket, he exited, stiff-spined.

'Sorry I kept you waiting,' Roarke began, then his eyes narrowed, darkened.

'No problem,' Eve said as he crossed to her. 'I was just . . . Hey—'

She jerked her chin as his hand cupped it, but his fingers held firm, turning her left cheek to the light. 'Your face is bruised.' His voice was cool on the statement, icily so. His eyes as they flicked over the injury betrayed nothing.

But his fingers were warm, tensed, and jolted something in her gut. 'A scuffle over a candy bar,' she said with a shrug.

His eyes met hers, held just an instant longer than comfortable. 'Who won?'

'I did. It's a mistake to come between me and food.'

'I'll keep that in mind.' He released her, dipped the hand that had touched her into his pocket. Because he wanted to touch her again. It worried him that he wanted, very much, to stroke away the bruise that marred her cheek. 'I think you'll approve of tonight's menu.'

'Menu? I didn't come here to eat, Roarke. I came here to look over your collection.'

'You'll do both.' He turned when Summerset brought in a tray that held an uncorked bottle of wine the color of ripened wheat and two crystal glasses.

'The forty-nine, sir.'

'Thank you. I'll pour out.' He spoke to Eve as he did so. 'I thought this vintage would suit you. What it lacks in subtlety . . .' He turned back, offering her a glass. 'It makes up for in sensuality.' He tapped his glass against hers so the crystal sang, then watched as she sipped.

God, what a face, he thought. All those angles and expressions, all that emotion and control. Just now she was fighting off showing both surprise and pleasure as the taste of the wine settled on her tongue. He was looking forward to the moment when the taste of her settled on his.

'You approve?' he asked.

'It's good.' It was the equivalent of sipping gold.

'I'm glad. The Montcart was my first venture into wineries. Shall we sit and enjoy the fire?'

It was tempting. She could almost see herself sitting there, legs angled toward the fragrant heat, sipping wine as the jeweled light danced.

'This isn't a social call, Roarke. It's a murder investigation.'

'Then you can investigate me over dinner.' He took her

arm, lifting a brow as she stiffened. 'I'd think a woman who'd fight for a candy bar would appreciate a two-inch fillet, medium rare.'

'Steak?' She struggled not to drool. 'Real steak, from a cow?'

A smile curved his lips. 'Just flown in from Montana. The steak, not the cow.' When she continued to hesitate, he tilted his head. 'Come now, lieutenant, I doubt if a little red meat will clog your considerable investigative skills.'

'Someone tried to bribe me the other day,' she muttered, thinking of Charles Monroe and his black silk robe.

'With?'

'Nothing as interesting as steak.' She aimed one long, level look. 'If the evidence points in your direction, Roarke, I'm still bringing you down.'

'I'd expect nothing less. Let's eat.'

He led her into the dining room. More crystal, more gleaming wood, yet another shimmering fire, this time cupped in rose-veined marble. A woman in a black suit served them appetizers of shrimp swimming in creamy sauce. The wine was brought in, their glasses topped off.

Eve, who rarely gave a thought to her appearance, wished she'd worn something more suitable to the occasion than jeans and a sweater.

'So, how'd you get rich?' she asked him.

'Various ways.' He liked to watch her eat, he discovered. There was a single-mindedness to it.

'Name one.'

'Desire,' he said, and let the word hum between them.

'Not good enough.' She picked up her wine again, meeting his eyes straight on. 'Most people want to be rich.'

'They don't want it enough. To fight for it. Take risks for it.'

'But you did.'

'I did. Being poor is . . . uncomfortable. I like comfort.'
He offered her a roll from a silver bowl as their salads were
served – crisp greens tossed with delicate herbs. 'We're not
so different, Eve.'

'Yeah, right.'

'You wanted to be a cop enough to fight for it. To take
risks for it. You find the breaking of laws uncomfortable. I
make money, you make justice. Neither is a simple matter.'
He waited a moment. 'Do you know what Sharon DeBlass
wanted?'

Her fork hesitated, then pierced a tender shoot of endive that
had been plucked only an hour before. 'What do you think she
wanted?'

'Power. Sex is often a way to gain it. She had enough money
to be comfortable, but she wanted more. Because money is also
power. She wanted power over her clients, over herself, and
most of all, she wanted power over her family.'

Eve set her fork down. In the firelight, the dancing glow
of candle and crystal, he looked dangerous. Not because
a woman would fear him, she thought, but because she
would desire him. Shadows played in his eyes, making them
unreadable.

'That's quite an analysis of a woman you claim you hardly
knew.'

'It doesn't take long to form an opinion, particularly if that
person is obvious. She didn't have your depth, Eve, your
control, or your rather enviable focus.'

'We're not talking about me.' No, she didn't want him to
talk about her – or to look at her in quite that way. 'Your
opinion is that she was hungry for power. Hungry enough to
be killed before she could take too big a bite?'

'An interesting theory. The question would be, too big a
bite of what? Or whom?'

The same silent servant cleared the salads, brought in

72

oversize china plates heavy with sizzling meat and thin, golden slices of grilled potatoes.

Eve waited until they were alone again, then cut into her steak. 'When a man accumulates a great deal of money, possessions, and status, he then has a great deal to lose.'

'Now we're speaking of me – another interesting theory.' He sat there, his eyes interested, yet still amused. 'She threatened me with some sort of blackmail and, rather than pay or dismiss her as ridiculous, I killed her. Did I sleep with her first?'

'You tell me,' Eve said evenly.

'It would fit the scenario, considering her choice of profession. There may be a blackout on the press on this particular case, but it takes little deductive power to conclude sex reared its head. I had her, then I shot her . . . if one subscribes to the theory.' He took a bite of steak, chewed, swallowed. 'There's a problem, however.'

'Which is?'

'I have what you might consider an old-fashioned quirk. I dislike brutalizing women, in any form.'

'It's old-fashioned in that it would be more apt to say you dislike brutalizing people, in any form.'

He moved those elegant shoulders. 'As I say, it's a quirk. I find it distasteful to look at you and watch the candlelight shift over a bruise on your face.'

He surprised her by reaching out, running a finger down the mark, very gently.

'I believe I would have found it even more distasteful to kill Sharon DeBlass.' He dropped his hand and went back to his meal. 'Though I have, occasionally, been known to do what is distasteful to me. When necessary. How is your dinner?'

'It's fine.' The room, the light, the food, was all more than fine. It was like sitting in another world, in another time. 'Who the hell are you, Roarke?'

He smiled and topped off their glasses. 'You're the cop. Figure it out.'

She would, she promised herself. By God she would, before it was done. 'What other theories do you have about Sharon DeBlass?'

'None to speak of. She liked excitement and risk and didn't flinch from causing those who loved her embarrassment. Yet she was . . .'

Intrigued, Eve leaned closer. 'What? Go ahead, finish.'

'Pitiable,' he said, in a tone that made Eve believe he meant no more and no less that just that. 'There was something sad about her under all that bright, bright gloss. Her body was the only thing about herself she respected. So she used it to give pleasure and to cause pain.'

'And did she offer it to you?'

'Naturally, and assumed I'd accept the invitation.'

'Why didn't you?'

'I've already explained that. I can elaborate and add that I prefer a different type of bedmate, and that I prefer to make my own moves.'

There was more, but he chose to keep it to himself.

'Would you like more steak, lieutenant?'

She glanced down, saw that she'd all but eaten the pattern off the plate. 'No. Thanks.'

'Dessert?'

She hated to turn it down, but she'd already indulged herself enough. 'No. I want to look at your collection.'

'Then we'll save the coffee and dessert for later.' He rose, offered a hand.

Eve merely frowned at it and pushed back from the table. Amused, Roarke gestured toward the doorway and led her back into the hall, up the curving stairs.

'It's a lot of house for one guy.'

'Do you think so? I'm more of the opinion that your

apartment is small for one woman.' When she stopped dead at the top of the stairs, he grinned. 'Eve, you know I own the building. You'd have checked after I sent my little token.'

'You ought to have someone out to look at the plumbing,' she told him. 'I can't keep the water hot in the shower for more than ten minutes.'

'I'll make a note of it. Next flight up.'

'I'm surprised you don't have elevators,' she commented as they climbed again.

'I do. Just because I prefer the stairs doesn't mean the staff shouldn't have a choice.'

'And staff,' she continued. 'I haven't seen one remote domestic in the place.'

'I have a few. But I prefer people to machines, most of the time. Here.'

He used a palm scanner, coded in a key, then opened carved double doors. The sensor switched on the lights as they crossed the threshold. Whatever she'd been expecting, it hadn't been this.

It was a museum of weapons: guns, knives, swords, cross-bows. Armor was displayed, from medieval ages to the thin, impenetrable vests that were current military issue. Chrome and steel and jeweled handles winked behind glass, shimmered on the walls.

If the rest of the house seemed another world, perhaps a more civilized one than what she knew, this veered jarringly in the other direction. A celebration of violence.

'Why?' was all she could say.

'It interests me, what humans have used to damage humans through history.' He crossed over, touching a wickedly toothed ball that hung from a chain. 'Knights farther back than Arthur carried these into jousts and battles. A thousand years . . .' He pressed a series of buttons on a display cabinet and took out a sleek, palm-sized weapon, the preferred killing tool of

75

twenty-first century street gangs during the Urban Revolt. 'And we have something less cumbersome and equally lethal. Progression without progress.'

He put the weapon back, closed and secured the case. 'But you're interested in something newer than the first, and older than the second. You said a thirty-eight, Smith & Wesson. Model Ten.'

It was a terrible room, she thought. Terrible and fascinating. She stared at him across it, realizing that the elegant violence suited him perfectly.

'It must have taken years to collect all of this.'

'Fifteen,' he said as he walked across the uncarpeted floor to another section. 'Nearly sixteen now. I acquired my first handgun when I was nineteen – from the man who was aiming it at my head.'

He frowned. He hadn't meant to tell her that.

'I guess he missed,' Eve commented as she joined him.

'Fortunately, he was distracted by my foot in his crotch. It was a nine-millimeter Baretta semiautomatic he'd smuggled out of Germany. He thought to use it to relieve me of the cargo I was delivering to him and save the transportation fee. In the end, I had the fee, the cargo, and the Baretta. And so, Roarke Industries was born out of his poor judgment. The one you're interested in,' he added, pointing as the wall display opened. 'You'll want to take it, I imagine, to see if it's been fired recently, check for prints, and so forth.'

She nodded slowly while her mind worked. Only four people knew the murder weapon had been left at the scene. Herself, Feeney, the commander, and the killer. Roarke was either innocent or very, very clever.

She wondered if he could be both.

'I appreciate your cooperation.' She took an evidence seal out of her shoulder bag and reached for the weapon that matched the one already in police possession. It took her only a heartbeat to realize it wasn't the one Roarke had pointed to.

Her eyes slid to his, held. Oh, he was watching her all right, carefully. Though she let her hand hesitate now over her selection, she thought they understood each other. 'Which?'

'This.' He tapped the display just under the .38. Once she'd sealed it and slipped it into her bag, he closed the glass. 'It's not loaded, of course, but I do have ammo, if you'd like to take a sample.'

'Thanks. Your cooperation will be noted in my report.'

'Will it?' He smiled, took a box out of a drawer, and offered it. 'What else will be noted, lieutenant?'

'Whatever is applicable.' She added the box of ammo to her bag, took out a notebook, and punched in her ID number, the date, and a description of everything she'd taken. 'Your receipt.' She offered him the slip after the notebook spit it out. 'These will be returned to you as quickly as possible unless they're called into evidence. You'll be notified one way or the other.'

He tucked the paper into his pocket, fingered what else he'd tucked there. 'The music room's in the next wing. We can have coffee and brandy there.'

'I doubt we'd share the same taste in music, Roarke.'

'You might be surprised,' he murmured, 'at what we share.' He touched her cheek again, this time sliding his hand around until it cupped the back of her neck. 'At what we will share.'

She went rigid and lifted a hand to shove his arm away. He simply closed his fingers over her wrist. She could have had him flat on his back in a heartbeat – so she told herself. Still, she only stood there, the breath backing up in her lungs and her pulse throbbing hard and thick.

He wasn't smiling now.

'You're not a coward, Eve.' He said it softly when his lips were an inch from hers. The kiss hovered there, a breath away

77

until the hand she'd levered against his arm changed its grip. And she moved into him.

She didn't think. If she had, even for an instant, she would have known she was breaking all the rules. But she'd wanted to see, wanted to know. Wanted to feel.

His mouth was soft, more persuasive than possessive. His lips nibbled hers open so that he could slide his tongue over them, between them, to cloud her senses with flavor.

Heat gathered like a fireball in her lungs even before he touched her, those clever hands molding over the snug denim over her hips, slipping seductively under her sweater to flesh.

With a kind of edgy delight, she felt herself go damp.

It was the mouth, just that generous and tempting mouth he'd thought he'd wanted. But the moment he'd tasted it, he'd wanted all of her.

She was pressed against him; that tough, angular body beginning to vibrate. Her small, firm breast weighed gloriously in his palm. He could hear the hum of passion that sounded in her throat, all but taste it as her mouth moved eagerly on his.

He wanted to forget the patience and control he'd taught himself to live by, and just ravage.

Here. The violence of the need all but erupted inside him. Here and now.

He would have dragged her to the floor if she hadn't struggled back, pale and panting.

'This isn't going to happen.'

'The hell it isn't,' he shot back.

The danger was shimmering around him now. She saw it as clearly as she saw the tools of violence and death surrounding them.

There were men who negotiated when they wanted something. There were men who just took.

'Some of us aren't allowed to indulge ourselves.'

'Fuck the rules, Eve.'

He stepped toward her. If she had stepped back, he would have pursued, like any hunter after the prize. But she faced him squarely, and shook her head.

'I can't compromise a murder investigation because I'm physically attracted to a suspect.'

'Goddamn it, I didn't kill her.'

It was a shock to see his control snap. To hear the fury and frustration in his voice, to witness it wash vividly across his face. And it was terrifying to realize she believed him, and not be sure, not be absolutely certain if she believed because she needed to.

'It's not as simple as taking your word for it. I have a job to do, a responsibility to the victim, to the system. I have to stay objective, and I—'

Can't, she realized. Can't.

They stared at each other as the communicator in her bag began to beep.

Her hands weren't quite steady as she turned away, took the unit out. She recognized the code for the station on the display and entered her ID. After a deep breath, she answered the request for voice print verification.

'Dallas, Lieutenant Eve. No audio please, display only.'

Roarke could just see her profile as she read the transmission. It was enough to measure the change in her eyes, the way they darkened, then went flat and cool.

She put the communicator away, and when she turned back to him, there was very little of the woman who'd vibrated in his arms in the woman who faced him now.

'I have to go. We'll be in touch about your property.'

'You do that very well,' Roarke murmured. 'Slide right into the cop's skin. And it fits you perfectly.'

'It better. Don't bother seeing me out. I can find my way.'

'Eve.'

She stopped at the doorway, looked back. There he was, a figure in black surrounded by eons of violence. Inside the cop's skin, the woman's heart stuttered.

'We'll see each other again.'

She nodded. 'Count on it.'

He let her go, knowing Summerset would slip out of some shadow to give her the leather jacket, bid her good night.

Alone, Roarke took the gray fabric button from his pocket, the one he'd found on the floor of his limo. The one that had fallen from the jacket of that drab gray suit she'd worn the first time he'd seen her.

Studying it, knowing he had no intention of giving it back to her, he felt like a fool.

# Chapter Six

A rookie was guarding the door to Lola Starr's apartment. Eve pegged him as such because he barely looked old enough to order a beer, his uniform looked as if it had just been lifted from the supply rack, and from the faint green cast of his skin.

A few months of working this neighborhood, and a cop stopped needing to puke at the sight of a corpse. Chemi-heads, the street LCs, and just plain bad asses liked to wale on each other along these nasty blocks as much for entertainment as for business profits. From the smell that had greeted her outside, someone had died out there recently, or the recycle trucks hadn't been through in the last week.

'Officer.' She paused, flashed her badge. He'd gone on alert the moment she'd stepped out of the pitiful excuse for an elevator. Instinct warned her, rightly enough, that without the quick ID, she'd have been treated to a stun from the weapon his shaky hand was gripping.

'Sir.' His eyes were spooked and unwilling to settle on one spot.

'Give me the status.'

'Sir,' he said again, and took a long unsteady breath. 'The landlord flagged down my unit, said there was a dead woman in the apartment.'

'And is there . . .' Her gaze flicked down to the name pinned over his breast pocket. 'Officer Prosky?'

'Yes, sir, she's . . .' He swallowed, hard, and Eve could see the horror flit over his face again.

'And how did you determine the subject is terminated, Prosky? You take her pulse?'

A flush, no healthier than the green hue, tinted his cheeks. 'No, sir. I followed procedure, preserved crime scene, notified headquarters. Visual confirmation of termination, the scene is uncorrupted.'

'The landlord went in?' All of this she could learn later, but she could see that he was steadying as she forced him to go over the steps.

'No, sir, he says not. After a complaint by one of the victim's clients who had an appointment for nine P.M., the landlord checked the apartment. He unlocked the door and saw her. It's only one room, Lieutenant Dallas, and she's – You see her as soon as you open the door. Following the discovery, the landlord, in a state of panic, went down to the street and flagged down my patrol unit. I immediately accompanied him back to the scene, made visual confirmation of suspicious death, and reported in.'

'Have you left your post, officer? However briefly?'

His eyes settled finally, met hers. 'No, sir, lieutenant. I thought I'd have to, for a minute. It's my first, and I had some trouble maintaining.'

'Looks like you maintained fine to me, Prosky.' Out of the crime bag she'd brought up with her, she took out the protective spray, used it. 'Make the calls to forensics and the ME. The room needs to be swept, and she'll need to be bagged and tagged.'

'Yes, sir. Should I remain on post?'

'Until the first team gets here. Then you can report in.' She finished coating her boots, glanced up at him. 'You married, Prosky?' she asked as she snapped her recorder to her shirt.

'No, sir. Sort of engaged though.'

82

'After you report in, go find your lady. The ones who go for the liquor don't last as long as the ones who have a nice warm body to lose it in. Where do I find the landlord?' she asked and turned the knob on the unsecured door.

'He's down in one-A.'

'Then tell him to stay put. I'll take his statement when I'm done here.'

She stepped inside, closed the door. Eve, no longer a rookie, didn't feel her stomach revolt at the sight of the body, the torn flesh, or the blood-splattered child's toys.

But her heart ached.

Then came the anger, a sharp red spear of it when she spotted the antique weapon cradled in the arms of a teddy bear.

'She was just a kid.'

It was seven A.M. Eve hadn't been home. She'd caught one hour's rough and restless sleep at her office desk between computer searches and reports. Without a Code Five attached to Lola Starr, Eve was free to access the data banks of the International Resource Center on Criminal Activity. So far, IRCCA had come up empty on matches.

Now, pale with fatigue, jittery with the false energy of false caffeine, she faced Feeney.

'She was a pro, Dallas.'

'Her fucking license was barely three months old. There were dolls on her bed. There was Kool-Aid in her kitchen.'

She couldn't get past it – all those silly, girlish things she'd had to paw through while the victim's pitiful body lay on the cheap, fussy pillows and dolls. Enraged, Eve slapped one of the official photos onto her desk.

'She looks like she should have been leading cheers at the high school. Instead, she's running tricks and collecting pictures of fancy apartments and fancier clothes. You figure she knew what she was getting into?'

'I don't figure she thought she'd end up dead,' Feeney said evenly. 'You want to debate the sex codes, Dallas?'

'No.' Wearily, she looked down at her hard copy again. 'No, but it bums me, Feeney. A kid like this.'

'You know better than that, Dallas.'

'Yeah, I know better.' She forced herself to snap back. 'Autopsy should be in this morning, but my prelim puts her dead for twenty-four hours minimum at discovery. You've identified the weapon?'

'SIG two-ten – a real Rolls-Royce of handguns, about 1980, Swiss import. Silenced. Those old timey silencers were only good for a couple, three shots. He'd have needed it because the victim's place wasn't soundproofed like DeBlass's.'

'And he didn't phone it in, which tells me he didn't want her found as quickly. Had to get himself someplace else,' she mused. Thoughtful, she picked up a small square of paper, officially sealed.

## TWO OF SIX

'One a week,' she said softly. 'Jesus Christ, Feeney, he isn't giving us much time.'

'I'm running her logs, trick book. She had a new client scheduled, 8:00 P.M., night before last. If your prelim checks, he's our guy.' Feeney smiled thinly. 'John Smith.'

'That's older than the murder weapon.' She rubbed her hands hard over her face. 'IRCCA's bound to spit our boy out from that tag.'

'They're still running data,' Feeney muttered. He was protective, even sentimental about the IRCCA.

'They're not going to find squat. We got us a time traveler, Feeney.'

He snorted. 'Yeah, a real Jules Verne.'

'We've got a twentieth-century crime,' she said through her

84

hands. 'The weapons, the excessive violence, the hand-printed note left on scene. So maybe our killer is some sort of historian, or buff anyway. Somebody who wishes things were what they used to be.'

'Lots of people think things would be better some other way. That's why the world's lousy with theme parks.'

Thinking, she dropped her hands. 'IRCCA isn't going to help us get into this guy's head. It still takes a human mind to play that game. What's he doing, Feeney? Why's he doing it?'

'He's killing LCs.'

'Hookers have always been easy targets, back to Jack the Ripper, right? It's a vulnerable job, even now with all the screening, we still get clients knocking LCs around, killing them.'

'Doesn't happen much,' Feeney mused. 'Sometimes with the S and M trade you get a party that gets too enthusiastic. Most LCs are safer than teachers.'

'They still run a risk, the oldest profession with the oldest crime. But things have changed, some things. People don't kill with guns as a rule anymore. Too expensive, too hard to come by. Sex isn't the strong motivator it used to be, too cheap, too easy to come by. We have different methods of investigation, and a whole new batch of motives. When you brush all that away, the one fact is that people still terminate people. Keep digging, Feeney. I've got people to talk to.'

'What you need's some sleep, kid.'

'Let him sleep,' Eve muttered. 'Let that bastard sleep.' Steeling herself, she turned to her tele-link. It was time to contact the victim's parents.

By the time Eve walked into the sumptuous foyer of Roarke's midtown office, she'd been up for more than thirty-two hours. She'd gotten through the misery of having to tell two shocked, weeping parents that their only daughter was dead. She'd stared at her monitor until the data swam in front of her eyes.

Her follow-up interview with Lola's landlord had been its own adventure. Since the man had had time to recover, he'd spent thirty minutes whining about the unpleasant publicity and the possibility of a drop-off in rentals.

So much, Eve thought, for human empathy.

Roarke Industries, New York, was very much what she'd expected. Slick, shiny, sleek, the building itself spread one hundred fifty stories into the Manhattan sky. It was an ebony lance, glossy as wet stone, ringed by transport tubes and diamond-bright skyways.

No tacky Glida-Grills on this corner, she mused. No street hawkers with their hot pocket PCs dodging security on their colorful air boards. Out-of-doors vending was off limits on this bite of Fifth. The zoning made things quieter, if a little less adventuresome.

Inside, the main lobby took up a full city block, boasting three tony restaurants, a high priced boutique, a handful of specialty shops, and a small theater that played art films.

The white floor tiles were a full yard square and gleamed like the moon. Clear glass elevators zipped busily up and down, people glides zigzagged left and right, while disembodied voices guided visitors to various points of interest or, if there was business to be conducted, the proper office.

For those who wanted to wander about on their own, there were more than a dozen moving maps.

Eve marched to a monitor and was politely offered assistance.

'Roarke,' she said, annoyed that his name hadn't been listed on the main directory.

'I'm sorry.' The computer's voice was that overly mannered tone that was meant to be soothing, and instead grated on

Eve's already raw nerves. 'I'm not at liberty to access that information.'

'Roarke,' Eve repeated, holding up her badge for the computer to scan. She waited impatiently as the computer hummed, undoubtedly checking and verifying her ID, notifying the man himself.

'Please proceed to the east wing, Lieutenant Dallas. You will be met.'

'Right.'

Eve turned down a corridor, passed a marble run that held a forest of snowy white impatiens.

'Lieutenant.' A woman in a killer red suit and hair as white as the impatiens smiled coolly. 'Come with me, please.'

The woman slipped a thin security card into a slot, laid her palm against a sheet of black glass for a handprint. The wall slid open, revealing a private elevator.

Eve stepped inside with her, and was unsurprised when her escort requested the top floor.

Eve had been certain Roarke would be satisfied with nothing but the top.

Her guide was silent on the ride up and exuded a discreet whiff of sensible scent that matched her sensible shoes and neat, sleek coif. Eve secretly admired women who put themselves together, top to toe, with such seeming effortlessness.

Faced with such quiet magnificence, she tugged self-consciously at her worn leather jacket and wondered if it was time she actually spent money on a haircut rather than hacking away at it herself.

Before she could decide on such earth-shattering matters, the doors whooshed open into a silent, white carpeted foyer the size of a small home. There were lush green plants – real plants: ficus, palm, what appeared to be a dogwood flowering off season. There was a sharp spicy scent from a bank of dianthus, blooming in shades of rose and vivid purple.

The garden surrounded a comfortable waiting area of mauve sofas and glossy wood tables, lamps that were surely solid brass with jeweled colored shades.

In the center of this was a circular workstation, equipped as efficiently as a cockpit with monitors and keyboards, gauges and tele-links. Two men and a woman worked at it busily, with a seamless ballet of competence in motion.

She was led past them into a glass-sided breezeway. A peek down, and she could see Manhattan. There was music piped in she didn't recognize as Mozart. For Eve, music began sometime after her tenth birthday.

The woman in the killer suit paused again, flashed her cool, perfect smile, then spoke into a hidden speaker. 'Lieutenant Dallas, sir.'

'Send her in, Caro. Thank you.'

Again Caro pressed her palm to a slick black glass. 'Go right in, lieutenant,' she invited as a panel slid open.

'Thanks.' Out of curiosity, Eve watched her walk away, wondering how anyone could stride so gracefully on three-inch heels. She walked into Roarke's office.

It was, as she expected, as impressive as the rest of his New York headquarters. Despite the soaring, three-sided view of New York, the lofty ceiling with its pinprick lights, the vibrant tones of topaz and emerald in the thickly cushioned furnishings, it was the man behind the ebony slab desk that dominated.

What in hell was it about him? Eve thought again as Roarke rose and slanted a smile at her.

'Lieutenant Dallas,' he said in that faint and fascinating Irish lilt, 'a pleasure, as always.'

'You might not think so when I'm finished.'

He lifted a brow. 'Why don't you come the rest of the way in and get started? Then we'll see. Coffee?'

'Don't try to distract me, Roarke.' She walked closer.

Then, to satisfy her curiosity, she took a brief turn around the room. It was as big as a heliport, with all the amenities of a first-class hotel: automated service bar, a padded relaxation chair complete with VR and mood settings, an oversize wall screen, currently blank. To the left, there was a full bath including whirl tub and drying tube. All the standard office equipment, of the highest high-tech, was built in.

Roarke watched her with a bland expression. He admired the way she moved, the way those cool, quick eyes took in everything.

'Would you like a tour, Eve?'

'No. How do you work with all this . . .' Using both hands, she gestured widely at the treated glass walls. 'Open.'

'I don't like being closed in. Are you going to sit, or prowl?'

'I'm going to stand. I have some questions to ask you, Roarke. You're entitled to have counsel present.'

'Am I under arrest?'

'Not at the moment.'

'Then we'll save the lawyers until I am. Ask.'

Though she kept her eyes level on his, she knew where his hands were, tucked casually in the pockets of his slacks. Hands revealed emotions.

'Night before last,' she said, 'between the hours of eight and ten P.M. Can you verify your whereabouts?'

'I believe I was here until shortly after eight.' With a steady hand he touched his desk log. 'I shut down my monitor at 8:17. I left the building, drove home.'

'Drove,' she interrupted, 'or were driven?'

'Drove. I keep a car here. I don't believe in keeping my employees waiting on my whims.'

'Damned democratic of you.' And, she thought, damned inconvenient. She'd wanted him to have an alibi. 'And then?'

'I poured myself a brandy, had a shower, changed. I had a late supper with a friend.'

'How late, and what friend?'

'I believe I arrived at about ten. I like to be prompt. At Madeline Montmart's townhouse.'

Eve had a quick vision of a curvy blond with a sultry mouth and almond eyes. 'Madeline Montmart, the actress?'

'Yes. I believe we had squab, if that's helpful.'

She ignored the sarcasm. 'No one can verify your movements between eight-seventeen and ten P.M.?'

'One of the staff might have noticed, but then, I pay them well and they're likely to say what I tell them to say.' His voice took on an edge. 'There's been another murder.'

'Lola Starr, licensed companion. Certain details will be released to the media within the hour.'

'And certain details will not.'

'Do you own a silencer, Roarke?'

His expression didn't change. 'Several. You look exhausted, Eve. Have you been up all night?'

'Goes with the job. Do you own a Swiss handgun, SIG two-ten, circa 1980?'

'I acquired one about six weeks ago. Sit down.'

'Were you acquainted with Lola Starr?' Reaching into her briefcase, she pulled out a photo she'd found in Lola's apartment. The pretty, elfin girl beamed out, full of sassy fun.

Roarke lowered his gaze to it as it landed on his desk. His eyes flickered. This time his voice was tinged with something Eve thought sounded like pity.

'She isn't old enough to be licensed.'

'She turned eighteen four months ago. Applied on her birthday.'

'She didn't have time to change her mind, did she?' His eyes lifted to Eve's. And yes, it was pity. 'I didn't know her. I don't use prostitutes – or children.' He picked up

90

the photo, skirted the desk, and offered it back to Eve. 'Sit down.'

'Have you ever—'

'Goddamn it, sit down.' In sudden fury, he took her shoulders, pushed her into a chair. Her case tipped, spilling out photos of Lola that had nothing to do with sassy fun.

She might have reached them first – her reflexes were as good as his. Perhaps she wanted him to see them. Perhaps she needed him to.

Crouching, Roarke picked up a photo taken at the scene. He stared at it. 'Christ Jesus,' he said softly. 'You believe I'm capable of this?'

'My beliefs aren't the issue. Investigating—' She broke off when his eyes whipped to hers.

'You believe I'm capable of this?' he repeated in an undertone that cut like a blade.

'No, but I have a job to do.'

'Your job sucks.'

She took the photos back, stored them. 'From time to time.'

'How do you sleep at night, after looking at something like this?'

She flinched. Though she recovered in a snap, he'd seen it. As intrigued as he was by her instinctive and emotional reaction, he was sorry he'd caused it.

'By knowing I'll take down the bastard who did it. Get out of my way.'

He stayed where he was, laid a hand on her rigid arm. 'A man in my position has to read people quickly and accurately, Eve. I'm reading you as someone close to the edge.'

'I said, get out of my way.'

He rose, but shifting his grip on her arm, pulled her to her feet. He was still in her way. 'He'll do it again,' Roarke said quietly. 'And it's eating at you wondering when and where and who.'

'Don't analyze me. We've got a whole department of shrinks on the payroll for that.'

'Why haven't you been to see one? You've been slipping through loopholes to avoid Testing.'

Her eyes narrowed.

He smiled, but there was no amusement in it.

'I have connections, lieutenant. You were due in Testing several days ago, standard department procedure after a justifiable termination, one you executed the night Sharon was killed.'

'Keep out of my business,' she said furiously. 'And fuck your connections.'

'What are you afraid of? What are you afraid they'll find if they get a look inside of that head of yours? That heart of yours?'

'I'm not afraid of anything.' She jerked her arm free, but he merely laid his hand on her cheek. A gesture so unexpected, so gentle, her stomach quivered.

'Let me help you.'

'I—' Something nearly spilled out, as the photos had. But this time her reflexes kept it tucked away. 'I'm handling it.' She turned away. 'You can pick up your property anytime after nine A.M. tomorrow.'

'Eve.'

She kept her eyes focused on the doorway, kept walking. 'What?'

'I want to see you tonight.'

'No.'

He was tempted – very tempted – to lunge after her. Instead, he stayed where he was. 'I can help you with the case.'

Cautious, she stopped, turned back. If he hadn't been experiencing an uncomfortable twist of sexual frustration, he might have laughed aloud at the combination of suspicion and derision in her eyes.

'How?'

'I know people Sharon knew.' As he spoke, he saw the derision alter to interest. But the suspicion remained. 'It doesn't take a long mental leap to realize you'll be looking for a connection between Sharon and the girl whose photos you're carrying. I'll see if I can find one.'

'Information from a suspect doesn't carry much weight in an investigation. But,' she added before he could speak, 'you can let me know.'

He smiled after all. 'Is it any wonder I want you naked, and in bed? I'll let you know, lieutenant.' And walked back behind his desk. 'In the meantime, get some sleep.'

When the door closed behind her, the smile went out of his eyes. For a long moment he sat in silence. Fingering the button he carried in his pocket, he engaged his private, secure line.

He didn't want this call on his log.

# Chapter Seven

Eve stepped up to the peep screen at Charles Monroe's door and started to announce herself when it slid open. He was in black tie, a cashmere cape swung negligently over his shoulders, offset by the cream of a silk scarf. His smile was every bit as well turned out as his wardrobe.

'Lieutenant Dallas. How lovely to see you again.' His eyes, full of compliments she knew she didn't deserve, skimmed over her. 'And how unfortunate I'm just on my way out.'

'I won't keep you long.' She stepped forward, he stepped back. 'A couple of questions, Mr Monroe, here, informally, or formally, at the station with your representative or counsel.'

His well shaped brows shot up. 'I see. I thought we'd progressed beyond that. Very well, lieutenant, ask away.' He let the door slide shut again. 'We'll keep it informal.'

'Your whereabouts night before last, between the hours of eight and eleven?'

'Night before last?' He slipped a diary out of his pocket, keyed it in. 'Ah, yes. I picked up a client at seven-thirty for an eight o'clock curtain at the Grande Theater. They're doing a reprise of Ibsen – depressing stuff. We sat third row, center. It ended just before eleven, and we had a late supper, catered. Here. I was engaged with her until three A.M.'

His smile flashed as he tucked the diary away again. 'Does that clear me?'

'If your client will corroborate.'

The smile faded into a look of pain. 'Lieutenant, you're killing me.'

'Someone's killing people in your profession,' she snapped back. 'Name and number, Mr Monroe.' She waited until he'd mournfully given the data. 'Are you acquainted with a Lola Starr?'

'Lola, Lola Starr . . . doesn't sound familiar.' He took out the diary again, scanning through his address section. 'Apparently not. Why?'

'You'll hear about it on the news by morning,' was all Eve told him as she opened the door again. 'So far, it's only been women, Mr Monroe, but if I were you, I'd be very careful about taking on new clients.'

With a headache drumming at her, she strode to the elevator. Unable to resist, she glanced toward the door of Sharon DeBlass's apartment, where the red police security light blinked.

She needed to sleep, she told herself. She needed to go home and empty her mind for an hour. But she was keying in her ID to disengage the seal, and walking into the home of a dead woman.

It was silent. And it was empty. She'd expected nothing else. Somehow she hoped there would be some flash of intuition, but there was only the steady pounding in her temples. Ignoring it, she went into the bedroom.

The windows had been sealed as well with concealing spray to prevent the media or the morbidly curious from doing fly-bys and checking out the scene. She ordered lights, and the shadows bounced back to reveal the bed.

The sheets had been stripped off and taken into forensics. Body fluids, hair, and skin had already been analyzed and logged. There was a stain on the floating mattress where blood had seeped through those satin sheets.

The pillowed headboard was splattered with it. She wondered if anyone would care enough to have it cleaned.

She glanced toward the table. Feeney had taken the small desktop PC so that he could search through the hard drive as well as the discs. The room had been searched and swept. There was nothing left to do.

Yet Eve went to the dresser, going methodically through the drawers again. Who would claim all these clothes? she wondered. The silks and lace, the cashmeres and satins of a woman who had preferred the textures of the rich against her skin.

The mother, she imagined. Why hadn't she sent in a request for the return of her daughter's things?

Something to think about.

She went through the closet, again going through skirts, dresses, trousers, the trendy capes and caftans, jackets and blouses, checking pockets, linings. She moved onto shoes, all kept neatly in acrylic boxes.

The woman had only had two feet, she thought with some annoyance. No one needed sixty pairs of shoes. With a little snort, she reached into toes, deep inside the tunnel of boots, into the springy softness of inflatable platforms.

Lola hadn't had so much, she thought now. Two pairs of ridiculously high heels, a pair of girlish vinyl straps, and a simple pair of air pump sneakers, all jumbled in her narrow closet.

But Sharon had been an organized as well as a vain soul. Her shoes were carefully stacked in rows of—

Wrong. Skin prickling, Eve stepped back. It was wrong. The closet was as big as a room, and every inch of space had been ruthlessly utilized. Now, there was a full foot empty on the shelves. Because the shoes were stacked six high in a row of eight.

It wasn't the way Eve had found them or the way she'd left

them. They'd been organized according to color and style. In stacks, she remembered perfectly, of four, a row of twelve.

Such a little mistake, she thought with a small smile. But a man who made one was bound to make another.


'Would you repeat that, lieutenant?'

'He restacked the shoe boxes wrong, commander.' Negotiating traffic, shivering as her car heater offered a tepid puff of air around her toes, Eve checked in. A tourist blimp crept by at low altitude, the guide's voice booming out tips on sky walk shopping as they crossed toward Fifth. Some idiotic road crew with a special daylight license power drilled a tunnel access on the corner of Sixth and Seventy-eighth. Eve pitched her voice above the din.

'You can review the discs of the scene. I know how the closet was arranged. It made an impression on me that any one person should have so many clothes, and keep them so organized. He went back.'

'Returned to the scene of the crime?' Whitney's voice was dry as dust.

'Clichés have a basis in fact.' Hoping for relative quiet, she jogged west down a cross street and ended up fuming behind a clicking microbus. Didn't anyone stay home in New York? 'Or they wouldn't be clichés,' she finished and switched to automatic drive so that she could warm her hands in her pockets. 'There were other things. She kept her costume jewelry in a partitioned drawer. Rings in one section, bracelets in another, and so on. Some of the chains were tangled when I looked again.'

'The sweepers—'

'Sir, I went through the place again after the sweepers. I know he's been there.' Eve bit back on frustration and reminded herself that Whitney was a cautious man. Administrators had to be. 'He got through the security, and he went

97

in. He was looking for something – something he forgot. Something she had. Something we missed.'

'You want the place swept again?'

'I do. And I want Feeney to go back over Sharon's files. Something's there, somewhere. And it concerns him enough to risk going back for it.'

'I'll signature the authorization. The chief isn't going to like it.' The commander was silent for a moment. Then, as if he'd just remembered it was a fully secured line, he snorted. 'Fuck the chief. Good eye, Dallas.'

'Thank you—' But he'd cut her off before she could finish being grateful.

Two of six, she thought, and in the privacy of her car, she shuddered from more than the cold. There were four more people out there whose lives were in her hands.

After pulling into her garage, she swore she'd call the damn mechanic the next day. If history ran true, it meant he'd have her vehicle in for a week, diddling with some idiotic chip in the heater control. The idea of the paperwork in accessing a replacement vehicle through the department was too daunting to consider.

Besides, she was used to the one she had, with all its little quirks. Everyone knew the uniforms copped the best air-to-land vehicles. Detectives had to make do with clinkers.

She'd have to rely on public transportation or just hook a car from the police garage and pay the bureaucratic price later.

Still frowning over the hassle to come and reminding herself to contact Feeney personally to have him go through a week's worth of security discs on the Gorham, she rode the elevator to her floor. Eve had no more than unkeyed her locks when her hand was on her weapon, drawing it.

The silence of her apartment was wrong. She knew instantly she wasn't alone. The prickle along her skin had her doing a quick sweep, arms and eyes, shifting fluidly left then right.

In the dim light of the room, the shadows hung and the silence remained. Then she caught a movement that had her tensed muscles rippling, her trigger finger poised.

'Excellent reflexes, lieutenant.' Roarke rose from the chair where he'd been lounging. Where he'd been watching her. 'So excellent,' he continued in that same mild tone as he touched on a lamp, 'that I have every faith you won't use that on me.'

She might have. She very well might have given him one good jolt. That would have wiped that complacent smile off his face. But any discharge of a weapon meant paperwork she wasn't prepared to face for simple revenge.

'What the fuck are you doing here?'

'Waiting for you.' His eyes remained on hers as he lifted his hands. 'I'm unarmed. You're welcome to check for yourself if you won't take my word for it.'

Very slowly, and with some reluctance, she holstered her weapon. 'I imagine you have a whole fleet of very expensive and very clever lawyers, Roarke, who would have you out before I finished booking you on a B and E. But why don't you tell me why I shouldn't put myself to the trouble, and the city to the expense of throwing you in a cage for a couple of hours?'

Roarke wondered if he'd become perverse that he could so enjoy the way she slashed at him. 'It wouldn't be productive. And you're tired, Eve. Why don't you sit down?'

'I won't bother to ask you how you got in here.' She could feel herself vibrating with temper, and wondered just how much satisfaction she'd gain from clamping his elegant wrists in restraints. 'You own the building, so that question answers itself.'

'One of the things I admire about you is that you don't waste time on the obvious.'

'My question is why.'

'I found myself thinking about you, on professional and personal levels, after you'd left my office.' He smiled, quick and charming. 'Have you eaten?'

'Why?' she repeated.

He stepped toward her so that the slant of light from the lamp played behind him. 'Professionally, I made a couple of calls that might be of interest to you. Personally . . .' He lifted a hand to her face, fingers just brushing her chin, his thumb skimming the slight dip. 'I found myself concerned by that fatigue in your eyes. For some reason I feel compelled to feed you.'

Though she knew it was the gesture of a cranky child, she jerked her chin free. 'What calls?'

He merely smiled again, moved to her tele-link. 'May I?' he said even as he keyed in the number he wanted. 'This is Roarke. You can send the meal up now.' He disengaged, smiled at her again. 'You don't object to pasta, do you?'

'Not on principle. But I object to being handled.'

'That's something else I like about you.' Because she wouldn't, he sat and, ignoring her frown, took out his cigarette case. 'But I find it easier to relax over a hot meal. You don't relax enough, Eve.'

'You don't know me well enough to judge what I do or don't do. And I didn't say you could smoke in here.'

He lighted the cigarette, eyeing her through the faint, fragrant haze. 'You didn't arrest me for breaking and entering, you're not going to arrest me for smoking. I brought a bottle of wine. I left it to breathe on the counter in the kitchen. Would you like some?'

'What I'd like—' She had a sudden flash, and the fury came so quickly she could barely see through it. In one leap, she was at her computer, demanding access.

That annoyed him – enough to have his voice tighten. 'If

I'd come in to poke through your files, I'd hardly have waited around for you.'

'The hell you wouldn't. That kind of arrogance is just like you.' But her security was intact. She wasn't sure if she was relieved or disappointed. Until she saw the small package beside her monitor. 'What's this?'

'I have no idea.' He blew out another stream of smoke. 'It was on the floor inside the door. I picked it up.'

Eve knew what it was – the size, the shape, the weight. And she knew when she viewed the disc she would see Lola Starr's murder.

Something about the way her eyes changed had him rising again, had his voice gentling. 'What is it, Eve?'

'Official business. Excuse me.'

She walked directly to the bedroom, closed and secured the door.

It was Roarke's turn to frown. He went into the kitchen, located glasses, and poured the burgundy. She lived simply, he thought. Very little clutter, very little that spoke of background or family. No mementos. He'd been tempted to wander into her bedroom while he'd had the apartment to himself and see what he might have discovered about her there, but he'd resisted.

It was not so much respect for her privacy as it was the challenge she presented that provoked him to discover her from the woman alone rather than her surroundings.

Still, he found the plain colors and lack of fuss illuminating. She didn't live here, as far as he could see, so much as she existed here. She lived, he deduced, in her work.

He sipped the wine, approved it. After dousing his cigarette, he carried both glasses back into the living room. It was going to be more than interesting to solve the puzzle of Eve Dallas.

When she came back in, nearly twenty minutes later, a white-coated waiter was just finishing setting up dishes on

101

a small table by the window. However glorious the scents, they failed to stir her appetite. Her head was pounding again, and she'd forgotten to take medication.

With a murmur, Roarke dismissed the waiter. He said nothing until the door closed and he was alone with Eve again. 'I'm sorry.'

'For what?'

'For whatever's upset you.' Except for that one flush of temper, she'd been pale when she'd come into the apartment. But her cheeks were colorless now, her eyes too dark. When he started toward her, she shook her head once, fiercely.

'Go away, Roarke.'

'Going away's easy. Too easy.' Very deliberately, he put his arms around her, felt her stiffen. 'Give yourself a minute.' His voice was smooth, persuasive. 'Would it matter, really matter to anyone but you, if you took one minute to let go?'

She shook her head again, but this time there was weariness in the gesture. He heard the sigh escape, and taking advantage, he drew her closer. 'You can't tell me?'

'No.'

He nodded, but his eyes flashed with impatience. He knew better; it shouldn't matter to him. She shouldn't. But too much about her mattered.

'Someone else then,' he murmured.

'There's no one else.' Then realizing how that might be construed, she pulled back. 'I didn't mean—'

'I know you didn't.' His smile was wry and not terribly amused. 'But there isn't going to be anyone else, for either of us, not for some time.'

Her step back wasn't a retreat, but a statement of distance. 'You're taking too much for granted, Roarke.'

'Not at all. Nothing for granted. You're work, lieutenant. A great deal of work. Your dinner's getting cold.'

She was too tired to make a stand, too tired to argue. She sat down, picked up her fork. 'Have you been to Sharon DeBlass's apartment during the last week?'

'No, why would I?'

She studied him carefully. 'Why would anyone?'

He paused a moment, then realized the question wasn't academic. 'To relieve the event,' he suggested. 'To be certain nothing was left behind that would be incriminating.'

'And as owner of the building, you could get in as easily as you got in here.'

His mouth tightened briefly. Annoyance, she judged, the annoyance of a man who was weary of answering the same questions. It was a small thing, but a very good sign of his innocence. 'Yes. I don't believe I'd have a problem. My master code would get me in.'

No, she thought, his master code wouldn't have broken the police security. That would require a different level, or an expert on security.

'I assume that you believe someone not in your department has been in that apartment since the murder.'

'You can assume that,' she agreed. 'Who handles your security, Roarke?'

'I use Lorimar for both my business and my home.' He lifted his glass. 'It's simpler that way, as I own the company.'

'Of course you do. I suppose you know quite a bit about security yourself.'

'You could say I have a long-standing interest in security matters. That's why I bought the company.' He scooped up the herbed pasta, held the fork to her lips, and was satisfied when she took the offered bite. 'Eve, I'm tempted to confess all, just to wipe that unhappy look off your face and see you eat with the enthusiasm I'd enjoyed last time. But whatever my crimes, and they are undoubtedly legion, they don't include murder.'

She looked down at her plate and began to eat. It frazzled

her that he could see she was unhappy. 'What did you mean when you said I was work?'

'You think things through very carefully, and you weigh the odds, the options. You're not a creature of impulse, and though I believe you could be seduced, with the right timing, and the right touch, it wouldn't be an ordinary occurrence.'

She lifted her gaze again. 'That's what you want to do, Roarke? Seduce me?'

'I will seduce you,' he returned. 'Unfortunately, not tonight. Beyond that, I want to find out what it is that makes you what you are. And I want to help you get what you need. Right now, what you need is a murderer. You blame yourself,' he added. 'That's foolish and annoying.'

'I don't blame myself.'

'Look in the mirror,' Roarke said quietly.

'There was nothing I could do,' Eve exploded. 'Nothing I could do to stop it. Any of it.'

'Are you supposed to be able to stop it, any of it? All of it?'

'That's exactly what I'm supposed to do.'

He tilted his head. 'How?'

She pushed away from the table. 'By being smart. By being in time. By doing my job.'

Something more here, he mused. Something deeper. He folded his hands on the table. 'Isn't that what you're doing now?'

The images flooded back into her brain. All the death. All the blood. All the waste. 'Now they're dead.' And the taste of it was bitter in her mouth. 'There should have been something I could have done to stop it.'

'To stop a murder before it happens, you'd have to be inside the head of a killer,' he said quietly. 'Who could live with that?'

'I can live with that.' She hurled it back at him. And it was pure truth. She could live with anything but failure. 'Serve and protect – it's not just a phrase, it's a promise. If I can't keep my word, I'm nothing. And I didn't protect them, any of them. I can only serve them after they're dead. Goddamn it, she was hardly more than a baby. Just a baby, and he cut her into pieces. I wasn't in time. I wasn't in time, and I should have been.'

Her breath caught on a sob, shocking her. Pressing a hand to her mouth, she lowered herself onto the sofa. 'God,' was all she could say. 'God. God.'

He came to her. Instinct had him taking her arms firmly rather than gathering her close. 'If you can't or won't talk to me, you have to talk to someone. You know that.'

'I can handle it. I—' But the rest of the words slid down her throat when he shook her.

'What's it costing you?' he demanded. 'And how much would it matter to anyone if you let it go? For one minute just let it go.'

'I don't know.' And maybe that was the fear, she realized. She wasn't sure if she could pick up her badge, or her weapon, or her life, if she let herself think too deeply, or feel too much. 'I see her,' Eve said on a deep breath. 'I see her whenever I close my eyes or stop concentrating on what needs to be done.'

'Tell me.'

She rose, retrieved her wine and his, and then returned to the sofa. The long drink eased her dry throat and settled the worst of the nerves. It was fatigue, she warned herself, that weakened her enough that she couldn't hold it in.

'The call came through when I was a half block away. I'd just closed another case, finished the data load. Dispatch called for the closest unit. Domestic violence – it's always messy, but I was practically on the doorstep. So I took it.

Some of the neighbors were outside, they were all talking at once.'

The scene came back to her, perfectly, like a video exactly cued. 'A woman was in her nightgown, and she was crying. Her face was battered, and one of the neighbors was trying to bind up a gash on her arm. She was bleeding badly, so I told them to call the MTs. She kept saying, "He's got her. He's got my baby."'

Eve took another drink. 'She grabbed me, bleeding on me, screaming and crying and telling me I had to stop him, I had to save her baby. I should have called for backup, but I didn't think I could wait. I took the stairs, and I could hear him before I got to the third floor where he was locked in. He was raging. I think I heard the little girl screaming, but I'm not sure.'

She closed her eyes then, praying she'd been wrong. She wanted to believe that the child had already been dead, already beyond pain. To have been that close, only steps away . . . No, she couldn't live with that.

'When I got to the door, I used the standard. I'd gotten his name from one of the neighbors. I used his name, and the child's name. It's supposed to make it more personal, more real if you use names. I identified myself and said I was coming in. But he just kept raging. I could hear things breaking. I couldn't hear the child now. I think I knew. Before I broke down the door, I knew. He'd used the kitchen knife to slice her to pieces.'

Her hand shook as she raised the glass again. 'There was so much blood. She was so small, but there was so much blood. On the floor, on the wall, all over him. I could see it was still dripping off the knife. Her face was turned toward me. Her little face, with big blue eyes. Like a doll's.'

She was silent for a moment, then set her glass aside. 'He was too wired up to be stunned. He kept coming. There was blood dripping off the knife, and splattered all over him, and he kept coming. So I looked in his eyes, right in his eyes. And I killed him.'

'And the next day,' Roarke said quietly, 'you dived straight into a murder investigation.'

'Testing's postponed. I'll get to it in another day or two.' She moved her shoulders. 'The shrinks, they'll think it's the termination. I can make them think that if I have to. But it's not. I had to kill him. I can accept that.' She looked straight into Roarke's eyes and knew she could tell him what she hadn't been able to say to herself. 'I wanted to kill him. Maybe even needed to. When I watched him die, I thought, He'll never do that to another child. And I was glad that I'd been the one to stop him.'

'You think that's wrong.'

'I know it's wrong. I know anytime a cop gets pleasure of any sort out of termination, she's crossed a line.'

He leaned forward so that their faces were close. 'What was the child's name?'

'Mandy.' Her breath hitched once before she controlled it. 'She was three.'

'Would you be torn up this way if you'd killed him before he'd gotten to her?'

She opened her mouth, closed it again. 'I guess I'll never know, will I?'

'Yes, you do.' He laid a hand over hers, watched her frown and look down at the contact. 'You know, I've spent most of my life with a basic dislike of police – for one reason or another. I find it very odd that I've met, under such extraordinary circumstances, one I can respect and be attracted to at the same time.'

She lifted her gaze again, and though the frown remained, she didn't draw her hand free of his. 'That's a strange compliment.'

'Apparently we have a strange relationship.' He rose, drawing her to her feet. 'Now you need to sleep.' He glanced toward the dinner she'd barely touched. 'You can heat that up when you've gotten your appetite back.'

'Thanks. Next time I'd appreciate you waiting until I'm home before you come in.'

'Progress,' he murmured when they'd reached the door. 'You accept there'll be a next time.' With a hint of a smile, he brought the hand he still held to his lips. He caught bafflement, discomfort and, he thought, a trace of embarrassment in her eyes as he brushed a light kiss over her knuckles. 'Until next time,' he said, and left.

Frowning, Eve rubbed her knuckles over her jeans as she headed to the bedroom. She stripped, letting her clothes lay wherever they dropped. She climbed into bed, shut her eyes, and willed herself to sleep.

She was just dozing off when she remembered Roarke had never told her who he'd called and what he'd discovered.

# *Chapter Eight*

In her office, with the door locked, Eve reviewed the disc of Lola Starr's murder with Feeney. She didn't flinch at the little popping sound of the silenced weapon. Her system no longer recoiled at the insult the bullet caused in flesh.

The screen held steady on the ending caption: Two of Six. Then it went blank. Without a word, Eve cued up the first murder, and they watched Sharon DeBlass die again.

'What can you tell me?' Eve asked when it was finished.

'Discs were made on a Trident MicroCam, the five thousand model. It's only been available about six months, very pricey. Big seller last Christmas, though. More than ten thousand moved in Manhattan alone during the traditional shopping season, not to mention how many went through the gray market. Not as much of a flood like less expensive models, but still too many to trace.'

He looked over at Eve with his drooping camel eyes. 'Guess who owns Trident?'

'Roarke Industries.'

'Give the lady a bouquet. I'd say the odds were pretty good the boss man owns one himself.'

'He'd certainly have access.' She made a note of it and resisted the memory of how his lips had felt brushing over her knuckles. 'The killer uses a fairly exclusive piece of equipment he manufactures himself. Arrogance or stupidity?'

'Stupidity doesn't fly with this boy.'

'No, it doesn't. The weapon?'

'We've got a couple thousand out there in private collections,' Feeney began, nibbling on a cashew. 'Three in the boroughs. Those are the ones that've been registered,' he added with a thin smile. 'The silencer doesn't have to be registered, as it doesn't qualify as deadly on its own. No way of tracing it.'

He leaned back, tapped the monitor. 'As far as the first disc, I've been running it. I came up with a couple of shadows. Makes me certain he recorded more than the murder. But I haven't been able to enhance anything. Whoever edited that disc knew all the tricks or had access to equipment that knew them for him.'

'What about the sweepers?'

'Commander ordered them for this morning, per your request.' Feeney glanced at his watch. 'Should be there now. I picked up the security discs on my way in, ran them. We've got a twenty-minute time lapse starting at three-ten, night before last.'

'Bastard waltzed right in,' she muttered. 'It's a shitty neighborhood, Feeney, but an upscale building. Nobody noticed him either time, which means he blends.'

'Or they're used to seeing him.'

'Because he was one of Sharon's regulars. Tell me why a man who was a regular client or an expensive, sophisticated, experienced prostitute, chose a green, low-scale what do you call it, ingenue like Lola Starr for his second hit?'

Feeney pursed his lips. 'He likes variety?'

Eve shook her head. 'Maybe he liked it so much the first time, he's not going to be choosy now. Four more to go, Feeney. He told us right off the bat we had a serial killer.

He announced it, letting us know Sharon wasn't particularly important. Just one of six.'

She blew out a breath, unsatisfied. 'So why'd he go back?' she said to herself. 'What was he looking for?'

'Maybe the sweepers'll tell us.'

'Maybe.' She picked up a list from her desk. 'I'm going to check out Sharon's client list again, then hit Lola's.'

Feeney cleared his throat, chose another cashew from his little bag. 'I hate to be the one to tell you, Dallas. The senator's demanding an update.'

'I have nothing to tell him.'

'You're going to have to tell him this afternoon. In East Washington.'

She stopped a pace in front of the door. 'Bullshit.'

'Commander gave me the news. We're on the two o'clock shuttle.' Feeney thought resignedly of how his stomach reacted to air travel. 'I hate politics.'

Eve was still gritting her teeth over her briefing with Whitney when she ran headlong into DeBlass's security outside his office in the New Senate Office Building, East Washington.

Their identification aside, both she and Feeney were scanned, and according to the revised Federal Property Act of 2022, were obliged to hand over their weapons.

'Like we're going to zap the guy while he's sitting at his desk,' Feeney muttered as they were escorted over red, white, and blue carpet.

'I wouldn't mind giving several of these guys a quick buzz.' Flanked by suits and shined shoes, Eve slouched in front of the glossy door of the senator's office, waiting for the internal camera to clear them.

'If you ask me, East Washington's been paranoid since the terrorist hit.' Feeney sneered into the camera. 'Couple dozen legislators get whacked, and they never forget it.'

The door opened, and Rockman, pristine in needle-thin pin stripes, nodded. 'Long memories are an advantage in politics, Captain Feeney. Lieutenant Dallas,' he added with another nod. 'We appreciate your promptness.'

'I had no idea the senator and my chief were so close,' Eve said as she stepped inside. 'Or that both of them would be so anxious to waste the taxpayers' money.'

'Perhaps they both consider justice priceless.' Rockman gestured them toward the gleaming desk of cherrywood – certainly priceless – where DeBlass waited.

He had, as far as Eve could see, benefited from the change of temperature in the country – too lukewarm in her opinion – and the repeal of the Two Term Bill. Under current law, a politician could now retain his seat for life. All he had to do was buffalo his constituents into electing him.

DeBlass certainly looked at home. His paneled office was as hushed as a cathedral and every bit as reverent with its altarlike desk, the visitor chairs as subservient as pews.

'Sit,' DeBlass barked, and folded his large-knuckled hands on the desk. 'My latest information is that you are no closer to finding the monster who murdered my granddaughter than you were a week ago.' His dark brows beetled over his eyes. 'I find this difficult to understand, considering the resources of the New York Police Department.'

'Senator.' Eve let Commander Whitney's terse instructions play in her head: Be tactful, respectful, and tell him nothing he doesn't already know. 'We're using those resources to investigate and gather evidence. While the department is not now prepared to make an arrest, every possible effort is being made to bring your granddaughter's murderer to justice. Her case is my first priority, and you have my word it will continue to be until it can be satisfactorily closed.'

The senator listened to the little speech with all apparent

interest. Then he leaned forward. 'I've been in the business of bullshit for more than twice your life, lieutenant. So don't pull out your tap dance with me. You have nothing.'

Fuck tact, Eve decided instantly. 'What we have, Senator DeBlass, is a complicated and delicate investigation. Complicated, given the nature of the crime; delicate, due to the victim's family tree. It's my commander's opinion that I'm the best choice to conduct the investigation. It's your right to disagree. But pulling me off my job to come here to defend my work is a waste of time. My time.' She rose. 'I have nothing new to tell you.'

With the vision of both their butts hanging in a sling, Feeney rose as well, all respect. 'I'm sure you understand, senator, that the delicacy of an investigation of this nature often means progress is slow. It's difficult to ask you to be objective when we're talking of your granddaughter, but Lieutenant Dallas and I have no choice but to be objective.'

With an impatient gesture, DeBlass waved them to sit again. 'Obviously my emotions are involved. Sharon was an important part of my life. Whatever she became, and however I was disappointed in her choices, she was blood.' He drew a deep breath, let it loose. 'I cannot and will not be placated with bits and pieces of information.'

'There's nothing else I can tell you,' Eve repeated.

'You can tell me about the prostitute who was murdered two nights ago.' His eyes flicked up to Rockman.

'Lola Starr,' he supplied.

'I imagine your sources of information on Lola Starr are as thorough as ours.' Eve chose to speak directly to Rockman. 'Yes, we believe that there is a connection between the two murders.'

'My granddaughter might have been misguided,' DeBlass broke in, 'but she did not socialize with people like Lola Starr.'

113

So, prostitutes had class systems, Eve thought wearily. What else was new? 'We haven't determined whether they knew each other. But there's little doubt that they both knew the same man. And that man killed them. Each murder followed a specific pattern. We'll use that pattern to find him. Before, we hope, he kills again.'

'You believe he will,' Rockman put in.

'I'm sure he will.'

'The murder weapon,' DeBlass demanded. 'Was it the same type?'

'It's part of the pattern,' Eve told him. She'd commit no more than that. 'There are basic and undeniable similarities between the two homicides. There's no doubt the same man is responsible.'

Calmer now, Eve stood again. 'Senator, I never knew your granddaughter and have no personal tie to her, but I'm personally offended by murder. I'm going after him. That's all I can tell you.'

He studied her for a moment, saw more than he'd expected to see. 'Very well, lieutenant. Thank you for coming.'

Dismissed, Eve walked with Feeney to the door. In the mirror she saw DeBlass signal to Rockman, Rockman acknowledged. She waited until she was outside before she spoke.

'The son of a bitch is going to tail us.'

'Huh?'

'DeBlass's guard dog. He's going to shadow us.'

'What the hell for?'

'To see what we do, where we go. Why do you tail anyone? We're going to lose him at the transport center,' she told Feeney as she flagged down a cab. 'Keep your eyes out and see if he follows you to New York.'

'Follows me? Where are you going?'

'I'm going to follow my nose.'

*

It wasn't a difficult maneuver. The west wing boarding terminal at National Transport was always bedlam. It was even worse at rush hour when all northbound passengers were jammed into the security line and herded along by computerized voices. Shuttles and runabouts were going to be jammed.

Eve simply lost herself in the crowd, crammed herself into a cross terminal transport to the south wing, and caught an underground to Virginia.

After settling in her tube, ignoring the four o'clocks who were heading to the suburban havens, she took out her pocket directory. She requested Elizabeth Barrister's address, then asked for directions.

So far her nose was just fine. She was on the right tube and would have to make only one change in Richmond. If her luck held, she could finish the trip and be back in her apartment in time for dinner.

With her chin on her fist, she toyed with the controls of her video screen. She would have bypassed the news – something she made a habit of doing – but when an all-too-familiar face flashed on-screen, she stopped scanning.

Roarke, she thought, narrowing her eyes. The guy sure kept popping up. Lips pursed, she tuned in the audio, plugged in her ear receiver.

'. . . in this international, multibillion dollar project, Roarke Industries, Tokayamo, and Europa will join hands,' the announcer stated. 'It's taken three years, but it appears that the much debated, much anticipated Olympus Resort will begin construction.'

Olympus Resort, Eve mused, flipping through her mental files. Some high-class, high-dollar vacation paradise, she recalled. A proposed space station built for pleasure and entertainment.

She snorted. Wasn't it just like him to spend his time and money on fripperies?

If he didn't lose his tailored silk shirt, she imagined he'd make another fortune.

'Roarke – one question, sir.'

She watched Roarke pause on his way down a long flight of marble steps and lift a brow – exactly as she remembered he did – at the reporter's interruption.

'Could you tell me why you've spent so much time and effort, and a considerable amount of your own capitol, on this project – one detractors say will never fly?'

'Fly is precisely what it will do,' Roarke replied. 'In a manner of speaking. As to why, the Olympus Resort will be a haven for pleasure. I can't think of anything more worthwhile on which to spend time, effort, and capital.'

You wouldn't, Eve decided, and glanced up just in time to realize she was about to miss her stop. She dashed to the doors of the tube, cursed the computer voice for scolding her for running, and made the change to Fort Royal.

When she came above ground again, it was snowing. Soft, lazy flakes drifted over her hair and shoulders. Pedestrians were stomping it to mush on the sidewalks, but when she found a cab and gave her destination, she found the swirl of white more picturesque.

There was still countryside to be had, if you possessed the money or the prestige. Elizabeth Barrister and Richard DeBlass possessed both, and their home was a striking two stories of rosy brick set on a sloping hill and flanked by trees.

Snow was pristine on the expansive lawn, ermine draped on the bare branches of what Eve thought might be cherry trees. The security gate was an artful symphony of curling iron. However decorative it might have been, Eve was certain it was as practical as a vault.

She leaned out the cab window, flashed her badge at the scanner. 'Lieutenant Dallas, NYPSD.'

'You are not listed in the appointment directory, Lieutenant Dallas.'

'I'm the officer in charge of the DeBlass case. I have some questions for Ms Barrister or Richard DeBlass.'

There was a pause, during which time Eve began to shiver in the cold.

'Please step out of the cab, Lieutenant Dallas, and up to the scanner for further identification.'

'Tough joint,' the cabbie muttered, but Eve merely shrugged and complied.

'Identification verified. Dismiss your transport, Lieutenant Dallas. You will be met at the gate.'

'Heard the daughter got whacked up in New York,' the cabbie said as Eve paid the fare. 'Guess they're not taking any chances. Want I should pull back a ways and wait for you?'

'No, thanks. But I'll ask for your number when I'm ready to go.'

With a half salute, the cabbie backed up, swung away. Eve's nose was beginning to numb when she saw the little electric cart slide through the gate. The curved iron opened.

'Please go inside, step into the cart,' the computer invited. 'You will be taken to the house. Ms Barrister will see you.'

'Terrific.' Eve climbed into the cart and let it take her noiselessly to the front steps of the brick house. Even as she started up them, the door opened.

Either the servants were required to wear boring black suits, or the house was still in mourning. Eve was shown politely into a room off the entrance hall.

Where Roarke's home had simply whispered money, this one said old money. The carpets were thick, the walls papered in silk. The wide windows offered a stunning view of rolling hills and falling snow. And solitude, Eve thought. The architect must have understood that those who lived here preferred to consider themselves alone.

'Lieutenant Dallas.' Elizabeth rose. There was nervousness in the deliberate movement, in the rigid stance and, Eve saw, in the shadowed eyes that held grief.

'Thank you for seeing me, Ms Barrister.'

'My husband's in a meeting. I can interrupt him if necessary.'

'I don't think it will be.'

'You've come about Sharon.'

'Yes.'

'Please sit down.' Elizabeth gestured toward a chair upholstered in ivory. 'Can I offer you anything?'

'No, thanks. I'll try not to keep you very long. I don't know how much of my report you've seen—'

'All of it,' Elizabeth interrupted. 'I believe. It seems quite thorough. As an attorney, I have every confidence that when you find the person who killed my daughter, you'll have built a strong case.'

'That's the plan.' Running on nerves, Eve decided, watching the way Elizabeth's long, graceful fingers clenched, unclenched. 'This is a difficult time for you.'

'She was my only child,' Elizabeth said simply. 'My husband and I were – are – proponents of the population adjustment theory. Two parents,' she said with a thin smile. 'One offspring. Do you have any further information to give me?'

'Not at this time. Your daughter's profession, Ms Barrister. Did this cause friction in the family?'

In another of her slow, deliberate gestures, Elizabeth smoothed down the ankle-skimming skirt of her suit. 'It was not a profession I dreamed of my daughter embracing. Naturally, it was her choice.'

'Your father-in-law would have been opposed. Certainly politically opposed.'

'The senator's views on sexual legislation are well known. As a leader of the Conservative Party, he is, of course, working

118

to change many of the current laws regarding what is popularly called the Morality Issue.'

'Do you share his views?'

'No, I don't, though I fail to see how that applies.'

Eve cocked her head. Oh, there was friction there, all right. Eve wondered if the streamlined attorney agreed with her outspoken father-in-law on anything. 'Your daughter was killed – possibly by a client, possibly by a personal friend. If you and your daughter were at odds over her lifestyle, it would be unlikely she would have confided in you about professional or personal acquaintances.'

'I see.' Elizabeth folded her hands and forced herself to think like a lawyer. 'You're assuming that, as her mother, as a woman who might have shared some of the same viewpoints, Sharon would talk to me, perhaps share with me some of the more intimate details of her life.' Despite her efforts, Elizabeth's eyes clouded. 'I'm sorry, lieutenant, that's not the case. Sharon rarely shared anything with me. Certainly not about her business. She was . . . aloof, from both her father and me. Really, from her entire family.'

'You wouldn't know if she had a particular lover – someone she was more personally involved with? One who might have been jealous?'

'No. I can tell you I don't believe she did. Sharon had . . .' Elizabeth took a steadying breath. 'A disdain for men. An attraction to them, yes, but an underlying disdain. She knew she could attract them. From a very early age, she knew. And she found them foolish.'

'Professional companions are rigidly screened. A dislike – or disdain, as you put it – is a usual reason for denial of licensing.'

'She was also clever. There was nothing in her life she wanted she didn't find a way to have. Except happiness. She was not a happy woman,' Elizabeth went on, and swallowed the lump that always seemed to hover in her throat. 'I spoiled her, it's true. I have no one to blame but myself for it. I wanted more children.' She pressed a hand to her mouth until she thought her lips had stopped trembling. 'I was philosophically opposed to having more, and my husband was very clear in his position. But that didn't stop the emotion of wanting children to love. I loved Sharon, too much. The senator will tell you I smothered her, babied her, indulged her. And he would be right.'

'I would say that mothering was your privilege, not his.'

This brought a ghost of a smile to Elizabeth's eyes. 'So were the mistakes, and I made them. Richard, too, though he loved her no less than I. When Sharon moved to New York, we fought with her over it. Richard pleaded with her. I threatened her. And I pushed her away, lieutenant. She told me I didn't understand her – never had, never would – and that I saw only what I wanted to see, unless it was in court; but what went on in my own home was invisible.'

'What did she mean?'

'That I was a better lawyer than a mother, I suppose. After she left, I was hurt, angry. I pulled back, quite certain she would come to me. She didn't, of course.'

She stopped speaking for a moment, hoarding her regrets. 'Richard went to see her once or twice, but that didn't work, and only upset him. We let it alone, let her alone. Until recently, when I felt we had to make a new attempt.'

'Why recently?'

'The years pass,' Elizabeth murmured. 'I'd hoped she would be growing tired of the lifestyle, perhaps have begun to regret the rift with family. I went to see her myself about a year ago. But she only became angry, defensive, then insulting when I tried to persuade her to come home. Richard, though he'd resigned himself, offered to go up and talk to her. But she refused to see him. Even Catherine tried,' she murmured and

120

rubbed absently at a pain between her eyes. 'She went to see Sharon only a few weeks ago.'

'Congresswoman DeBlass went to New York to see Sharon?'

'Not specifically. Catherine was there for a fund-raiser and made a point to see and try to speak with Sharon.' Elizabeth pressed her lips together. 'I asked her to. You see, when I tried to open communications again, Sharon wasn't interested. I'd lost her,' Elizabeth said quietly, 'and moved too late to get her back. I didn't know how to get her back. I'd hoped that Catherine could help, being family, but not Sharon's mother.'

She looked over at Eve again. 'You're thinking that I should have gone again myself. It was my place to go.'

'Ms Barrister—'

But Elizabeth shook her head. 'You're right, of course. But she refused to confide in me. I thought I should respect her privacy, as I always had. I was never one of those mothers who peeked into her daughter's diary.'

'Diary?' Eve's antenna vibrated. 'Did she keep one?'

'She always kept a diary, even as a child. She changed the password in it regularly.'

'And as an adult?'

'Yes. She'd refer to it now and again – joke about the secrets she had and the people she knew who would be appalled at what she'd written about them.'

There'd been no personal diary in the inventory, Eve remembered. Such things could be as small as a woman's thumb. If the sweepers missed it the first time . . .

'Do you have any of them?'

'No.' Abruptly alert, Elizabeth looked up. 'She kept them in a deposit box, I think. She kept them all.'

'Did she use a bank here in Virginia?'

'Not that I'm aware of. I'll check and see what I can find out for you. I can go through the things she left here.'

121

'I'd appreciate that. If you think of anything – anything at all – a name, a comment, no matter how casual, please contact me.'

'I will. She never spoke of friends, lieutenant. I worried about that, even as I used it to hope that the lack of them would draw her back home. Out of the life she'd chosen. I even used one of my own, my own friends, thinking he would be more persuasive than I.'

'Who was that?'

'Roarke.' Elizabeth teared up again, fought them back. 'Only days before she was murdered, I called him. We've known each other for years. I asked him if he would arrange for her to be invited to a certain party I knew he'd be attending. If he'd seek her out. He was reluctant. Roarke isn't one to meddle in family business. But I used our friendship. If he would just find a way to befriend her, to show her that an attractive woman doesn't have to use her looks to feel worthwhile. He did that for me, and for my husband.'

'You asked him to develop a relationship with her?' Eve said carefully.

'I asked him to be her friend,' Elizabeth corrected. 'To be there for her. I asked him because there's no one I trust more. She'd cut herself off from all of us, and I needed someone I could trust. He would never hurt her, you see. He would never hurt anyone I loved.'

'Because he loves you?'

'Cares.' Richard DeBlass spoke from the doorway. 'Roarke cares very much for Beth and for me, and a few select others. But loves? I'm not sure he'd let himself risk quite that unstable an emotion.'

'Richard.' Elizabeth's control wobbled as she got to her feet. 'I wasn't expecting you quite yet.'

'We finished early.' He came to her, closed his hands over hers. 'You should have called me, Beth.'

'I didn't—' She broke off, looked at him helplessly. 'I'd hoped to handle it alone.'

'You don't have to handle anything alone.' He kept his hand closed over his wife's as he turned to Eve. 'You'd be Lieutenant Dallas?'

'Yes, Mr DeBlass. I had a few questions and hoped it would be easier if I asked them in person.'

'My wife and I are willing to cooperate in any way we can.' He remained standing, a position Eve judged as one of power and of distance.

There was none of Elizabeth's nerves or fragility in the man who stood beside her. He was taking charge, Eve decided, protecting his wife and guarding his own emotions with equal care.

'You were asking about Roarke,' he continued. 'May I ask why?'

'I told the lieutenant that I'd asked Roarke to see Sharon. To try to . . .'

'Oh, Beth.' In a gesture that was both weary and resigned, he shook his head. 'What could he do? Why would you bring him into it?'

She stepped away from him, her face so filled with despair, Eve's heart broke. 'I know you told me to let it alone, that we had to let her go. But I had to try again. She might have connected with him, Richard. He has a way.' She began to speak quickly now, her words tumbling out, tripping over each other. 'He might have helped her if I'd asked him sooner. With enough time, there's very little he can't do. But he didn't have enough time. Neither did my child.'

'All right,' Richard murmured, and laid a hand on her arm. 'All right.'

She controlled herself again, drew back, drew in. 'What can I do now, lieutenant, but pray for justice?'

'I'll get you justice, Ms Barrister.'

123

She closed her eyes and clung to that. 'I think you will. I wasn't sure of that, even after Roarke called me about you.'

'He called you – to discuss the case?'

'He called to see how we were – and to tell me he thought you'd be coming to see me personally before long.' She nearly smiled. 'He's rarely wrong. He told me I'd find you competent, organized, and involved. You are. I'm grateful I've had the opportunity to see that for myself and to know that you're in charge of my daughter's murder investigation.'

'Ms Barrister,' Eve hesitated only a moment before deciding to take the risk. 'What if I told you Roarke is a suspect?'

Elizabeth's eyes went wide, then calmed again almost immediately. 'I'd say you were taking an extraordinarily big wrong step.'

'Because Roarke is incapable of murder?'

'No, I wouldn't say that.' It was a relief to think of it, if only for a moment, in objective terms. 'Incapable of a senseless act, yes. He might kill cold-bloodedly, but never the defenseless. He might kill, I wouldn't be surprised if he had. But would he do to anyone what was done to Sharon – before, during, after? No. Not Roarke.'

'No,' Richard echoed, and his hand searched for his wife's again. 'Not Roarke.'

Not Roarke, Eve thought again when she was back in her cab and headed for the underground. Why the hell hadn't he told her he'd met Sharon DeBlass as a favor to her mother? What else hadn't he told her?

Blackmail. Somehow she didn't see him as a victim of blackmail. He wouldn't give a damn what was said or broadcast about him. But the diary changed things and made blackmail a new and intriguing motive.

Just what had Sharon recorded about whom, and where were the goddamn diaries?

# Chapter Nine

'No problem reversing the tail,' Feeney said as he shoveled in what passed for breakfast at the eatery at Cop Central. 'I see him cue in on me. He's looking around for you, but there's plenty of bodies. So I get on the frigging plane.'

Feeney washed down irradiated eggs with black bean coffee without a wince. 'He gets on, too, but he sits up in First Class. When we get off, he's waiting, and that's when he knows you're not there.' He jabbed at Eve with his fork. 'He was pissed, makes a quick call. So I get behind him, trail him to the Regent Hotel. They don't like to tell you anything at the Regent. Flash your badge and they get all offended.'

'And you explained, tactfully, about civic duty.'

'Right.' Feeney pushed his empty plate into the recycler slot, crushed his empty cup with his hand, and sent it to follow. 'He made a couple of calls – one to East Washington, one to Virginia. Then he makes a local – to the chief.'

'Shit.'

'Yeah. Chief Simpson's pushing buttons for DeBlass, no question. Makes you wonder what buttons.'

Before Eve could comment, her communicator beeped. She pulled it out and answered the call from her commander.

'Dallas, be in Testing. Twenty minutes.'

'Sir, I'm meeting a snitch on the Colby matter at oh nine hundred.'

'Reschedule.' His voice was flat. 'Twenty minutes.'

Slowly, Dallas replaced her communicator. 'I guess we know one of the buttons.'

'Seems like DeBlass is taking a personal interest in you.' Feeney studied her face. There wasn't a cop on the force who didn't despise Testing. 'You going to handle it okay?'

'Yeah, sure. This is going to tie me up most of the day, Feeney. Do me a favor. Do a run on the banks in Manhattan. I need to know if Sharon DeBlass kept a safe deposit box. If you don't find anything there, spread out to the other boroughs.'

'You got it.'

The Testing section was riddled with long corridors, some glassed, some done in pale green walls that were supposed to be calming. Doctors and technicians wore white. The color of innocence and, of course, power. When she entered the first set of reinforced glass doors, the computer politely ordered her to surrender her weapon. Eve took it out of her holster, set it on the tray, and watched it slide away.

It made her feel naked even before she was directed into Testing Room I-C and told to strip.

She laid her clothes on the bench provided and tried not to think about the techs watching her on their monitors or the machines with the nastily silent glide and their impersonal blinking lights.

The physical exam was easy. All she had to do was stand on the center mark in the tubelike room and watch the lights blip and flash as her internal organs and bones were checked for flaws.

Then she was permitted to don a blue jumpsuit and sit while a machine angled over to examine her eyes and ears. Another, snicking out from one of the wall slots, did a standard reflex test. For the personal touch, a technician entered to take a blood sample.

*Please exit door marked Testing 2-C. Phase one is complete, Dallas, Lieutenant Eve.*

In the adjoining room, Eve was instructed to lie on a padded table for the brain scan. Wouldn't want any cops out there with a brain tumor urging them to blast civilians, she thought wearily.

Eve watched the techs through the glass wall as the helmet was lowered onto her head.

Then the games began.

The bench adjusted to a sitting position and she was treated to virtual reality. The VR put her in a vehicle during a high-speed chase. Sounds exploded in her ears: the scream of sirens, the shouts of conflicting orders from the communicator on the dash. She could see that it was a standard police unit, fully charged. The control of the vehicle was hers, and she had to swerve and maneuver to avoid flattening a variety of pedestrians the VR hurled in her path.

In one part of her brain she was aware her vitals were being monitored: blood pressure, pulse, even the amount of sweat that crawled on her skin, the saliva that pooled and dried in her mouth. It was hot, almost unbearably hot. She narrowly missed a food transport that lumbered into her path.

She recognized her location. The old ports on the east side. She could smell them: water, bad fish, and old sweat. Transients wearing their uniform of blue coveralls were looking for a handout or a day's labor. She flew by a group of them jostling for position in front of a placement center.

*Subject armed. Rifle torch, hand explosive. Wanted for robbery homicide.*

Great, Eve thought as she careened after him. Fucking great. She punched the accelerator, whipped the wheel, and kissed off the fender of the target vehicle in a shower of sparks. A spurt of flame whooshed by her ear as he fired at her. The proprietor of a port side roach coach dived for cover,

127

along with several of his customers. Rice noodles flew along with curses.

She rammed the target again, ordering her backup to maneuver into a pincer position.

This time her quarry's vehicle shuddered, tipped. As he fought for control, she used hers to batter his to a stop. She shouted the standard identification and warning as she bolted from the vehicle. He came out blasting, and she brought him down.

The shock from her weapon jolted his nervous system. She watched him jitter, wet himself, then collapse.

She'd hardly taken a breath to readjust when the bastard techs tossed her into a new scene. The screams, the little girl's screams; the raging roar of the man who was her father.

They had reconstructed it almost too perfectly, using her own report, visuals of the site, and the mirror of her memory they'd lifted in the scan.

Eve didn't bother to curse them, but held back her hate, her grief, and sent herself racing up the stairs and back into her nightmare.

No more screams from the little girl. She beat on the door, calling out her name and rank. Warning the man on the other side of the door, trying to calm him.

'Cunts. You're all cunts. Come on in, cunt bitch. I'll kill you.'

The door folded like cardboard under her ramming shoulder. She went in, weapon drawn.

'She was just like her mother – just like her fucking mother. Thought they'd get away from me. Thought they could. I fixed it. I fixed them. I'm going to fix you, cunt cop.'

The little girl was staring at her with big, dead eyes. Doll's eyes. Her tiny, helpless body mutilated, blood spreading like a pool. And dripping from the knife.

She told him to freeze: '*You son of a bitch*, drop the weapon.

128

*Drop the fucking knife!'* But he kept coming. Stunned him. But he kept coming.

The room smelled of blood, of urine, of burned food. The lights were too bright, unshaded and blinding so that everything, everything stood out in jarring relief. A doll with a missing arm on the ripped sofa, a crooked window shield that let in a hard red glow from the neon across the street, the overturned table of cheap molded plastic, the cracked screen of a broken 'link.

The little girl with dead eyes. The spreading pool of blood. And the sharp, sticky gleam of the blade.

'I'm going to ram this right up your cunt. Just like I did to her.'

Stunned again. His eyes were wild, jagged on homemade Zeus, that wonderful chemical that made gods out of men, with all the power and insanity that went with delusions of immortality.

The knife, with the scarlet drenched blade hacked down, whistled.

And she dropped him.

The jolt zipped through his nervous system. His brain died first, so that his body convulsed and shuddered as his eyes turned to glass. Strapping down on the need to scream, she kicked the knife away from his still twitching hand and looked at the child.

The big doll's eyes stared at her, and told her – again – that she'd been too late.

Forcing her body to relax, she let nothing into her mind but her report.

The VR section was complete. Her vitals were checked again before she was taken to the final testing phase. The one-on-one with the psychiatrist.

Eve didn't have anything against Dr Mira. The woman was dedicated to her calling. In private practice, she could have

129

earned triple the salary she pulled in under the Police and Security Department.

She had a quiet voice with the faintest hint of upper class New England. Her pale blue eyes were kind – and sharp. At sixty, she was comfortable with middle age, but far from matronly.

Her hair was a warm honey brown and scooped up in the back in a neat yet complicated twist. She wore a tidy, rose toned suit with a sedate gold circle on the lapel.

No, Eve had nothing against her personally. She just hated shrinks.

'Lieutenant Dallas.' Mira rose from a soft blue scoop chair when Eve entered.

There was no desk, no computer in sight. One of the tricks, Eve knew, to make the subjects relax and forget they were under intense observation.

'Doctor.' Eve sat in the chair Mira indicated.

'I was just about to have some tea. You'll join me?'

'Sure.'

Mira moved gracefully to the server, ordered two teas, then brought the cups to the sitting area. 'It's unfortunate that your testing was postponed, lieutenant.' With a smile, she sat, sipped. 'The process is more conclusive and certainly more beneficial when run within twenty-four hours of an incident.'

'It couldn't be helped.'

'So I'm told. Your preliminary results are satisfactory.'

'Fine.'

'You still refuse autohypnosis?'

'It's optional.' Hating the defensive sound of her voice.

'Yes, it is.' Mira crossed her legs. 'You've been through a difficult experience, lieutenant. There are signs of physical and emotional fatigue.'

'I'm on another case, a demanding one. It's taking a lot of my time.'

'Yes, I have that information. Are you taking the standard sleep inducers?'

Eve tested the tea. It was, as she'd suspected, floral in scent and flavor. 'No. We've been through that before. Night pills are optional, and I opt no.'

'Because they limit your control.'

Eve met her eyes. 'That's right. I don't like being put to sleep, and I don't like being here. I don't like brain rape.'

'You consider Testing a kind of rape?'

There wasn't a cop with a brain who didn't. 'It's not a choice, is it?'

Mira kept her sigh to herself. 'The termination of a subject, no matter the circumstances, is a traumatic experience for a police officer. If the trauma effects the emotions, the reactions, the attitude, the officer's performance will suffer. If the use of full force was caused by a physical defect, that defect must be located and repaired.'

'I know the company line, doctor. I'm cooperating fully. But I don't have to like it.'

'No, you don't.' Mira neatly balanced the cup on her knee. 'Lieutenant, this is your second termination. Though that is not an unusual amount for an officer with your length of duty, there are many who never need to make that decision. I'd like to know how you feel about the choice you made, and the results.'

I wish I'd been quicker, Eve thought. I wish that child was playing with her toys right now instead of being cremated.

'As my only choice was to let him carve me into pieces, or stop him, I feel just fine about the decision. My warning was issued and ignored. Stunning was ineffective. The evidence that he would, indeed, kill was lying on the floor between us in a puddle of blood. Therefore, I have no problem with the results.'

'You were disturbed by the death of the child?'

131

'I believe anyone would be disturbed by the death of a child. Certainly that kind of vicious murder of the defenseless.'

'And do you see the parallel between the child and yourself?' Mira asked quietly. She could see Eve draw in and close off. 'Lieutenant, we both know I'm fully aware of your background. You were abused, physically, sexually, and emotionally. You were abandoned when you were eight.'

'That has nothing to do with—'

'I think it may have a great deal to do with your mental and emotional state,' Mira interrupted. 'For two years between the ages of eight and ten, you lived in a communal home while your parents were searched for. You have no memory of the first eight years of your life, your name, your circumstances, your birthplace.'

However mild they were, Mira's eyes were sharp and searching. 'You were given the name Eve Dallas and eventually placed in foster care. You had no control over any of this. You were a battered child, dependent on the system, which in many ways failed you.'

It took every ounce of will for Eve to keep her eyes and her voice level. 'As I, part of the system, failed to protect the child. You want to know how I feel about that, Dr Mira?'

Wretched. Sick. Sorry.

'I feel that I did everything I could do. I went through your VR and did it again. Because there was no changing it. If I could have saved the child, I would have saved her. If I could have arrested the subject, I would have.'

'But these matters were not in your control.'

Sneaky bitch, Eve thought. 'It was in my control to terminate. After employing all standard options, I exercised my control. You've reviewed the report. It was a clean, justifiable termination.'

Mira said nothing for a moment. Her skills, she knew, had never been able to more than scrape at Eve's outer wall of defense. 'Very well, lieutenant. You're cleared to resume duty without restriction.' Mira held up a hand before Eve could rise. 'Off the record.'

'Is anything?'

Mira only smiled. 'It's true that very often the mind protects itself. Yours refuses to acknowledge the first eight years of your life. But those years are a part of you. I can get them back for you when you're ready. And Eve,' she added in that quiet voice, 'I can help you deal with them.'

'I've made myself what I am, and I can live with it. Maybe I don't want to risk living with the rest.' She got up and walked to the door. When she turned back, Mira was sitting just as she had been, legs crossed, one hand holding the pretty little cup. The scent of brewed flowers lingered in the air.

'A hypothetical case,' Eve began and waited for Mira's nod.

'A woman, with considerable social and financial advantages, chooses to become a whore.' At Mira's lifted brow, Eve swore impatiently. 'We don't have to pretty up the terminology here, doctor. She chose to make her living from sex. Flaunted it in front of her well-positioned family, including her arch-conservative grandfather. Why?'

'It's difficult to come up with one specific motive from such general and sketchy information. The most obvious would be the subject could find her self-worth only in sexual skill. She either enjoyed or detested the act.'

Intrigued, Eve stepped away from the door. 'If she detested it, why would she become a pro?'

'To punish.'

'Herself?'

'Certainly, and those close to her.'

To punish, Eve mused. The diary. Blackmail.

'A man kills,' she continued. 'Viciously, brutally. The killing is tied to sex, and is executed in a unique and distinctive fashion. He records it, has bypassed a sophisticated

133

security system. A recording of the murder is delivered to the investigating officer. A message is left at the scene, a boastful message. What is he?'

'You don't give me much,' Mira complained, but Eve could see her attention was caught. 'Inventive,' she began. 'A planner, and a voyeur. Confident, perhaps smug. You said distinctive, so he wishes to leave his mark, and he wants to show off his skill, his brain. Using your observation and deductive talents, lieutenant, did he enjoy the act of murder?'

'Yes. I think he reveled in it.'

Mira nodded. 'Then he will certainly enjoy it again.'

'He already has. Two murders, barely a week apart. He won't wait long before the next, will he?'

'It's doubtful.' Mira sipped her tea as if they were discussing the latest spring fashions. 'Are the two murders connected in any way other than the perpetrator and the method?'

'Sex,' Eve said shortly.

'Ah.' Mira tilted her head. 'With all our technology, with the amazing advances that have been made in genetics, we are still unable to control human virtues and flaws. Perhaps we are too human to permit the tampering. Passions are necessary to the human spirit. We learned that early this century when genetic engineering nearly slipped out of control. It's unfortunate that some passions twist. Sex and violence. For some it's still a natural marriage.'

She stood then to take the cups and place them beside the server. 'I'd be interested in knowing more about this man, lieutenant. If and when you decide you want a profile, I hope you'll come to me.'

'It's Code Five.'

Mira glanced back. 'I see.'

'If we don't tie this up before he hits again, I may be able to swing it.'

'I'll make myself available.'

'Thanks.'

'Eve, even strong, self-made women have weak spots. Don't be afraid of them.'

Eve held Mira's gaze for another moment. 'I've got work to do.'

Testing left her shaky. Eve compensated by being surly and antagonistic with her snitch and nearly losing a lead on a case involving bootlegged chemicals. Her mood was far from cheerful when she checked back in to Cop Central. There was no message from Feeney.

Others in her department knew just where she'd spent the day and did their best to stay out of her way. As a result, she worked in solitude and annoyance for an hour.

Her last effort was to put through a call to Roarke. She was neither surprised nor particularly disappointed when he wasn't available. She left a message on his E-mail requesting an appointment, then logged out for the day.

She intended to drown her mood in cheap liquor and mediocre music at Mavis's latest gig at the Blue Squirrel.

It was a joint, which put it one slippery step up from a dive. The light was dim, the clientele edgy, and the service pitiful. It was exactly what Eve was looking for.

The music struck her in one clashing wave when she walked in. Mavis was managing to lift her appealing screech of a voice over the band, which consisted of one multitattooed kid on a melody master.

Eve snarled off the offer from a guy in a hooded jacket to buy her a drink inone of the private smoking booths. She jockeyed her way to a table, pressed in an order for a screamer, and settled back to watch Mavis perform.

She wasn't half bad, Eve decided. Not half good either, but the customers weren't choosy. Mavis was wearing paint tonight, her busty little body a canvas for splatters and streaks of orange and violet, with strategically brushed splotches of emerald. Bracelets and chains jangled as she jittered around the small, raised stage. One step below, a mass of humanity gyrated in sympathy.

Eve watched a small, sealed package pass from hand to hand on the edge of the dance floor. Drugs, of course. They'd tried a war on them, legalizing them, ignoring them, and regulating them. Nothing seemed to work.

She couldn't raise the interest to make a bust and lifted a hand in a wave to Mavis instead.

The vocal part of the song ended – such as it was. Mavis leaped offstage, wiggled through the crowd, and plopped a painted hip on the edge of Eve's table.

'Hey, stranger.'

'Looking good, Mavis. Who's the artist?'

'Oh, this guy I know.' She shifted, tapped an inch-long fingernail on the left cheek of her butt. 'Caruso. See, he signed me. Got the job free for passing his name around.' Her eyes rounded when the waitress set the long, slim glass filled with frothy blue liquid in front of Eve. 'A screamer? Wouldn't you rather I find a hammer and just knock you unconscious?'

'It's been a shitty day,' Eve muttered and took the first shocking sip. 'Jesus. These never get any better.'

Worried, Mavis leaned closer. 'I can cut out for a little while.'

'No, I'm okay.' Eve risked her life with another sip. 'I just wanted to check out your gig, let off some steam. Mavis, you're not using, are you?'

'Hey, come on.' More concerned than insulted, Mavis shook Eve's shoulder. 'I'm clean, you know that. Some shit gets passed around in here, but it's all minor league. Some happy pills, some calmers, a few mood patches.' She pokered up. 'If

136

you're looking to make a bust, you could at least do it on my night off.'

'Sorry.' Annoyed with herself, Eve rubbed her hands over her face. 'I'm not fit for human consumption at the moment. Go back and sing. I like hearing you.'

'Sure. But if you want company when you split, just give me a sign. I can fix it.'

'Thanks.' Eve sat back, closed her eyes. It was a surprise when the music slowed, even mellowed. If you didn't look around, it wasn't so bad.

For twenty credits she could have hooked on mood enhancer goggles, treated herself to lights and shapes that fit the music. At the moment, she preferred the dark behind her eyes.

'This doesn't seem quite your den of iniquity, lieutenant.'

Eve opened her eyes and stared up at Roarke. 'Every time I turn around.'

He sat across from her. The table was small enough that their knees bumped. His way of adjusting was to slide his thighs against hers. 'You called me, remember, and you'd left this address when you logged out.'

'I wanted an appointment, not a drinking buddy.'

He glanced at the drink on the table, leaned over to take a sniff. 'You're not going to get one with that poison.'

'This joint doesn't run to fine wine and aged scotch.'

He laid a hand over hers for the simple purpose of watching her scowl and jerk away. 'Why don't we go somewhere that does?'

'I'm in a pisser of a mood. Roarke. Give me an appointment, at your convenience, then take off.'

'An appointment for what?' The singer caught his attention. He cocked a brow, watching her roll her eyes and gesture. 'Unless she's having some sort of seizure, I believe the vocalist is signaling you.'

Resigned, Eve glanced over, shook her head. 'She's a friend

of mine.' She shook her head more emphatically when Mavis grinned and turned both thumbs up. 'She thinks I got lucky.'

'You did.' Roarke picked the drink up and set it on an adjoining table where greedy hands fought over it. 'I just saved your life.'

'Goddamn it—'

'If you want to get drunk, Eve, at least do it with something that will leave you most of your stomach lining.' He scanned the menu, winced. 'Which means nothing that can be purchased here.' He took her hand as he rose. 'Come on.'

'I'm fine right here.'

All patience, he bent down until his face was close to hers. 'What you are is hoping to get drunk enough so that you can take a few punches at someone without worrying about the consequences. With me, you don't have to get drunk, you don't have to worry. You can take all the punches you want.'

'Why?'

'Because you have something sad in your eyes. And it gets to me.' While she was dealing with the surprise of that statement, he hauled her to her feet and toward the door.

'I'm going home,' she decided.

'No, you're not.'

'Listen, pal—'

That was as far as she got before her back was shoved against the wall and his mouth crushed hard on hers. She didn't fight. The wind had been knocked out of her by the suddenness, and the rage under it, and the shock of need that slammed into her like a fist.

It was quick, seconds only, before her mouth was free. 'Stop it,' she demanded, and hated that her voice was only a shaky whisper.

'Whatever you think,' he began, struggling for his own composure, 'there are times when you need someone. Right now, it's me.' Impatience shimmering around him, he pulled her outside. 'Where's your car?'

She gestured down the block and let him propel her down the sidewalk. 'I don't know what your problem is.'

'It seems to be you. Do you know how you looked?' he demanded as he yanked open the car door. 'Sitting in that place with your eyes closed, shadows under them?' Picturing it again only fired his anger. He shoved her into the passenger seat and rounded the car to take the driver's position himself. 'What's your fucking code?'

Fascinated with the whiplash temper, she shifted to key it in herself. With the lock released, he pressed the starter and pulled away from the curb.

'I was trying to relax,' Eve said carefully.

'You don't know how,' he shot back. 'You've packed it in, but you haven't gotten rid of it. You're walking a real straight line, Eve, but it's a damn thin one.'

'That's what I'm trained to do.'

'You don't know what you're up against this time.'

Her fingers curled into a fist at her side. 'And you do.'

He was silent for a moment, banking his own emotions. 'We'll talk about it later.'

'I like now better. I went to see Elizabeth Barrister yesterday.'

'I know.' Calmer, he adjusted to the jerky rhythm of her car. 'You're cold. Turn up the heater.'

'It's busted. Why didn't you tell me that she'd asked you to meet Sharon, to talk to her?'

'Because Beth asked me in confidence.'

'What's your relationship with Elizabeth Barrister?'

'We're friends.' Roarke slanted her a look. 'I have a few. She and Richard are among them.'

'And the senator?'

'I hate his fucking, pompous, hypocritical guts,' Roarke said

139

calmly. 'If he gets his party's nomination for president, I'll put everything I've got into his opponent's campaign. If it's the devil himself.'

'You should learn to speak your mind, Roarke,' she said with a ghost of a smile. 'Did you know that Sharon kept a diary?'

'It's a natural assumption. She was a businesswoman.'

'I'm not talking about a log, business records. A diary, a personal diary. Secrets, Roarke. Blackmail.'

He said nothing as he turned the idea over. 'Well, well. You found your motive.'

'That remains to be seen. You have a lot of secrets, Roarke.'

He let out a half laugh as he stopped at the gates of his estate. 'Do you really think I'd be a victim of blackmail, Eve? That some lost, pitiful woman like Sharon could unearth information you can't and use it against me?'

'No.' That was simple. She put a hand on his arm. 'I'm not going inside with you.' That was not.

'If I were bringing you here for sex, we'd have sex. We both know it. You wanted to see me. You want to shoot the kind of weapon that was used to kill Sharon and the other, don't you?'

She let out a short breath. 'Yes.'

'Now's your chance.'

The gates opened. He drove through.

# *Chapter Ten*

The same stone-faced butler stood guard at the door. He took Eve's coat with the same faint disapproval.

'Send coffee down to the target room, please,' Roarke ordered as he led Eve up the stairs.

He was holding her hand again, but Eve decided it was less a sentimental gesture than one to make sure she didn't balk. She could have told him she was much too intrigued to go anywhere, but found she enjoyed that ripple of annoyance under his smooth manner.

When they'd reached the third floor, he went through his collection briskly, choosing weapons without fuss or hesitation. He handled the antiques with the competence of experience and, she thought, habitual use.

Not a man who simply bought to own, but one who made use of his possessions. She wondered if he knew that counted against him. Or if he cared.

Once his choices were secured in a leather case, he moved to a wall.

Both the security console and the door itself were so cleverly hidden in a painting of a forest, she would never have found it. The trompe l'oeil slid open to an elevator.

'This car only opens to a select number of rooms,' he explained as Eve stepped into the elevator with him. 'I rarely take guests down to the target area.'

'Why?'

'My collection, and the use of it, are reserved for those who can appreciate it.'

'How much do you buy through the black market?'

'Always a cop.' He flashed that grin at her, and she was sure, tucked his tongue in his cheek. 'I buy only through legal sources, naturally.' His eyes skimmed down to her shoulder bag. 'As long as you've got your recorder on.'

She couldn't help but smile back. Of course she had her recorder on. And of course he knew it. It was a measure of her interest that she opened the bag, took out her recorder, and manually disengaged.

'And your backup?' he said smoothly.

'You're too smart for your own good.' Willing to take the chance, she slipped a hand into her pocket. The backup unit was nearly paper thin. She used a thumbnail to deactivate it. 'What about yours?' She glanced around the elevator as the doors opened. 'You'd have video and audio security in every corner of this place.'

'Of course.' He took her hand again and drew her out of the car.

The room was high ceilinged, surprisingly spartan given Roarke's love of comfort. The lights switched on the moment they stepped in, illuminating plain, sand colored walls, a bank of simple high-backed chairs, and tables when a tray holding a silver coffeepot and china cups had already been set.

Ignoring them, Eve walked over to a long, glossy black console. 'What does it do?'

'A number of things.' Roarke set the case he carried down on a flat area. He pressed his palm to an identiscreen. There was a soft green glow beneath it as his print was read and accepted, then lights and dials glowed on.

'I keep a supply of ammunition here.' He pressed a series

of buttons. A cabinet in the base of the console slid open. 'You'll want these.' From a second cabinet, he took earplugs and safety glasses.

'This is, what, like a hobby?' Eve asked as she adjusted the glasses. The small, clear lenses cupped her eyes, the attached earplugs fit snugly.

'Yes. Like a hobby.'

His voice came with a faint echo through her ear protectors, linking them, closing out the rest. He chose the .38, loaded it.

'This was standard police issue in the mid-twentieth century. Toward the second millennium, nine millimeters were preferred.'

'The RS-fifties were the official weapon of choice during the Urban Revolt and into the third decade of the twenty-first century.'

He lifted a brow, pleased. 'You've been doing your homework.'

'Damn right.' She glanced at the weapons in his hand. 'Into the mind of a killer.'

'Then you'd be aware that the hand laser you have strapped to your side didn't gain popular acceptance until about twenty-five years ago.'

She watched with a slight frown as he slapped the cylinder shut. 'The NS laser, with modifications, has been standard police issue since 2023. I didn't notice any lasers in your collection.'

His eyes met hers, and there was a laugh in them. 'Cop toys only. They're illegal, lieutenant, even for collectors.' He pressed a button. Against the far wall a hologram flashed, so lifelike that Eve blinked and braced before she caught herself.

'Excellent image,' she murmured, studying the big, bull-shouldered man holding a weapon she couldn't quite identify.

'He's a replica of a typical twentieth-century thug. That's an AK-forty-seven he's holding.'

'Right.' She narrowed her eyes at it. It was more dramatic than in the photos and videos she'd studied. 'Very popular with urban gangs and drug dealers of the era.'

'An assault weapon,' Roarke murmured. 'Fashioned to kill. Once I activate, if he hits target, you'd feel a slight jolt. Low level electrical shock, rather than the much more dramatic insult of a bullet. Want to try it?'

'You go first.'

'Fine.' Roarke activated. The hologram lunged forward, swinging up his weapon. The sound effects kicked in instantly.

The thunder of noise had Eve jerking back a step. Snarled obscenities, street sounds, the terrifyingly rapid explosion of gunfire.

She watched, slack jawed, as the image spurted what looked entirely too much like blood. The wide chest seemed to erupt with it as the man flew back. The weapon spiraled out of his hand. Then both vanished.

'Jesus.'

A little surprised that he'd been showing off, like a kid at an arcade, Roarke lowered his weapon. 'It hardly makes the point of what something like this can do to flesh and bone if the image isn't realistic.'

'Guess not.' She had to swallow. 'Did he hit you?'

'Not that time. Of course, one on one, and when you can fully anticipate your opponent, doesn't make it very difficult to win your round.'

Roarke pushed more buttons, and the dead gunman was back, whole and ready to rock. Roarke took his stance with the ease and automation, Eve thought, of a veteran cop. Or, to borrow his word, a thug.

Abruptly, the image lunged, and as Roarke fired, other holograms appeared in rapid succession. A man with some sort of wicked looking handgun, a snarling woman aiming a long barreled weapon – a .44 Magnum, Eve decided – a small, terrified child carrying a ball.

They flashed and fired, cursed, screamed, bled. When it was over, the child was sitting on the ground weeping, all alone.

'A random choice like that's more difficult,' Roarke told her. 'Caught my shoulder.'

'What?' Eve blinked, focused on him again. 'Your shoulder.'

He grinned at her. 'Don't worry, darling. It's just a flesh wound.'

Her heart was thudding in her ears, no matter how ridiculous she told herself was her reaction. 'Hell of a toy, Roarke. Real fun and games time. Do you play often?'

'Now and again. Ready to try it?'

If she could handle a session with VR, Eve decided, she could handle this. 'Yeah, run another random pattern.'

'That's what I admire about you, lieutenant.' Roarke selected ammo, loaded fresh. 'You jump right in. Let's try a dry run first.'

He brought up a simple target, circles and a bull's-eye. He stepped behind her, putting the .38 in her hands, his over them. He pressed his cheek to hers. 'You have to sight it, as it doesn't sense heat and movement as your weapon does.' He adjusted her arms until he was satisfied. 'When you're ready to fire, you want to squeeze the trigger, not pump it. It's going to jerk a bit. It's not as smooth or as silent as your laser.'

'I've got that,' she muttered. It was foolish to be susceptible to his hands over hers, the press of his body, the smell of him. 'You're crowding me.'

He turned his head, just enough to have his lips brushing up to her earlobe. It was innocently unpierced, rather sweet, like a child's.

'I know. You need to brace yourself more than you're used to. Your reaction will be to flinch. Don't.'

'I don't flinch.' To prove it, she squeezed the trigger. Her arms jerked, annoying her. She shot again, and a third time, missing the heart of the target by less than an inch. 'Christ, you feel it, don't you?' She rolled her shoulders, fascinated by the way they sang in response to the weapon in her hands.

'It makes it more personal. You've got a good eye.' He was impressed, but his tone was mild. 'Of course, it's one thing to shoot at a circle, another to shoot at a body. Even a reproduction.'

A challenge? she noted. Well, she was up for it. 'How many more shots in this?'

'We'll reload it full.' He programmed in a series. Curiosity and, he had to admit, ego had him choosing a tough one. 'Ready?'

She flicked a glance at him, adjusted her stance. 'Yeah.'

The first image was an elderly woman clutching a shopping bag with both hands. Eve nearly took the bystander's head off before her finger froze. A movement flickered to the left, and she shot a mugger before he could bring an iron pipe down on the old woman. A slight sting in her left hip had her shifting again, and taking out a blad man with a weapon similar to her own.

They came fast and hard after that.

Roarke watched her, mesmerized. No, she didn't flinch, he mused. Her eyes stayed flat and cool. Cop's eyes. He knew her adrenaline was up, her pulse hammering. Her movements were quick but as smooth and studied as a dance. Her jaw was set, her hands steady.

And he wanted her, he realized as his gut churned. Quite desperately he wanted her.

'Caught me twice,' she said almost to herself. She opened the chamber herself, reloaded as she'd seen Roarke do. 'Once in the hip, once in the abdomen. That makes me dead or in dire straits. Run another.'

He obliged her, then tucked his hands in his pockets and watched her work.

When she was done, she asked to try the Swiss model. She found she preferred the weight and the response of it. Definitely an advantage over a revolver, she reflected. Quicker, more responsive, better fire power, and a reload took seconds.

Neither weapon fit as comfortably in her hand as her laser, yet she found both primitively and horribly efficient.

And the damage they caused, the torn flesh, the flying blood, turned death into a gruesome affair.

'Any hits?' Roarke asked.

Though the images were gone, she stared at the wall, and the afterimages that played in her mind. 'No. I'm clean. What they do to a body,' she said softly, and put the weapon down. 'To have used these – to have faced having to use them day after day, and know going in they could be used against you. Who could face that,' she wondered, 'without going a little insane?'

'You could.' He removed his eye and ear protectors. 'Conscience and dedication to duty don't have to equal any kind of weakness. You got through Testing. It cost you, but you got through it.'

Carefully, she set her protectors beside his. 'How do you know?'

'How do I know you were in Testing today? I have contacts. How do I know it cost you?' He cupped her chin. 'I can see it,' he said softly. 'Your heart wars with your head. I don't think you realize that's what makes you so good at your job. Or so fascinating to me.'

'I'm not trying to fascinate you. I'm trying to find a man who used those weapons I just fired; not for defense, but for pleasure.' She looked straight into his eyes. 'It isn't you.'

'No, it isn't me.'

'But you know something.'

He brushed the pad of his thumb over, into the dip in her chin before dropping his hand. 'I'm not at all sure that I do.' He crossed over to the table, poured coffee. 'Twentieth-century weapons, twentieth-century crimes, with twentieth-century motives?' He flicked a glance at her. 'That would be my take.'

'It's a simple enough deduction.'

'But tell me, lieutenant, can you play deductive games in history, or are you too firmly entrenched in the now?'

She'd wondered the same herself, and she was learning. 'I'm flexible.'

'No, but you're smart. Whoever killed Sharon had a knowledge, even an affection, perhaps an obsession with the past.' His brow lifted mockingly. 'I do have a knowledge of certain pieces of the past, and undoubtedly an affection for them. Obsession?' He lifted a careless shoulder. 'You'd have to judge for yourself.'

'I'm working on it.'

'I'm sure you are. Let's take a page out of old-fashioned deductive reasoning, no computers, no technical analysis. Study the victim first. You believe Sharon was a blackmailer. And it fits. She was an angry woman, a defiant one who needed power. And wanted to be loved.'

'You figured all that out after seeing her twice?'

'From that.' He offered the coffee to her. 'And from talking to people who knew her. Friends and associates found her a stunning, energetic woman, yet a secretive one. A woman who dismissed her family, yet thought of them often. One who loved to live, yet one who brooded regularly. I imagine we've covered much of the same ground.'

Irritation jumped in. 'I wasn't aware you were covering any ground, Roarke, in a police investigation.'

'Beth and Richard are my friends. I take my friendships seriously. They're grieving, Eve. And I don't like knowing Beth is blaming herself.'

She remembered the haunted eyes and nerves. She sighed. 'All right, I can accept that. Who have you talked to?'

'Friends, as I said, acquaintances, business associates.' He set his coffee aside as Eve sipped hers and paced. 'Odd, isn't it, how many different opinions and perceptions you find on one woman. Ask this one, and you'll hear Sharon was loyal, generous. Ask another and she was vindictive, calculating. Still another saw her as a party addict who could never find enough excitement, while the next tells you she enjoyed quiet evenings on her own. Quite a role player, our Sharon.'

'She wore different faces for different people. It's common enough.'

'Which face, or which role, killed her?' Roarke took out a cigarette, lighted it. 'Blackmail.' Thoughtfully he blew out a fragrant stream of smoke. 'She would have been good at it. She liked to dig into people and could dispense considerable charm while doing it.'

'And she dispensed it on you.'

'Lavishly.' That careless smile flashed again. 'I wasn't prepared to exchange information for sex. Even if she hadn't been my friend's daughter and a professional, she wouldn't have appealed to me in that way. I prefer a different type.' His eyes rested on Eve's again, broodingly. 'Or thought I did. I haven't yet figured out why the intense, driven, and prickly type appeals to me so unexpectedly.'

She poured more coffee, looked at him over the rim. 'That isn't flattering.'

'It wasn't meant to be. Though for someone who must have a very poor-sighted hairdresser and doesn't choose the standard enhancements, you are surprisingly easy to look at.'

'I don't have a hairdresser, or time for enhancements.' Or, she decided, the inclination to discuss them. 'To continue the deduction. If Sharon DeBlass was murdered by one of her blackmail victims, where does Lola Starr come in?'

'A problem, isn't it?' Roarke took a contemplative drag. 'They don't appear to have anything in common other than their choice of profession. It's doubtful they knew each other or shared the same taste in clients. Yet there was one who, at least briefly, knew them both.'

'One who chose them both.'

Roarke lifted a brow, nodded. 'You put it better.'

'What did you mean when you said I didn't know what I was getting into?'

His hesitation was so brief, so smoothly covered, it was barely noticeable. 'I'm not sure if you understand the power DeBlass has or can use. The scandal of his granddaughter's murder could add to it. He wants the presidency, and he wants to dictate the mood and moral choices of the country and beyond.'

'You're saying he could use Sharon's death politically? How?'

Roarke stubbed his cigarette out. 'He could paint his granddaughter as a victim of society, with sex for profit as the murder weapon. How can a world that allows legalized prostitution, full conception control, sexual adjustment, and so forth not take responsibility for the results?'

Eve could appreciate the debate, but shook her head. 'DeBlass also wants to eliminate the gun ban. She was shot by a weapon not really available under current law.'

'Which makes it more insidious. Would she have been able to defend herself if she, too, had been armed?' When Eve started to disagree, he shook his head. 'It hardly matters what

150

the answer is, only the question itself. Have we forgotten our founders and the basic tenets of their blueprint for the country? Our right to bear arms. A woman murdered in her own home, her own bed, a victim of sexual freedom and defenselessness. More, yes, much more, of moral decline.'

He strolled over to disengage the console. 'Oh, you'll argue that murder by handgun was the rule rather than the exception when anyone with the desire and the finances could purchase one, but he'll drown that out. The Conservative Party is gaining ground, and he's the spearhead.'

He watched her assimilate as she poured yet more coffee. 'Has it occurred to you that he might not want the murderer caught?'

Off guard, she looked up. 'Why wouldn't he? Over and above the personal, wouldn't that give him even more ammunition? "Here's the low-life, immoral scum that murdered my poor, misguided granddaughter."'

'That's a risk, isn't it? Perhaps the murderer is a fine, upstanding pillar of his community who was equally misguided. But a scapegoat is certainly required.'

He waited a moment, watching her think it through. 'Who do you think made certain you went to Testing in the middle of this case? Who's watching every step you take, monitoring every stage of your investigation? Who'd digging into your background, your personal life as well as your professional one?'

Shaken, she set her cup down. 'I suspect DeBlass put the pressure on about Testing. He doesn't trust me, or he hasn't decided I'm competent to head the investigation. And he had Feeney and me followed from East Washington.' She let out a long breath. 'How do you know he's digging on me? Because you are?'

He didn't mind the anger in her eyes, or the accusation. He preferred it to the worry another might have shown. 'No,

151

because I'm watching him while he's watching you. I decided I'd find it more satisfying to learn about you from the source, over time, than by reading reports.'

He stepped closer, skimmed his fingers over her choppy hair. 'I respect the privacy of the people I care about. And I care about you, Eve. I don't know why, precisely, but you pull something from me.'

When she started to step back, he tightened his fingers. 'I'm tired of every time I have a moment with you, you put murder between us.'

'There is murder between us.'

'No. If anything, that's what brought us here. Is that the problem? You can't shed Lieutenant Dallas long enough to feel?'

'That's who I am.'

'Then that's who I want.' His eyes had darkened with impatient desire. The frustration he felt was only with himself, for being so impossibly driven he might, at any moment, beg. 'Lieutenant Dallas wouldn't be afraid of me, even if Eve might.'

The coffee had wired her. That's what had her system so jittery with nerves. 'I'm not afraid of you, Roarke.'

'Aren't you?' He moved closer, curling his hands on the lapels of her shirt. 'What do you think will happen if you step over the line?'

'Too much,' she murmured. 'Not enough. Sex isn't high on my priority list. It's distracting.'

The temper in his eyes lighted to a laugh. 'Damn right it is. When it's done well. Isn't it time you let me show you?'

She gripped his arms, not sure if she intended to move in or away. 'It's a mistake.'

'So we'll have to make it count,' he muttered before his mouth captured hers.

She moved in.

Her arms went around him, fingers diving into his hair. Her body slammed into his, vibrating as the kiss grew rough, then nearly brutal. His mouth was hot, almost vicious. The shock of it sent flares of reaction straight to her center.

Already, his fast, impatient hands were tugging her shirt from her jeans, finding her skin. In response, she dragged at his, desperate to get through silk and to flesh.

He had a vision of himself dragging her to the floor, pounding himself into her until her screams echoed like gunshots, and his release erupted like blood. It would be quick, and fierce. And over.

With the breath shuddering in his lungs, he jerked back. Her face was flushed, her mouth already swollen. He'd torn her shirt at the shoulder.

A room filled with violence, the smell of gunsmoke still stinking the air, and weapons still within reach.

'Not here.' He half carried, half dragged her to the elevator. By the time the doors opened, he'd ripped aside the torn sleeve. He shoved her against the back wall as the doors closed them in, and fumbled with her holster. 'Take this damn thing off. Take it off.'

She hit the release and let the holster dangle from one hand as she fought open his buttons with the other. 'Why do you wear so many clothes?'

'I won't next time.' He ripped the tattered shirt aside. Beneath she wore a thin, nearly transparent undershirt that revealed small, firm breasts and hardened nipples. He closed his hands over them, watched her eyes glaze. 'Where do you like to be touched?'

'You're doing fine.' She had to brace a hand on the side wall to keep from buckling.

When the doors opened again, they were fused together. They circled out with his teeth nipping and scraping along her throat. She let her bag and her holster drop.

She got a glimpse of the room: wide windows, mirrors, muted colors. She could smell flowers and felt the give of carpet under her feet. As she struggled to release his slacks, she caught sight of the bed.

'Holy God.'

It was huge, a lake of midnight blue cupped between high carved wood. It stood on a platform beneath a domed sky window. Across from it was a fireplace of pale green stone where fragrant wood sizzled.

'You sleep here?'

'I don't intend to sleep tonight.'

He interrupted her gawking by pulling her up the two stairs to the platform and tumbling her onto the bed.

'I have to check in by oh seven hundred.'

'Shut up, lieutenant.'

'Okay.'

With a half laugh, she rolled on top of him and fastened her mouth to his. Wild, reckless energy was bursting inside her. She couldn't move quickly enough, her hands weren't fast enough to satisfy the craving.

She fought off her boots, let him peel the jeans over her hips. A wave of pleasure rippled through her when she heard him groan. It had been a long time since she'd felt the tension and heat of a man's body – a very long time since she'd wanted to.

The need for release was driving and fierce. The moment they were naked, she would have straddled him and satisfied it. But he flipped their positions, muffled her edgy protests with a long, rough kiss.

'What's your hurry?' he murmured, sliding a hand down to take her breast and watching her face while his thumb quietly tortured her nipple. 'I haven't even looked at you.'

'I want you.'

'I know.' He levered back, running a hand from her shoulder

to her thigh while his gaze followed the movement. The blood was pounding in his loins. 'Long, slim . . .' His hand squeezed lightly on her breast. 'Small. Very nearly delicate. Who would have guessed?'

'I want you inside me.'

'You only want one aspect inside you,' he murmured.

'Goddamn it,' she began, then groaned when he dipped his head and took her breast into his mouth.

She writhed against him, against herself as he suckled, so gently at first it was torture, then harder, faster until she had to bite back a scream. His hands continued to skim over her, kindling exotic little fires of need.

It wasn't what she was used to. Sex, when she chose to have it, was quick, simple, and satisfied a basic need. But this was tangling emotions, a war on the system, a battering of the senses.

She struggled to get a hand between them, to reach him where he lay hard and heavy against her. Pure panic set in when he braceleted her wrists and levered her hands over her head.

'Don't.'

He'd nearly released her in reflex before he saw her eyes. Panic yes, even fear, but desire, too. 'You can't always be in control, Eve.' As he spoke he ran his free hand over her thigh. She trembled, and her eyes unfocused when his fingers brushed the back of her knee.

'Don't,' she said again, fighting for air.

'Don't what? Find a weakness, exploit it?' Experimentally, he caressed that sensitive skin, tracing his fingers up toward the heat, then back again. Her breath was coming in pants now as she fought to roll away from him.

'Too late, it seems,' he murmured. 'You want the kick without the intimacy?' He began a trail of slow, open-mouthed kisses at the base of her throat, working his way down while her body shivered like a plucked wire beneath his. 'You don't need a partner for that. And you have one tonight. I intend to give as much pleasure as I get.'

'I can't.' She strained against him, bucked, but each frantic movement brought only a new and devastating sensation.

'Let go.' He was mad to have her. But her struggle to hold back both challenged and infuriated.

'I can't.'

'I'm going to make you let go, and I'm going to watch it happen.' He slid back up her, feeling every tremble and quake, until his face was close to hers again. He pressed his palm firmly on the mound between her thighs.

Her breath hissed out. 'You bastard. I can't.'

'Liar,' he said quietly, then slid a finger down, over her, into her. His groan melded with hers as he found her tight, hot, wet. Clinging to control, he focused on her face, the change from panic to shock, from shock to glazed helplessness.

She felt herself slipping, battled back, but the pull was too strong. Someone screamed as she fell, then her body imploded. One moment the tension was vicious, then the spear of pleasure arrowed into her, so sharp, so hot. Dazed, disoriented, she went limp.

He went mad.

He dragged her up so that she was kneeling, her head heavy on his shoulder. 'Again,' he demanded, dragging her head back by the hair and plundering her mouth. 'Again, goddamn it.'

'Yes.' It was building so quickly. The need like teeth grinding inside her. Free, her hands raced over him, and her body arched fluidly back so that his lips could taste where and how they liked.

Her next climax ripped through him like claws. With something like a snarl, he shoved her onto her back, levered her hips high, and drove himself inside her. She closed around him, a hot, greedy fist.

Her nails scraped at his back, her hips pistoned as he plunged. When her hands slid weakly from his sweat-slicked shoulders, he emptied himself into her.

# Chapter Eleven

She didn't speak for a long time. There really wasn't anything to say. She had taken an inappropriate step with her eyes wide open. If there were consequences, she would pay them.

Now, she needed to gather whatever dignity she could scrape together and get out.

'I have to go.' With her face averted, she sat up and wondered how she was going to find her clothes.

'I don't think so.' Roarke's voice was lazy, confident, and infuriating. Even as she started to get off the bed, he snagged her arm, overbalanced her, and had her on her back again.

'Look, fun's fun.'

'It certainly is. I don't know as I'd qualify what just happened here as fun. I say it was too intense for that. I haven't finished with you, lieutenant.' When her eyes narrowed, he grinned. 'Good, that's what I wanted to—'

He lost his breath and with it the words when her elbow shot into his stomach. In the blink of an eye, she'd reversed their positions. That well-aimed elbow was now pressing dangerously on his windpipe.

'Listen, pal, I come and go as I please, so check your ego.'

Like a white flag, he lifted his palms out for peace. Her elbow lifted a half inch before he shifted and sprang.

She was tough, strong, and smart. That was only one more

reason why, after a sweaty struggle, she was infuriated to find herself under him again.

'Assaulting an officer will earn you one to five, Roarke. That's in a cage, not cushy home detention.'

'You're not wearing your badge. Or anything else, for that matter.' He gave her a friendly nip on the chin. 'Be sure to put that in your report.'

So much for dignity, she decided. 'I don't want to fight with you.' It pleased her that her voice was calm, even reasonable. 'I just have to go.'

He shifted, watched as her eyes widened, then fluttered half closed when he slipped inside her again. 'No, don't shut your eyes.' His voice was whisper rough.

So she watched him, incapable of resisting the fresh onslaught of pleasure. He kept the rhythm slow now, with long, deep strokes that stirred the soul.

Her breath quickened, thickened. All she could see was his face, all she could feel was that lovely, fluid slide of his body in hers, the tireless friction of it that had an orgasm shivering through her like gold.

His fingers linked with hers, and his lips curved on hers. She felt his body tighten an instant before he buried his face in her hair. They lay quiet, bodies meshed but still. He turned his head, pressed a kiss to her temple.

'Stay,' he murmured. 'Please.'

'Yes.' She closed her eyes now. 'All right, yes.'

They didn't sleep. It wasn't fatigue so much as bafflement that assaulted Eve when she stepped into Roarke's shower in the early hours of the morning.

She didn't spend nights with men. Always she'd been careful to keep sex simple, straightforward and, yes, impersonal. Yet here she was, the morning after, letting herself be pummeled by the hot pulse of his shower sprays. For hours,

159

she'd let herself be pummeled by him. He'd assaulted then invaded parts of her she'd thought impregnable.

She was trying to regret it. It seemed important that she realize and recognize her mistake, and move on. But it was difficult to regret anything that made her body feel so alive and kept the dreams at bay.

'You look good wet, lieutenant.'

Eve turned her head as Roarke stepped through the criss crossing sprays. 'I'm going to need to borrow a shirt.'

'We'll find you one.' He pressed a knob on the tiled walls, cupped his hand under a fount to catch a puddle of clear, creamy liquid.

'What are you doing?'

'Washing your hair,' he murmured and proceeded to stroke and massage the shampoo into her short, sopping cap of hair. 'I'm going to enjoy smelling my soap on you.' His lips curved. 'You're a fascinating woman, Eve. Here we are, wet, naked, both of us half dead from a very memorable night, and still you watch me with very cool, very suspicious eyes.'

'You're a suspicious character, Roarke.'

'I think that's a compliment.' He bent his head to bite her lip, as the steam rose and the spray began to pulse like a heartbeat. 'Tell me what you meant, the first time I made love to you, when you said, "I can't."'

He angled her head back, and Eve closed her eyes in defense as water chased the shampoo away. 'I don't remember everything I said.'

'You remember.' From another fount, he drew pale green soap that smelled of wild forests. Watching her, he slicked it over her shoulders, down her back, then around and up to her breasts. 'Hadn't you had an orgasm before?'

'Of course I have.' True, she'd always equated them with the subtle pop of a cork from a bottle of stress, not the

160

violent explosion that destroyed a lifetime of restraint. 'You're flattering yourself, Roarke.'

'Am I?' Didn't she know that those cool eyes, that wall of resistance she was scrambling to rebuild was an irresistible challenge? Obviously not, he mused. He tugged lightly at her soap-slicked nipples, smiling when she sucked in a breath. 'I'm about to flatter myself again.'

'I haven't got time for this,' she said quickly, and found her back pressed against the tile wall. 'It was a mistake in the first place. I have to go.'

'It won't take long.' He felt a hard slap of lust when he cupped her hips, lifted her. 'It wasn't a mistake then, or now. And I have to have you.'

His breath was coming faster. It stunned him how much he could want her still, baffled him that she could be blind to how helpless he was under the clawing need for her. It infuriated him that she could, simply by existing, be his weakness.

'Hold onto me,' he demanded, his voice harsh, edgy. 'Goddamn it, hold onto me.'

She already was. He pierced her, pinned her to the wall with an erection that filled her to bursting. Her frantic, helpless mewing echoed off the walls. She wanted to hate him for that, for making her a victim of her own rampant passions. But she held onto him, and let herself spin dizzily out of control.

He climaxed violently, slapped a hand on the wall, his arm rigid to maintain balance as her legs slid slowly off his hips. Suddenly he was angry, furious that she could strip away his finesse until he was no more than a beast rutting.

'I'll get you a shirt,' he said briskly, then stepped out, flicking a towel from a rack, and leaving her alone in the billowing steam.

By the time she was dressed, frowning over the feel of raw

161

silk against her skin, there was a tray of coffee waiting in the sitting area of the bedroom.

The morning news chattered quietly on the view screen, the curiosity corner at the lower left running fields of figures. The stock exchange. The monitor on a console was open to a newspaper. Not the *Times* or one of the New York tabs, Eve noted. It looked like Japanese.

'Do you have time for breakfast?' Roarke sat, sipping his coffee. He wasn't able to give his full attention to the morning data. He'd enjoyed watching her dress: the way her hands had hesitated over his shirt before she'd shrugged into it, how her fingers had run quickly up the buttons, the quick wriggle of hip as she'd tugged on jeans.

'No, thanks.' She wasn't sure of her moves now. He'd fucked her blind in the shower, then had withdrawn to play well-mannered host. She strapped into her holster before crossing to accept the coffee he'd already poured her.

'You know, lieutenant, you wear your weapon the way other women wear pearls.'

'It's not a fashion accessory.'

'You misunderstand. To some, jewelry is as vital as limbs.' He tilted his head, studying her. 'The shirt's a bit large, but it suits you.'

Eve thought anything she could wear on her back that cost close to a week's pay couldn't suit her. 'I'll get it back to you.'

'I have several others.' He rose, unnerving her again by tracing a fingertip over her jaw. 'I was rough before. I'm sorry.'

The apology, so quiet and unexpected, embarrassed her. 'Forget it.' She shifted away, drained her cup, set it aside.

'I won't forget it; neither will you.' He took her hand, lifted it to his lips. Nothing could have pleased him more than the quick suspicion on her face. 'You won't forget me, Eve. You'll think of me, perhaps not fondly, but you'll think of me.'

'I'm in the middle of a murder investigation. You're part of it. Sure, I'll think of you.'

'Darling,' he began, and watched with amusement as his use of the endearment knitted her brow. 'You'll be thinking of what I can do *to* you. Unfortunately, I won't be able to do more than imagine it myself for a few days.'

She tugged her hand free and reached, casually she hoped, for her bag. 'Going somewhere?'

'The preliminary work on the resort requires my attention, and my presence on FreeStar One for a number of meetings with the directorship. I'll be tied up, a few hundred thousand miles away, for a day or two.'

An emotion moved through her she wasn't ready to admit was disappointment. 'Yeah, I heard you wrapped the deal on that major indulgence for the bored rich.'

He only smiled. 'When the resort's complete, I'll take you there. You may form another opinion. In the meantime, I have to ask you for your discretion. The meetings are confidential. There's still a loose end or two to tie up, and it wouldn't do for my competitors to know we're getting under way so quickly. Only a few key people will know I'm not here in New York.'

She finger combed her hair. 'Why did you tell me?'

'Apparently, I've decided you're a key.' As disconcerted by that as she, Roarke led the way to the door. 'If you need to contact me, tell Summerset. He'll put you through.'

'The butler?'

Roarke smiled as they descended the stairs. 'He'll see to it,' was all he said. 'I should be gone about five days, a week at the most. I want to see you again.' He stopped, took her face in his hands. 'I need to see you again.'

Her pulse jumped, as if it had nothing to do with the rest of her. 'Roarke, what's going on here?'

'Lieutenant.' He leaned forward, touched his lips to hers.

163

'Indications are we're having a romance.' Then he laughed, kissed her again, hard and quick. 'I believe I could have held a gun to your head and you wouldn't have looked as terrified. Well, you'll have several days to think it through, won't you?'

She had a feeling several years wouldn't be enough.

There, at the base of the stairs, was Summerset, stone-faced, stiff-necked, holding her jacket. She took it and glanced back at Roarke as she shrugged it on.

'Have a good trip.'

'Thanks.' Roarke laid a hand on her shoulder before she could walk out the door. 'Eve, be careful.' Annoyed with himself, he dropped his hands. 'I'll be in touch.'

'Sure.' She hurried out, and when she glanced back, the door was closed. When she opened her car door, she noticed the electronic memo on the driver's seat. Scooping it up, she got behind the wheel. As she headed toward the gate, she flicked on the memo. Roarke's voice drawled out.

'I don't like the idea of you shivering unless I cause it. Stay warm.'

Frowning, she tucked the memo in her pocket before experimentally touching the temperature gauge. The blast of heat had her yelping in shock.

She grinned all the way to Cop Central.

Eve closed herself in her office. She had two hours before her official shift began, and she wanted to use every minute of it on the DeBlass-Starr homicides. When her shift kicked in, her duties would spread to a number of cases in varying degrees of progress. This time was her own.

As a matter of routine, she cued IRCCA to transmit any and all current data and ordered it in hard copy to review later. The transmission was depressingly brief and added nothing solid.

Back, she thought, to deductive games. On her desk she'd

spread out photos of both victims. She knew them intimately now, these women. Perhaps now, after the night she'd spent with Roarke, she understood something of what had driven them.

Sex was a powerful tool to use or have used against you. Both of these women had wanted to wield it, to control it. In the end, it had killed them.

A bullet in the brain had been the official cause of death, but Eve saw sex as the trigger.

It was the only connection between them, and the only link to their murderer.

Thoughtfully, she picked up the .38. It was familiar in her hand now. She knew exactly how it felt when it fired, the way the punch of it sung up the arm. The sound it made when the mechanism and basic physics sent the bullet flying.

Still holding the gun, she cued up the disc she'd requisitioned and watched Sharon DeBlass's murder again.

What did you feel, you bastard? she wondered. What did you feel when you squeezed the trigger and sent that slug of lead into her, when the blood spewed out, when her eyes rolled up dead?

What did you feel?

Eyes narrowed, she reran the disc. She was almost immune to the nastiness of it now. There was, she noted, the slightest waver in the video, as if he'd jostled the camera.

Did you arm jerk? she wondered. Did it shock you, the way her body flew back, how far the blood splattered?

Is that why she could hear the soft sob of breath, the slow exhale before the image changed?

What did you feel? she asked again. Revulsion, pleasure, or just cold satisfaction?

She leaned closer to the monitor. Sharon was carefully arranged now, the scene set as the camera panned her objectively and, yes, Eve thought, coldly.

Then why the jostle? Why the sob?

And the note. She picked up the sealed envelope and read it again. How did you know you'd be satisfied to stop at six? Have you already picked them out? Selected them?

Dissatisfied, she ejected the disc, replaced it and the .38. Loading the Starr disc, taking the second weapon, Eve ran through the process again.

No jostle this time, she noted. No quick, indrawn breath. Everything's smooth, precise, exact. You knew this time, she thought, how it would feel, how she'd look, how the blood would smell.

But you didn't know her. Or she didn't know you. You were just John Smith in her book, marked as a new client.

How did you choose her? And how are you going to pick the next one?

Just before nine, when Feeney knocked on her door, she was studying a map of Manhattan. He stepped behind her, leaned over her shoulder, and breathed candy mints.

'Thinking of relocating?'

'I'm trying geography. Widen view five percent,' she ordered the computer. The image adjusted. 'First murder, second murder,' she said, nodding toward the tiny red pulses on Broadway and in the West Village. 'My place.' There was a green pulse just off Ninth Avenue.

'Your place?'

'He knows where I live. He's been there twice. These are three places we can put him. I was hoping I'd be able to confine the area, but he spreads himself out. And the security.' She indulged in one little sigh, as she eased back in her chair. 'Three different systems. Starr's was all but nonexistent. Electronic doorman, inoperable – and it had been, according to other residents, for a couple of weeks. DeBlass had top grade, key code for entry, hand plate, full building security – audio and video. Had to be breached on-site. Our time lag

166

only hits one elevator, and the victim's hallway. Mine's not as fancy. I could breach the entry, any decent B and E man could. But I've got a System Five thousand police lock on the door. You have to be a real pro to pop it without the master code.'

Drumming her fingers on the desk, she scowled at the map. 'He's a security expert, knows his weapons – old weapons, Feeney. He'd cued in enough to department procedure to tag me for the primary investigator within hours of the first hit. He doesn't leave fingerprints or bodily fluids. Not even a fucking pubic hair. What does that tell you?'

Feeney sucked air through his teeth, rocked back on his heels. 'Cop. Military. Maybe paramilitary or government security. Could be a security hobbyist; there are plenty of them. Possible professional criminal, but unlikely.'

'Why unlikely?'

'If the guy was making a living off crime, why murder? There's no profit in either of these hits.'

'So, he's taking a vacation,' Eve said, but it didn't play for her.

'Maybe. I've run known sex offenders, crossed with IRCCA. Nobody pops who fits the MO. You look at this report yet?' he asked, indicating the IRCCA transmission.

'No. Why?'

'I already tagged it this morning. You might be surprised that there were about a hundred gun assaults last year, country wide. About that many accidental, too.' He jerked a shoulder. 'Bootlegged, homemade, black market, collectors.'

'But nobody fits our profile.'

'Nope.' He chewed contemplatively. 'Perverts either, though it's a real education to scan the data. Got a favorite. This guy in Detroit, hit on four before they tagged him. Liked to pick up a lonely heart, go back to her place. He'd tranq her, then he'd strip her down, spray her with glow-in-the-dark red paint, top to toe.'

'Weird.'

'Lethal. Skin's gotta breathe, so she'd suffocate, and while she was smothering to death, he'd play with her. Wouldn't bang her, no sperm or penetration. He'd just run his eager little hands over her.'

'Christ, that's sick.'

'Yeah, well, anyway. He gets a little too eager, a little too impatient with one, starts rubbing her before she's dry, you know. Some of the paint rubs off, and she starts to come around. So he panics, runs. Now our girl's naked, covered with paint, wobbly from the tranq, but she's pissed, runs right outside on the street and starts screaming. The unit comes by, catches on quick 'cause she's glowing like a laser show, and starts a standard search. Our boy's only a couple of blocks away. So they catch him . . .'

'Don't say it.'

'Red-handed,' Feeney said with a wicked grin. 'Kiss my ass, that's a good one. Caught him red-handed.' When Dallas just rolled her eyes, Feeney decided the guys in his division would appreciate the story more.

'Anyway, we maybe got a pervert. I'll bump up the pervs and the pros. Maybe we'll get lucky. I like the idea of that better than a cop.'

'So do I.' Lips pursed, she swiveled to look at him. 'Feeney, you've got a small collection, know something about antique firearms.'

He held out his arms, wrists tight together. 'I confess. Book me.'

She nearly smiled. 'You know any other cops who collect?'

'Sure, a few. It's an expensive hobby, so most of the ones I know collect reproductions. Speaking of expensive,' he added, fingering her sleeve. 'Nice shirt. You get a raise?'

'It's borrowed,' she muttered, and was surprised that she had to control a flush. 'Run them for me, Feeney. The ones that have genuine antiques.'

'Ah, Dallas.' His smile faded away at the thought of focusing in on his own people. 'I hate that shit.'

'So do I. Run them anyway. Keep it to the city for now.'

'Right.' He blew out a breath, wondered if she realized his name would be on the list. 'Hell of a way to start the day. Now I've got a present for you, kid. There was a memo on my desk when I got in. The chief's on his way in to the commander's office. He wants both of us.'

'Fuck that.'

Feeney just looked at his watch. 'I make it in five minutes. Maybe you want to put on a sweater or something, so Simpson doesn't get a good look at that shirt and decide we're overpaid.'

'Fuck that, too.'

Chief Edward Simpson was an imposing figure. Well over six feet, fighting trim, he preferred dark suits and vivid ties. His waving brown hair was tipped with gray.

It was well known throughout the department that those distinguished highlights were added by his personal cosmetician. His eyes were a steely blue – a color his polls indicated inspired voter confidence – that rarely showed humor, his mouth a thin comma of command. Looking at him, you thought of power and authority.

It was disillusioning to know how carelessly he used both to do laps in the heady pool of politics.

He sat down, steepling his long, creamy hands that winked with a trio of gold rings. His voice, when he spoke, had an actor's resonance.

'Commander, captain, lieutenant, we have a delicate situation.'

169

And an actor's timing. He paused, let those hard blue eyes scan each face in turn.

'You're all aware of how the media enjoys sensationalism,' he continued. 'Our city has, in the five years of my jurisdiction, lowered its crime rate by five percent. A full percentage a year. However, with recent events, it isn't the progress that will be touted by the press. Already there are headlines of these two killings. Stories that question the investigation and demand answers.'

Whitney, detesting Simpson in every pore, answered mildly. 'The stories lack details, chief. The Code Five on the DeBlass case makes it impossible to cooperate with the press or feed it.'

'By not feeding it,' Simpson snapped back. 'We allow them to speculate. I'll be making a statement this afternoon.' He held up a hand even as Whitney started to protest. 'It's necessary to give the public something to assess, and by assessing feel confident that the department has the matter under control. Even if that isn't the case.'

His eyes zeroed in on Eve. 'As the primary, lieutenant, you'll attend the press conference as well. My office is preparing a statement for you to give.'

'With all respect, Chief Simpson, I can't divulge to the public any details of the case that could undermine the investigation.'

Simpson plucked a piece of lint from his sleeve. 'Lieutenant, I have thirty years of experience. I believe I know how to handle a press conference. Secondly,' he continued, dismissing her by turning back to Commander Whitney, 'it's imperative that the link the press has made between the DeBlass and Starr homicides be broken. The department can't be responsible for embarrassing Senator DeBlass personally, or damaging his position, by joining these cases at the hip.'

'The murderer did that for us,' Eve said between her teeth.

Simpson spared her a glance. 'Officially, there is no connection. When asked, deny.'

'When asked,' Eve corrected. 'Lie.'

'Save your personal ethics. This is reality. A scandal that starts here and reverberates to East Washington will come back on us like a monsoon. Sharon DeBlass has been dead over a week, and you have nothing.'

'We have the weapon,' she disagreed. 'We have possible motive as blackmail, and a list of suspects.'

His color came up as he rose out of the chair. 'I'm head of this department, lieutenant, and the mess you make is left to me to clean. It's time you stop digging at dirt and close the case.'

'Sir.' Feeney stepped forward. 'Lieutenant Dallas and I—'

'Can both be on Traffic Detail in a fucking heartbeat,' Simpson finished.

Fists clenched, Whitney lunged to his feet. 'Don't threaten my officers, Simpson. You play your games, smile for the cameras, and rub asses with East Washington, but don't you come in on my turf and threaten my people. They're on and they stay on. You want to change that, you try going through me.'

Simpson's color deepened further. In fascination, Eve watched a vein throb at his temple. 'Your people press the wrong buttons on this, it'll be your ass. I've got Senator DeBlass under control for the moment, but he's not happy having the primary running off to pressure his daughter-in-law, to invade the privacy of her grief and ask her embarrassing, irrelevant questions. Senator DeBlass and his family are victims, not suspects, and are to be accorded respect and dignity during this investigation.'

'I accorded Elizabeth Barrister and Richard DeBlass respect and dignity.' Very deliberately Eve shut down her temper. 'The interview was conducted with their consent and cooperation.

I was not aware that I was required to receive permission from you or the senator to proceed as I see warranted on this case.'

'And I will not have the press speculating that this department harasses grieving parents, or why the primary resisted required testing after a termination.'

'Lieutenant Dallas's testing was postponed at my order,' Whitney said with snarling fury. 'And with your approval.'

'I'm well aware of that.' Simpson angled his head. 'I'm talking about speculation in the press. We will, all of us, be under a microscope until this man is stopped. Lieutenant Dallas's record and her actions will be up for public dissection.'

'My record'll stand it.'

'And your actions,' Simpson said with a faint smile. 'How will you answer the fact that you're jeopardizing the case and your position by indulging in a personal relationship with a suspect? And what do you think my official position will be if and when it comes out that you spent the night with that suspect?'

Control kept her in place, made her eyes flat, had her voice even. 'I'm sure you'd hang me to save yourself, Chief Simpson.'

'Without hesitation,' he agreed. 'Be at City Hall. Noon, sharp.'

When the door clinked shut behind him, Commander Whitney sat again. 'Dickless son of a bitch.' Then his eyes, still sharp as razors, cut into Eve. 'What the fuck are you doing?'

Eve accepted – was forced to accept – that her privacy was no longer an issue. 'I spent the night with Roarke. It was a personal decision, on my personal time. In my professional opinion, as primary investigator, he has been eliminated as a suspect. It doesn't negate the fact that my behavior was inadvisable.'

'Inadvisable,' Whitney exploded. 'Try asinine. Try career suicide. Goddamn it, Dallas, can't you hold your glands in check? I don't expect this from you.'

She didn't expect it from herself. 'It doesn't affect the investigation, or my ability to continue it. If you think differently, you're wrong. If you pull me off, you'll have to take my badge, too.'

Whitney stared at her another moment, swore again. 'You make damn sure Roarke is eliminated from the short list, Dallas. Damn sure he's eliminated or booked within thirty-six hours. And you ask yourself a question.'

'I've already asked it,' she interrupted, with a giddy relief only she knew she experienced when he didn't call for her badge – yet. 'How did Simpson know where I spent last night? I'm being monitored. Second question is why. Is it on Simpson's authority, is it DeBlass? Or, did someone leak the information to Simpson in order to damage my credibility and therefore, the investigation.'

'I expect you to find out.' He jerked a thumb toward the door. 'Watch yourself at that press conference, Dallas.'

They'd taken no more than three strides down the corridor when Feeney erupted. 'What the hell are you thinking of? Jesus Christ, Dallas.'

'I didn't plan it, okay?' She jabbed for an elevator, jammed her hands in her pockets. 'Back off.'

'He's on the short list. He's one of the last people we know of who saw Sharon DeBlass alive. He's got more money than God, and can buy anything, including immunity.'

'He doesn't fit type.' She stormed into the elevator, barked out her floor. 'I know what I'm doing.'

'You don't know shit. All the years I've known you, I've never seen you so much as stub your toe on a guy. Now you've fallen fucking over on one.'

'It was just sex. Not all of us have a nice comfortable life

173

with a nice comfortable wife. I wanted someone to touch me, and he wanted to be the one. It's none of your goddamn business who I sleep with.'

He caught her arm before she could storm out of the elevator. 'The hell with that. I care about you.'

She fought back the rage at being questioned, at being probed, at having her most private moments invaded. She turned back, lowering her voice so that those who walked the corridor wouldn't overhear.

'Am I a good cop, Feeney?'

'You're the best I ever worked with. That's why—'

She held up a hand. 'What makes a good cop?'

He sighed. 'Brains, guts, patience, nerve, instinct.'

'My brains, my guts, my instincts tell me it's not Roarke. Every time I try to turn it around and point it at him, I hit a wall. It's not him. I've got the patience, Feeney, and the nerve to keep at it until we find out who.'

His eyes stayed on hers. 'And if you're wrong this time, Dallas?'

'If I'm wrong, they won't have to ask for my badge.' She had to take a steadying breath. 'Feeney, if I'm wrong about this, about him, I'm finished. All the way finished. Because if I'm not a good cop, I'm nothing.'

'Jesus, Dallas, don't—'

She shook her head. 'Run the cop list for me, will you? I've got some calls to make.'

# Chapter Twelve

Press conferences left a bad taste in Eve's mouth. She stood on the steps of City Hall, on a stage set by Simpson with his patriotic tie and his gold I Love New York lapel pin. In his Big Brother of the City mode, his voice rose and fell while he read his statement.

A statement, Eve thought in disgust, that was riddled with lies, half truths, and plenty of self aggrandizements. According to Simpson he would have no rest until the murderer of young Lola Starr was brought to justice.

When questioned as to whether there was any connection between the Starr homicide and the mysterious death of Senator DeBlass's granddaughter, he flatly denied it.

It wasn't his first mistake and, Eve thought glumly, it would hardly be his last.

The words were barely out of his mouth when he was peppered with shouts from Channel 75's on-air ace, Nadine Furst.

'Chief Simpson, I have information that indicates the Starr homicide is linked with the DeBlass case – not only because both women were engaged in the same profession.'

'Now, Nadine.' Simpson flashed his patient, avuncular smile. 'We all know that information is often passed to you and your associates, and it's often inaccurate. That's why I set up the Data Verification Center in the first year of my term as chief of police. You have only to check with the DVC for accuracy.'

Eve managed to hold back a snort, but Nadine, with her sharp cat's eyes and lightning brain didn't bother. 'My source claims that Sharon DeBlass's death was not an accident – as the DVC claims – but murder. That both DeBlass and Starr were killed by the same method and the same man.'

This caused an uproar in the huddle of news teams, a scatter shot of demands and questions that had Simpson sweating under his monogrammed shirt.

'The department stands behind its position that there is no connection between these unfortunate incidents,' Simpson shouted out, but Eve saw little lights of panic flickering in his eyes. 'And my office stands behind the investigators.'

Those jittery eyes shot to Eve, and she knew, in that instant, what it was to be picked up bodily and thrown to the wolves.

'Lieutenant Dallas, a veteran officer with more than ten years of experience on the force, is in charge of the Starr homicide. She'll be happy to answer your questions.'

Trapped, Eve stepped forward while Simpson bent down so that his weasley aide could whisper rapid-fire advice in his ear.

Questions rained down on her, and she waited, filtering them until she found one she could deal with.

'How was Lola Starr murdered?'

'In order to protect the credibility of the investigation, I'm not at liberty to divulge the method.' She suffered through the shouts, cursing Simpson. 'I will state that Lola Starr, an eighteen-year-old licensed companion, was murdered, with violence and premeditation. Evidence indicates that she was murdered by a client.'

That fed them for awhile, Eve noted. Several reporters checked their links with base.

'Was it a sexual crime?' someone shouted out, and Eve lifted a brow.

'I've just stated that the victim was a prostitute and that she was killed by a client. Put it together.'

'Was Sharon DeBlass also killed by a client?' Nadine demanded.

Eve met those cagey feline eyes levelly. 'The department has not issued any official statement that Sharon DeBlass was murdered.'

'My source names you as primary in both cases. Will you confirm?'

Boggy ground. Eve stepped onto it. 'Yes. I'm the primary on several ongoing investigations.'

'Why would a ten-year vet be assigned to an accidental death?'

Eve smiled. 'Want me to define bureaucracy?'

That drew some chuckles, but it didn't pull Nadine off the scent.

'Is the DeBlass case still ongoing?'

Any answer would stir a hornet's nest. Eve opted for the truth. 'Yes. And it will remain ongoing until I, as primary, am satisfied with its disposition. However,' she continued, rolling over the shouts. 'No more emphasis will be given to Sharon DeBlass's death than any other. Including Lola Starr. Any case that comes across my desk is treated equally, regardless of family or social background. Lola Starr was a young woman from a small family. She had no social status, no influential background, no important friends. Now, after a few short months in New York, she's dead. Murdered. She deserves the best I can give her, and that's what she's going to get.'

Eve scanned the crowd, zeroed in on Nadine. 'You want a story, Ms Furst. I want a killer. I figure my wants are more important than yours, so that's all I have to say.'

She turned on her heel, shot Simpson one fulminating look,

then strode away. She could hear him fighting off questions as she headed for her car.

'Dallas.' Nadine, in low-heeled shoes built for style and movement, raced after her.

'I said I'm finished. Talk to Simpson.'

'Hey, if I want to wade through bullshit, I can call the DVC. That was a pretty impassioned statement. Didn't sound like Simpson's speech writer.'

'I like to talk for myself.' Eve reached her car and started to open the door when Nadine touched her shoulder.

'You like to play it straight. So do I. Look, Dallas, we've got different methods, but similar goals.' Satisfied that she had Eve's attention, she smiled. When her lips curved, her face turned into a tidy triangle, dominated by those upslanted green eyes. 'I'm not going to pull out the old public's right to know.'

'You'd be wasting your time.'

'What I am going to say is we've got two women dead in a week. My information, and my gut tells me they were both murdered. I don't figure you're going to confirm that.'

'You figure right.'

'What I want's a deal. You let me know if I'm on the right track, and I hold off going out with anything that undermines your investigation. When you've got something solid and you're ready to move on it, you call me. I get an exclusive on the arrest – live.'

Almost amused, Dallas leaned against her car. 'What are you going to give me for that, Nadine? A handshake and a smile?'

'For that I'm going to give you everything my source has passed to me. Everything.'

Now she was interested. 'Including the source?'

'I couldn't do that if I had to. Point is, I don't. What I do have, Dallas, is a disc, delivered to me at the studio. On

178

the disc are copies of police reports, including autopsies on both victims, and a couple of nasty little videos of two dead women.'

'Fuck that. If you had half of what you're telling me, you'd have been on air in a heartbeat.'

'I thought about it,' Nadine admitted. 'But this is bigger than ratings. Hell of a lot bigger. I want a story, Dallas, one that's going to cop me the Pulitzer, the International News Award, and a few other major prizes.'

Her eyes changed, darkened. She wasn't smiling anymore. 'But I saw what someone did to those woman. Maybe the story comes first with me, but it's not all. I pushed Simpson today, and I pushed you. I liked the way you pushed back. You can deal with me, or I can go out on my own. Your choice.'

Eve waited. A fleet of taxis cruised by, and a maxibus with its humming electric motor. 'We deal.' Before Furst's eyes could light in triumph, Eve turned on her. 'You cross me on this, Nadine, you cross me by so much as an inch, and I'll bury you.'

'Fair enough.'

'The Blue Squirrel, twenty minutes.'

The afternoon crowd at the club was too bored to do much more than huddle over their drinks. Eve found a corner table, ordered a Pepsi Classic and the veggie pasta. Nadine slid in across from her. She chose the chicken plate with no-oil fries. An indication, Eve thought glumly, of the wide difference between a cop's salary and a reporter's.

'What have you got?' Eve demanded.

'A picture's worth several hundred thousand words.' Nadine took a personal palm computer out of her bag – her red leather bag, Eve noted with envy. She had a weakness for leather and bold colors that she could rarely indulge.

Nadine popped in the disc, handed Eve the PPC. There was

little use in swearing, Eve decided as she watched her own reports flick on-screen. Brooding, she let the disc run over Code Five data, through official medical reports, the ME's findings. She stopped it when the videos began. There was no need to check out death over a meal.

'Is it accurate?' Nadine asked when Eve passed back the computer.

'It's accurate.'

'So the guy's some sort of gun freak, a security expert who patronizes companions.'

'The evidence indicates that profile.'

'How far have you narrowed it down?'

'Obviously, not far enough.'

Nadine waited while their food was served. 'There's got to be a lot of political pressure on you – the DeBlass end.'

'I don't play politics.'

'Your chief does.' Nadine took a bite of her chicken. Eve smirked as she winced. 'Christ, this is terrible.' Philosophically, she shifted to the fries. 'It's no secret DeBlass is front runner for the Conservative Party's nomination this summer. Or that the asshole Simpson is shooting for governor. Given the show this afternoon, it looks like cover-up.'

'At this point, publicly, there is no connection between the cases. But I meant what I said about equality, Nadine. I don't care who Sharon DeBlass's granddaddy is. I'm going to find the guy who did her.'

'And when you do, is he going to be charged with both murders, or only with Starr's?'

'That's up to the prosecuting attorney. Personally, I don't give a shit, as long as I hang him.'

'That's the difference between you and me, Dallas.' Nadine waved a fry, then bit in. 'I want it all. When you get him, and I break the story, the PA's not going to have a choice. The fallout's going to keep DeBlass busy for months.'

180

'Now who's playing politics?'

Nadine lifted a shoulder. 'Hey, I just report the story, I don't make it. And this one's got it all. Sex, violence, money. Having a name like Roarke's involved is going to shoot the ratings through the roof.'

Very slowly, Eve swallowed pasta. 'There's no evidence linking Roarke to the crimes.'

'He knew DeBlass – he's a friend of the family. Christ, he owns the building where Sharon was killed. He's got one of the top weapon collections in the world, and rumor is he's an expert shot.'

Eve picked up her drink. 'Neither murder weapon can be traced to him. He has no connection with Lola Starr.'

'Maybe not. But even as a periphery character, Roarke sells news. And it's no state secret that he and the senator have bumped heads in the past. The man's got ice in his veins,' she added with a shrug. 'I don't imagine he'd have any problem with a couple of cold-blooded killings. But . . .' She paused to lift her own drink. 'He's also a fanatic about privacy. It's hard to picture him bragging about the murders by sending discs to reporters. Somebody does that, they want publicity as much as they want to get away with the crime.'

'An interesting theory.' Eve had had enough. A headache was beginning to brew behind her eyes, and the pasta wasn't going to sit well. She rose, then leaned over the table close to Nadine. 'I'll give you another one, formulated by a cop. Do you want to know who your source is, Nadine?'

Her eyes glittered. 'Damn right.'

'Your source is the killer.' Eve paused, watching the light go out of Nadine's eyes. 'I'd watch my step if I were you, friend.'

Eve strode off, heading around behind the stage. She hoped Mavis was in the narrow cubicle that served as a dressing room. Just then, she needed a pal.

Eve found her, huddled under a blanket and sneezing into a tattered tissue.

'Got a fucking cold.' Mavis glared out of puffy eyes and blew like a bullhorn. 'I had to be crazy, wearing nothing but goddamn paint for twelve hours in goddamn lousy February.'

Warily, Eve kept her distance. 'Are you taking anything?'

'I'm taking everything.' She gestured to a tabletop littered with over-the-counter drugs and touch-up cosmetics. 'It's a fucking pharmaceutical conspiracy, Eve. We've wiped out just about every known plague, disease, and infection. Oh, we come up with a new one every now and again, to give the researchers something to do. But none of these bright-eyed medical types, none of the medi-computers can figure out how to cure the common fucking cold. You know why?'

Even couldn't stop the smile. She waited patiently until Mavis finished another bout of explosive sneezing. 'Why?'

'Because the pharmaceutical companies need to sell drugs. You know what a damn sinus tab costs? You can get anticancer injections cheaper. I swear it.'

'You can go to the doctor, get a prescription to eradicate the symptoms.'

'I got that, too. Damn stuff's only good for eight hours, and I've got a performance tonight. I have to wait until seven o'clock to take it.'

'You should be home in bed.'

'They're exterminating the building. Some wise guy said he saw a cockroach.' She sneezed again, then peered owlishly at Eve from under unpainted lashes. 'What are you doing here?'

'I had some business. Look, get some rest. I'll see you later.'

'No, stick around. I'm boring myself.' She reached for a bottle of some nasty looking pink liquid and glugged it down. 'Hey, nice shirt. You get a bonus or something?'

'Or something.'

'So, sit down. I was going to call you, but I've been too busy hacking up my lungs. That was Roarke who came in our fine establishment last night, wasn't it?'

'Yeah, it was Roarke.'

'I almost passed out when he walked up to your table. What's the story? You helping him with some security or something?'

'I slept with him,' Eve blurted out, and Mavis responded with a fit of helpless choking.

'You – Roarke.' Eyes watering, she reached for more tissue. 'Jesus, Eve. Jesus Christ, you never sleep with anybody. And you're telling me you slept with Roarke?'

'That's not precisely accurate. We didn't sleep.'

Mavis let out a moan. 'You didn't sleep. How long?'

Eve jerked a shoulder. 'I don't know. I stayed the night. Eight, nine hours, I guess.'

'Hours.' Mavis shuddered delicately. 'And you just kept going.'

'Pretty much.'

'Is he good? Stupid question,' she said quickly. 'You wouldn't have stayed otherwise. Wow, Eve, what got into you? Besides his incredibly energetic cock?'

'I don't know. It was stupid.' She dragged her hands through her hair. 'It's never been like that for me before. I didn't think it could – that I could. It's just never been important, then all of a sudden – shit.'

'Honey.' Mavis snaked a hand from under her blanket and took Eve's tensed fingers. 'You've been blocking off normal needs all your life because of things you barely remember. Somebody just found a way to get through. You should be happy.'

'It puts him in the pilot's seat, doesn't it?'

'Oh, that's bullshit,' Mavis interrupted before Eve could go on. 'Sex doesn't have to be a power trip. It sure as hell doesn't have to be a punishment. It's supposed to be fun. And now and again, if you're lucky, it gets to be special.'

'Maybe.' She closed her eyes. 'Oh God, Mavis, my career's on the line.'

'What are you talking about?'

'Roarke's involved in a case I'm working on.'

'Oh shit.' She had to break off and blow again. 'You're not going to have to bust him for something, are you?'

'No.' Then more emphatically. 'No. But if I don't tie it all up fast, with a nice, tidy bow, I'll be out. I'll be finished. Somebody's using me, Mavis.' Her eyes sharpened again. 'They're clearing the path in one direction, tossing roadblocks in the other. I don't know why. If I don't find out, it's going to cost me everything I have.'

'Then you're going to have to find out, aren't you?' Mavis squeezed Eve's fingers.

She would find out, Eve promised herself. It was after ten P.M. when she let herself into the lobby of her building. If she didn't want to think just then, it wasn't a crime. She'd had to swallow a reprimand from the chief's office for veering from the official statement during the press conference.

The commander's unofficial support didn't quite ease the sting.

Once she was inside her apartment she checked her E-mail. She knew it was foolish, this nagging hope that she'd find a message from Roarke.

There wasn't one. But what she found had her flesh crawling with ice.

The video message was unnamed, sent from a public access. The little girl. Her dead father. The blood.

Eve recognized the angles of the official department record, the one taken to document the site of murder and justified termination.

The audio came over it. A playback of her auto-record of the child's screams. Her beating on the door. The warning, and all the horror that followed.

'You bastard,' she whispered. 'You're not going to get to me with this. You're not going to use that baby to get to me.'

But her fingers shook as she ejected the disc. And she jolted when her intercom rang.

'Who is it?'

'Hennessy from apartment two-D.' The pale, earnest face of her downstairs neighbor flicked on screen. 'I'm sorry, Lieutenant Dallas. I didn't know what to do exactly. We've got trouble down here in the Finestein apartment.'

Eve sighed and let the image of the elderly couple flip into her mind. Quiet, friendly, television addicts. 'What's the problem?'

'Mr Finestein's dead, lieutenant. Keeled over in the kitchen while his wife was out playing mah-jongg with friends. I thought maybe you could come down.'

'Yeah.' She sighed again. 'I'll be there. Don't touch anything, Mr Hennessy, and try to keep people out of the way.' Out of habit she called dispatch, reported an unattended death and her presence on the scene.

She found the apartment quiet, with Mrs Finestein sitting on the living room sofa with her tiny white hands folded in her lap. Her hair was white as well, a snowfall around a face that was beginning to line despite antiaging creams and treatments.

The old woman smiled gently at Eve.

'I'm so sorry to trouble you, dear.'

'It's okay. Are you all right?'

'Yes, I'm fine.' Her soft blue eyes stayed on Eve's. 'It was our weekly game, the girls and mine. When I got home, I found him in the kitchen. He'd been eating a custard pie. Joe was overly fond of sweets.'

She looked over at Hennessy, who stood, shifting uncomfortably from foot to foot. 'I didn't know quite what to do, and went knocking on Mr Hennessy's door.'

'That's fine. If you'd stay with her for a minute please,' she said to Mr Hennessy.

The apartment was set up similarly to her own. It was meticulously neat, despite the abundance of knickknacks and memorabilia.

At the kitchen table with its centerpiece of china flowers, Joe Finestein had lost his life, and considerable dignity.

His head was slumped, half in, half out of a fluffy custard pie. Eve checked for a pulse, found none. His skin had cooled considerably. At a guess, she put his death at one-fifteen, give or take a couple of hours.

'Joseph Finestein,' she recited dutifully. 'Male, approximately one hundred and fifteen years of age. No signs of forced entry, no signs of violence. There are no marks on the body.'

She leaned closer, looked into Joe's surprised and staring eyes, sniffed the pie. After finishing her prelim notes, she went back to relieve Hennessy and interview the deceased's widow.

It was midnight before she was able to crawl into bed. Exhaustion snatched at her like a cross and greedy child. Oblivion was what she wanted, what she prayed for.

No dreams, she ordered her subconscious. Take the night off.

Even as she closed her eyes, her bedside 'link blipped.

'Fry in hell, whoever you are,' she muttered, then dutifully wrapped the sheet around her naked shoulders and switched it on.

'Lieutenant.' Roarke's image smiled at her. 'Did I wake you?'

'You would have in another five minutes.' She shifted as the audio hissed with a bit of space interference. 'I guess you got where you were going all right.'

'I did. There was only a slight delay in transport. I thought I might catch you before you turned in.'

'Any particular reason?'

'Because I like looking at you.' His smile faded as he stared at her. 'What's wrong, Eve?'

Where do you want me to start? she thought, but shrugged. 'Long day – ending with one of your other tenants here croaking in his late night snack. He went facedown in a custard pie.'

'There are worse ways to go, I suppose.' He turned his head, murmured to someone nearby. Eve saw a woman move briskly behind Roarke and out of view. 'I've just dismissed my assistant,' he explained. 'I wanted to be alone when I asked if you're wearing anything under that sheet.'

She glanced down, lifted a brow. 'Doesn't look like it.'

'Why don't you take it off?'

'No way I'm going to satisfy your prurient urges by inter-space transmission, Roarke. Use your imagination.'

'I am. I'm imagining what I'm going to do to you the next time I get my hands on you. I advise you to rest up, lieutenant.'

She wanted to smile and couldn't. 'Roarke, we're going to have to talk when you get back.'

'We can do that as well. I've always found conversations with you stimulating, Eve. Get some sleep.'

'Yeah, I will. See you, Roarke.'

'Think of me, Eve.'

He ended the transmission, then sat alone, brooding at the blank monitor. There'd been something in her eyes, he thought. He knew the moods of them now, could see beyond the training into the emotion.

187

The something had been worry.

Turning his chair, he looked out at his view of star splattered space. She was too far away for him to do any more than wonder about her.

And to ask himself, again, why she mattered so much.

# Chapter Thirteen

Eve studied the report of the bank search for Sharon DeBlass's deposit box with frustration. No record, no record, no record.

Nothing in New York, New Jersey, Connecticut. Nothing in East Washington or Virginia.

She had rented one somewhere, Eve thought. She'd had diaries, and had kept them tucked away someplace where she could get to them safely and quickly.

In those diaries, Eve was convinced, was a motive for murder.

Unwilling to tag Fenney for another, broader search, she began one herself, starting with Pennsylvania, working west and north toward the borders of Canada and Quebec. In slightly less than twice the time it would have taken Feeney, she came up blank again.

Then, working south, she struck out with Maryland, and down to Florida. Her machine began to chug noisily at the work. Eve issued a warning snarl and a sharp bump to the console. She swore she'd risk the morass of requisition for a new unit if this one just held out for one more case.

More from stubbornness than hope, she did a scan of the Midwest, heading toward the Rockies.

You were too smart, Sharon, Eve thought, as the negative results flickered by. Too smart for your own good. You wouldn't have gone out of the country, or off planet where you'd have to go through a customs scan every trip. Why go far away, someplace where you'd need transport or travel docs? You might want immediate access.

If your mother knew you kept diaries, maybe other people knew it, too. You bragged about it because you liked to make people uncomfortable. And you knew they were safely tucked away.

But close, damn it, Eve thought, closing her eyes to bring the woman she was coming to know so well into full focus. Close enough so that you could feel the power, use it, toy with people.

But not so simple that just anyone could track it down, gain access, spoil the game. You used an alias. Rented your safe box under another name – just in case. And if you were smart enough to use an alias, you'd have used one that was basic, that was familiar. One you wouldn't have to hassle over.

It was so simple, Eve realized as she keyed in Sharon Barrister. So simple both she and Feeney had overlooked it.

She hit pay dirt at the Brinkstone International Bank and Finance, Newark, New Jersey.

Sharon Barrister not only had a safe-deposit box, she had a brokerage account in the amount of $326,000.85.

Grinning at the screen, she hit her tie-in with the PA. 'I need a warrant,' she announced.

Three hours later, she was back in Commander Whitney's office, trying not to gnash her teeth. 'She's got another one somewhere,' Eve insisted. 'And the diaries are in it.'

'Nobody's stopping you from looking for it, Dallas.'

'Fine, that's fine.' She whirled around the office as she spoke. Energy was pumping now, and she wanted action. 'What are we going to do about this?'

She jerked a hand at the file on his desk.

'You've got the disc I took from the safe-deposit box and

the print out I ran. It's right there, commander. A blackmail list: names and amounts. And Simpson's name is there, in tidy alphabetical order.'

'I can read, Dallas.' He resisted the urge to rub at the tension gathering at the base of his skull. 'The chief isn't the only person named Simpson in the city, much less the country.'

'It's him.' She was fuming and there was no place to put the steam. 'We both know it. There are a number of other interesting names there, too. A governor, a Catholic bishop, a respected leader of the International Organization of Women, two high-ranking cops, an ex-Vice President—'

'I'm aware of the names,' Whitney interrupted. 'Are you aware of your position, Dallas, and the consequences?' He held up a hand to silence her. 'A few neat columns of names and numbers don't mean squat. This data gets out of this office, and it's over. You're finished and so's the investigation. Is that what you want?'

'No, sir.'

'You get the diaries, Dallas, find the connection between Sharon DeBlass and Lola Starr, and we'll see where we go from there.'

'Simpson's dirty.' She leaned over the desk. 'He knew Sharon DeBlass; he was being blackmailed. And he's doing everything he can to undermine the investigation.'

'Then we'll have to work around him, won't we?' Whitney put the file in his lock box. 'No one knows what we have in here, Dallas. Not even Feeney. Is that clear?

'Yes, sir.' Knowing she had to be satisfied with that, she started for the door. 'Commander, I'd like to point out that there's a name absent from that list. Roarke's not on it.'

Whitney met her eyes, nodded. 'As I said, Dallas. I can read.'

Her message light was blinking when she got back to her

office. A check of her E-mail turned up two calls from the medical examiner. Impatiently, Eve put the hot lead aside and returned the call.

'Finished running the tests on your neighbor, Dallas. You hit the bull's-eye.'

'Oh, hell.' She ran her hands over her face. 'Send through the results. I'll take it from here.'

Hetta Finestein opened her door with a puff of lavender sachet and the yeasty smell of homemade bread.

'Lieutenant Dallas.'

She smiled her quiet smile and stepped back in invitation. Inside, the viewing screen was tuned to a chatty talk show where interested members of the home audience could plug in and shoot their holographic images to the studio for fuller interaction. The topic seemed to be higher state salaries for professional mothers. Just now the screen was crowded with women and children of varying sizes and vocal opinions.

'How nice of you to come by. I've had so many visitors today. It's a comfort. Would you like some cookies?'

'Sure,' Eve agreed, and felt like slime. 'Thanks.' She sat on the couch, let her eyes scan the tidy little apartment. 'You and Mr Finestein used to run a bakery?'

'Oh, yes.' Hetta's voice carried from the kitchen, along with her bustling movements. 'Until just a few years ago. We did very well. People love real cooking, you know. And if I do say so myself, I have quite a hand with pies and cakes.'

'You do a lot of baking here, at home.'

Hetta came in with a tray of golden cookies. 'One of my pleasures. Too many people never know the joy of a home-baked cookie. So many children never experience real sugar. It's hideously expensive, of course, but worth it.'

Eve sampled a cookie and had to agree. 'I guess you must have baked the pie your husband was eating when he died.'

192

'You won't find store-bought or simulations in my house,' Hetta said proudly. 'Of course, Joe would gobble everything up almost as soon as I took it out of the oven. There's not an AutoChef on the market as reliable as a good baker's instincts and creativity.'

'You did bake the pie, Mrs Finestein.'

The woman blinked, lowered her lashes. 'Yes, I did.'

'Mrs Finestein, you know what killed your husband?'

'Yes, I do.' She smiled softly. 'Gluttony. I told him not to eat it. I specifically told him not to eat it. I said it was for Mrs Hennessy across the hall.'

'Mrs Hennessy.' That jolted Eve back several mental paces. 'You—'

'Of course, I knew he'd eat it, anyway. He was very selfish that way.'

Eve cleared her throat. 'Could we, ah, turn the program off?'

'Hmm? Oh, I'm sorry.' The flustered hostess tapped her cheeks with her hands. 'That's so rude. I'm so used to letting it play all day I don't even notice it. Um, program – no, screen off.'

'And the audio,' Eve said patiently.

'Of course.' Shaking her head as the sound continued to run, Hetta looked sheepish. 'I've just never gotten the hang of the thing since we switched from remote to voice. Sound off, please. There, that's better, isn't it.'

The woman could bake a poisoned pie, but couldn't control her own television, Eve thought. It took all kinds. 'Mrs Finestein, I don't want you to say any more until I've read you your rights. Until you're sure you understand them. You're under no obligation to make any statement,' Eve began, while Hetta continued to smile gently.

Hetta waited until the recitation was over. 'I didn't expect to get away with it. Not really.'

'Get away with what, Mrs Finestein?'

'Poisoning Joe. Although . . .' She pursed her lips like a child. 'My grandson's a lawyer – a very clever boy. I think he'd say that since I did tell Joe, very specifically told him not to eat that pie, it was more Joe's doing than mine. In any case,' she said and waited patiently.

'Mrs Finestein, are you telling me that you added synthetic cyanide compound to a custard pie with the intention of killing your husband?'

'No, dear. I'm telling you I added cyanide compound, with a nice dose of extra sugar to a pie, and told my husband not to touch it. "Joe," I said, "Don't you so much as sniff this custard pie. I baked it special, and it's not for you. You hear me, Joe?"'

Hetta smiled again. 'He said he heard me all right, and then just before I left for my evening with the girls, I told him again, just to be sure. 'I mean it, Joe. You let that pie be.' I expected he would eat it, though, but that was up to him, wasn't it? Let me tell you about Joe,' she continued conversationally, and picked up the cookie tray to urge another on Eve. When Eve hesitated, she laughed gaily. 'Oh, dear, these are quite safe, I promise you. I just gave a dozen to the nice little boy upstairs.'

To prove her point she chose one herself and bit in.

'Now, where was I? Oh, yes, about Joe. He's my second husband, you know. We've been married fifty years come April. He was a good partner, and quite a fine baker himself. Some men should never retire. The last few years he's been very hard to live with. Cross and complaining all the time, forever finding fault. And never would get flour on his fingers. Not that he'd pass by an almond tart without gobbling it down.'

Because it sounded almost reasonable, Eve waited a moment. 'Mrs Feinstein, you poisoned him because he ate too much?'

Hetta's rosy cheeks rounded. 'It does seem that way. But

194

it goes deeper. You're so young, dear, and you don't have family, do you?'

'No.'

'Families are a source of comfort, and a source of irritation. No one outside can ever understand what goes on in the privacy of a home. Joe wasn't an easy man to live with, and I'm afraid, though I'm sorry to speak ill of the dead, that he had developed bad habits. He'd find a real glee in upsetting me, in ruining my small pleasures. Why just last month he deliberately ate half the Tower of Pleasure Cake I'd baked for the International Betty Crocker cook-off. Then he told me it was dry.' Her voice huffed out in obvious insult. 'Can you imagine?'

'No,' Eve said weakly. 'I can't.'

'Well, he did it just to make me mad. It was the way he wielded power, you see. So I baked the pie, told him not to touch it, and went out to play mah-jongg with the girls. I wasn't at all surprised when I got back and found he hadn't listened. He was a glutton, you see.' She gestured with the cookie before delicately finishing the last bite. 'That's one of the seven deadly sins, gluttony. It just seemed right that he would die by sin. Are you sure you won't have another cookie?'

The world was certainly a mad place, Eve decided, when old women poisoned custard pies. And, she thought, with Hetta's quiet, old-fashioned, grandmotherly demeanor, the woman would probably get off.

If they sent her up, she'd get kitchen duty and happily bake pastries for the other inmates.

Eve filed her report, caught a quick dinner in the eatery, then went back to work on the still simmering lead.

She'd no more than cleared half the New York banks when the call came through. 'Yeah, Dallas.'

Her answer was the image that flowed onto her screen.

195

A dead woman, arranged all too familiarly on blood-soaked
sheets.

## THREE OF SIX

She stared at the message imposed over the body and snarled
at her computer.

'Trace address. Now, goddamn it.'

After the computer obliged, she tagged Dispatch.

'Dallas, Lieutenant Eve, ID 5347BQ. Priority A. Any available units to 156 West Eighty-ninth, apartment twenty-one
nineteen. Do not enter premises. Repeat, do not enter premises.
Detain any and all persons exiting building. Nobody goes in
that apartment, uniform or civilian. My ETA, ten minutes.'

'Copy, Dallas, Lieutenant, Eve.' The droid on duty spoke
coolly and without rush. 'Units five-oh and three-six available
to respond. Will await your arrival. Priority A. Dispatch,
out.'

She grabbed her bag and her field kit and was gone.

Eve entered the apartment alone, weapon out and ready. The
living room was tidy, even homey with its thick cushions and
fringed area rugs. There was a book on the sofa and a slight
dip in the cushion, indicating someone had spent some time
curled up and reading. Frowning over the image, she moved
to a door beyond.

The small room was set up as an office, the workstation
tidy as a pin, with little hints of personality in the basket of
perfumed silk flowers, the bowl of colorful gumdrops, the
shiny white mug decorated with a glossy red heart.

The workstation faced the window, the window faced the
sheer side of another building, but no one had bothered with
a privacy screen. Lining one wall was a clear shelf holding
several more books, a large drop box for discs, another for

196

E-memos, a small treasure trove of pricey graphite pencils and recycled legal pads. Cuddled between was a lopsided baked clay blob that might have been a horse, and had certainly been made by a child.

Eve turned out of the room and opened the opposing door.

She knew what to expect. Her system didn't revolt. The blood was still very fresh. With only a small sigh, she holstered her weapon, knowing she was alone with the dead.

Through the thin protective spray on her hands, she felt the body. It hadn't had time to cool.

She'd been positioned on the bed, and the weapon had been placed neatly between her legs.

Eve pegged it as a Ruger P-90, a sleek combat weapon popular as home defense during the Urban Revolt. Light, compact, and fully automatic.

No silencer this time. But she'd be willing to bet the bedroom was soundproofed – and that the killer had known it.

She moved over to the fussily female circular dresser, opened a small burlap bag that was currently a fashion rage. Inside she found the dead woman's companion's license.

Pretty woman, she mused. Nice smile, direct eyes, really stunning coffee-and-cream complexion.

'Georgie Castle,' Eve recited for the record. 'Female. Age fifty-three. Licensed companion. Death probably occurred between seven and seven-forty-five P.M., cause of death gunshot wounds. ME to confirm. Three visible points of violence: forehead, mid-chest, genitalia. Most likely induced with antique combat style handgun left at scene. No signs of struggle, no appearance of forced entry or robbery.'

A whisper of a sound behind her had Eve whipping out her weapon. Crouched, eyes hard and cold, she stared at a fat gray cat who slid into the room.

'Jesus, where'd you come from?' She let out a long, cleansing breath as she replaced her weapon. 'There's a cat,' she added for the record, and when it blinked at her, flashing one gold and one green eye, she bent down to scoop it up.

The purring sounded like a small, well oiled engine.

Shifting him, she took out her communicator and called for a homicide team.

A short time later, Eve was in the kitchen, watching the cat sniff with delicate disdain at a bowl of food she'd unearthed when she heard the raised voices outside the apartment door.

When she went to investigate, she found the uniform she'd posted trying to restrain a frantic and very determined woman.

'What's the problem here, officer?'

'Lieutenant.' With obvious relief, the uniform deferred to her superior. 'The civilian demands entry. I was—'

'Of course I demand entry.' The woman's dark red hair, cut in a perfect wedge, moved and settled around her face with each jerky movement. 'This is my mother's home. I want to know what you're doing here.'

'And your mother is?' Eve prompted.

'Mrs. Castle. Mrs Georgie Castle. Was there a break-in?' Anger turned to worry as she tried to squeeze past Eve. 'Is she all right? Mom?'

'Come with me.' Eve took a firm hold of her arm and steered her inside and into the kitchen. 'What's your name?'

'Samantha Bennett.'

The cat left his bowl and walked over to curl around and through Samantha's legs. In a gesture Eve recognized as habitual and automatic, Samantha bent to give the cat one quick scratch between the ears.

'Where's my mother?' Now that the worry was heading toward fear, Samantha's voice cracked.

There was no part of the job Eve dreaded more than this, no aspect of police work that scraped at her heart with such dull blades.

'I'm sorry, Ms Bennett. 'I'm very sorry. Your mother's dead.'

Samantha said nothing. Her eyes, the same warm honey tone as her mother's, unfocused. Before she could fold, Eve eased her into a chair. 'There's a mistake,' she managed. 'There has to be a mistake. We're going to the movies. The nine o'clock show. We always go to the movies on Tuesdays.' She stared up at Eve with desperately hopeful eyes. 'She can't be dead. She's barely fifty, and she's healthy. She's strong.'

'There's no mistake. I'm sorry.'

'There was an accident?' Those eyes filled now, flowed over. 'She had an accident?'

'It wasn't an accident.' There was no way but one to get it down. 'Your mother was murdered.'

'No, that's impossible.' The tears kept flowing. Her voice hitched over them as she continued to shake her head in denial. 'Everyone liked her. Everyone. No one would hurt her. I want to see her. I want to see her now.'

'I can't let you do that.'

'She's my mother.' Tears plopped on her lap even as her voice rose. 'I have the right. I want to see my mother.'

Eve clamped both hands on Samantha's shoulders, forcing her back into the chair she'd sprung from. 'You're not going to see her. It wouldn't help her. It wouldn't help you. What you're going to do is answer my questions, and that's going to help me find who did this to her. Now, do you want me to get you something? Call anyone for you?'

'No. No.' Samantha fumbled in her purse for a tissue. 'My husband, my children. I'll have to tell them. My father. How can I tell them?'

'Where is your father, Samantha?'

'He lives – he lives in Westchester. They divorced about two years ago. He kept the house because she wanted to move

199

into the city. She wanted to write books. She wanted to be a writer.'

Eve turned to the filtered water unit on the counter, glugged out a glass, pressed it on Samantha. 'Do you know how your mother made her living?'

'Yes.' Samantha pressed her lips together, crushed the damp tissue in her chilled fingers. 'No one could talk her out of it. She used to laugh and say it was time she did something shocking, and what wonderful research it was for her books. My mother—' Samantha broke off to drink. 'She got married very young. A few years ago, she said she needed to move on, see what else there was. We couldn't talk her out of that, either. You could never talk her out of anything.'

She began to weep again, covering her face and sobbing silently. Eve took the barely touched glass, waited, let the first wave of grief and shock roll. 'Was it a difficult divorce? Was your father angry?'

'Baffled. Confused. Sad. He wanted her back, and always said this was just one of her phases. He—' The question behind the question abruptly struck her. She lowered her hands. 'He would never hurt her. Never, never, never. He loved her. Everyone did. You couldn't help it.'

'Okay.' Eve would deal with that later. 'You and your mother were close?'

'Yes, very close.'

'Did she ever talk to you about her clients?'

'Sometimes. It embarrassed me, but she'd find a way to make it all so outrageously funny. She could do that. Called herself Granny Sex, and you had to laugh.'

'Did she ever mention anyone who made her uneasy?'

'No. She could handle people. It was part of her charm. She was only going to do this until she was published.'

'Did she ever mention the names Sharon DeBlass or Lola Starr?'

'No.' Samantha started to drag her hair back, then her hand froze in midair. 'Starr, Lola Starr. I heard, on the news, I heard about her. She was murdered. Oh God. Oh God.' She lowered her head and her hair fell in wings to shield her face.

'I'm going to have an officer take you home, Samantha.'

'I can't leave. I can't leave her.'

'Yes, you can. I'm going to take care of her.' Eve laid her hands over Samantha's. 'I promise you, I'll take care of her for you. Come on now.' Gently, she helped Samantha to her feet. She wrapped an arm around the distraught woman's waist as she led her to the door. She wanted her out before the team had finished in the bedroom. 'Is your husband home?'

'Yes. He's home with the children. We have two children. Two years, and six months. Tony's home with the children.'

'Good. What's your address?'

The shock was settling in. Eve hoped the numbness she could read on Samantha's face would help as the woman recited an upscale address in Westchester.

'Officer Banks.'

'Yes, lieutenant.'

'Take Mrs Bennett home. I'll call for another officer for the door. Stay with the family as long as you're needed.'

'Yes, sir.' With compassion, Banks guided Samantha toward the elevators. 'This way, Mrs Bennett,' she murmured.

Samantha leaned drunkenly on Banks. 'You'll take care of her?'

Eve met Samantha's ravaged eyes. 'I promise.'

An hour later, Eve walked into the station house with a cat under her arm.

'Hey there, lieutenant, caught yourself a cat burglar.' The desk sergeant snorted at his own humor.

'You're a laugh riot, Riley. Commander still here?'

'He's waiting for you. You're to go up as soon as you show.'

201

He leaned forward to scratch the purring cat. 'Hooked yourself another homicide?'

'Yeah.'

A kissing sound had her glancing over at a leering hunk in a spandex jumpsuit. The jumpsuit, and the blood trickling at the side of his mouth were approximately the same color. His accessories were a set of thin, black restraints that secured one arm to a nearby bench. He rubbed his crotch with his free hand and winked at her.

'Hey, baby. Got something here for you.'

'Tell Commander Whitney I'm on my way,' she told Riley as the desk sergeant rolled his eyes.

Unable to resist, she swung by the bench, leaned close enough to smell sour vomit. 'That was a charming invitation,' she murmured, then arched a brow when the man peeled open his fly patch and wagged his personality at her. 'Oh, look, kitty. A teeny-tiny little penis.' She smiled, leaned just a bit closer. 'Better take care of it, asshole, or my pussy here might mistake it for a teeny-tiny little mouse and bite it off.'

It made her feel better to see what there was of his pride and joy shrivel before he closed his flaps. The good humor lasted almost until she stepped into the elevator and ordered Commander Whitney's floor.

He was waiting, with Feeney, and the report she'd transmitted directly from the crime scene. In the nature of the repetition required in police work, she went over the same ground verbally.

'So that's the cat,' Feeney said.

'I didn't have the heart to dump him on the daughter in the state she was in.' Eve shrugged. 'And I couldn't very well just leave him there.' With her free hand, she reached into her bag. 'Her discs. Everything's labeled. I scanned through her appointments. The last one of the day was at six-thirty. John Smith. The weapon.' She laid the bagged weapon on Commander Whitney's desk. 'Looks like Ruger P-ninety.'

Feeney took a look, nodded. 'You're learning, kid.'

'I've been boning up.'

'Early twenty-first, probably oh eight, oh nine.' Feeney stated as he turned the sealed weapon in his hands. 'Prime condition. Serial number's intact. Won't take long to run it,' he added, but moved his shoulders. 'But he's too smart to use a registered.'

'Run it,' Whitney ordered, and gestured to the auxiliary unit across the room. 'I've got surveillance on your building, Dallas. If he tries to slip you another disc, we'll spot him.'

'If he stays true to form, it'll be within twenty-four hours. He's holding to the pattern so far, though each of his victims has been a distinctly different type: with DeBlass you've got the glitz, the sophistication; with Starr you've got fresh, childlike; and with this one, we've got comfort, still young but mature.

'We're still interviewing neighbors, and I'm going to hit the family again, look into the divorce. It looks to me like she took this guy spur of the moment. She had a standing date with her daughter for Tuesdays. I'd like Feeney to run her 'link, see if he called her direct. We're not going to be able to keep this from the media, commander. And they're going to hit us hard.'

'I'm already working on media control.'

'It may be hotter than we think.' Feeney looked up from the terminal. His eyes lingered on Eve's, made her blood chill.

'The murder weapon's registered. Purchased through silent auction at Sotheby's last fall. Roarke.'

Eve didn't speak for a moment. Didn't care. 'It breaks pattern,' she managed. 'And it's stupid. Roarke's not a stupid man.'

'Lieutenant—'

'It's a plant, commander. An obvious one. A silent auction.

Any second-rate hacker can use someone's ID and bid. How was it paid for?' she snapped at Feeney.

'I'll need to access Sotheby's records after they open tomorrow.'

'My bet's cash, electronic transfer. The auction house gets the money, why should they question it?' Her voice might have been calm, but her mind was racing. 'And the delivery. Odds are electronic pick-up station. You don't need ID for an EPS; all you do is key in the delivery code.'

'Dallas.' Whitney spoke patiently. 'Pick him up for questioning.'

'I can't.'

His eyes remained level, cool. 'That's a direct order. If you have a personal problem, save it for personal time.'

'I can't pick him up,' she repeated. 'He's on the FreeStar space station, a fair distance from the murder scene.'

'If he put out that he'd be on FreeStar—'

'He didn't,' she interrupted. 'And that's where the killer made a mistake. Roarke's trip is confidential, with only a few key people apprised. As far as it's generally known, he's right here in New York.'

Commander Whitney inclined his head. 'Then we'd better check his whereabouts. Now.'

Her stomach churned as she engaged Whitney's 'link. Within seconds she was listening to Summerset's prune voice. 'Summerset, Lieutenant Dallas. I have to contact Roarke.'

'Roarke is in meetings, lieutenant. He can't be disturbed.'

'He told you to put me through, goddamn it. This is police business. Give me his access number or I'm coming over there and hauling your bony ass in for obstructing justice.'

Summerset's face puckered up. 'I am not authorized to give out that data. I will, however, transfer you. Please stand by.'

Eve's palms began to sweat as the screen went to holding blue. She wondered whose idea it was to pipe in the sugary music. Certainly not Roarke's. He had too much class.

Oh God, what was she going to do if he wasn't where he said he'd be?

The blue screen contracted into a pinpoint, then opened up. There was Roarke, a trace of impatience in his eyes, a half smile on his mouth.

'Lieutenant. You've caught me at a bad time. Can I get back to you?'

'No.' She could see from the corner of her eye that Feeney was already tracing the transmission. 'I need to verify your whereabouts.'

'My whereabouts?' His brow cocked. He must have seen something in her face, though Eve would have sworn she kept it as smooth and unreadable as stone. 'What's wrong, Eve? What's happened?'

'Your whereabouts, Roarke. Please verify.'

He remained silent, studying her. Eve heard someone speak to him. He flicked away the interruption with a dismissing gesture. 'I'm in the middle of a meeting in the presidential chamber of Station FreeStar, the location of which is Quadrant Six, Slip Alpha. Scan,' he ordered, and the intergalactic 'link circled the room. A dozen men and women sat at a wide, circular table.

The long, bowed port showed a scatter of stars and the perfect blue-green globe of Earth.

'Location of transmission confirmed,' Feeney said in an undertone. 'He's just where he says he is.'

'Roarke, please switch to privacy mode.'

Without a flicker of expression, he lifted a headset. 'Yes, lieutenant?'

'A weapon registered to you was confiscated at a homicide. I have to ask you to come in for questioning at the first possible opportunity. You're free to bring your attorney. I'm advising you to bring your attorney,' she added, hoping he understood the emphasis. 'If you don't comply within forty-eight hours, the Station Guard will escort you back on-planet. Do you understand your rights and obligations in this matter?'

'Certainly. I'll make arrangements. Good-bye, lieutenant.'

The screen went blank.

# *Chapter Fourteen*

More shaken than she cared to admit, Eve entered Dr Mira's office the following morning. At Mira's invitation, she took a seat, folded her hands to keep them from any telltale restless movements.

'Have you had time to profile?'

'You requested urgent status.' Indeed, Mira had been up most of the night, reading reports, using her training and her psych diagnostics to compose a profile. 'I'd like more time to work on this, but I can give you an overall view.'

'Okay.' Eve leaned forward. 'What is he?'

'*He* is almost certainly correct. Traditionally, crimes of this nature are not committed within the same sex. He's a man, above average intelligence, with sociopathic and voyeuristic tendencies. He's bold, but not a risk taker, though he probably sees himself as such.'

In her graceful way, she linked her fingers together, crossed her legs. 'His crimes are well thought out. Whether or not he has sex with his victims is incidental. His pleasure and satisfaction comes from the selection, the preparation, and the execution.'

'Why prostitutes?'

'Control. Sex is control. Death is control. And he needs to control people, situations. The first murder was probably impulse.'

'Why?'

'He was caught off guard by the violence, his own capability of violence. He had a reaction, a jerk of a movement, the indrawn breath, the shaky exhale. He recovered, systematically protected himself. He doesn't want to be caught, but he wants – needs to be admired, feared. Hence the recordings.

'He uses collector's weapons,' she continued in that same moderate voice, 'a status symbol of money. Again, power and control. He leaves them behind so that they can show he's unique among men. He appreciates the overt violence of guns and the impersonal aspect of them. The kill from a comfortable distance, the aloofness of that. He's decided on the number he'll kill to show that he's organized, precise. Ambitious.'

'Could he have had the six women in mind from the beginning? Six targets?'

'The only verified connection between the three victims is their profession,' Mira began, and saw that Eve had already reached the same conclusion, but wanted it confirmed. 'He had the profession in mind. It would be my opinion the women are incidental. It's likely he holds a high-level position, certainly a responsible one. If he has a sexual or marriage partner, he or she is subservient. His opinion of women is low. He debases and humiliates them after death to show his disgust and his superiority. He doesn't perceive these as crimes but as moments of personal power, personal statement.

'The prostitute, male or female, remains a profession of low esteem in many minds. Women are not his equals; a prostitute is beneath his contempt, even when he uses her for his own release. He enjoys his work, lieutenant. He enjoys it very much.'

'Is it work, doctor, or a mission?'

'He has no mission. Only ambitions. It isn't religion, not a moral statement, not a societal stance.'

'No, the statement's personal, the stance is control.'

'I would agree,' Mira said, pleased with the straightforward workings of Eve's mind. 'It is, to him, an interest, a new and somewhat fascinating hobby that he has discovered himself adept at. He's dangerous, lieutenant, not simply because he has no conscience, but because he's good at what he does. And his success feeds him.'

'He'll stop at six,' Eve murmured. 'With this method. But he'll find another creative way to kill. He's too vain to go back on his word to the authorities, but he's enjoying his hobby too much to give it up.'

Mira angled her head. 'One would think, lieutenant, that you've already read my report. I believe you're coming to understand him very well.'

Eve nodded. 'Yeah, piece by piece.' There was a question she had to ask, one she had suffered over through a long, sleepless night. 'To protect himself, to make the game more difficult, would he hire someone, pay someone to kill a victim he'd chosen while he was alibied?'

'No.' Mira's eyes softened with compassion as she watched Eve's close in relief. 'In my opinion, he needs to be there. To watch, to record, most of all to experience. He doesn't want vicarious satisfaction. Nor does he believe you'll outsmart him. He enjoys watching you sweat, lieutenant. He's an observer of people, and I believe he focused on you the moment he learned you were primary. He studies you, and knows you care. He sees that as a weakness to exploit, and does so by presenting you with the murders – not at your place of work, but where you live.'

'He sent the last disc. It was in my morning mail drop, posted from a midtown slot about an hour after the murder. We had my building under surveillance. He'd have figured that and found a way to get around it.'

'He's a born button pusher.' Mira handed Eve a disc and a hard copy of the initial profile. 'He is an intelligent and a mature man. Mature enough to restrain his impulses, a man of means and imagination. He would rarely show his emotions, rarely have them to show. It's an intellect with him – and, as you said, vanity.'

'I appreciate you getting this for me so quickly.'

'Eve,' Mira said before Eve could rise. 'There's an addendum. The weapon that was left at the last murder. The man who committed these crimes would not make so foolish a mistake to leave a traceable weapon behind. The diagnostic rejected it at a probability of ninety-three point four percent.'

'It was there,' Eve said flatly. 'I bagged it myself.'

'As I'm sure he wanted you to. It's likely he enjoyed implicating someone else to further bog the system, twist the investigation process. And it's likely he chose this particular person to upset you, to distract you, even to hurt you. I've included that in the profile. Personally, I want to tell you that I'm concerned about his interest in you.'

'I'm going to see to it that he's a hell of a lot more concerned with my interest in him. Thank you, doctor.'

Eve went directly to Whitney's office to deliver the psychiatric profile. With any luck at all, Feeney would have verified her suspicions about the purchase and delivery of the murder weapon.

If she was right, and she had to believe she was, that and the weight of Mira's profile would clear Roarke.

She already knew, by the way Roarke had looked at her – through her – during their last transmission, that her professional duties had destroyed whatever personal bridge they'd been building.

She was only more sure of it when she was cleared into the office, and found Roarke there.

He must have used a private transport, she decided. It would have been impossible for him to have arrived so quickly through normal channels. He only inclined his head, said nothing as she crossed to give Commander Whitney the disc and file.

'Dr Mira's profile.'

'Thank you, lieutenant.' His eyes shifted to Roarke's. 'Lieutenant Dallas will show you to an interview area. We appreciate your cooperation.'

Still, he said nothing, only rose and waited for Eve to go to the door. 'You're entitled to have your attorney present,' she began as she called for an elevator.

'I'm aware of that. Am I being charged with any crime, lieutenant?'

'No.' Cursing him, she stepped inside, requested Area B. 'This is just standard procedure.' His silence continued until she wanted to scream. 'Damn it, I don't have a choice here.'

'Don't you?' he murmured and preceded her out of the car when the doors opened.

'This is my job.' The doors of the interview area whisked open, then snapped closed behind them. The surveillance cameras any petty thief would know were hidden in every wall engaged automatically. Eve took a seat at a small table and waited for him to sit across from her.

'These proceedings are being recorded. Do you understand?'

'Yes.'

'Lieutenant Dallas, ID 5347BQ, interviewer. Subject, Roarke. Initial date and time. Subject has waived the presence of an attorney. Is that correct?'

'Yes, the subject has waived the presence of an attorney.'

'Are you acquainted with a licensed companion, Georgie Castle?'

'No.'

'Have you been to 156 West Eighty-ninth Street?'

'No, I don't believe I have.'

'Do you own a Ruger P-ninety, automatic combat weapon, circa 2005?'

'It's likely that I own a weapon of that make and era. I'd have to check to be certain. But for argument's sake, we'll say I do.'

'When did you purchase said weapon?'

'Again, I'd have to check.' He never blinked, never took his eyes from hers. 'I have an extensive collection, and don't carry all the details of it in my head or in my pocket log.'

'Did you purchase said weapon at Sotheby's?'

'It's possible. I often add to my collection through auctions.'

'Silent auctions?'

'Occasionally.'

Her stomach, already knotted, began to roll. 'Did you add to your collection with the aforesaid weapon at a silent auction at Sotheby's on October second of last year?'

Roarke slipped his log out of his pocket, skimmed back to the date. 'No. I don't have a record of that. It seems I was in Tokyo on that date, engaged in meetings. You can verify that easily.'

Damn you, damn you, she thought. You know that's no answer. 'Representatives are often used in auctions.'

'They are.' Watching her dispassionately, he tucked the log away again. 'If you check with Sotheby's, you'll be told that I don't use representatives. When I decide to acquire something, it's because I've seen it – with my own eyes. Gauged its worth to me. If and when I decide to bid, I do so personally. In a silent auction, I would either attend, or participate by 'link.'

'Isn't it traditional to use a sealed electronic bid, or a representative authorized to go to a certain ceiling?'

'I don't worry about traditions overmuch. The fact is, I could change my mind as to whether I want something. For one reason or another, it could lose its appeal.'

212

She understood the underlying meaning of his statement, tried to accept that he was done with her. 'The aforesaid weapon, registered in your name and purchased through silent auction at Sotheby's in October of last year was used to murder Georgie Castle at approximately seven-thirty last evening.'

'You and I both know I wasn't in New York at seven-thirty last evening.' His gaze skimmed over her face. 'You traced the transmission, didn't you?'

She didn't answer. Couldn't. 'Your weapon was found at the scene.'

'Have we established it was mine?'

'Who has access to your collection?'

'I do. Only I do.'

'Your staff?'

'No. If you recall, lieutenant, my display cases are locked. Only I have the code.'

'Codes can be broken.'

'Unlikely, but possible,' he agreed. 'However, unless my palm print is used for entry, any case that is opened by any means triggers an alarm.'

Goddamn it, give me an opening. Couldn't he see she was pleading with him, trying to save him? 'Alarm's can be bypassed.'

'True. When any case is opened without my authorization, all entry to the room is sealed off. There's no way to get out, and security is notified simultaneously. I can assure you, lieutenant, it's quite foolproof. I believe in protecting what's mine.'

She glanced up as Feeney came in. He jerked his head, and she rose.

'Excuse me.'

When the doors shut behind them, he dipped his hands into his pockets. 'You called it, Dallas. Electronic bid, cash deal, delivered to an EPS. The head snoot at Sotheby's claims this

213

was an unusual procedure for Roarke. He always attends in person, or by direct 'link. Never used this line before in the fifteen years or so he's dealt with them.'

She allowed herself one satisfied breath. 'That checks with Roarke's statement. What else?'

'Ran an undercheck on the registration. The Ruger only appeared on the books in Roarke's name a week ago. No way in hell we can pin it on him. The commander says to spring him.'

She couldn't afford to be relieved, not yet, and only nodded. 'Thanks, Feeney.'

She slipped back inside. 'You're free to go.'

He stood as she stepped backward through the open door. 'Just like that?'

'We have no reason, at this time, to detain or inconvenience you any further.'

'Inconvenience?' He walked toward her until the doors snicked shut at his back. 'Is that what you call this? An inconvenience?'

He was, she told herself entitled to his anger, to his bitterness. She was obliged to do her job. 'Three women are dead. Every possibility has to be explored.'

'And I'm just one of your possibilities?' He reached out, the sudden violent movement of his hands closing over her shirt, surprising her. 'Is that what it comes down to between us?'

'I'm a cop. I can't afford to overlook anything, to assume anything.'

'To trust,' he interrupted. 'Anything. Or anyone. If it had leaned a little the other way, would you have locked me up? Would you have put me in a cage, Eve?'

'Back off.' Eyes blazing, Feeney strode down the corridor. 'Back fucking off.'

'Leave us alone, Feeney.'

'Hell I will.' Ignoring Eve, he shoved against Roarke. 'Don't you come down on her, big shot. She went to bat for you. And the way things stand, it could have cost her the job. Simpson's already prepping her as sacrificial lamb because she was dumb enough to sleep with you.'

'Shut up, Feeney.'

'Goddamn it, Dallas.'

'I said shut up.' Calm again, detached, she looked at Roarke. 'The department appreciates your cooperation,' she said to Roarke and, prying his hand from her shirt, turned and hurried off.

'What the hell did you mean by that?' Roarke demanded.

Feeney only snorted. 'I got better things to do than waste my time on you.'

Roarke backed him into a wall. 'You're going to be free to book me for assaulting an officer in about two breaths, Feeney. Tell me what you meant about Simpson?'

'You want to know, big shot?' Feeney looked around for a place of comparative privacy, jerked a head toward the door of a men's room. 'Come into my office, and I'll tell you.'

She had the cat for company. Eve was already regretting the fact that she'd have to turn the useless, overweight feline over to Georgie's family. She should have done so already, but found solace in even a pitiful furball's worth of companionship.

Nonetheless, she was nothing but irritated by the beep of her intercom. Human company was not welcomed. Particularly, as she checked her viewing screen, Roarke.

She was raw enough to take the coward's way. Leaving the summons unanswered, she walked back to the couch, curled up with the cat. If she'd had a blanket handy, she'd have pulled it over her head.

The sound of her locks disengaging moments later had her

springing to her feet. 'You son of a bitch,' she said when Roarke walked in. 'You cross too many lines.'

He simply tucked his master code back in his pocket. 'Why didn't you tell me?'

'I don't want to see you.' She hated that her voice sounded desperate rather than angry. 'Take a hint.'

'I don't like being used to hurt you.'

'You do fine on your own.'

'You expect me to have no reaction when you accuse me of murder? When you believe it?'

'I never believed it.' It came out in a hiss, a passionate whisper. 'I never believed it,' she repeated. 'But I put my personal feelings aside and did my job. Now get out.'

She headed for the door. When he grabbed her, she swung out, fast and hard. He didn't even attempt to block the blow. Calmly he wiped the blood from his mouth with the back of his hand while she stood rigid, her breathing fast and audible.

'Go ahead,' he invited. 'Take another shot. You needn't worry. I don't hit women – or murder them.'

'Just leave me alone.' She turned away, gripped the back of the sofa where the cat sat eyeing her coolly. The emotions were welling up, threatening to fill her chest to bursting. 'You're not going to make me feel guilty for doing what I had to do.'

'You sliced me in two, Eve.' It infuriated him anew to admit it, to know she could so easily devastate him. 'Couldn't you have told me you believe in me?'

'No.' She squeezed her eyes tight. 'God, don't you realize it would have been worse if I had? If Whitney couldn't believe I'd be objective, if Simpson even got a whiff that I showed you any degree of preferential treatment, it would have been worse. I couldn't have moved on the psych profile so fast. Couldn't have put Feeney on a priority basis to check the trail of the weapon to eliminate probable cause.'

'I hadn't thought of that,' he said quietly. 'I hadn't thought.'

When he laid a hand on her shoulder, she shrugged it off, turned on him with blazing eyes.

'Goddamn it, I told you to bring an attorney. I told you. If Feeney hadn't hit the right buttons, they could have held you. You're only out because he did, and the profile didn't fit.'

He touched her again; she jerked back again. 'It appears I didn't need an attorney. All I needed was you.'

'It doesn't matter.' She battled control back into place. 'It's done. The fact that you have an unassailable alibi for the time of the murder, and that the gun was an obvious plant shifts the focus away from you.' She felt sick, unbearably tired. 'It may not eliminate you completely, but Dr Mira's profiles are gold. Nobody overturns her diagnostics. She's eliminated you, and that carries a lot of weight with the department and the PA.'

'I wasn't worried about the department or the PA.'

'You should have been.'

'It seems you've worried enough for me. I'm very sorry.'

'Forget it.'

'I've seen shadows under your eyes too often since I've known you.' He traced a thumb along them. 'I don't like being responsible for the ones I see now.'

'I'm responsible for myself.'

'And I had nothing to do with putting your job in jeopardy?'

Damn Feeney, she thought viciously. 'I make my own decisions. I pay my own consequences.'

Not this time, he thought. Not alone. 'The night after we'd been together, I called. I could see you were worried, but you brushed it off. Feeney told me exactly why you were worried that night. Your angry friend wanted to pay me back for making you unhappy. He did.'

'Feeney had no right—'

'Perhaps not. He wouldn't have had to if you'd confided in me.' He took both her arms to stop her quick movement. 'Don't turn away from me,' he warned, his voice low. 'You're good at shutting people out, Eve. But it won't work with me.'

'What did you expect, that I'd come crying to you? "Roarke, you seduced me, and now I'm in trouble. Help." The hell with that, you didn't seduce me. I went to bed with you because I wanted to. Wanted to enough that I didn't think about ethics. I got slammed for it, and I'm handling it. I don't need help.'

'Don't want it, certainly.'

'Don't need it.' She wouldn't humiliate herself by struggling away now, but stood passive. 'The commander's satisfied that you're not involved in the murders. You're clear, so other than what the department will officially term an error in judgment on my part, so am I. If I'd been wrong about you, it'd be different.'

'If you'd been wrong about me, it would have cost you your badge.'

'Yes. I'd have lost my badge. I'd have lost everything. I'd have deserved to. But it didn't happen, so it's over. Move on.'

'Do you really think I'm going to walk away?'

It weakened her, that soft, gentle lilt that came into his voice. 'I can't afford you, Roarke. I can't afford to get involved.'

He stepped forward, laid his hands on the back of the couch, caged her in. 'I can't afford you, either. It doesn't seem to matter.'

'Look—'

'I'm sorry I hurt you,' he murmured. 'Very sorry that I didn't trust you, then accused you of not trusting me.'

'I didn't expect you to think any differently. To act any differently.'

That stung more than the blow to the face. 'No. I'm sorry for that, too. You risked a great deal for me. Why?'

There were no easy answers. 'I believed you.'

He pressed his lips to her brow. 'Thank you.'

'It was a judgment call,' she began, letting out a shaky breath when he touched his mouth to her cheek.

'I'm going to stay with you tonight.' Then to her temple. 'I'm going to see that you sleep.'

'Sex as a sedative?'

He frowned, but brushed his lips lightly over hers. 'If you like.' He lifted her off her feet, flustering her. 'Let's see if we can find the right dosage.'

Later, with the lights still on low, he watched her. She slept facedown, a limp sprawl of exhaustion. To please himself, he stroked a hand down her back – smooth skin, slim bones, lean muscle. She didn't stir.

Experimentally, he let his fingers comb through her hair. Thick as mink pelt, shades of aged brandy and old gold, poorly cut. It made him smile as he traced those fingers over her lips. Full, firm, fiercely responsive.

However surprised he was that he'd been able to take her beyond what she'd experienced before, he was overwhelmed by the knowledge that had, unknowingly, taken him.

How much farther, he wondered, would they go?

He knew it had ripped him when he'd believed she'd thought him guilty. The sense of betrayal, disillusionment was huge, weakening, and something he hadn't felt in too many years to count.

She'd taken him back to a point of vulnerability he'd escaped from. She could hurt him. They could hurt each other. That was something he would have to consider carefully.

But at the moment, the pressing question was who wanted to hurt them both. And why.

He was still gnawing at the problem when he took her hand, linked fingers, and let himself slide into sleep with her.

# Chapter Fifteen

He was gone when she woke. It was better that way. Mornings after carried a casual intimacy that made her nervous. She was already more involved with him than she had ever been with anyone. That click between them had the potential, she knew, to reverberate through the rest of her life.

She took a quick shower, bundled into a robe, then headed into the kitchen. There was Roarke, in trousers and a shirt he'd yet to button, scanning the morning paper on her monitor.

Looking, she realized with a quick tug-of-war of delight and dismay, very much at home.

'What are you doing?'

'Hmmm?' He glanced up, reached behind him to open the AutoChef. 'Making you coffee.'

'Making me coffee?'

'I heard you moving around.' He took the cups out, carried them to where she was still hovering in the doorway. 'You don't do that often enough.'

'Move around?'

'No.' He chuckled and touched her lips to hers. 'Smile at me. Just smile at me.'

Was she smiling? She hadn't realized. 'I thought you'd left.' She walked around the small table, glanced at the monitor. The stock reports. Naturally. 'You must have gotten up early.'

'I had some calls to make.' He watched her, enjoying the way she raked her fingers through her damp hair. A nervous habit he was certain she was unaware of. He picked up the portalink he'd left on the table, slipped it back into his pocket. 'I had a conference call scheduled with the station – five A.M. our time.'

'Oh.' She sipped her coffee, wondering how she had ever lived without the zip of the real thing in the morning. 'I know those meetings were important. I'm sorry.'

'We'd managed to hammer down most of the details. I can handle the rest from here.'

'You're not going back?'

'No.'

She turned to the AutoChef, fiddled with her rather limited menu. 'I'm out of most everything. Want a bagel or something?'

'Eve.' Roarke set his coffee down, laid his hands on her shoulders. 'Why don't you want me to know you're pleased I'm staying?'

'Your alibi holds. It's none of my business if you—' She broke off when he turned her to face him. He was angry. She could see it in his eyes and prepared for the argument to come. She hadn't prepared for the kiss, the way his mouth closed firmly over hers, the way her heart rolled over slow and dreamy in her chest.

So she let herself be held, let her head nestle in the curve of his shoulder. 'I don't know how to handle this,' she murmured. 'I don't have any precedent here. I need rules, Roarke. Solid rules.'

'I'm not a case you need to solve.'

'I don't know what you are. But I know this is going too fast. It shouldn't have even started. I shouldn't have been able to get started with you.'

He drew her back so that he could study her face. 'Why?'

221

'It's complicated. I have to get dressed. I have to get to work.'

'Give me something.' His fingers tightened on her shoulders. 'I don't know what you are, either.'

'I'm a cop,' she blurted out. 'That's all I am. I'm thirty years old and I've only been close to two people in my entire life. And even with them, it's easy to hold back.'

'Hold back what?'

'Letting it matter too much. If it matters too much, it can grind you down until you're nothing. I've been nothing. I can't be nothing ever again.'

'Who hurt you?'

'I don't know.' But she did. She did. 'I don't remember, and I don't want to remember. I've been a victim, and once you have, you need to do whatever it takes not to be one again. That's all I was before I got into the academy. A victim, with other people pushing the buttons, making the decisions, pushing me one way, pulling me another.'

'Is that what you think I'm doing?'

'That's what's happening.'

There were questions he needed to ask. Questions, he could see by her face, that needed to wait. Perhaps it was time he took a risk. He dipped a hand into his pocket, drew out what he carried there.

Baffled, Eve stared down at the simple gray button in his palm. 'That's off my suit.'

'Yes. Not a particularly flattering suit – you need stronger colors. I found it in my limo. I meant to give it back to you.'

'Oh.' But when she reached out, he closed his fingers over the button.

'A very smooth lie.' Amused, he laughed at himself. 'I had no intention of giving it back to you.'

'You got a button fetish, Roarke?'

'I've been carrying this around like a schoolboy carries a lock of his sweetheart's hair.'

Her eyes came back to his, and something sweet moved through her. Sweeter yet as she could see he was embarrassed. 'That's weird.'

'I thought so, myself.' But he slipped the button back in his pocket. 'Do you know what else I think, Eve?'

'I don't have a clue.'

'I think I'm in love with you.'

She felt the color drain out of her cheeks, felt her muscles go lax, even as her heart shot like a missile to her throat. 'That's . . .'

'Yes, difficult to come up with the proper word, isn't it?' He slid his hands down her back, up again, but brought her no closer. 'I've been giving it a lot of thought and haven't hit on one myself. But I should circle back to my point.'

She moistened her lips. 'There's a point?'

'A very interesting and important point. I'm every bit as much in your hands as you are in mine. Every bit as uncomfortable, though perhaps not as resistant, to finding myself in that position. I'm not going to let you walk away until we've figured out what to do about it.'

'It, ah, complicates things.'

'Outrageously,' he agreed.

'Roarke, we don't even know each other. Outside of the bedroom.'

'Yes, we do. Two lost souls. We've both turned away from something and made ourselves something else. It's hardly a wonder that fate decided to throw a curve into what had been, for both of us, a straight path. We have to decide how far we want to follow the curve.'

'I have to concentrate on the investigation. It has to be my priority.'

'I understand. But you're entitled to a personal life.'

223

'My personal life, this part of it, grew out of the investigation. And the killer's making it more personal. Planting that
gun so that suspicion would swing toward you was a direct
response to my involvement with you. He's focused on me.'

Roarke's hand jerked up to the lapels of her robe. 'What do
you mean?'

Rules, she reminded herself. There were rules. And she was
about to break them. 'I'll tell you what I can while I'm getting
dressed.'

Eve went to the bedroom with the cat sliding and weaving in
front of her. 'Do you remember that night you were here when
I got home? The package that you'd found on the floor?'

'Yes, it upset you.'

With a half laugh she peeled out of her robe. 'I've got a rep
for having the best poker face in the station.'

'I made my first million gambling.'

'Really?' She tugged a sweater over her head, reminded
herself not to be distracted. 'It was a recording of Lola Starr's
murder. He sent me Sharon DeBlass's as well.'

A cold lance of fear stabbed. 'He was in your apartment.'

She was busy discovering she had no clean underwear and
didn't notice the iced edge of his voice. 'Maybe, maybe not.
I think not. No signs of forced entry. He could have shoved it
under the door. That's what he did the first time. He mailed
Georgie's disc. We had the building under surveillance.'

Resigned, she pulled slacks over bare skin. 'He either knew
it or smelled it. But he saw I got the discs, all three of them.
He knew I was primary almost before I did.'

She searched for socks, got lucky, and found a pair that
matched. 'He called me, transmitted the video of Georgie
Castle's murder scene minutes after he'd whacked her.' She
sat on the edge of the bed, pulled on the socks. 'He planted
a weapon, made sure it was traceable. To you. Not to knock
how inconvenient a murder charge would have made your life,

Roarke, if I hadn't had the commander behind me on this, I'd have been off the case, and out of the department in a blink. He knows what goes on inside Cop Central. He knows what's going on in my life.'

'Fortunately, he didn't know that I wasn't even on the planet.'

'That was a break for both of us.' She located her boots, tugged them on. 'But it's not going to stop him.' She rose, picked up her holster. 'He's still going to try to get to me, and you're his best bet.'

Roarke watched her automatically check her laser before strapping it on. 'Why you?'

'He doesn't have a high opinion of women. I'd have to say it burns his ass to have a female heading the investigation. It lowers his status.' She shrugged, raked her fingers through her hair to whip it into place. 'At least that's the shrink's opinion.'

Philosophically, she pried the cat free when he started to climb up her leg, gave him a light toss to the bed where he turned his butt in her direction and began to wash.

'And is it the shrink's opinion that he could try to eliminate you by more direct means?'

'I don't fit the pattern.'

Fighting back the slippery edge of fear, Roarke fisted his hands in his pockets. 'And if he breaks the pattern?'

'I can handle myself.'

'It's worth risking your life for three women who are already dead?'

'Yes.' She heard the fury pulsing in his voice and faced it. 'It's worth risking my life to find justice for three women who are already dead, and to try to prevent three more from dying. He's only half through. He's left a note under each body. He's wanted us to know, right from the start that he had a plan. And he's daring us to stop him. One of six, two of six, three of six. I'll do whatever it takes to keep him from having the fourth.'

'Full-out guts. That's what I first admired about you. Now it terrifies me.'

For the first time she moved to him, laid a hand on his cheek. Almost as soon as she had, she dropped her hand and stepped back again, embarrassed. 'I've been a cop for ten years, Roarke, never had more than some bumps and bruises. Don't worry about it.'

'I think you're going to have to get used to having someone worry about you, Eve.'

That hadn't been the plan. She walked out of the bedroom to get her jacket and bag. 'I'm telling you this so that you'll understand what I'm up against. Why I can't split my energies and start analyzing what's between us.'

'There'll always be cases.'

'I hope to God there won't always be cases like this one. This isn't murder for gain, or out of passion. It isn't desperate or frenzied. It's cold and calculated. It's . . .'

'Evil?'

'Yes.' It relieved her that he'd said it first. It didn't sound so foolish. 'Whatever we've done in genetic engineering, in vitro, with social programs, we still can't control basic human failings: violence, lust, envy.'

'The seven deadly sins.'

She thought of the old woman and her poisoned pie. 'Yeah. I've got to go.'

'Will you come to me when you're off duty tonight?'

'I don't know when I'll log out. It could be—'

'Will you come?'

'Yeah.'

Then he smiled, and she knew he was waiting for her to make the move. She was sure he knew just how hard it was for her to cross to him, to bring her lips up, to press them, however casually, to his.

'See you.'

226

'Eve. You should have gloves.'

She decoded the door, tossed a quick smile over her shoulder. 'I know – but I just keep losing them.'

Her up mood lasted until she walked into her office and found DeBlass and his aide waiting for her.

Deliberately, DeBlass stared at his gold watch. 'More banker's hours than police hours, Lieutenant Dallas.'

She knew damn well it was only minutes past eight, but shrugged out of her jacket. 'Yeah, it's a pretty lush life around here. Is there something I can do for you, senator?'

'I'm aware there's been yet another murder. I'm obviously dissatisfied with your progress. However, I'm here for damage control. I do not want my granddaughter's name linked with the two other victims.'

'You want Simpson for that, or his press secretary.'

'Don't smirk at me, young woman.' DeBlass leaned forward. 'My granddaughter is dead. Nothing can change that. But I will not have the DeBlass name sullied, muddied by the death of two common whores.'

'You seem to have a low opinion of women, senator.' She was careful not to smirk this time, but watched him, and considered.

'On the contrary; I revere them. Which is why those who sell themselves, those who disregard morality and common decency, revolt me.'

'Including your granddaughter?'

He lurched out of his chair, his face purpling, eyes bulging. Eve was quite certain he would have struck her if Rockman hadn't stepped between them.

'Senator, the lieutenant is only baiting you. Don't give her the satisfaction.'

'You will not besmirch my family.' DeBlass was breathing fast, and Eve wondered if he had any history of heart trouble.

227

'My granddaughter paid dearly for her sins, and I will not see the rest of my loved ones dragged down into public ridicule. And I will not tolerate your vile insinuations.'

'Just trying to get my facts straight.' It was fascinating watching him battle for composure. He was having a rough time of it, she noted, hands shaking, chest heaving. 'I'm trying to find the man who killed Sharon, senator. I assume that's also high on your agenda.'

'Finding him won't get her back.' He sat again, obviously exhausted by the outburst. 'What's important now is to protect what's left. To do that, Sharon must be segregated from the other women.'

She didn't like his opinion, but neither did she care for his color. It was still alarmingly high. 'Can I get you some water, Senator DeBlass?'

He nodded, waved at her. Eve slipped into the corridor and dispensed a cup of bottled water. When she came back, his breathing was more regular, his hands a bit steadier.

'The senator has been overtaxing himself,' Rockman put in. 'His Morals Bill goes before the House tomorrow. The pressure of this family tragedy is a great weight.'

'I appreciate that. I'm doing everything I can to close the case.' She tilted her head. 'Political pressure is also a great weight on an investigation. I don't care to be monitored on my personal time.'

Rockman gave her a mild smile. 'I'm sorry. Could you qualify that?'

'I was monitored, and my personal relationship with a civilian reported to Chief Simpson. It's no secret that Simpson and the senator are tight.'

'The senator and Chief Simpson have a personal and a political allegiance,' Rockman agreed. 'However, it would hardly be ethical, or in the senator's best interest, to monitor a member of the police force. I assure you, lieutenant, Senator

DeBlass has been much too involved with his own grief and his responsibilities to the country to worry about your . . . personal relationships. It has come to our attention, however, through Chief Simpson, that you've had a number of liaisons with Roarke.'

'An amoral opportunist.' The senator set his cup aside with a snap. 'A man who would stop at nothing to add to his own power.'

'A man,' Eve added, 'who has been cleared of any connection with this investigation.'

'Money buys immunity,' DeBlass said in disgust.

'Not in this office. I'm sure you'll request the report from the commander. In the meantime, whether or not it assuages your grief, I intend to find the man who killed your granddaughter.'

'I suppose I should commend your dedication.' DeBlass rose. 'See that your dedication doesn't jeopardize my family's reputation.'

'What changed your mind, senator?' Eve wondered. 'The first time we spoke, you threatened to have my job if I didn't bring Sharon's murderer to justice, and quickly.'

'She's buried,' was all he said, and strode out.

'Lieutenant.' Rockman kept his voice low. 'I will repeat that the pressure on Senator DeBlass is enormous, enough to crush a lesser man.' He let out a slow breath. 'The fact is, it's destroyed his wife. She's had a breakdown.'

'I'm sorry.'

'The doctors don't know if she'll recover. This additional tragedy has his son crazed with grief; his daughter has closed herself off from her family and gone into retreat. The senator's only hope of restoring his family is to let Sharon's death, the horror of it, pass.'

'Then it might be wise for the senator to take a step back and leave due process to the department.'

'Lieutenant – Eve,' he said with that rare and quick flash of charm. 'I wish I could convince him of that. But I believe that would be as fruitless an endeavor as convincing you to let Sharon rest in peace.'

'You'd be right.'

'Well then.' He laid a hand on her arm briefly. 'We must all do what we can to set things right. It was good to see you again.'

Eve closed the door behind him and considered. DeBlass certainly had the kind of hair-trigger temper that could lead to violence. She was almost sorry he didn't also have the control, the calculation, to have meticulously planned three murders.

In any case, she'd have a hard time connecting a rabidly right-wing senator to a couple of New York prostitutes.

Maybe he was protecting his family, she mused. Or maybe he was protecting Simpson, a political ally.

That was crap, Eve decided. He might work on Simpson's behalf if the chief was involved in the Starr and Castle homicides. But a man didn't protect the killer of his grandchild.

Too bad she wasn't looking for two men, Eve mused. Regardless, she was going to do some pecking away at Simpson's underpinnings.

Objectively, she warned herself. And it wouldn't do to forget that there was a strong possibility that DeBlass didn't know one of his favorite political cronies had been blackmailed by his only granddaughter.

She'd have to find out.

But for now, she had another hunch to follow. She located Charles Monroe's number and put through a call.

His voice was smeared with sleep, his eyes heavy. 'You spend all your time in bed, Charles?'

'All I can, Lieutenant Sugar.' He rubbed a hand over his face and grinned at her. 'That's how I think of you.'

'Well, don't. Couple of questions.'

'Ah, can't you come on over and ask in person? I'm warm and naked and all alone.'

'Pal, don't you know there's a law against soliciting a police officer?'

'I'm talking freebie here. I told you – we'd keep it strictly personal.'

'We're keeping it strictly impersonal. You had an associate. Georgie Castle. Did you know her?'

The seductive smile faded from his face. 'Yeah, actually, I did. Not well, but I met her at a party about a year ago. She was new in the business. Fun, attractive. Game, you know. We hit it off.'

'In what way?'

'In a friendly way. We had a drink now and again. Once when Sharon had an overbooking, I had her send a couple of clients Georgie's way.'

'They knew each other.' Eva pounced on it. 'Sharon and Gerogie?'

'I don't think so. As far as I remember, Sharon contacted Georgie, asked her if she was interested in a couple of fresh tricks. Georgie gave it the green light, and that was that. Oh, yeah, Sharon said something about Georgie sending her a dozen roses. Real ones, like a thank-you gift. Sharon got a real kick out of the old-fashioned etiquette.'

'Just an old-fashioned girl,' Eve said under her breath.

'When I heard Georgie was dead, it hit hard. I gotta tell you. With Sharon it was a jolt, but not that much of a surprise. She lived on the edge. But Georgie, she was centered, you know?'

'I may need to follow up on this, Charles. Stay available.'

'For you—'

'Knock it off,' she ordered, before he could get cute. 'What do you know about Sharon's diaries?'

'She never let me read one,' he said easily. 'I used to tease her about them. Seems to me she said she'd kept them since she was a kid. You got one? Hey, am I in it?'

'Where'd she keep them?'

'In her apartment, I guess. Where else?'

That was the question, Eve mused. 'If you think of anything else about Georgie or about the diaries, contact me.'

'Day or night, Lieutenant Sugar. Count on me.'

'Right.' But she was laughing when she broke transmission.

The sun was just setting when she arrived at Roarke's. She didn't consider herself off duty. The favor she was going to ask had been simmering in her mind all day. She'd decided on it, rejected it, and generally vacillated until she'd disgusted herself.

In the end, she'd left the station for the first time in months right on the dot of the end of her shift. With what limited progress she'd made, she'd hardly needed to be there at all.

Feeney had hit nothing but a dead end in his search for a second lock box. He had, with obvious reluctance, given her the list of cops she'd requested. Eve intended to run a make on each of them – on her own time and in her own way.

With some regreat, she realized she was going to use Roarke.

Summerset opened the door with his usual disdain. 'You're earlier than expected, lieutenant.'

'If he isn't in, I can wait.'

'He's in the library.'

'Which is where, exactly?'

Summerset permitted himself the tiniest huff. If Roarke hadn't ordered him to show the woman in immediately he would have shuffled her off to some small, poorly lit room. 'This way, please.'

'What exactly is it about me that rubs you wrong, Summer-set?'

With his back poker straight, he led her up a flight and down the wide corridor. 'I have no idea what you mean, lieutenant. The library,' he announced in reverent terms, and opened the door for her.

She'd never in her life seen so many books. She never would have believed so many existed outside of museums. The walls were lined with them so that the two-level room positively reeked with books.

On the lower level, on what was surely a leather sofa, Roarke lounged, a book in his hand, the cat on his lap.

'Eve. You're early.' He set the book aside, picked up the cat as he rose.

'Jesus, Roarke, where did you get all these?'

'The books?' He let his gaze roam the room. Firelight danced and shifted over colorful spines. 'Another of my interests. Don't you like to read?'

'Sure, now and again. But discs are so much more convenient.'

'And so much less aesthetic.' He stroked the cat's neck and sent him into ecstasy. 'You're welcome to borrow any you like.'

'I don't think so.'

'How about a drink?'

'I could handle that.'

His 'link beeped. 'This is the call I've been waiting for. Why don't you get us both a glass of wine I've had breathing over on the table?'

'Sure.' She took the cat from him and walked over to oblige. Because she wanted to eavesdrop, she forced herself to stay the length of the room away from where he sat murmuring.

It gave her a chance to browse the books, to puzzle over

the titles. Some she had heard of. Even with a state education, she'd been required to read Steinbeck and Chaucer, Shakespeare and Dickens. The curriculum had taken her through King and Grisham, Morrison and Grafton.

But there were dozens, perhaps hundreds of names here she'd never heard of. She wondered if anyone could handle so many books, much less read them.

'I'm sorry,' he said when the call was complete. 'That couldn't wait.'

'No problem.'

He took the wine she'd poured him. 'The cat's becoming quite attached to you.'

'I don't think he has any particular loyalties.' But Eve had to admit, she enjoyed the way he curled under her stroking hand. 'I don't know what I'm going to do about him. I called Georgie's daughter and she said she just couldn't face taking him. Pressing the matter only made her cry.'

'You could keep him.'

'I don't know. You have to take care of pets.'

'Cats are remarkably self-sufficient.' He sat on the sofa and waited for her to join him. 'Want to tell me about your day?'

'Not very productive. Yours?'

'Very productive.'

'A lot of books,' Eve said lamely, knowing she was stalling.

'I have an affection for them. I could barely read my name when I was six. Then I came across a battered copy of Yeats. An Irish writer of some note,' he said when Eve looked blank. 'I badly wanted to figure it out, so I taught myself.'

'Didn't you go to school?'

'Not if I could help it. You've got trouble in your eyes, Eve,' he murmured.

She blew out a breath. What was the use of stalling when

he could see right through her? 'I've got a problem. I want to do a run on Simpson. Obviously, I can't go through channels or use either my home or office units. The minute I tried to dig on the chief of police, I'd be flagged.'

'And you're wondering if I have a secured, unregistered system. Of course I do.'

'Of course,' she muttered. 'A nonregistered system is in violation of Code four fifty-three-B, section thirty-five.'

'I can't tell you how aroused it makes me when you quote codes, lieutenant.'

'It's not funny. And what I'm going to ask you to do is illegal. It's a serious offense to electronically breach the privacy of a state official.'

'You could arrest both of us afterward.'

'This is serious, Roarke. I go by the book, and now I'm asking you to help me break the law.'

He rose, drew her to her feet. 'Darling Eve, you have no idea how many I've already broken.' He fetched the wine bottle, letting it dangle from two fingers of the hand he slipped around her waist. 'I ran an underground dice game when I was ten,' he began, leading her from the room. 'A legacy from my dear old father who'd earned himself a knife through the gullet in a Dublin alley.'

'I'm sorry.'

'We weren't close. He was a bastard and no one loved him, least of all me. Summerset, we'll have dinner at seven-thirty,' Roarke added as he turned toward the stairs. 'But he taught me, by means of a fist to the face, to read the dice, the cards, the odds. He was a thief, not a good one, as his end proved. I was better. I stole, I cheated, I spent some time learning the smuggling trade. So you see, you're hardly corrupting me with such a nominal request.'

She didn't look at him as he decoded a locked door on the second floor. 'Do you . . .'

'Do I steal, cheat, and smuggle now?' He turned and touched a hand to her face. 'Oh, you'd hate that, wouldn't you? I almost wish I could say yes, then give it all up for you. I learned a long time ago that there are gambles more exciting for their legitimacy. And winning is so much more satisfying when you've dealt from the top of the deck.'

He pressed a kiss to her brow, then stepped into the room. 'But, we have to keep our hand in.'

# *Chapter Sixteen*

Compared to the rest of the house she'd seen, this room was spartan, designed rigidly for work. No fancy statues, dripping chandeliers. The wide, U-shaped console, the base for communication, research, and information retrieving devices, was unrelieved black, studded with controls, sliced with slots and screens.

Eve had heard that IRCCA had the swankiest base system in the country. She suspected Roarke's matched it.

Eve was no compu-jock, but she knew at a glance that the equipment here was vastly superior to any the New York Police and Security Department used – or could afford – even in the lofty Electronic Detection Division.

The long wall facing the console was taken up by six large monitor screens. A second, auxiliary station held a sleek little tele-link, a second laser fax, a hologram send-receive unit, and several other pieces of hardware she didn't recognize.

The trio of comp stations boasted personal monitors with attached 'links.

The floor was glazed tile, the diamond patterns in muted colors that bled together like liquid. The single window looked over the city and pulsed with the last lights of the setting sun.

It seemed even here, Roarke demanded ambiance.

'Quite a setup,' Eve commented.

'Not quite as comfortable as my office, but it has the basics.'
He moved behind the main console, placed his palm on the
identiscreen. 'Roarke. Open operations.'

After a discreet hum, the lights on the console glowed
on. 'New palm and voice print clearance,' he continued and
gestured to Eve. 'Cleared for yellow status.'

At his nod, Eve pressed her hand to the screen, felt the faint
warmth of the reading. 'Dallas.'

'There you are.' Roarke took his seat. 'The system will
accept your voice and hand commands.'

'What's yellow status?'

He smiled. 'Enough to give you everything you need to
know – not quite enough to override my commands.'

'Hmmm.' She scanned the controls, the patiently blink-
ing lights, the myriad screens and gauges. She wished for
Feeney and his computer-minded brain. 'Search on Edward
T. Simpson, Chief of Police and Security, New York City.
All financial data.'

'Going right to the heart,' Roarke murmured.

'I don't have time to waste. This can't be traced?'

'Not only can't it be traced, but there'll be no record of the
search.'

'Simpson, Edward T.,' the computer announced in a warm,
female tone. 'Financial records. Searching.'

At Eve's lifted brow, Roarke grinned. 'I prefer to work with
melodious voices.'

'I was going to ask,' she returned, 'how you can access data
without alerting the Compuguard.'

'No system's foolproof, or completely breach resistant –
even the ubiquitous Compuguard. The system is an excellent
deterrent to your average hacker or electronic thief. But with
the right equipment, it can be compromised. I have the right
equipment. Here comes the data. On viewing screen one,' he
ordered.

Eve glanced up and saw Simpson's credit report flash onto the large monitor. It was the standard business: vehicle loans, mortgages, credit card balances. All the automatic E-transactions.

'That's a hefty AmEx bill,' she mused. 'And I don't think it's common knowledge he owns a place on Long Island.'

'Hardly murderous motives. He maintains a Class A rating, which means he pays what he owes. Ah, here's a bank account. Screen two.'

Eve studied the numbers, dissatisfied. 'Nothing out of line, pretty average deposits and withdrawals – mostly automatic bill paying transfers that jibe with the credit report. What's Jeremy's?'

'Men's clothier,' Roarke told her with the smallest sneer of disdain. 'Somewhat second rate.'

She wrinkled her nose. 'Hell of a lot to spend on clothes.'

'Darling, I'm going to have to corrupt you. It's only too much if they're inferior clothes.'

She sniffed, stuck her thumbs in the front pockets of her baggy brown trousers.

'Here's his brokerage account. Screen three. Spineless,' Roarke added after a quick scan.

'What do you mean?'

'His investments, such as they are. All no risk. Government issue, a few mutual funds, a smattering of blue chip. Everything on-planet.'

'What's wrong with that?'

'Nothing if you're content to let your money gather dust.' He slanted her a look. 'Do you invest, lieutenant?'

'Yeah, right.' She was still trying to make sense of the abbreviations and percentage points. 'I watch the stock reports twice a day.'

'Not a standard credit account.' He nearly shuddered.

'So what?'

'Give me what you have, I'll double it within six months.'

She only frowned, struggling to read the brokerage report. 'I'm not here to get rich.'

'Darling,' he corrected in that flowing Irish lilt. 'We all are.'

'How about contributions, political, charities, that kind of thing?'

'Access tax saving outlay,' Roarke ordered. 'Viewing screen two.'

She waited, impatiently tapping a hand on her thigh. Data scrolled on. 'He puts his money where his heart is,' she muttered, scanning his payments to the Conservative Party, DeBlass's campaign fund.

'Not particularly generous otherwise. Hmm.' Roarke's brow lifted. 'Interesting, a very hefty gift to Moral Values.'

'That's an extremist group, isn't it?'

'I'd call it that, the faithful prefer to think of it as an organization dedicated to saving all of us sinners from ourselves. DeBlass is a strong proponent.'

But she was flipping through her own mental files. 'They're suspected of sabotaging the main data banks at several large contraception control clinics.'

Roarke clucked his tongue. 'All those women deciding for themselves if and when they want to conceive, how many children they want. What's the world coming to? Obviously, someone has to bring them back to their senses.'

'Right.' Dissatisfied, Eve stuck her hands in her pockets. 'It's a dangerous connection for someone like Simpson. He likes to play middle of the road. He ran on a Moderate ticket.'

'Cloaking his Conservative ties and leanings. In the last few years he's been cautiously removing the layers. He wants to be governor, perhaps believes DeBlass can put him there. Politics is a bartering game.'

'Politics. Sharon DeBlass's blackmail disc was heavy on politicians. Sex, murder, politics,' Eve murmured. 'The more things change . . .'

'Yes, the more they remain the same. Couples still indulge in courting rituals, humans still kill humans, and politicians still kiss babies and lie.'

Something wasn't quite right, and she wished for Feeney again. Twentieth-century murders, she thought, twentieth-century motives. There was one other thing that hadn't changed over the last millennium. Taxes.

'Can we get his IRS data? The past three years?'

'That's a little trickier.' His mouth had already quirked up at the challenge.

'It's also a federal offense. Listen, Roarke—'

'Just hold on a minute.' He pressed a button and a manual keyboard slipped out of the console. With some surprise, Eve watched his fingers fly over the keys. 'Where'd you learn to do that?' Even with required department training, she was barely competent on manual.

'Here and there,' he said absently, 'in my misspent youth. I have to get around the security. It's going to take some time. Why don't you pour us some more wine?'

'Roarke, I shouldn't have asked.' An attack of conscience had her walking to him. 'I can't let this come back on you—'

'Ssh.' His brows drew together in concentration as he maneuvered his way through the security labyrinth.

'But—'

He head snapped up, impatience vivid in his eyes. 'We've already opened the door, Eve. Now we go through, or we turn away from it.'

Eve thought of three women, dead because she hadn't been able to stop it. Hadn't known enough to stop it. With a nod, she turned away again. The clatter of the keyboard resumed.

241

She poured the wine, then moved to stand in front of the screens. Tidy as they came, she mused. Top credit rating, prompt payment of debts, conservative and, she assumed, relatively small investments. Surely that was more money than average spent on clothes, wine shops, and jewelry. But it wasn't a crime to have expensive taste. Not when you paid for it. Even the second home wasn't a criminal offense.

Some of the contributions were dicey for a registered Moderate, but still, not criminal.

She heard Roarke curse softly and looked back. But he was hunkered over the keyboard. She might not have been there. Odd, she wouldn't have guessed he had the technical skills to access manually. According to Feeney, it was almost a lost art except in tech-clerks and hackers.

Yet here he was, the rich, the privileged, the elegant, clattering over a problem usually delegated to a low-paid, overworked office drone.

For a moment, she let herself forget about the business at hand and smiled at him.

'You know, Roarke, you're kind of cute.'

She realized it was the first time she'd really surprised him. His head came up, and his eyes were startled – for perhaps two heartbeats. Then that sly smile came into them. The one that made her own pulse jitter.

'You're going to have to do better than that, lieutenant. I've got you in.'

'No shit?' Excitement flooded through her as she whirled back to the screens. 'Put it up.'

'Screens four, five, six.'

'There's his bottom line.' She frowned over gross income. 'It's about right, wouldn't you say – salarywise.'

'A bit of interest and dividends from investments.' Roarke scrolled pages. 'A few honorariums for personal appearances and speeches. He lives close, but just within his means, according to all of the data shown.'

'Hell.' She tossed back wine. 'What other data is there?'

'For a sharp woman, that's an incredibly naive question. Underground accounts,' he explained. 'Two sets of books is a tried and true and very traditional method of hiding illicit income.'

'If you had illicit income, why would you be stupid enough to document it?'

'A question for the ages. But people do. Oh yes, they do. Yes,' he said, answering her unspoken question as to his own bookkeeping methods. 'Of course I do.'

She shot him a hard look. 'I don't want to know about it.'

He only moved his shoulders. 'The point being, because I do, I know how it's done. Everything's above board here, wouldn't you say?' With a few commands he had the IRS reports merged on one screen. 'Now let's go down a level. Computer, Simpson, Edward T., foreign accounts.'

'No known data.'

'There's always more data,' Roarke murmured, undeterred. He went back to the keyboard, and something began to hum.

'What's that noise?'

'It's just telling me I'm hitting a wall.' Like a laborer, he flicked open the buttons at his cuffs, rolled up his sleeves. The gesture made Eve smile. 'And if there's a wall, there's something behind it.'

He continued to work, one handed, and sipped his wine. When he repeated his command, the response had shifted.

'Data protected.'

'Ah, now we've got it.'

'How can you—'

'Ssh,' he ordered again and had Eve subsiding into impatient silence. 'Computer, run numerical and alphabetical combinations for passkey.'

Pleased with the progress, he pushed back. 'This will take a little time. Why don't you come here?'

'Can you show me how you—' She broke off, shocked, when Roarke pulled her into his lap. 'Hey, this is important.'

'So's this.' He took her mouth, sliding his hand up her hip to just under the curve of her breast. 'It could take an hour, maybe more, to find the key.' Those quick, clever hands were already moving under her sweater. 'You don't like to waste time, as I recall.'

'No, I don't.' It was the first time in her life she'd ever sat on anyone's lap, and the sensation wasn't at all unpleasant. She was sinking, but the next mechanical hum had her pulling back. Speechless, she stared at the bed gliding out of a panel in the side wall. 'The man who has everything,' she managed.

'I will have.' He hooked an arm under her legs, lifted her. 'Very shortly.'

'Roarke.' She had to admit, maybe just this once, she enjoyed being swept up and carried off.

'Yes.'

'I always thought too much emphasis, in society, advertisement, entertainment, was put on sex.'

'Did you?'

'I did.' Grinning, she shifted her body, quick and agile, and overbalanced him. 'I've changed my mind,' she said as they tumbled onto the bed.

She'd already learned that lovemaking could be intense, overwhelming, even dangerously exciting. She hadn't known it could be fun. It was a revelation to find that she could laugh and wrestle over the bed like a child.

Quick, nipping kisses, ticklish groping, breathless giggles. She couldn't remember ever giggling before in her life as she pinned Roarke to the mattress.

'Gotcha.'

'You do indeed.' Delighted with her, he let her hold him

down, rain kisses over his face. 'Now that you have me, what are you going to do about it?'

'Use you, of course.' She bit down, none too gently, on his bottom lip. 'Enjoy you.' With her brows arched, she unfastened his shirt, spread it open. 'You do have a terrific body.' To please herself, she ran her hands over his chest. 'I used to think that sort of thing was overrated, too. After all, anyone with enough money can have one.'

'I didn't buy mine,' Roarke said, surprised into defending his physique.

'No, you've got a gym in this place, don't you?' Bending, she let her lips cruise over his shoulder. 'You'll have to show it to me sometime. I think I'd like watching you sweat.'

He rolled her over, reversing positions. He felt her freeze, then relax under his restraining hands. Progress, he thought. The beginnings of trust. 'I'm ready to work out with you, lieutenant, anytime.' He tugged the sweater over her head. 'Anytime at all.'

He released her hands. It moved him to have her reach up, draw him down to her to embrace.

So strong, he thought, as the tone of the lovemaking changed from playful to tender. So soft. So troubled. He took her slowly, and very gently over the first rise, watched her crest, listened to the low, humming moan as her system absorbed each velvet shock.

He needed her. It still had the power to shake him to know just how much he needed her. He knelt, lifting her. Her legs wrapped silkily around him, her body bowed fluidly back. He could take his mouth over her, tasting warm flesh while he moved inside her, deep, steady, slow.

Each time she shuddered, a fresh stream of pleasure rippled through him. Her throat was a slim white feast he couldn't resist. He laved it, nipped, nuzzled while the pulse just under that sensitized flesh throbbed like a heart.

And she gasped his name, cupping his head in her hands, pressing him against her as her body rocked, rocked, rocked.

She discovered lovemaking made her loose, and warm. The slow arousal, the long, slow finish energized her. She didn't feel awkward climbing back into her clothes with the scent of him clinging to her. She felt smug.

'I feel good around you.' It surprised her to say it aloud, to give him – or anyone – even so slight an advantage.

He understood that such an admission, for her, was tantamount to a shouted declaration of devotion from other women.

'I'm glad.' He traced a fingertip down her cheek, dipped it into the faint dent in her chin. 'I like the idea of staying around you.'

She turned away at that, crossed over to watch the number sequences fly by on the console screen. 'Why did you tell me about being a kid in Dublin, about your father, the things you did?'

'You won't stay with someone you don't know.' He studied her back as he tucked his shirt into his trousers. 'You'd told me a little, so I told you a little. And I think, eventually, you'll tell me who hurt you when you were a child.'

'I told you I don't remember.' She hated even the whisper of panic in her voice. 'I don't need to.'

'Don't tighten up.' He murmured to her as he walked over to massage her shoulders. 'I won't press you. I know exactly what it is to remake yourself, Eve. To distance yourself from what was.'

What good would it do to tell her that no matter how far, how fast you ran, the past always stayed two paces behind you?

Instead, he wrapped his arms around her waist, satisfied when she closed her hands over his. He knew she was studying the screens across the room. Knew the instant she saw it.

246

'Son of a bitch, look at the numbers: income, outgo. They're too damn close. They're practically exact.'

'They are exact,' Roarke corrected, and released the woman, knowing the cop would want to stand clear. 'To the penny.'

'But that's impossible.' She struggled to do the math in her head. 'Nobody spends exactly what they make – not on record. Everyone carries at least a little cash – for the occasional vendor on the sidewalk, the Pepsi machine, the kid who brings the pizza. Sure, it's mostly plastic or electronic, but you've got to have some cash floating around.'

She paused, turned around. 'You'd already seen it. Why the hell didn't you say something?'

'I thought it would be more interesting to wait until we found his cache.' He glanced down as the blinking yellow light for searching switched to green. 'And it appears we have. Ah, a traditional man, our Simpson. As I suspected, he relies on the well respected and discreet Swiss. Display data on screen five.'

'Jesus fucking Christ.' Eve gaped at the bank listings.

'That's in Swiss francs,' Roarke explained. 'Translate to USD, screen six. About triple his tax portfolio here, wouldn't you say, lieutenant?'

Her blood was up. 'I knew he was taking. Goodamn it, I knew it. And look at the withdrawals, Roarke, in the last year. Twenty-five thousand a quarter, every quarter. A hundred thousand.' She turned back to Roarke, and her smile was thin. 'That matches the figure on Sharon's list. Simpson – one hundred K. She was bleeding him.'

'You may be able to prove it.'

'I damn well will prove it.' She began to pace. 'She had something on him. Maybe it was sex, maybe it was graft. Probably a combination of a lot of ugly little sins. So he paid her to keep her quiet.'

Eve thrust her hands into her pockets, pulled them out again.

'Maybe she upped the ante. Maybe he was just sick and tired of shelling out a hundred a year for insurance. So he offs her. Somebody keeps trying to scuttle the investigation. Somebody with the power and the information to complicate things. It points right at him.'

'What about the two other victims?'

She was working on it. Goddamn it, she was working on it. 'He used one prostitute. He could have used others. Sharon and the third victim knew each other – or of each other. One of them might have known Lola, mentioned her, even suggested her as a change of pace. Hell, she could have been a random choice. He got caught up in the thrill of the first murder. It scared him, but it was also a high for him.'

She stopped prowling the room long enough to flick a glance at Roarke. He'd taken out a cigarette, lighted it, watching her.

'DeBlass is one of his backers,' she continued. 'And Simpson's come out strongly in favor of DeBlass's upcoming Morals Bill. They're just prostitutes, he's thinking. Just legal whores, and one of them was threatening him. How much more of a danger to him would she have been once he put in his bid for governor?'

She stopped pacing again, turned back. 'And that's just shit.'

'I thought it sounded quite reasonable.'

'Not when you look at the man.' Slowly, she rubbed her fingers between her brows. 'He doesn't have the brains for it. Yeah, I think he could kill, Christ knows he's into control, but to pull off a series of murders this slick? He's a desk man – an administrator, an image, not a cop. He can't even remember a penal code without an aide prompting him. Graft's easy, it's just business. And to kill out of panic or passion or fury, yes. But to plan, to execute the plan step by step? No. He isn't even smart enough to juggle his public records well.'

248

'So he had help.'

'Possible. Maybe if I could put pressure on him, I'd find out.'

'I can help you there.' Roarke took a final, thoughtful drag before crushing out his cigarette. 'What do you think the media would do if it received an anonymous transmission of Simpson's underground accounts?'

She dropped the hand she'd lifted to rake through her hair. 'They'd hang him. If he knows anything, even with a fleet of lawyers around him, we might be able to shake something loose.'

'Just so. Your call, lieutenant.'

She thought of rules, of due process, of the system she'd made herself an intregal part of. And she thought of three dead women – three more she might be able to protect.

'There's a reporter. Nadine Furst. Give it to her.'

She wouldn't stay with him. Eve knew a call would come, and it was best if she were home and alone when it did. She didn't think she would sleep, but she drifted into dreams.

She dreamed first of murder. Sharon, Lola, Georgie, each of them smiling toward the camera. That instant of fear a lightning bolt in the eyes before they flew back on sex-warmed sheets.

Daddy. Lola had called him Daddy. And Eve stumbled painfully into an older, more terrifying dream.

She was a good girl. She tried to be good, not to cause trouble. If you caused trouble, the cops came and got you, and put you in a deep, dark hole where bugs skittered and spiders crept toward you on silent, slithery legs.

She didn't have friends. If you had friends you had to make up stories about where the bruises came from. How you were clumsy when you weren't clumsy. How you'd fallen when you hadn't fallen. Besides, they never lived in one place very long. If you did, the fucking social workers came nosing around, asking questions. It was the fucking social workers who called the cops that put you away in that dark, bug crawling hole.

Her Daddy had warned her.

So she was a good girl, without any friends, who moved from place to place when she was taken.

But it didn't seem to make any difference.

She could hear him coming. She always heard him. Even if she was sound asleep, the creeping shuffle of his bare feet on the floor woke her as quickly as a thunder clap.

Oh, please, oh, please, oh please. She would pray, but she wouldn't cry. If she cried she was beaten, and he did the secret things anyway. The painful and secret thing that she knew, even at five, was somehow bad.

He told her she was good. The whole time he did the secret thing he would tell her she was good. But she knew she was bad, and she would be punished.

Sometimes he tied her up. When she heard her door open, she whimpered softly, praying he wouldn't tie her this time. She wouldn't fight, she wouldn't, if he just didn't tie her up. If he just didn't hold his hand over her mouth, she wouldn't scream or call out.

'Where's my little girl? Where's my good little girl?'

Tears gathered in the corners of her eyes as his hands slipped under the sheets, poking, probing, pinching. She could smell his breath on her face, sweet, like candy.

His fingers rammed inside her, his other hand coming down hard over her mouth as she drew in breath to scream. She couldn't help it.

'Be quiet.' His breath was coming in short gasps, in a sickening arousal she didn't understand. His fingers dug into her cheeks where bruises would form by morning. 'Be a good girl. There's a good girl.'

She couldn't hear his grunts for the screaming inside her head. She screamed it over and over and over.

No, Daddy. No, Daddy.

'*No!*' The scream ripped out of Eve's throat as she reared up in bed. Gooseflesh prickled on her clammy skin, and she shivered and shivered as she tugged the blankets up.

Didn't remember. Wouldn't remember, she comforted herself and drew up her knees, pressed her forehead against them. Just a dream, and it was already fading. She could will it away – had done so before – until there was nothing left but the faint nausea.

Still shaky, she got up, wrapped herself in her robe to combat the chill. In the bath she ran water over her face until she was breathing evenly again. Steadier, she got herself a tube of Pepsi, huddled back into bed, and switched on one of the twenty-four-hour news stations.

And settled down to wait.

It was the lead story at six A.M., the headline read by a cat-eyed Nadine. Eve was already dressed when the call came through summoning her to Cop Central.

# Chapter Seventeen

Whatever personal satisfaction Eve felt on finding herself part of the team who questioned Simpson, she hid it well. In deference to his position, they used the office of Security Administration rather than an interrogation area.

The clear wrap of windows and the glossy acrylic table didn't negate the fact that Simpson was in deep trouble. The beading of sweat above his top lip indicated he knew just how deep.

'The media is trying to injure the department,' Simpson began, using the statement meticulously prepared by his senior aide. 'With the very visible failure of the investigation into the brutal deaths of three women, the media is attempting to incite a witch-hunt. As chief of police, I'm an obvious target.'

'Chief Simpson.' Not by the flicker of an eyelash did Commander Whitney expose his inner glee. His voice was grave, his eyes somber. His heart was celebrating. 'Regardless of the motive, it will be necessary for you to explain the discrepancy in your books.'

Simpson sat frozen while one of his attorneys leaned over and murmured in his ear.

'I have not admitted to any discrepancy. If one exists, I'm unaware of it.'

'Unaware, Chief Simpson, of more than two million dollars?'

'I've already contacted my accounting firm. Obviously, if there is a mistake of some nature, it was made by them.'

'Will you confirm or deny that the account numbered four seventy-eight nine one one two seven, four ninety-nine is yours?'

After another brief consultation, Simpson nodded. 'I will confirm that.' To lie would only tighten the noose.

Whitney glanced at Eve. They'd agreed the account was an IRS matter. All they'd wanted was for Simpson to confirm.

'Will you explain, Chief Simpson, the withdrawal of one hundred thousand dollars, in twenty-five thousand dollar increments, every three months during the past year?'

Simpson tugged at the knot of his tie. 'I see no reason to explain how I spend my money, Lieutenant Dallas.'

'Then perhaps you can explain how it is those same amounts were listed by Sharon DeBlass and accredited to you.'

'I don't know what you're talking about.'

'We have evidence that you paid to Sharon DeBlass one hundred thousand dollars, in twenty-five thousand dollar increments in one year's period.' Eve waited a beat. 'That's quite a large amount between casual acquaintances.'

'I have nothing to say on the matter.'

'Was she blackmailing you?'

'I have nothing to say.'

'The evidence says it for you,' Eve stated. 'She was blackmailing you; you were paying her off. I'm sure you're aware there are only two ways to stop extortion, Chief Simpson. One, you cut off the supply. Two . . . you eliminate the blackmailer.'

'This is absurd. I didn't kill Sharon. I was paying her like clockwork. I—'

'Chief Simpson.' The elder of the team of lawyers put a hand on Simpson's arm, squeezed. He turned his mild gaze to Eve. 'My client has no statement to make regarding Sharon

DeBlass. Obviously, we will cooperate in any way with the Internal Revenue Service's investigation into my client's records. At this time, however, no charges have been made. We're here only as a courtesy, and to show our goodwill.'

'Were you acquainted with a woman known as Lola Starr?' Eve shot out.

'My client has no comment.'

'Did you know licensed companion, Georgie Castle?'

'Same response,' the lawyer said patiently.

'You've done everything you could to roadblock this murder investigation from the beginning. Why?'

'Is that a statement of fact, Lieutenant Dallas?' the lawyer asked. 'Or an opinion?'

'I'll give you facts. You knew Sharon DeBlass, intimately. She was hosing you for a hundred grand a year. She's dead, and someone is leaking confidential information on the investigation. Two more women are dead. All the victims made their living through legal prostitution – something you oppose.'

'My opposition of prostitution is a political, moral, and a personal stance,' Simpson said tightly. 'I will support wholeheartedly any legislation that outlaws it. But I would hardly eliminate the problem by picking off prostitutes one at a time.'

'You own a collection of antique weapons,' Eve persisted.

'I do,' Simpson agreed, ignoring his attorney. 'A small, limited collection. All registered, secured, and inventoried. I'll be more than happy to turn them over to Commander Whitney for testing.'

'I appreciate that,' Whitney said, shocking Simpson by agreeing. 'Thank you for your cooperation.'

Simpson rose, his face a battleground of emotion. 'When this matter is cleared up, I won't forget this meeting.' His eyes rested briefly on Eve. 'I won't forget who attacked the office of Chief of Police and Security.'

Commander Whitney waited until Simpson sailed out, followed by his team of attorneys. 'When this is settled, he won't get within a hundred yards of the office of Chief of Police and Security.'

'I needed more time to work on him. Why'd you let him walk?'

'His isn't the only name on the DeBlass list,' Whitney reminded her. 'And there's no tie, as yet, between him and the other two victims. Whittle the list down, get me a tie, and I'll give you all the time you need.' He paused, shuffling through the hard copies of the documents that had been transmitted to his office. 'Dallas, you seemed very prepared for this interview. Almost as if you'd been expecting it. I don't suppose I need remind you that tampering with private documents is against the law.'

'No, sir.'

'I didn't think I did. Dismissed.'

As she headed for the door, she thought she heard him murmur 'Good job' but she might have been mistaken.

She was taking the elevator to her own section when her communicator blipped. 'Dallas.'

'Call for you. Charles Monroe.'

'I'll get back to him.'

She snagged a cup of sludge masquerading as coffee, and what might have been a doughnut as she passed through the bullpen area of the records section. It took nearly twenty minutes for her to requisition copies of the discs for the three homicides.

Closeting herself in her office, she studied them again. She reviewed her notes, made fresh ones.

The victim was on the bed each time. The bed rumpled each time. They were naked each time. Their hair was mussed.

255

Eyes narrowed, she ordered the image of Lola Starr to freeze, pull into close-up.

'Skin reddened left buttocks,' she murmured. 'Missed that before. Spanking? Domination thrill? Doesn't appear to be bruising or welting. Have Feeney enhance and determine. Switch to DeBlass tape.'

Again, Eve ran it. Sharon laughed at the camera, taunted it, touching herself, shifting. 'Freeze image. Quadrant – shit – try sixteen, increase. No marks,' she said. 'Continue. Come on, Sharon, show me the right side, just in case. Little more. Freeze. Quadrant twelve, increase. No marks on you. Maybe you did the spanking, huh? Run Castle disc. Come on Georgie, let's see.'

She watched the woman smile, flirt, lift a hand to smooth down her tousled hair. Eve already knew the dialogue perfectly: *'That was wonderful. You're terrific.'*

She was kneeling, sitting back on her haunches, her eyes pleasant and companionable. Silently, Eve began to urge her to move, just a little, shift over. Then Georgia yawned delicately, turned to fluff the pillows.

'Freeze. Oh yeah, paddled you, didn't he? Some guys get off on playing bad girl and Daddy.'

She had a flash, like a stab of a knife through the brain. Memories sliced through her, the solid slap of a hand on her bottom, stinging, the heavy breathing. *'You have to be punished, little girl. Then Daddy's going to kiss it better. He's going to kiss it all better.'*

'Jesus.' She rubbed shaking hands over her face. 'Stop. Put it away. Put it away.'

She reached for cold coffee and found only dregs. The past was past, she reminded herself, and had nothing to do with her. Nothing to do with the job at hand.

'Victim Two and Three show marks of abuse on buttocks. No marks on Victim One.' She let out a long breath, took in a slow one. Steadier. 'Break in pattern. Apparent emotional reaction during first murder, absent in subsequent two.'

Her 'link buzzed, she ignored it.

'Possible theory: Perpetrator gained confidence, enjoyment in subsequent murders. Note: No security on Victim Two. Time lapse on security cameras, Victim Three, thirty-three minutes less than Victim One. Possible theory: More adept, more confident, less inclined to play with victim. Wants the kick faster.'

Possible, possible, she thought, and her computer agreed after a jittery wheeze, with a ninety-six-three probability factor. But something else was clicking as she ran the three discs so closely together, interchanging sections.

'Split screen,' she ordered, 'Victims One and Two, from beginning.'

Sharon's cat smile, Lola's pout. Both women looked toward the camera, toward the man behind it. Spoke to him.

'Freeze images,' Eve said so softly only the sharp ears of the computer could have heard her. 'Oh God, what have we here?'

It was a small thing, a slight thing, and with the eyes focused on the brutality of the murders, easily missed. But she saw it now, through Sharon's eyes. Through Lola's.

Lola's gaze was angled higher.

The height of the beds could account for it, Eve told herself as she added Georgie's image to the screen. Each woman had their head tilted. After all, they were sitting, he very likely standing. But the angle of the eyes, the point at which they stared . . . Only Sharon's was different.

Still watching the screen, Eve called Dr Mira.

'I don't care what she's doing,' Eve spat out at the drone working reception. 'It's urgent.'

She snarled as she was put on hold and her ears assaulted with mindless, sugary music.

'Question,' she said the moment Mira was on the line.

'Yes, lieutenant.'

'Is it possible we have two killers?'

'A copycat? Unlikely, lieutenant, given as much of the method and style of the murders has been kept under wraps.'

'Shit leaks. I've got breaks in pattern. Small ones, but definite breaks.' Impatient, she outlined them. 'Theory, doctor. The first murder committed by someone who knew Sharon well, who killed on impulse, then had enough control to clean up behind himself well. The second two are reflections of the first crime, fined down, though thorough, committed by someone cold, calculating, with no connection to his victims. And goddamn it, he's taller.'

'It's a theory, lieutenant. I'm sorry, but it's just as likely, even more so, that all three murders were committed by one man who grows more calculating with each success. In my professional opinion, no one who wasn't privy to the first crime, to the stages of it, could have so perfectly mirrored the events in the second two.'

Her computer had ditched her theory as well, with a forty-eight-five. 'Okay, thanks.' Deflated, Eve disconnected. Stupid to be disappointed, she told herself. How much worse could it be if she were after two men instead of one?

Her 'link buzzed again. Teeth bared in annoyance, she flipped on. 'Dallas, What?'

'Hey, Lieutenant Sugar, a guy might think you didn't care.'

'I don't have time to play, Charles.'

'Hey, don't cut me off. I got something for you.'

'Or for lame innuendos—'

'No, really. Boy, flirt with a woman once or twice and she never takes you seriously.' His perfect face registered hurt. 'You asked me to call if I remembered anything, right?'

'Right.' Patience, she warned herself. 'So, did you?'

'It was the diaries that got me thinking. You know how I said she was always recording everything. Since you're looking for them, I figure they weren't over at her place.'

'You should be a detective.'

'I like my line of work. Anyhow, I started wondering where she might put them for safekeeping. And I remembered the safe-deposit box.'

'We've already checked it. Thanks, anyway.'

'Oh. Well, how'd you get into it without me? She's dead.'

Eve paused on the point of cutting him off. 'Without you?'

'Yeah. A couple, three years ago, she asked me to sign for one for her. Said she didn't want her name on the record.'

Eve's heart began to thump. 'Then what good would it do her?'

Charles's smile was sheepish and charming. 'Well, technically, I signed her on as my sister. I've got one in Kansas City. So we listed Sharon as Annie Monroe. She paid the rent, and I just forgot about it. I can't even say for sure if she kept it, but I thought you might want to know.'

'Where's the bank?'

'First Manhattan, on Madison.'

'Listen to me, Charles. You're home, right?'

'That's right.'

'You stay there. Right there. I'll be over in fifteen minutes. We're going to go banking, you and me.'

'If that's the best I can do. Hey, did I give you a hot lead, Lieutenant Sugar?'

'Just stay put.'

She was up and shrugging into her jacket when her 'link buzzed again. 'Dallas.'

'Dispatch, Dallas. We have a transmission on hold for you. Video blocked. Refuses to identify.'

'Tracing?'

'Tracing now.'

'Then put it through.' She swung up her bag as the audio clicked. 'This is Dallas.'

'Are you alone?' It was a female voice, tremulous.

'Yes. Do you want me to help you?'

'It wasn't my fault. You have to know it wasn't my fault.'

'No one's blaming you.' Training had Eve picking up on both fear and grief. 'Just tell me what happened.'

'He raped me. I couldn't stop him. He raped me. He raped her, too. Then he killed her. He could kill me.'

'Tell me where you are.' She studied her screen, waiting for the trace to come through. 'I want to help, but I have to know where you are.'

Breath hitching, a whimper. 'He said it was supposed to be a secret. I couldn't tell. He killed her so she couldn't tell. Now there's me. No one will believe me.'

'I believe you. I'll help you. Tell me—' She swore as the transmission broke. 'Where?' she demanded after switching to dispatch.

'Front Royal, Virginia. Number seven oh three, five five five, thirty-nine oh eight. Address—'

'I don't need it. Get me Captain Ryan Feeney in EDD. Fast.'

Two minutes wasn't fast enough. Eve nearly drilled a hole in her temple rubbing it while she waited. 'Feeney, I've got something, and it's big.'

'What?'

'I can't go into it yet, but I need you to go pick up Charles Monroe.'

'Christ, Eve, have we got him?'

'Not yet. Monroe's going to take you to Sharon's other safe box. You take good care of him, Feeney. We're going to need him. And you take damn good care of whatever you find in the box.'

'What are you going to be doing?'

'I've got to catch a plane.' She broke transmission, then called Roarke. It took another three minutes of very precious time before he came on-line.

'I was about to call you, Eve. It looks like I have to fly to Dublin. Care to join me?'

'Roarke, I need your plane. Now. I have to get to Virginia fast. If I go through channels or take public transport—'

'The plane will be ready for you. Terminal C, Gate 22.'

She closed her eyes. 'Thanks. I owe you.'

Her gratitude lasted until she arrived at the gate and found Roarke waiting for her.

'I don't have time to talk.' Her voice was a snap, her long legs eating up the distance from gate to lift.

'We'll talk on the plane.'

'You're not going with me. This is official—'

'This is my plane, lieutenant,' he interrupted smoothly as the lift closed them in together, gliding silently up.

'Can't you do anything without strings?'

'Yes. This isn't one of them.' The hatch opened. The flight attendant waited efficiently.

'Welcome aboard, sir, lieutenant. Can I offer you refreshments?'

'No, thank you. Have the pilot take off as soon as we're cleared.' Roarke took his seat while Eve stood fuming. 'We can't take off until you're seated and secured.'

'I thought you were going to Ireland.' She could argue with him just as easily sitting down.

'It's not a priority. This is. Eve, before you state your case, I'll outline mine. You're going to Virginia in quite a rush. That points to the DeBlass case and some new information. Beth and Richard are friends, close friends. I don't have many close friends, nor do you. Reverse situations. What would you do?'

261

She drummed her fingers on the arm of her chair as the plane began to taxi. 'This can't be personal.'

'Not for you. For me, it's very personal. Beth contacted me even as I was arranging for the plane to be readied. She asked me to come.'

'Why?'

'She wouldn't say. She didn't have to – she only had to ask.'

Loyalty was a trait Eve had a difficult time arguing against. 'I can't stop you from going, but I'm warning you, this is department business.'

'And the department is in upheaval this morning,' he said evenly, 'because of certain information leaked to the media – by an unnamed source.'

She hissed out a breath. Nothing like backing yourself into a corner. 'I'm grateful for your help.'

'Enough to tell me the outcome?'

'I imagine the cap will be off by the end of the day.' She moved her shoulders restlessly, staring out the window, willing the miles away. 'Simpson's going to try to ditch the whole business on his accounting firm. I can't see him pulling it off. The IRS'll get him for tax fraud. I imagine the internal investigation will uncover where he got the money. Considering Simpson's imagination, I'd bet on the standard kickbacks, bribes, and graft.'

'And the blackmail?'

'Oh, he was paying her. He admitted as much before his lawyer shut him up. And he'll cop to it, once he realizes paying blackmail's a lot less dicey than accessory to murder.'

She took out her communicator, requested Feeney's access.

'Yo, Dallas.'

'Did you get them?'

Feeney held a small box up so that she could see it in the

262

tiny viewing screen. 'All labeled and dated. About twenty years' worth.'

'Start with the last entry, work back. I should hit destination in about twenty minutes. I'll contact you as soon as I can for a status report.'

'Hey, Lieutenant Sugar.' Charles edged his way on-screen and beamed at her. 'How'd I do?'

'You did good. Thanks. Now, until I say different, forget about the safe box, the diaries, everything.'

'What diaries?' he said with a wink. He blew her a kiss before Feeney elbowed him aside.

'I'm heading back to Cop Central now. Stay in touch.'

'Out.' Eve switched off, slipped the communicator back in her pocket.

Roarke waited a beat. 'Lieutenant Sugar?'

'Shut up, Roarke.' She closed her eyes to ignore him, but couldn't quite wipe the smirk off her face.

When they landed, she was forced to admit that Roarke's name worked even faster than a badge. In minutes they were in a powerful rental car and eating up the miles to Front Royal. She might have objected about being delegated to the passenger seat, but she couldn't fault his driving.

'Ever done the Indy?'

'No.' He spared her a brief glance as they bulleted up Route 95 at just under a hundred. 'But I've driven in a few Grand Prix.'

'Figures.' She tapped her fingers against the chicken stick when he shot the car into a vertical rise, skimmed daringly – and illegally – over the top of a small jam of cars. 'You say Richard is a good friend. How would you describe him?'

'Intelligent, dedicated, quiet. He rarely speaks unless he has something to say. Overshadowed by his father, often at odds with him.'

'How would you describe his relationship with his father?'

He brought the vehicle down again, wheels barely skidding on the road surface. 'From the little he might have said, and the things Beth let drop, I'd have to say combative, frustrated.'

'And his relationship with his daughter?'

'The choices she made were in direct opposition to his lifestyle, his, well, morals, if you wish. He's a staunch believer in freedom of choice and expression. Still, I can't imagine any father wanting his daughter to become a woman who sells herself for a living.'

'Wasn't he involved in designing his father's security for the last senatorial campaign?'

He took the vehicle up again, maneuvered it off the road, muttering something about a shortcut. In the time he took to skim through a glade of trees, over a few residential buildings, and down again onto a quiet suburban street, he was silent, he was silent.

She stopped counting the traffic violations.

'Family loyalty transcends politics. A man with DeBlass's views is either well loved or well hated. Richard may disagree with his father, but he'd hardly want him assassinated. And as he specializes in security law, it follows he'd assist his father in the matter.'

A son protects his father, Eve thought. 'And how far would DeBlass go to protect his son?'

'From what? Richard is a moderate's moderate. He maintains a low profile, supports his causes quietly. He—' The import of the question struck. 'You're off target,' Roarke said between his teeth. 'Way off target.'

'We'll see.'

The house on the hill looked peaceful. Under the cold blue sky, it sat serenely, warmly, with a few brave crocuses beginning to peep out of the winter stung grass.

Appearances, Eve thought, were deceiving more often than not. She knew this wasn't a home of easy wealth, quiet happiness, and tidy lives. She was certain now that she knew what had gone on behind those rosy walls and gleaming glass.

Elizabeth opened the door herself. If anything, she was paler and more drawn than when Eve had last seen her. Her eyes were puffy from weeping, and the mannishly tailored suit she wore bagged at the hips from recent weight loss.

'Oh, Roarke.' As Elizabeth went into his arms, Eve could all but hear the fragile bones knocking together. 'I'm sorry I dragged you out here. I shouldn't have bothered you.'

'Don't be silly.' He tilted her face up with a gentleness that tugged at the heart Eve was struggling to hold distant. 'Beth, you're not taking care of yourself.'

'I can't seem to function, to think, or to do. Everything's crumbling away at my feet, and I—' She broke off, remembering abruptly that they weren't alone. 'Lieutenant Dallas.'

Eve caught the quick accusation in Elizabeth's eyes when she looked at Roarke. 'He didn't bring me, Ms Barrister. I brought him. I received a call this morning from this location. Did you make it?'

'No.' Elizabeth stepped back. Her hands reached for each other, twisted. 'No, I didn't. It must have been Catherine. She arrived here last night, suddenly. Hysterical, overwrought. Her mother has been hospitalized, and the prognosis is poor. I can only think the stress of the last few weeks has been too much for her. That's why I called you, Roarke. Richard's at his wit's end. I don't seem to be any help. We needed someone.'

'Why don't we go in and sit down?'

'They're in the parlor.' In a jittery move, Elizabeth turned to look down the hall. 'She won't take a sedative, she won't explain. She refused to let us do more than call her husband and son and tell them she was here, and not to come. She's frantic at the idea they might be in some sort of danger. I suppose what happened to Sharon has made her worry more about her own child. She's obsessed with saving him from God knows what.'

'If she called me,' Eve put in. 'Then maybe she'll talk to me.'

'Yes. Yes, all right.'

She led the way down the hall, and into the tidy, sunwashed parlor. Catherine DeBlass sat on a sofa, leaning into her brother's arms. Eve couldn't be sure if he was comforting, or restraining.

Richard raised stricken eyes to Roarke's. 'It's good of you to come. We're a mess, Roarke.' His voice shook, nearly broke. 'We're a mess.'

'Elizabeth.' Roarke crouched in front of Catherine. 'Why don't you ring for coffee?'

'Oh, of course. I'm sorry.'

'Catherine.' His voice was gentle, as was the hand he laid on her arm. But the touch had Catherine jerking up, her eyes going wide.

'Don't. What – what are you doing here?'

'I came to see Beth and Richard. I'm sorry you're not well.'

'Well?' She gave what might have been a laugh as she curled into herself. 'None of us will ever be well again. How can we? We're all tainted. We're all to blame.'

'For what?'

She shook her head, pushed herself into the far corner of the sofa. 'I can't talk to you.'

'Congresswoman DeBlass, I'm Lieutenant Dallas. You called me a little while ago.'

'No, no I didn't.' Panicked, Catherine wrapped her arms tightly around her chest. 'I didn't call. I didn't say anything.'

As Richard leaned over to touch her, Eve shot him a warning glance. Deliberately, she put herself between them, sat and

266

took Catherine's frigid hand. 'You wanted me to help. And I will help you.'

'You can't. No one can. I was wrong to call. We have to keep it in the family. I have a husband, I have a little boy.' Tears began to swim in her eyes. 'I have to protect them. I have to go away, far away, so I can protect them.'

'We'll protect them,' Eve said quietly. 'We'll protect you. It was too late to protect Sharon. You can't blame yourself.'

'I didn't try to stop it,' Catherine said in a whisper. 'Maybe I was even glad, because it wasn't me anymore. It wasn't me.'

'Ms DeBlass, I can help you. I can protect you and your family. Tell me who raped you.'

Richard let out a hiss of shock. 'My God, what are you saying? What—'

Eve turned on him, eyes fierce. 'Be quiet. There's no more secrets here.'

'Secrets,' Catherine said between trembling lips. 'It has to be a secret.'

'No, it doesn't. This kind of secret hurts. It crawls inside you and eats at you. It makes you scared, and it makes you guilty. The ones who want it to be secret use that – the guilt, the fear, the shame. The only way you can fight back is to tell. Tell me who raped you.'

Catherine's breath shuddered out. She looked at her brother, terror bright in her eyes. Eve turned her face back, held it.

'Look at me. Just me. And tell me who raped you. Who raped Sharon?'

'My father.' The words burst from her in a howl of pain. 'My father. My father. My father.' She buried her face in her hands and sobbed.

'Oh God.' Across the room, Elizabeth stumbled back into the server droid. China shattered. Coffee seeped dark into the lovely rug. 'Oh my God. My baby.'

Richard shot off the couch, reaching her as she swayed. He

267

caught her hard against him. 'I'll kill him for this. I'll kill him.' Then he pressed his face into her hair. 'Beth. Oh, Beth.'

'Do, what you can for them,' Eve murmured to Roarke as she gathered Catherine to her.

'You thought it was Richard,' Roarke said in an undertone.

'Yes.' Her eyes were dull and flat when she lifted them to his. 'I thought it was Sharon's father. Maybe I didn't want to think that something so foul could flourish in two generations.'

Roarke leaned forward. His face was hard as rock. 'One way or the other, DeBlass is a dead man.'

'Help your friends,' Eve said evenly. 'I have work to do here.'

# Chapter Eighteen

She let Catherine cry it out, though she knew, too well, that the tears wouldn't wash the wound clean. She knew, too, that she wouldn't have been able to handle the situation alone. It was Roarke who calmed Elizabeth and Richard, who ordered in the domestic droid to gather up the broken crockery, who held their hands, and when he gauged the time was right, it was he who gently suggested bringing Catherine some tea.

Elizabeth fetched it herself, carefully closing the parlor doors behind her before she carried the cup to her sister-in-law. 'Here, darling, drink a little.'

'I'm sorry.' Catherine put both shaky hands around the cup to warm them. 'I'm sorry. I thought it had stopped. I made myself believe it had stopped. I couldn't live otherwise.'

'It's all right.' Her face blank, Elizabeth went back to her husband.

'Ms DeBlass, I need you to tell me everything. Congresswoman DeBlass?' Eve waited until Catherine focused on her again. 'Do you understand this is being recorded?'

'He'll stop you.'

'No, he won't. That's why you called me, because you know I'll stop him.'

'He's afraid of you,' Catherine whispered. 'He's afraid of you. I could tell. He's afraid of women. That's why he hurts

269

them. I think he may have given something to my mother. Broke her mind. She knew.'

'Your mother knew your father was abusing you?'

'She knew. She pretended she didn't, but I could see it in her eyes. She didn't want to know – she just wanted everything quiet and perfect, so she could give her parties and be the senator's wife.' She lifted a hand, shielding her eyes. 'When he would come into my room at night, I could see it on her face the next morning. But when I tried to talk to her, to tell her to make him stop, she pretended she didn't know what I meant. She told me to stop imagining things. To be good, to respect the family.'

She lowered her hand again, cupped her tea with both hands, but didn't drink. 'When I was little, seven or eight, he would come in at night and touch me. He said it was all right, because he was Daddy, and I was going to pretend to be Mommy. It was a game, he said, a secret game. He told me I had to do things – to touch him. To—'

'It's all right,' Eve soothed as Catherine began to tremble violently. 'You don't have to say. Tell me what you can.'

'You had to obey him. You had to. He was a force in our house. Richard?'

'Yes.' Richard caught his wife's hand in his and squeezed, squeezed. 'I know.'

'I couldn't tell you because I was ashamed, and I was afraid, and Mom just looked away, so I thought I had to do it.' She swallowed hard. 'On my twelfth birthday, we had a party. Lots of friends, and a big cake, and the ponies. You remember the ponies, Richard?'

'I remember.' Tears tracked silently down his cheeks. 'I remember.'

'And that night, the night of my birthday, he came. He said I was old enough now. He said he had a present for me, a special present because I was growing up. And he raped me.'

She buried her face in her hands and rocked. 'He said it was a present. Oh God. And I begged him to stop, because it hurt. And because I was old enough to know it was wrong, it was evil. I was evil. But he didn't stop. And he kept coming back. All those years until I could get away. I went to college, far away, where he couldn't touch me. And I told myself it never happened. It never, never happened.

'I tried to be strong, to make a life. I got married because I thought I would be safe. Justin was so kind, so gentle. He never hurt me. And I never told him. I thought if he knew, he'd despise me. So I kept telling myself it never happened.'

She lowered her hands and looked at Eve. 'I believed it, sometimes. Most of the time. I could lose myself in my work, in my family. But then I could see, I knew he was doing the same thing to Sharon. I wanted to help, but I didn't know how. So I pushed it away, just like my mother did. He killed her. Now he'll kill me.'

'Why do you think he killed Sharon?'

'She wasn't weak like me. She turned it on him, used it against him. I heard them arguing. Christmas Day. When we all went to his house to pretend we were a family. I saw them go into his office, and I followed them. I opened the door, and I watched and I listened through the crack. He was so furious with her because she was making a public mockery of everything he stood for. And she said, "You made me what I am, you bastard." It warmed me to hear that. It made me want to cheer. She stood up to him. She threatened to expose him unless he paid her. She had it all documented, she said, every dirty detail. So he'd have to play the game her way. They fought, hurling words at each other. And then . . .'

Catherine glanced over at Elizabeth, at her brother, then looked away. 'She took off her blouse.' Elizabeth's moan had Catherine trembling again. 'She told him he could have her, just like any client. But he'd pay more. A lot more. He

271

was looking at her. I knew the way he was looking at her, his eyes glazed over, his mouth slack. He grabbed her breasts. She looked at me. Right at me. She'd known I was there, and she looked at me with such disgust. Maybe even with hate, because she knew I'd do nothing. I closed the door, closed it and ran. I was sick. Oh, Elizabeth.'

'It's not your fault. She must have tried to tell me. I never saw, I never heard. I never thought. I was her mother, and I didn't protect her.'

'I tried to talk to her.' Catherine gripped her hands together. 'When I went to New York for the fund-raiser. She said I'd chosen my way, and she'd chosen hers. And hers was better. I played politics, kept my head buried, and she played with power and kept her eyes opened.

'When I heard she was dead, I knew. At the funeral I watched him, and he watched me watching him. He came up to me, put his arms around me, held me close as if in comfort. And he whispered to me to pay attention. To remember, and to see what happened when families don't keep secrets. And he said what a fine boy Franklin was. What big plans he had for him. He said how proud I should be. And how careful.' She closed her eyes. 'What could I do? He's my child.'

'No one's going to hurt your son.' Eve closed a hand over Catherine's rigid ones. 'I promise you.'

'I'll never know if I could have saved her. Your child, Richard.'

'You can know you're doing everything possible now.' Hardly aware she'd taken Catherine's hand, Eve tightened her grip in reassurance. 'It's going to be difficult for you, Ms DeBlass, to go over all of this again, as you'll have to. To face the publicity. To testify, should it come to trial.'

'He'll never let it go to trial,' Catherine said wearily.

'I'm not going to give him a choice.' Maybe not on murder, she thought. Not yet. But she had him cold on sexual abuse.

'Ms Barrister, I think your sister-in-law should rest now. Could you help her upstairs?'

'Yes, of course.' Elizabeth rose, walked over to help Catherine to her feet. 'Let's go lie down for a bit, darling.'

'I'm sorry.' Catherine leaned heavily against Elizabeth as she was led from the room. 'God forgive me, I'm so sorry.'

'There's a psychiatric counselor attached to the department, Mr DeBlass. I think your sister should see her.'

'Yes.' He said it absently, staring at the closed door. 'She'll need someone. Something.'

You all will, Eve thought. 'Are you up to a few questions?'

'I don't know. He's a tyrant, difficult. But this makes him a monster. How am I to accept that my own father is a monster?'

'He has an alibi for the night of your daughter's death,' Eve pointed out. 'I can't charge him without more.'

'An alibi?'

'The record shows that Rockman was with your father, working with him in his East Washington office until nearly two on the night of your daughter's death.'

'Rockman would say whatever my father told him to say.'

'Including covering up murder?'

'It's simply a matter of the easiest way out. Why should anyone believe my father is connected?' He shuddered once, as if blasted with a sudden chill. 'Rockman's statement merely detaches his employer from any suspicion.'

'How would your father travel back and forth to New York from East Washington if he wanted no record of the trip?'

'I don't know. If his shuttle went out, there would be a log.'

'Logs can be altered,' Roarke said.

'Yes.' Richard looked up as if remembering all at once that his friend was there. 'You'd know more about that than I.'

'A reference to my smuggling days,' Roarke explained to Eve. 'Long behind me. It can be done, but it would require some payoffs. The pilot, perhaps the mechanic, certainly the air engineer.'

'So I know where to put the pressure on.' And if Eve could prove his shuttle had taken the trip on that night, she'd have probable cause. Enough to break him. 'How much do you know about your father's weapon collection?'

'More than I care to.' Richard rose on unsteady legs. He went to a cabinet, splashed liquor into a glass. He drank it fast, like medicine. 'He enjoys his guns, often shows them off. When I was younger, he tried to interest me in them. Roarke can tell you, it didn't work.'

'Richard believes guns are a dangerous symbol of power abuse. And I can tell you that yes, DeBlass occasionally used the black market.'

'Why didn't you mention that before?'

'You didn't ask.'

She let it drop, for now. 'Does your father have a knowledge of security – the technical aspects?'

'Certainly. He takes pride in knowing how to protect himself. It's one of the few things we can discuss without disagreeing.'

'Would you consider him an expert?'

'No,' Richard said slowly. 'A talented amateur.'

'His relationship with Chief Simpson? How would you describe it?'

'Self-serving. He considered Simpson a fool. My father enjoys utilizing fools.' Abruptly, he sank into a chair. 'I'm sorry. I can't do this. I need some time. I need my wife.'

'All right. Mr DeBlass, I'm going to order surveillance on your father. You won't be able to reach him without being monitored. Please don't try.'

'You think I'll try to kill him?' Richard gave a mirthless

laugh and stared down at his own hands. 'I want to. For what he did to my daughter, to my sister, to my life. I wouldn't have the courage.'

When they were outside again, Eve headed straight for the car without looking at Roarke. 'You suspected this?' she asked.

'That DeBlass was involved? Yes, I did.'

'But you didn't tell me.'

'No.' Roarke stopped her before she could wrench open the door. 'It was a feeling, Eve. I had no idea about Catherine. Absolutely none. I suspected that Sharon and DeBlass were having an affair.'

'That's too clean a word for it.'

'I suspected it,' he continued, 'because of the way she spoke of him during our single dinner together. But again, it was a feeling, not a fact. That feeling would have done nothing to enhance your case. And,' he added, turning her to face him, 'once I got to know you, I kept that feeling to myself, because I didn't want to hurt you.' She jerked her head away. He brought it patiently back with his fingertips. 'You had no one to help you?'

'It isn't about me.' But she let out a shuddering breath. 'I can't think about it, Roarke. I can't. I'll mess up if I do, and if I mess up, he could get away with it. With rape and murder, with abusing the children he should have been protecting. I won't let him.'

'Didn't you say to Catherine that the only way to fight back was to tell?'

'I have work to do.'

He fought back frustration. 'I assume you'll want to go to the Washington Airport where DeBlass keeps his shuttle.'

'Yes.' She climbed in the car when Roarke walked around to get in the driver's side. 'You can drop me at the nearest transport station.'

275

'I'm sticking, Eve.'

'All right, fine. I need to check in.'

As he drove down the winding lane, she put in a call to Feeney. 'I've got something hot here,' she said before he could speak. 'I'm on my way to East Washington.'

'You've got something hot?' Feeney's voice was almost a song. 'Didn't have to look farther than her final entry, Dallas, logged the morning of her murder. God knows why she took it to the bank. Blind luck. She had a date at midnight. You'll never guess who.'

'Her grandfather.'

Feeney goggled, sputtered. 'Fuck it, Dallas, how'd you get it?'

Eve closed her eyes briefly. 'Tell me it's documented, Feeney. Tell me she names him.'

'Calls him the senator – calls him her old fart of a grand-daddy. And she writes pretty cheerfully about the five thousand she charges him for each boink. Quote: "It's almost worth letting him slobber all over me – and there's a lot of energy left in dear old Granddad. The bastard. Five thousand every couple of weeks isn't such a bad deal. I sure as hell give him his money's worth. Not like when I was a kid and he used me. Table's turned. I won't turn into a dried up prune like poor Aunt Catherine. I'm thriving on it now. And one day, when it bores me enough, I'm sending my diaries to the media. Multiple copies. It drives the bastard crazy when I threaten to do that. Maybe I'll twist the knife a little tonight. Give the senator a good scare. Christ, it's wonderful to have the power to make him squirm after all he's done to me."'

Feeney shook his head. 'It was a long-time deal, Dallas. I've run through several entries. She earned a nice income from blackmail, and names names and deeds. But this puts the senator at her place on the night of her death. And that puts his balls in the old nutcracker.'

'Can you get me a warrant?'

'Commander's orders are to patch it through the minute you called in. He says to pick him up. Murder One, three counts.'

She let out a slow breath. 'Where do I find him?'

'He's at the Senate building, hawking his Morals Bill.'

'Fucking perfect. I'm on my way.' She switched off, turned to Roarke. 'How much faster can this thing go?'

'We'll find out.'

If Whitney's orders hadn't come through with the warrant, instructing her to be discreet, Eve would have marched onto the Senate floor and cuffed him in front of his associates. Still, there was considerable satisfction in the way it went down.

She waited while he completed his impassioned speech on the moral decline of the country, the insidious corruption that stemmed from promiscuity, conception control, genetic engineering. He expounded on the lack of morality in the young, the dearth of organized religion in the home, the school, the workplace. Our one nation under God had become godless. Our constitutional right to bear arms sundered by the liberal left. He touted figures on violent crime, on urban decay, on bootlegged drugs, all a result, the senator claimed, of our increasing moral decline, our softness on criminals, our indulgence in sexual freedom without responsibility.

It made Eve sick to listen.

'In the year 2016,' she said softly, 'at the end of the Urban Revolt, before the gun ban, there were over ten thousand deaths and injuries from guns in the borough of Manhattan alone.'

She continued to watch DeBlass sell his snake oil while Roarke laid a hand at the base of her spine.

'Before we legalized prostitution, there was a rape or attempted rape every three seconds. Of course, we still have rape, because it has much less to do with sex than with power, but the figures have dropped. Licensed prostitutes don't have pimps, so they aren't beaten, battered, killed. And they can't use drugs. There was a time when women went to butchers to deal with an unwanted pregnancy. When they had to risk their lives or ruin them. Babies were born blind, deaf, deformed before genetic engineering and the research it made possible to repair in vitro. It's not a perfect world, but you listen to him and you realize it could be a lot worse.'

'Do you know what the media is going to do to him when this hits?'

'Crucify him,' Eve murmured. 'I hope to God it doesn't make him a martyr.'

'The voice of the moral right suspected of incest, trucking with prostitutes, committing murder. I don't think so. He's finished.' Roarke nodded. 'In more ways than one.'

Eve heard the thunderous applause from the gallery. From the sound of it, DeBlass's team had been careful to pepper the spectators with their own.

Discretion be damned, she thought as the gavel was struck and an hour's recess was called. She moved through the milling aides, assistants, and pages until she came to DeBlass. He was being congratulated on his eloquence, slapped on the back by his senatorial supporters.

She waited until he saw her, until his gaze skimmed over her, then Roarke, until his mouth tightened. 'Lieutenant. If you need to speak with me, we can adjourn briefly to my office. Alone. I can spare ten minutes.'

'You're going to have plenty of time, senator. Senator DeBlass, you're under arrest for the murders of Sharon DeBlass, Lola Starr, and Georgie Castle.' As he blustered in protest and the murmurs began, she lifted her voice. 'Additional charges include the incestuous rapes of Catherine DeBlass, your daughter, and Sharon DeBlass, your granddaughter.'

He was still standing, frozen in shock when she linked the

restraints over his wrist, turned him, and secured his hands behind his back. 'You are under no obligation to make a statement.'

'This is an outrage.' He exploded over the standard recitation of revised Miranda. 'I'm a senator of the United States. This is federal property.'

'And these two federal agents will escort you,' she added. 'You are entitled to an attorney or representative.' As she continued to recite his rights, a flash from her eyes had the federal deputies and onlookers backing off. 'Do you understand these rights?'

'I'll have your badge, you bitch.' He began to wheeze as she muscled him through the crowd.

'I'll take that as a yes. Catch your breath, senator. We can't have you popping off with a cardiac.' She leaned closer to his ear. 'And you won't have my badge, you bastard. I'm going to have your ass.' She turned him over to the federal agents. 'They're waiting for him in New York,' she said briefly.

She could hardly be heard now. DeBlass was screaming, demanding immediate release. The Senate had erupted with voices and bodies. Through it, she spotted Rockman. He came toward her, his face a cold mask of fury.

'You're making a mistake, lieutenant.'

'No, I'm not. But you made one in your statement. The way I see it, that's going to make you accessory after the fact. I'm going to start working on that when I get back to New York.'

'Senator DeBlass is a great man. You're nothing but a pawn for the Liberal Party and their plans to destroy him.'

'Senator DeBlass is an incestuous child molester. A rapist and a murderer. And what I am, pal, is the cop who's taking him down. You'd better call a lawyer unless you want to sink with him.'

Roarke had to force himself not to snatch her up as she swept

279

through the hallowed Senate halls. Members of the media were already leaping toward her, but she cut through them as if they weren't there.

'I like your style, Lieutenant Dallas,' he said when they'd fought their way to the car. 'I like it a lot. And by the way, I don't think I'm in love with you anymore. I know I am.'

She swallowed hard on the nausea rising in her throat. 'Let's get out of here. Let's get the hell out of here.'

Sheer force of will kept her steady until she got to the plane. It kept her voice flat and expressionless as she reported in to her superior. Then she stumbled, and shoving away from Roarke's supporting arms, rushed into the head to be wretchedly and violently ill.

On the other side of the door, Roarke stood helplessly. If he understood her at all, it was to know that comforting would make it worse. He murmured instructions to the flight attendant and took his seat. While he waited, he stared out at the tarmac.

He looked up when the door opened. She was ice pale, her eyes too big, too dark. Her usually smooth gait was coltish and stiff.

'Sorry. I guess it got to me.'

When she sat, he offered a mug. 'Drink this. It'll help.'

'What is it?'

'It's tea, a whiff of whiskey.'

'I'm on duty,' she began, but his quick, vicious eruption cut her off.

'Drink, goddamn it, or I'll pour it into you.' He flipped a switch and ordered the pilot to take off.

Telling herself it was easier than arguing, she lifted the mug, but her hands weren't steady. She barely managed to get a sip through her chattering teeth before she set it aside.

She couldn't stop shaking. When Roarke reached for her,

she drew herself back. The sickness was still there, sliding slyly through her stomach, making her head pound evilly.

'My father raped me.' She heard herself say it. The shock of it, hearing her own voice say the words, mirrored in her eyes. 'Repeatedly. And he beat me, repeatedly. If I fought or I didn't fight, it didn't matter. He still raped me. He still beat me. And there was nothing I could do. There's nothing you can do when the people who are supposed to take care of you abuse you that way. Use you. Hurt you.'

'Eve.' He took her hand then, holding firm when she tried to yank free. 'I'm sorry. Terribly sorry.'

'They said I was eight when they found me, in some alley in Dallas. I was bleeding, and my arm was broken. He must have dumped me there. I don't know. Maybe I ran away. I don't remember. But he never came for me. No one ever came for me.'

'Your mother?'

'I don't know. I don't remember her. Maybe she was dead. Maybe she was like Catherine's mother and pretended not to know. I only get flashes, nightmares of the worst of it. I don't even know my name. They weren't able to identify me.'

'You were safe then.'

'You've never been shuffled through the system. There's no feeling of safety. Only impotence. They strip you bare with good intentions.' She sighed, let her head fall back, her eyes close. 'I didn't want to arrest DeBlass, Roarke. I wanted to kill him. I wanted to kill him with my own hands because of what happened to me. I let it get personal.'

'You did your job.'

'Yeah. I did my job. And I'll keep doing it.' But it wasn't the job she was thinking of now. It was life. Hers, and his. 'Roarke, you've got to know I've got some bad stuff inside. It's like a virus that sneaks around the system, pops out when your resistance is low. I'm not a good bet.'

'I like long odds.' He lifted her hand, kissed it. 'Why don't we see it through? Find out if we can both win.'

'I've never told anybody before.'

'Did it help?'

'I don't know. Maybe. Christ, I'm so tired.'

'You could lean on me.' He slipped an arm around her, nestled her head in the curve of his shoulder.

'For a little while,' she murmured. 'Until we get to New York.'

'For a little while then.' He pressed his lips to her hair and hoped she would sleep.

# Chapter Nineteen

DeBlass wouldn't talk. His lawyers put the muzzle on him early, and they put in on tight. The interrogation process was slow, and it was tedious. There were times Eve thought he would burst, when the temper that reddened his face would tip the scales in her favor.

She'd stopped denying it was personal. She didn't want a tricky, media blitzed trial. She wanted a confession.

'You were engaged in an incestuous affair with your grand-daughter, Sharon DeBlass.'

'My client has not confirmed those allegations.'

Eve ignored the lawyer, watched DeBlass's face. 'I have here a transcript of a portion of Sharon DeBlass's diary, dated on the night of her murder.'

She shoved the paper across the table. DeBlass's lawyer, a trim, tidy man with a neat sandy beard and mild blue eyes picked it up, studied it. Whatever his reaction was, he hid it behind cool indifference.

'This proves nothing, lieutenant, as I'm sure you know. The destructive fantasies of a dead woman. A woman of dubious reputation who has long been estranged from her family.'

'There's a pattern here, Senator DeBlass.' Eve stubbornly continued to address the accused rather than his knight at arms. 'You sexually abused your daughter, Catherine.'

'Preposterous,' DeBlass blurted out before his attorney lifted a hand to silence him.

'I have a statement, signed and verified before witnesses from Congresswoman Catherine DeBlass.' Eve offered it, and the lawyer nipped it out of her fingers before the senator could move.

He scanned it, then folded his carefully manicured hands over it. 'You may not be aware, lieutenant, that there is an unfortunate history of mental disorder here. Senator DeBlass's wife is even now under observation for a breakdown.'

'We are aware.' She spared the lawyer a glance. 'And we will be investigating her condition, and the cause of it.'

'Congresswoman DeBlass has also been treated for symptoms of depression, paranoia, and stress,' the lawyer continued in the same neutral tone.

'If she has, Senator DeBlass, we'll find that the roots of it are due to your systematic and continued abuse of her as a child. You were in New York on the night of Sharon DeBlass's murder,' she said, switching gears smoothly. 'Not, as you previously claimed, in East Washington.'

Before the lawyer could block her, she leaned forward, her eyes steady on DeBlass's face. 'Let me tell you how it went down. You took your private shuttle, paying the pilot and the flight engineer to doctor the log. You went to Sharon's apartment, had sex with her, recorded it for your own purposes. You took a weapon with you, a thirty-eight caliber Smith & Wesson antique. And because she taunted you, because she threatened you, because you couldn't take the pressure of possible exposure any longer, you shot her. You shot her three times, in the head, in the heart and in the genitalia.'

She kept the words coming fast, kept her face close to his. It pleased her that she could smell his sweat. 'The last shot was pretty clever. Messed up any chance for us to verify sexual activity. You ripped her open at the crotch. Maybe it was symbolic, maybe it was self-preservation. Why'd you take the gun with you? Had you planned it? Had you decided to end it once and for all?'

DeBlass's eyes darted left and right. His breathing grew hard and fast.

'My client does not acknowledge ownership of the weapon in question.'

'Your client's scum.'

The lawyer puffed up. 'Lieutenant Dallas, you're speaking of a United States Senator.'

'That makes him elected scum. It shocked you, didn't it, senator? All the blood, the noise, the way the gun jerked in your hand. Maybe you hadn't really believed you could go through with it. Not when push came to shove and you had to pull the trigger. But once you had, there was no going back. You had to cover it up. She would have ruined you, she never would have let you have peace. She wasn't like Catherine. Sharon wouldn't fade into the background and suffer all the shame and the guilt and the fear. She used it against you, so you had to kill her. Then you had to cover your tracks.'

'Lieutenant Dallas—'

She never took her eyes from DeBlass, and ignoring the lawyer's warning, kept beating at him. 'That was exciting, wasn't it? You could get away with it. You're a United States senator, the victim's grandfather. Who would believe it of you? So you arranged her on the bed, indulged yourself, your ego. You could do it again, and why not? The killing had stirred something in you. What better way to hide than to make it seem as if there was some maniac at large?'

She waited while DeBlass reached for a glass of water and drank thirstily. 'There was a maniac at large. You printed out the note, slipped it under her. And you dressed, calmer now, but excited. You set the 'link to call the cops at two fifty-five.

285

You needed enough time to go down and fix the security tapes. Then you got back on your shuttle, flew back to East Washington, and waited to play the outraged grandfather.'

Through it all, DeBlass said nothing. But a muscle jerked in his cheek and his eyes couldn't find a place to land.

'That's a fascinating story, lieutenant,' the lawyer said. 'But it remains that – a story. A supposition. A desperate attempt by the police department to fight their way out of a difficult situation with the media and the people of New York. And, of course, it's perfect timing that such ridiculous and damaging accusation should be levied against the senator just as his Morals Bill is coming up for debate.'

'How did you pick the other two? How did you select Lola Starr and Georgie Castle? Have you already picked the fourth, the fifth, the sixth? Do you think you could have stopped there? Could you have stopped when it made you feel so powerful, so invincible, so righteous?'

DeBlass wasn't red now. He was gray, and his breathing was harsh and choppy. When he reached for a glass again, his hand jerked and sent it rolling to the floor.

'This interview is over.' The lawyer stood, helped DeBlass to his feet. 'My client's health is precarious. He requires medical attention immediately.'

'Your client's a murderer. He'll get plenty of medical attention in a penal colony, for the rest of his life.' She pressed a button. When the doors of the interrogation room opened, a uniform stepped in. 'Call the MTs,' she ordered. 'The senator's feeling a little stressed. It's going to get worse,' she warned, turning back to DeBlass. 'I haven't even gotten started.'

Two hours later, after filing reports and meeting with the prosecuting attorney, Eve fought her way through traffic. She had read a good portion of Sharon DeBlass's diaries. It was something she needed to set aside for now, the pictures of a twisted man and how he had turned a young girl into a woman almost as unbalanced as he.

Because she knew it could have been, all too easily, her story. Choices were there to be taken, she thought, brooding. Sharon's had killed her.

She wanted to blow off some steam, go over the events step by step with someone who would listen, appreciate, support. Someone who, for a little while, would stand between her and the ghosts of what was. And what could have been.

She headed for Roarke's.

When the call came through on her car 'link, she prayed it wasn't a summons back to duty. 'Dallas.'

'Hey, kid.' It was Feeney's tired face on-screen. 'I just watched the interrogation discs. Good job.'

'Didn't get as far as I'd like, fencing with the damn lawyer. I'm going to break him, Feeney. I swear it.'

'Yeah, my money's on you. But, ah, I got to tell you something that's not going to go down well. DeBlass had a little heart blip.'

'Christ, he's not going to code out on us?'

'No. No, they medicated him. Some talk about getting him a new one next week.'

'Good.' She blew out a stream of breath. 'I want him to live a long time – behind bars.'

'We've got a strong case. The prosecutor's ready to canonize you, but in the meantime, he's sprung.'

She hit the brakes. A volley of testy horn blasts behind her had her whipping over to the edge of Tenth and blocking the turning lane. 'What the hell do you mean, he's sprung?'

Feeney winced, as much in empathy as reaction. 'Released on his own recognizance. U.S. senator, lifetime of patriotic duty, salt of the earth, dinky heart – and a judge in his pocket.'

'Fuck that.' She pulled her hair until the pain equaled her frustration. 'We got him on murder, three counts. Prosecutor said she was going for no bail.'

'She got shot down. DeBlass's lawyer made a speech that would have wrung tears from a stone and had a corpse saluting the flag. DeBlass is back in East Washington by now, under doctor's orders to rest. He got a thirty-six-hour hold on further interrogation.'

'Shit.' She punched the wheel with the heel of her hand. 'It's not going to make any difference,' she said grimly. 'He can play the ill elder statesman, he can do a tap dance at the fucking Lincoln Memorial, I've got him.'

'Commander's worried that the time lag will give DeBlass an opportunity to pool his resources. He wants you back working with the prosecutor, going over everything we've got by oh eight hundred tomorrow.'

'I'll be there. Feeney, he's not going to slip out of this noose.'

'Just make sure you've got the knot nice and tight, kid. See you at eight.'

'Yeah.' Steaming, she swung back into traffic. She considered going home, burying herself in the chain of evidence. But she was five minutes from Roarke's. Eve opted to use him as a sounding board.

She could count on him to play devil's advocate if she needed it, to point out flaws. And, she admitted, to calm her down so that she could think without all these violent emotions getting in the way. She couldn't afford those emotions, couldn't afford to let Catherine's face pop into her head, as it had time and time again. The shame and the fear and the guilt.

It was impossibly hard to separate it. She knew she wanted DeBlass to pay every bit as much for Catherine as for the three dead women.

She was cleared through Roarke's gate, drove quickly up the sloped driveway. Her pulse began to thud as she raced up the steps. Idiot, she told herself. Like some hormonal plagued teenager. But she was smiling when Summerset opened the door.

'I need to see Roarke,' she said, brushing by him.

'I'm sorry, lieutenant. Roarke isn't at home.'

'Oh.' The sense of deflation made her feel ridiculous. 'Where is he?'

Summerset's face pokered up. 'I believe he's in a meeting. He was forced to cancel an important trip to Europe, and was therefore compelled to work late.'

'Right.' The cat pranced down the steps and immediately began twining himself through Eve's legs. She picked him up, stroked his underbelly. 'When do you expect him?'

'Roarke's time is his business, lieutenant. I don't presume to expect him.'

'Look, pal, I haven't been twisting Roarke's arm to get him to spend his valuable time with me. So why don't you pull the stick out of your ass and tell me why you act like I'm some sort of embarrassing rodent whenever I show up.'

Shock turned Summerset's face paper white. 'I am not comfortable with crude manners, Lieutenant Dallas. Obviously, you are.'

'They fit me like old slippers.'

'Indeed.' Summerset drew himself up. 'Roarke is a man of taste, of style, of influence. He has the ear of presidents and kings. He has escorted women of unimpeachable breeding and pedigree.'

'And I've got lousy breeding and no pedigree.' She would have laughed if the barb hadn't stuck so close to the heart. 'It seems even a man like Roarke can find the occasional mongrel appealing. Tell him I took the cat,' she added and walked out.

*

It helped to tell herself Summerset was an insufferable snob. And the cat's silent interest as she vented on the drive home was curiously smoothing. She didn't need some tight-assed butler's approval. As if in agreement, the cat walked over onto her lap and began to knead her thighs.

She winced a little as his claws nipped through her trousers, but didn't move him aside. 'I guess we've got to come up with a name for you. Never had a pet before,' she murmured. 'I don't know what Georgie called you, but we'll start fresh. Don't worry, we won't go for anything wimpy like Fluffy.'

She pulled into her garage, parked, saw the yellow light blipping on the wall of her spot. A warning that her payment on the space was overdue. If it went red, the barricade would engage and she'd be screwed.

She swore a little, more from habit than heat. She hadn't had time to pay bills, damn it, and now realized she could face an evening of catching up playing the credit juggle with her bank account.

Hauling the cat under her arm, she walked to the elevator. 'Fred, maybe.' She tilted her head, stared into his unreadable two-toned eyes. 'No, you don't look like Fred. Jesus, you must weigh twenty pounds.' Shifting her bag, she stepped into the car. 'We'll give the name some thought, Tubbo.'

The minute she set him down inside the apartment, he darted for the kitchen. Taking her responsibilities as pet owner seriously, and deciding it was one way to postpone crunching figures, Eve followed and came up with a saucer of milk and some leftover Chinese that smelled slightly off.

The cat apparently had no delicacies when it came to food, and attacked the meal with gusto.

She watched him a moment, letting her mind drift. She'd

wanted Roarke. Needed him. That was something else she'd have to give some thought to.

She didn't know how seriously to take the fact that he claimed to be in love with her. Love meant different things to different people. It had never been a part of her life.

She poured herself a half glass of wine, then merely frowned into it.

She felt something for him, certainly. Something new, and uncomfortably strong. Still, it was best to let things coast as they were. Decisions made quickly were almost always regretted quickly.

Why the hell hadn't he been home?

She set the untouched wine aside, dragged a hand through her hair. That was the biggest problem with getting used to someone, she thought. You were lonely when they weren't there.

She had work to do, she reminded herself. A case to close, a little Russian roulette with her credit status. Maybe she'd indulge in a long, hot bath, letting some of the stress steam away before prepping for her morning meeting with the prosecutor.

She left the cat gulping sweet and sour and went to the bedroom. Instincts, sluggish after a long day and personal questions, kicked in a moment too late.

Her hand was on her weapon before she fully registered the move. But it dropped away slowly as she stared into the long barrel of the revolver.

Colt, she thought. Forty-five. The kind that tamed the American west, six bullets at a time.

'This isn't going to help your boss's case, Rockman.'

'I disagree.' He stepped from behind the door, kept the gun pointed at her heart. 'Take your weapon out slowly, lieutenant, and drop it.'

She kept her eyes on his. The laser was fast, but it wouldn't be faster than a cocked .45. At this range, the hole it would put in her would make a nasty impression. She dropped her weapon.

'Kick it toward me. Ah!' He smiled pleasantly as her hand slid toward her pocket. 'And the communicator. I prefer keeping this between you and me. Good,' he said when her unit hit the floor.

'Some people might find your loyalty to the senator admirable, Rockman. I find it stupid. Lying to give him an alibi is one thing. Threatening a police officer is another.'

'You're a remarkably bright woman, lieutenant. Still, you make remarkably foolish mistakes. Loyalty isn't an issue here. I'd like you to remove your jacket.'

She kept her moves slow, her eyes on his. When the jacket was off one shoulder, she engaged the recorder in its pocket. 'If holding me at gunpoint isn't due to loyalty to Senator DeBlass, Rockman, what is it?'

'It's a matter of self-preservation and great pleasure. I'd hoped for the opportunity to kill you, lieutenant, but didn't see clearly how to work it into the plan.'

'What plan is that?'

'Why don't you sit down? The side of the bed. Take off your shoes and we'll chat.'

'My shoes?'

'Yes, please. This gives me my first, and I'm sure only opportunity to discuss what I've managed to accomplish. Your shoes?'

She sat, choosing the side of the bed nearest her 'link. 'You've been working with DeBlass through it all, haven't you?'

'You want to ruin him. He could have been president, and eventually the Chair of the World Federation of Nations. The tide's swinging, and he could have swept it along and sat in the Oval Office. Beyond.'

'With you at his side.'

'Of course. And with me at his side, we would have taken the country, then the world, in a new direction. The right direction. One of strong morals, strong defense.'

She took her time, letting one shoe drop before unstrapping the other. 'Defense – like your old pals in SafeNet?'

His smile was hard, his eyes bright. 'This country has been run by diplomats for too long. Our generals discuss and negotiate rather than command. With my help, DeBlass would have changed that. But you were determined to bring him down, and me with him. There's no chance for the presidency now.'

'He's a murderer, a child abuser—'

'A statesman,' Rockman interrupted. 'You'll never bring him to trial.'

'He'll be brought to trial, and he'll be convicted. Killing me won't stop it.'

'No, but it will destroy your case against him – posthumously on both parts. You see, when I left him less than two hours ago, Senator DeBlass was in his office in East Washington. I stood by him as he chose a four fifty-seven Magnum, a very powerful gun. And I watched as he put the barrel into his mouth, and died like a patriot.'

'Christ.' It jolted her, the image of it. 'Suicide.'

'The warrior falling on his sword.' Admiration shone in Rockman's voice. 'I told him it was the only way, and he agreed. He would never have been able to tolerate the humiliation. When his body is found, when yours is found, the senator's reputation will be intact once again. It will be proven that he was dead hours before you. He couldn't have killed you, and as the method will be exactly as the other murders, and as there will be two more, as promised, the evidence against him will cease to matter. He'll be mourned. I'll lead the charge of fury and insult – and step into his bloody shoes.'

293

'This isn't about politics. Goddamn you.' She rose then, braced for the blow. She was grateful he didn't use the gun, but the back of his hand to knock her back. She turned with it, fell heavily onto the night table. The glass she'd left there shattered to the floor.

'Get up.'

She moaned a little. Indeed, the flash of pain had her cheek singing and her vision blurred. She pushed herself up, turned, careful to keep her body in front of the 'link she'd switched on manually.

'What good is it going to do to kill me, Rockman?'

'It will do me a great deal of good. You were the spearhead of the investigation. You're sexually involved with a man who was an early suspect. Your reputation, and your motives will come under close scrutiny after your death. It's always a mistake to give a woman authority.'

She wiped the blood from her mouth. 'Don't like women, Rockman?'

'They have their uses, but under it all, they're whores. Perhaps you didn't sell your body to Roarke, but he bought you. Your murder won't really break the pattern I've established.'

'You've established?'

'Did you really believe DeBlass was capable of planning out and executing such a meticulous series of murders?' He waited until he saw that she understood. 'Yes, he killed Sharon. An impulse. I wasn't even aware he was considering it. He panicked afterward.'

'You were there. You were with him the night he killed Sharon.'

'I was waiting for him in the car. I always accompanied him on his trysts with her. Driving him so that only I, who he trusted, would be involved.'

'His own granddaughter.' Eve didn't dare turn to be certain she was transmitting. 'Didn't it disgust you?'

294

'She disgusted me, lieutenant. She used his weakness. Every man's entitled to one, but she used it, exploited it, then threatened him. After she was dead, I realized it was for the best. She would have waited until he was president, then twisted the knife.'

'So you helped him cover it up.'

'Of course.' Rockman lifted his shoulders. 'I'm glad we have this opportunity. It was frustrating for me not to be able to take credit. I'm delighted to share it with you.'

Ego, she remembered. Not just intelligence, but ego and vanity. 'You had to think fast,' she commented. 'And you did. Fast and brilliantly.'

'Yes.' His smile spread. 'He called me on the car 'link, told me to come up quickly. He was half mad with fear. If I hadn't calmed him, she might have succeeded in ruining him.'

'You can blame her?'

'She was a whore. A dead whore.' He shrugged it off, but held the gun steady. 'I gave the senator a sedative, and I cleaned up the mess. As I explained to him, it was necessary to make Sharon only part of the whole. To use her failings, her pathetic choice of profession. It was a simple matter to doctor the security discs. The senator's penchant for recording his sexual activities gave me the idea to use that as part of the pattern.'

'Yes,' she said through numbed lips. 'That was clever.'

'I wiped the place down, wiped the gun. Since he'd been sensible enough not to use one that was registered, I left it behind. Again, establishing pattern.'

'So you used it,' Eve said quietly. 'Used him, used Sharon.'

'Only fools waste opportunities. He was more himself once we were away,' Rockman mused. 'I was able to outline the rest of my plan. Using Simpson to apply pressure, leak information. It was unfortunate that the senator didn't remember until later to tell me about Sharon's diaries. I had to risk going

295

back. But, as we know now, she was clever enough to hide them well.'

'You killed Lola Starr and Georgie Castle. You killed them to cover up the first murder.'

'Yes. But unlike the senator, I enjoyed it. From beginning to end. It was a simple matter to select them, choose names, locations.'

It was a little difficult at the moment to enjoy the fact that she'd been right, and her computer wrong. Two killers after all. 'You didn't know them? You didn't even know them?'

'Did you think I should?' He laughed at that. 'Who they were hardly mattered. Only what. Whores offend me. Women who spread their legs to weaken a man offend me. You offend me, lieutenant.'

'Why the discs?' Where the hell was Feeney? Why wasn't a roving unit breaking down her door right now? 'Why did you send me the discs?'

'I liked watching you scramble around like a mouse after cheese – a woman who believed she could think like a man. I pointed you at Roarke, but you let him talk you onto your back. All too typical. You disappointed me. You were emotional, lieutenant: over the deaths, over that little girl you didn't save. But you got lucky. Which is why you're about to become very unlucky.'

He sidestepped over to the dresser where he had a camera waiting. He switched it on. 'Take off your clothes.'

'You can kill me,' she said as her stomach began to churn. 'But you're not going to rape me.'

'You'll do exactly what I want you to do. They always do.' He lowered the gun until it pointed at her midsection. 'With the others, it was a shot to the head first. Instant death, probably painless. Do you have any idea what sort of pain you'll experience with a forty-five slug in your gut? You'll be begging me to kill you.'

His eyes lit brilliantly. 'Strip.'

Eve's hands fell to her sides. She'd face the pain, but not the nightmare. Neither of them saw the cat slink into the room.

'Your choice, lieutenant,' Rockman said, then jerked when the cat brushed between his legs.

Eve sprang forward, head low, and used the force of her body to drive him against the wall.

# *Chapter Twenty*

Feeney stopped on his way back from the eatery, a half a soy burger in his hand. He loitered by the coffee dispenser, gossiping with a couple of cops on robbery detail. They swapped stories, and Feeney decided he could use one more cup of coffee before calling it a night.

He nearly bypassed his office altogether, with visions of an evening in front of the TV screen and a nice cold beer swimming in his head. His wife might even be up for a little cuddle if he was lucky.

But he was a creature of habit. He breezed in to make certain his precious computer was secured for the night. And heard Eve's voice.

'Hey, Dallas, what brings you—' He stopped, scanning his empty office. 'Working too hard,' he muttered, then heard her again.

'You were with him. You were with him the night he killed Sharon.'

'Oh my Jesus.'

He could see little on the screen: Eve's back, the side of the bed. Rockman was blocked from view, but the audio was clear. Feeney was already praying when he called Dispatch.

Eve heard the cat's annoyed screech when her foot stomped his tail, heard too, the clatter as the gun hit the floor. Rockman had her in height, he had her in weight. And he'd recovered from her full body slam too quickly. He proved graphically that he was military trained.

She fought viciously, unable to restrain herself to the cool, efficient moves of hand to hand. She used nails and teeth.

The shortened blow to the ribs stole her breath. She knew she was going down, and she made sure she took him with her. They hit the floor hard, and though she rolled, he came down on top of her.

Lights starred behind her eyes when her head rapped hard against the floor.

His hand was around her throat, bruising her windpipe. She went for the eyes, missed, and raked furrows down his cheek that had him howling like an animal. If he'd used his other hand for a blow to the face, he might have stunned her, but he was too focused on reaching the gun. Her stiff-handed chop to his elbow had his hand shaking from her throat. Painfully gasping in air, she scrambled with him for the gun.

His hand closed over it first.

Roarke tucked a package under his arm as he walked into the lobby of Eve's building. He enjoyed the fact that she'd come to him. It was a habit he didn't intend to see her break. He thought now that she'd closed her case, he could talk her into taking a couple of days off. He had an island in the West Indies he thought she'd enjoy.

He pressed her intercom, and was smiling over the image of swimming naked with her in clear blue water, making love under a hot, white sun when all hell broke loose behind him.

'Get the hell out of the way.' Feeney came in like a steamroller, a dozen uniforms in his wake. 'Police business.'

'Eve!' Roarke's blood drained even as he muscled his way onto the elevator.

Feeney ignored him and barked into his communicator.

'Secure all exits. Get those fucking sharpshooters in position.'

Roarke fisted his hand uselessly at his sides. 'DeBlass?'

'Rockman,' Feeney corrected, counting every beat of his own heart. 'He's got her. Stay out of the way, Roarke.'

'The fuck I will.'

Feeney flicked his eyes over, measured. No way he was going to spare a couple of cops to restrain a civilian, and he had a hunch this civilian would go to the wall, as he would, for Eve.

'Then do what I tell you.'

They heard the gunshot as the elevator doors opened.

Roarke was two steps ahead of Feeney when he rammed Eve's apartment door. He swore, reared back. They hit it together.

The pain was like being stabbed with ice. Then it was gone, numbed with fury. Eve clamped her hand over the wrist of his gun hand, dug her short nails into his flesh. Rockman's face was close to hers, his body pinning her in an obscene parody of love. His wrist was slippery with his own blood where she clawed at it.

She swore as she lost her grip, as he began to smile.

'You fight like a woman.' He shook his hair back from his eyes, and the blood from his torn cheek welled red. 'I'm going to rape you. The last thing you'll know before I kill you is that you're no better than a whore.'

She sagged, and aroused with victory, he ripped at her blouse.

His smile shattered when she pumped her fist into his mouth. Blood splattered over her like warm rain. She hit him again, heard the crunch of cartilage as his nose fountained more blood. Quick as a snake, she scissored up.

And again, she jabbed at him, an elbow to the jaw, torn

300

knuckles to the face, screaming and cursing as if her words would pummel him as well as her fists.

She didn't hear the battering of the door, the crash of it falling in. With rage behind her, she shoved Rockman to his back, straddled him, and continued to plunge her fists into his face.

'Eve. Sweet God.'

It took Roarke and Feeney together to haul her off. She fought, snarling, until Roarke pressed her face into his shoulder.

'Stop. It's done. It's over.'

'He was going to kill me. He killed Lola and Georgie. He was going to kill me, but he was going to rape me first.' She pulled back, wiped at the blood and sweat on her face. 'That's where he made a mistake.'

'Sit down.' His hands were trembling and slicked with blood when he eased her onto the bed. 'You're hurt.'

'Not yet. It'll start in a minute.' She gathered in a breath, let it out. She was a cop, damn it, she reminded herself. She was a cop, and she'd act like one. 'You got the transmission,' she said to Feeney.

'Yeah.' He took out a handkerchief to wipe his clammy face.

'Then what the hell took you so long?' She managed a ghost of a smile. 'You look a little upset, Feeney.'

'Shit. All in a day's work.' He flipped on his communicator. 'Situation under control. We need an ambulance.'

'I'm not going to any health center.'

'Not for you, champ. For him.' He glanced down at Rockman, who managed a weak groan.

'Once you clean him up, book him for the murders of Lola Starr and Georgie Castle.'

'You sure about that?'

Her legs were a bit wobbly, but she rose and picked up her

301

jacket. 'Got it all.' She held out the recorder. 'DeBlass did Sharon, but our boy here is accessory after the fact. And I want him charged with the attempted rape and murder of a police officer. Toss in B and E for the hell of it.'

'You got it.' Feeney tucked the recorder into his pocket. 'Christ, Dallas, you're a mess.'

'I guess I am. Get him out of here, will you, Feeney?'

'Sure thing.'

'Let me help you.' Roarke bent down, lifted Rockman by the lapels. He jerked the man up, steadied him. 'Look at me, Rockman. Vision clear?'

Rockman blinked blood out of his eyes. 'I can see you.'

'Good.' Roarke's arm shot up, quick as a bullet, and his fist connected with Rockman's already battered face.

'Oops,' Feeney said mildly, when Rockman crumbled to the floor again. 'Guess he's not too steady on his feet.' He bent over himself, slipped on the cuffs. 'Maybe a couple of you boys ought to carry him out. Hold the ambulance for me. I'll ride with him.'

He took out an evidence bag, slipped the gun into it. 'Nice piece – ivory handle. Bet it packs a wallop.'

'Tell me about it.' Her hand went automatically to her arm.

Feeney stopped admiring the gun and gaped at her. 'Shit, Dallas, you shot?'

'I don't know.' She said it almost dreamily, surprised when Roarke ripped off the sleeve of her already tattered shirt. 'Hey.'

'Grazed her.' His voice was hollow. He ripped the sleeve again, used it to stanch the wound. 'She needs to be looked at.'

'I figure I can leave that to you,' Feeney remarked. 'You might want to stay somewhere else tonight, Dallas. Let a team come in and clean this up for you.'

'Yeah.' She smiled as the cat leaped onto the bed. 'Maybe.'

He whistled through his teeth. 'Busy day.'

'It comes and goes,' she murmured, stroking the cat. Galahad, she thought, her white knight.

'See you around, kid.'

'Yeah. Thanks, Feeney.'

Determined to get through, Roarke crouched in front of her. He waited until Feeney's whistling faded away. 'Eve, you're in shock.'

'Sort of. I'm starting to hurt though.'

'You need a doctor.'

She moved her shoulders. 'I could use a pain pill, and I need to clean up.'

She looked down at herself, took inventory calmly. Her blouse was torn, spotted with blood. Her hands were a mess, ripped and swollen knuckles – she couldn't quite make a fist. A hundred bruises were making themselves known and the wound on her arm where the bullet had nicked it was turning to fire.

'I don't think it's as bad as it looks,' she decided, 'but I'd better check.'

When she started to rise, he picked her up. 'I kind of like when you carry me. Makes me all wobbly inside. Then I feel stupid about it after. There's stuff in the bathroom.'

Since he wanted to see the damage for himself, he carried her in, set her on the toilet. He found strong, police issue pain pills in a nearly empty medicine cabinet. He offered one, and water, before dampening a cloth.

She pushed at her hair with her good arm. 'I forgot to tell Feeney. DeBlass is dead. Suicide. What they used to call eating your gun. Hell of a phrase.'

'Don't worry about it now.' Roarke worked on the bullet wound first. It was a nasty gash, but the bleeding had already slowed. Any competent MT could close it in a matter of minutes. It didn't make his hands any steadier.

'There were two killers.' She frowned at the far wall. 'That was the problem. I clicked onto it, but then I let it go. Data indicated low probability percentage. Stupid.'

Roarke rinsed out the cloth and started on her face. He was deliriously relieved that most of the blood on it wasn't hers. Her mouth was cut, her left eye already beginning to swell. There was raw color along her cheekbone.

He managed to take a full, almost easy breath. 'You're going to have a hell of a bruise.'

'I've had them before.' The medication was seeping in, turning pain into a mist. She only smiled when he stripped her to the waist and began checking for other injuries. 'You've got great hands. I love when you touch me. Nobody ever touched me like that. Did I tell you?'

'No.' And he doubted she'd remember she was telling him now. He'd make sure to remind her.

'And you're so pretty. So pretty,' she repeated, lifting a bleeding hand to his face. 'I keep wondering what you're doing here.'

He took her hand, wrapped a cloth gently around it. 'I've asked myself the same question.'

She grinned foolishly, let herself float. Need to file my report, she thought hazily. Soon. 'You don't really think we're going to make anything out of this, do you? Roarke and the cop?'

'I guess we'll have to find out.' There were plenty of bruises, but the bluing along her ribs worried him most.

'Okay. Maybe I could lie down now? Can we go to your place, 'cause Feeney's going to send a team in to record the scene and all that. If I could just take a little nap before I go in to make my report.'

'You're going to the closest health center.'

'No, uh-uh. Can't stand them. Hospitals, health centers, doctors.' She gave him a glassy-eyed smile and lifted her arms. 'Let me sleep in your bed, Roarke. Okay? The great big one, up on the platform, under the sky.'

For lack of anything closer to hand, he took off his jacket and slipped it around her. When he picked her up again, her head lolled on his shoulder.

'Don't forget Galahad. The cat saved my life. Who'd have thought?'

'Then he gets caviar for the whole of his nine lives.' Roarke snapped his fingers and the cat fell happily into step.

'Door's broken.' Eve chuckled as Roarke stepped around it and into the hall. 'Landlord's going to be pissed. But I know how to get around him.' She pressed a kiss to Roarke's throat. 'I'm glad it's over,' she said, sighing. 'I'm glad you're here. Be nice if you stuck around.'

'Count on it.' Shifting her, he bent down and retrieved the package he'd dropped in the hallway in his race to her door. There was a fresh pound of coffee inside. He figured he'd need it as a bribe when she woke up and found herself in a hospital bed.

'Don't wanna dream tonight,' she murmured as she drifted off.

He stepped into the elevator, the cat at his feet. 'No.' He brushed his lips over Eve's hair. 'No dreams tonight.'

If you enjoyed *Naked in Death*,
you won't want to miss J. D. Robb's
new crime novel . . .

# GLORY

## IN

# DEATH

Here is a special excerpt
from this thrilling novel featuring
New York police lieutenant Eve Dallas . . .

The dead were her business. She lived with them, worked with them, studied them. She dreamed of them. And because that didn't seem to be enough, in some deep, secret chamber of her heart, she mourned for them.

A decade as a cop had toughened her, given her a cold, clinical, and often cynical eye toward death and its many causes. It made scenes such as the one she viewed now, on a rainy night on a dark street nasty with litter, almost too usual. But still, she felt.

Murder no longer shocked, but it continued to repel.

The woman had been lovely. Long trails of her golden hair spread out like rays on the dirty sidewalk. Her eyes, wide and still with that distressed expression death often left in them, were a deep purple against cheeks bloodlessly white and wet with rain.

She'd worn an expensive suit, the same rich color as her eyes. The jacket was neatly buttoned in contrast to the jerked-up skirt that exposed her trim thighs. Jewels glittered on her fingers, at her ears, against the sleek lapel of the jacket. A leather bag with a gold clasp lay near her outstretched fingers.

Her throat had been viciously slashed.

Lieutenant Eve Dallas crouched down beside death and studied it carefully. The sights and scents were familiar, but each time, every time, there was something new. Both victim and killer left their own imprint, their own style, and made murder personal.

The scene had already been recorded. Police sensors and the more intimate touch of the privacy screen were in place to keep the curious barricaded and to preserve the murder site. Street traffic, such as it was in this area, had been diverted. Air traffic was light at this hour of the night and caused little distraction. The backbeat from the music of the sex club across the street thrummed busily in the air, punctuated by the occasional howl from the celebrants. The colored lights from its revolving sign pulsed against the screen, splashing garish colors over the victim's body.

Eve could have ordered it shut down for the night, but it seemed an unnecessary hassle.

A uniform stood by continuing video and audio. Beside the screen a couple of forensics sweepers huddled against the driving rain and talked shop and sports. They hadn't bothered to look at the body yet, hadn't recognized her.

Was it worse, Eve wondered, and her eyes hardened as she watched the rain through blood, when you knew the victim?

She'd had only a professional relationship with Prosecuting Attorney Cicely Towers, but enough of one to have formed a definite opinion of a strong woman. A successful woman, Eve thought, a fighter, one who had pursued justice doggedly.

Had she been pursuing it here, in this miserable neighborhood?

With a sigh, she reached over, opened the elegant and expensive bag to corroborate her visual ID. 'Cicely Towers,' she said for the recorder. 'Female, age 45, divorced. Resides 2132 East 83rd, number 61-B. No robbery. Victim still wearing jewelry. Approximately . . .' She flipped through the wallet. 'Twenty in hard bills, fifty credit tokens, six credit cards left at scene. No overt signs of struggle or sexual assault.'

She looked back at the woman sprawled on the sidewalk.

What the hell were you doing here, Towers? she wondered. Here, away from the power center, away from your classy home address?

And dressed for business, she thought. Eve knew Cicely Towers's authoritative wardrobe well, had admired it in court and at City Hall. Strong colors – always camera ready – coordinated accessories, always with a feminine touch.

She rose, rubbed absently at the wet knees of her jeans.

'Homicide,' Eve said briefly. 'Bag her.'

It was past ten when she made it back to Cop Central. In concession to her hollow stomach, she zipped through the eatery, disappointed but not surprised to find most of the good stuff long gone by that hour. She settled for a soy muffin and what the eatery liked to pretend was coffee.

She sipped and munched while she scanned the final autopsy report on her monitor.

The time of death remained as issued in the prelim. The cause was a severed jugular and the resulting loss of blood and oxygen. The victim had enjoyed a meal of sea scallops and wild greens, wine, real coffee and fresh fruit with whipped cream. Ingestion estimated at five hours before death.

The call had come in quickly. Cicely Towers had lay dead only ten minutes before a cab driver, brave or desperate enough to work the neighborhood, had spotted the body and reported it. The first cruiser had arrived three minutes later.

Her killer had moved fast, Eve mused. Then again, it was easy to fade in a neighborhood like that, to slip into a car, a doorway, a club. There would have been blood; the jugular gushed and sprayed. But the rain would have been an asset, washing it from the murderer's hands.

She would have to comb the neighborhood, ask questions

311

that were unlikely to receive any sort of viable answers. Still, bribes often worked where procedure, or threats, wouldn't.

She was studying the police photo of Cicely Towers with her necklace of blood when her link beeped.

'Dallas, Homicide.'

A face flashed on her screen, young, beaming, and sly. 'Lieutenant, what's the word?'

Eve didn't swear, though she wanted to. Her opinion of reporters wasn't terribly high, but C. J. Morse was on the lowest end of her scale. 'You don't want to hear the word I've got for you, Morse.'

His moonpie face split with a smile. 'Come on, Dallas, the public's right to know. Remember?'

'I've got nothing for you.'

'Nothing? You want me to go on air saying that Lieutenant Eve Dallas, the finest of New York's finest has come up empty in the investigation of the murder of one of the city's most respected, most prominent and most visible public figures? I could do that, Dallas,' he said, clicking his tongue. 'I could, but it wouldn't look good for you.'

'And you figure that matters to me.' Her smile was thin and laser sharp, and her finger hovered over the disconnect. 'You figure wrong.'

'Maybe not to you personally, but in reflecting on the department.' His girlishly long lashes fluttered. 'On Commander Whitney for pulling strings to put you on as primary. And there's the backwash on Roarke.'

Her finger twitched, then curled into her palm. 'Cicely Towers's murder is a priority with the department, with Commander Whitney and with me.'

'I'll quote you.'

Fucking little bastard. 'And my work with the department has nothing to do with Roarke.'

'Hey, brown-eyes, anything that touches you touches Roarke